The Reluctant Lady

A Regency Historical Romance

by Kate Morrell

Copyright © 2010 Kate Morrell
All rights reserved.
ISBN:1514772965
ISBN-13:9781514772966

DEDICATION

At long last I can keep my promise and dedicate my first novel
to my much loved and much missed
Uncle Vernon.

He was the funniest man I ever met, though I can't remember
a single joke he told. Yet playing knockout whist with him one
memorable night, I thought it might
be possible to die of laughter.

He also had a great and kind heart, and left the world a lesser
place when he departed it much too soon.

ACKNOWLEDGMENTS

Thank you to Judith for all your feedback, support and for making me do it.

Thank you to Alison and Luigi at LBA for taking me on and giving me hope.

Thank you to Allison Hunter for the excellent advice. I probably should have taken more of it.

Thank you to Roy for being my trusty steed.

Chapter One
A Quarrel at Christopher's

4th April, 1814

'Four o' the clock and all's well!' called the Watch, his voice and enthusiasm dampened by one of London's notorious soot-laden fogs. Even the cheery glow of the new gas streetlamps failed to lift the smoky indigo gloom that shrouded the city.

But these were promising conditions for a figure that lurked impatiently awaiting a rare opportunity.

At last, muffled sounds of drunken laughter heralded a jolly band of young bucks turning from Piccadilly into the unlit side street where Christopher's, a popular gaming hell, was to be found. As they passed, he stepped swiftly out of the mists and attached himself to their group, his presence going largely unnoticed as they made jovial progress past shuttered windows and shadowy doorways.

Christopher's was not shuttered and its emerald silk curtains gleamed invitingly. The men bundled up the steps, and there was much banter and cheering as the burly man at the door admitted them.

In the hubbub, none noticed that the stranger, who would otherwise have been excluded, had entered in their wake.

Although he surrendered his overcoat, hat and gloves as they did, he did not follow them into the room, but stood in the doorway, his clear, grey eyes adjusting to the shimmering brilliance of the well-lit saloon. He was a handsome youth, with tawny gold hair, swept back in natural waves from a noble brow. Though his linen was clean, his clothes were not fine, although his slender figure carried them well, making the best of a well-worn corbeau jacket and old, much-polished shoes.

His eyes skimmed the room - past the tables of seated players and those standing chatting languidly; past the footmen, impassive but for their eyes, on constant watch for a raised finger or a beckoning look.

For an instant, he saw himself reflected, pale and tense, in one of the large mirrors cleverly placed behind the supper tables, to double the apparent size of the spread. But his eyes moved swiftly on.

Stepping forward, he looked through the broad archway that led into a larger drawing room to the rear. Here, it seemed, he had found his quarry, as his gaze alighted on Rafael Wolvenden, 3rd Viscount Rothsea, the saturnine young man holding the bank at one of the larger tables.

As the young man approached, two of the players struggled to their feet. One yawned and stretched, while the other rubbed his tired eyes and spoke.

'Desolated to deprive you of any more of my blunt, Rafe,' said Mr Deverell. Then, catching his friend's infectious yawn, he finished rather indistinctly: 'But Gil and I have a horse running at Newmarket this afternoon that has a fair chance of finishing in the money.'

'Ever the optimist, Dev?' replied Lord Rothsea, as he gathered up the cards. 'Have any of your cattle *ever* finished in the money?'

'Capricious Fate has yet to smile,' conceded his friend. 'But Bonnie Bay Lass will change all that! Care to come and watch our triumph?'

Lord Rothsea grinned at his friend's indefatigable confidence.

'No, I thank you. I'm off to the Fall for Easter,' he said, speaking of Seaton Fall, his favourite country seat. 'Come and stay when the racing is done and I'll have my chef make up a crow pie for *one of us* to eat.'

Mr Deverell laughed as Rafe's quizzing expression left him in no doubt which one of them his friend thought would be eating his words. Then laying a hand on one of the other players' shoulders, he said: 'You coming, Denny?'

'Oh, aye, might as well,' said The Honourable Richard Dennington, standing unsteadily and smoothing his waistcoat with loving care. 'Deal me out, Rafe.'

'By all means, Denny,' replied Rafe, with a languid wave of a hand. 'Just take that dashed ugly waistcoat to Newmarket and leave it there. Can't think where you find the dreadful things.'

'This beauty?' cried Denny, looking down at the gaudy magnificence of his peacock's-eye patterned waistcoat.

'No, Denny, don't try and defend your waistcoat, old man,' said Dev, pulling him towards the door. 'We'll be here all night and I want to watch our horse win.'

'Night! It's past four. Oh, very well,' conceded Denny. 'I shan't rise to your baiting, Rafe, for I know it's mere envy.'

'Harry, there's room for one more, if you can stomach Denny's waistcoat,' Sir Edward Gilbert directed his invitation to the distinctly bosky Lord Stowe, who sat on Rothsea's right.

'Alas, I'm dining with m'mother and sister this evening, Gil,' said Lord Stowe, with a rueful look. 'They came to town early to get tricked out for the season.'

'Poor chap,' said Gil sympathetically, as he left with an airy wave of his fingers.

'Good fellow, Gil,' said Lord Stowe, when he was out of earshot.

'My dear Harry,' remarked Rafe. 'One of your greatest charms and abiding weaknesses is that you think everyone a good fellow … even your humble servant,' a gesture of one long tanned hand indicating himself.

Though Rafe might deprecate himself, he was as fine a specimen of his class as might be found in England. His face was arrestingly handsome – fine-boned, lightly tanned, with dark flying eyebrows over thickly-lashed startling cobalt-blue eyes that had a ring of darker blue at the outer edge. The intelligent expression within them animated his handsome features, even when he appeared bored. He was taller than most, with the strong, athletic build of a sportsman, and a lazy grace that gave his movements a feline charm. His beautiful hands belied their strength – he was a devil with fists or pistols, but, sadly, he had the fiend's own temper too.

At present, however, Rafe was not looking his best. Those striking blue eyes were red-rimmed with tiredness and intoxication, his square jaw was darkly shadowed with twenty hours' growth, and though he had started the evening a picture of immaculate elegance, his cravat was now rather mangled and his silk twill jacket looked as though he had slept in it.

Rafe's dark brows and tanned, unshaven face made him look rather satyr-like beside Harry's blond good looks. Harry had an open, affable expression that lent his own handsome face a candour and approachability that rendered him instantly and universally likable. He was the genial centre of a group of friends that had come together at Eton and Cambridge and now, having been wonderfully and expensively prepared for something, spent their days doing nothing, as befitted their station in life.

Harry smiled hazily at Rafe's comment but then saw his friend's expression darken as the tawny-haired youth took Denny's vacated seat. Like Rafe, he thought the stranger much too young for the game and although clearly of gentlemanly birth, his clothes betrayed his lack of funds. This seemed confirmed by the way the boy looked at the money as he made his bet, and then the suppressed tension with which he watched the turn of the cards.

An experienced gambler, Rafe had seen this kind of desperation many times before. He darted a disapproving glance towards Harry, who shrugged powerlessly. The other players, either too drunk or too absorbed in the game to notice, had accepted the poor fellow. So, though he was not happy about the youth's presence at the table, Rafe said nothing. Who was he, after all, to be lecturing the young man? This was how wealth changed hands. Rafe could not be sorry as he had benefited so richly himself.

Well, let the boy's father ride rusty over him, thought Rafe grimly, *If he loses, he loses. It's not my concern.*

At first the boy won, and at one point during the hour that followed he had upwards of two thousand guineas in front of him in notes and vowels. But like any gambler for whom winning was a novelty, he could not choose the right moment to leave the game. Not when he had two thousand guineas; not when his luck began to turn; not even when he had lost his original stake.

Rafe saw the boy tremble a little when this inevitable moment came and he pitied him. But his sympathy evaporated when, with a hectic glitter in his eyes, the youth looked across the table at him and asked in a low voice: 'Will you take my note, my lord?'

'I will not,' replied Rafe with stern calm, reviewing his cards. 'I have no wish to offend you, so let us say that I prefer not to encourage the folly of youth, and leave it at that.'

There was an uncomfortable pause.

'You do not scruple to cheat, my lord, so why should you baulk at the honest folly of others?' This was said with such a clear, quiet voice that its meaning was missed by the others at the table for a full second or more. Then there was a collective gasp at this most unspeakable of insults.

'Good God!' breathed Harbury, his glass stilled on its way to his lips.

'Take it back, man! Apologise!' exclaimed Harry. Then, turning swiftly towards his friend with ready apprehension of his quick temper, he added: 'He's nine parts drunk, Rafe, and can't know what he's saying!'

But it was too late. A spark of fury had flared in Rafe's blue eyes the instant the fell words had left the boy's mouth. If the lad had taken back the insult immediately and unreservedly, he might, just might, have spared him. But he had not. Even now, grey eyes locked with blue and neither looked away.

'I am not so drunk that I can believe it is by luck that my lord Rothsea wins every hand that he deals,' hissed the youth, sealing his fate.

There was another gasp at this outrageous insinuation and at the brazen willingness with which the lad raced to his doom.

'He's won every hand that *I've* dealt,' responded Harry, anxious to do what he could to avoid the inevitable duel. 'And Harbury here too! Do you imagine that we dealt him favourable cards?'

'Perhaps he did not rely on those you dealt.'

'Good God, man! What are you saying?!' said one of the other gentlemen, his voice suddenly loud in the hush that fell upon the room as players strained to witness the drama unfolding at Rothsea's table.

'Oh, I think he has made his opinions perfectly clear,' murmured Rafe, his voice deceptively silky, veiling a white-hot fury, as he and his accuser continued to glare at one another.

'You're a bad loser and damned fool!' exclaimed Harry, trying to break the deadlock. 'In heaven's name, withdraw your remark, or you leave Lord Rothsea no choice.'

'There are no terms in which he could frame an apology that would make me consider accepting it,' snarled Rafe.

'Then it is fortunate that I have no intention of attempting it,' said the youth with calculated insolence. 'I think you a cheat and your infamous luck of your own fabrication. There! Is that plain enough for you?' he growled, standing slowly and leaning a little across the table as he spoke.

'You impudent little cur!' replied Rafe wrathfully. 'Yes, that last was your death warrant. Have your seconds advise my friend Harry here when and where you wish to die.' He threw a swift enquiring glance at Harry, who nodded reluctantly, confirming that he would act for him.

'I would meet you *now*, my lord, in the park opposite. I have to leave town this morning, so we must conclude our business now,' the young man insisted. 'And you need not be quite so cocksure about putting a period to my existence. I am an excellent shot.'

'Good grief!' exclaimed Harry. 'It's just not done, sir! You must postpone your journey, and attend to this matter in the proper form.'

'Out of the question! Or are you both cheat *and* coward?' he sneered at Rafe.

At this, Rafe's tenuous hold on his temper snapped, and he reached out as if to grab the young man's throat, but was quickly restrained.

'Aye! I'm for you! I can send you to an early grave as soon as you please, you insolent dog!' spat Rafe. His fiery temper, never difficult to spark, was now beyond reason.

Shaking off the restraining hands of his friends, Rafe signalled one of the footmen and despatched him to fetch a pair of pistols from his house, a short distance away in Albemarle Street.

'A duel in Green Park! But you will be seen by the Watch!' cried Harry appalled.

'In this fog?' scoffed the youth. 'We will be lucky to see each other across twelve paces.'

'And who will act for you? You must have a second, sir!' Harry persisted.

'I shall act for myself.'

'No ... no, that will not do! You may be the best shot in England, but it will be a miracle if you are not wounded,' Harry groaned as he realised, with great reluctance, what must be done. 'I will second you. Harbury, would you act for Rafe?'

Lord Harbury agreed unhappily, and went off to engage the surgeon who had the misfortune to live next door to the gaming house.

While Rafe paced like a caged panther and the establishment was in uproar around them, the grey-eyed youth was surprisingly calm. He asked a footman for writing materials, and his hand shook only slightly as he tore a leaf of the house's distinctive lilac paper in two and scrawled briefly on each half. One, which contained his direction, he handed to Harry. The other contained a short message, barely four lines, but the man held it for a long moment staring into the distance, before bestowing it carefully in an inside pocket of his jacket.

Within fifteen minutes, the footman's return with the pistols signalled their departure, and though many in the room would have loved to witness the contest, duels were private affairs, so the company could only watch in tense silence as Harry and the principals left the saloon. Then the room erupted into heated discussion as the betting book was called for and wagers laid on the outcome.

Harbury had succeeded in rousing the surgeon, who looked groggy and dishevelled, having dressed all by guess. Only a promised douceur of twenty guineas had persuaded him to attend, and there was an awkward moment when all realised that only Rafe had the ready cash to supply this.

Dawn was lifting the gloom. They moved through creamy mist redolent of morning fires and horse dung, as they crossed Piccadilly into Green Park. Under normal circumstances, it would be an unthinkable location for a duel, but such was the density of the murk that within a few minutes they might have been anywhere.

Rafe's hot temper was already beginning to cool, and he was regretting the haste with which this scrambled affair had been arranged. As his eyes met the youth's momentarily, he felt a renewed twinge of conscience at the thought of taking the life of one so young. Rafe decided merely to wound him.

His opponent had seen this wavering.

'Shoot to kill, Rothsea, for I certainly shall!' he said, whipping up his lordship's temper. 'I hope to make this the last day you ever cheat a man at play!'

'Be damned to you, insolent devil!' barked Rafe, livid once more. 'I shall certainly make this day *your* last.'

The youth had given Rafe an intolerable insult, even Harry was stunned by its venom, but he tried desperately to persuade Rafe merely to clip the poor fellow.

'He's just a boy, Rafe!' pleaded Harry in a desperate whisper at Rafe's shoulder, as Harbury measured the distance – a lethal eight paces because of the fog - and drew the heel of his Hessian across the furthest mark, where the young man now stood. 'Don't kill him, for heaven's sake!'

'Stand away, Harry!' snarled Rafe, taking position, and Harry retreated to stand midway between them and then stepped backwards from the line of fire, shaking his head in sad resignation.

Harbury and the surgeon had retired some thirty feet away; Harbury bearing the hats and coats of both principals. Though he could see neither in the mists, of habit the surgeon turned away from the combatants, unhappily twisting his hands together now that this was clearly a killing affair.

With obvious reluctance, Harry took a kerchief from his pocket, lifted it and then let it fall.

At this, a startling double crack of gunfire split the air. By the time the others reacted, Rafe had dashed to reach the mortally wounded youth as he crumpled to the ground.

Tossing aside his pistol, smoke still curling wickedly from its barrel, Rafe knelt to support the young man's shoulders with one strong arm. The boy's head lolled weakly against the crook of his elbow, and with surprising gentleness, Rafe brushed back the tumbled gold locks from his face. It had lost its vengeful glint, and now looked touchingly innocent and fearful, as the poor lad clung to the last moments of life.

Rafe's arms suddenly shook, as something in the boy's expression awakened a dreadful memory that he had thought long since subdued. In that instant, not grey eyes but familiar blue stared up at him in terror, sensing approaching death and soundlessly begging Rafe to save him. Ten years had passed since that awful day, yet for those few seconds, the remembered anguish was as vivid and biting as a whip's lash.

Harry's hand on his shoulder steadied him and brought him sharply back to the present.

'Why, lad? Why?' demanded Rafe hoarsely, his wild rage turning to bitterest remorse, then he frowned pityingly as the poor boy seemed to utter gibberish.

'Tal Hairn,' the youth gasped, blood foaming in his mouth and the light dying in his eyes. 'Save Merry ... S-save Merry ..."

At that same moment, the 'Merry' he spoke of was anxiously pacing the bare floorboards of their rented rooms in a dismal little house on Newport Street, to the north-east of Covent Garden, a very far cry from the glamour of Mayfair.

Yet, though this willowy youth wore breeches and ran frantic fingers through short, cropped curls brushed *á la Brutus*, Merry was not a boy, but was in fact the dead man's sister. Almost as tall as her brother, so convincing was her imitation, that in all the years of her masquerade, no one had ever suspected her real sex. Indeed, Merry herself was in danger of forgetting it.

But at this moment, Merry's only thought was for her missing brother, Bryn.

He had left yesterday evening in a rare state of nervous excitement, declining her company, which should have alerted her. Even more disturbing, it now seemed that he had taken all their money. Ordinarily, this would have been little enough, but just two days ago, Merry had won two hundred guineas on a cumulative wager at very long odds. In their straitened circumstances, it was a dazzling sum. Ever the practical one, Merry had proposed buying a small cottage in the country and at last settling down to a quiet, honest life.

Bryn had been less enthusiastic.

'We're the Griffiths of Tal Hairn, Merry,' he'd said. 'We weren't born to live in some pokey cottage in the middle of nowhere, tutoring hayseeds to make a crust.'

As the heir, Bryn felt the Griffiths' degrading reversal in fortune as keenly as their father had.

'Tal Hairn was lost twenty years ago, Bryn,' Merry had retorted. 'We are the Griffiths of Nowhere now.' Then gesturing to encompass the dingy room, she added: 'I, for one, would prefer a pokey cottage of our own to these squalid digs at the rates Jenkins charges … and is tutoring any less noble than running brandy or gambling for our bread?'

Merry thought she had won the argument about how to use their windfall, but inexplicably and quite out of character, Bryn had taken it all without asking, and had not returned. Not for a moment did she imagine that her brother had left her. It was unthinkable. They were bonded by love and duty. But staring out of the window, she worried that he might have been set upon and robbed, and even now could be lying injured somewhere in the chill fog.

It was not for his sake alone that she fretted. Last night had been the longest time she had been entirely on her own, and by dawn the solitude had become unbearable. In their hand to mouth existence, Merry had often experienced hunger and privation, but she had never known loneliness. After just one night, she now numbered it amongst her few fears.

Harry and Harbury had buttoned the dead boy into his greatcoat, clapping his hat firmly down at an angle to hide much of his slack-jawed face, and then hailed a cab, pretending that their 'friend' was dead drunk. Some twenty minutes later, they lifted their charge from the hackney in Newport Street and exchanged a look eloquent of their utter lack of relish for the grim task ahead.

But before Harry could reach up and knock on the grimy door, it was opened by an anxious youth, who bore an uncanny resemblance to the one they were supporting, but for a pair of thick-rimmed spectacles, slightly askew, and a smattering of freckles across his nose and cheeks. He still had the softness and slightness of childhood about his face and form, so Harry guessed that he was fourteen at most. At first, this seemed confirmed by the boy's voice, which, though a little husky, had not yet broken.

'Bryn!' cried Merry in concern, and then looked up in anxious enquiry at the two strangers.

'Your brother?' asked Harry.

Merry nodded dumbly, and then remembering her manners, she bowed and said: 'Thank you for bringing my brother home, sirs. Pray follow me.'

As she led the way, it was clear that Merry was a little stunned that such fine gentlemen should take pains to deliver her brother to their lodgings. But as they carried Bryn into the room, their grave demeanour spoke more eloquently than words that their burden was not merely injured or drunk.

Merry gasped as the realisation jolted through her. Shocked grief harrowed her young face and panic blazed in her eyes, before she managed manfully to suppress it. Struggling for breath, her shaking hand dragged helplessly at her cheap cravat, as the men laid the body on the threadbare divan, where it sprawled unnaturally in a ghastly parody of sleep.

'What happened?' Merry managed to ask in an unsteady whisper.

'It was a duel,' replied Harry, his eyes skidding swiftly around the drab little room, so devoid of possessions.

'A duel?' echoed Merry in disbelief.

'Called Lord Rothsea a cheat,' mumbled Harbury.

'And for this he was killed?' cried Merry aghast.

'Rothsea couldn't delope. Would have looked like he was guilty. And your brother *didn't* delope,' replied Harbury, as if explaining the obvious.

'Could Lord Rothsea not have wounded my brother? Is he such a terrible shot?' demanded Merry, her voice rising with wrath.

There was an embarrassed clearing of throats.

'Best shot I know,' responded Harry grimly.

'So he meant to kill him?' she deduced bleakly.

The question met with silence.

'Murder!' blurted Merry, in a throbbing voice.

'More like suicide,' mumbled Harbury. 'Rothsea's reputation is no secret.'

Merry snorted, dismissing this hateful suggestion without a blink. Bryn would *never* do such a cowardly thing. He could not have known he would be killed, but it was passing strange that Bryn, with his gentle temper, should instigate a duel.

'No, no!' lied Harry hastily, to spare the poor child. 'It was a drunken quarrel, that's all.'

'*Was* Rothsea cheating?' demanded Merry.

'Good God, no!' said Harry.

'No need to cheat. Rich as Croesus,' confirmed Harbury.

'He is just a very good player and bested your brother,' finished Harry.

Merry shook her head, struggling to take it all in, then another fear stilled her breath.

'How much did Bryn lose?' she asked, with unnatural calm.

'Everything, as far as I could tell,' replied Harry, seeing in Merry's over-bright eyes a flash of wild despair swiftly masked.

Numb with shock, Merry stared at her brother. He had gambled all their security on the main chance. Now, he lay dead, leaving her destitute. Her head spun with a tumult of emotion, in which grief jarred against anger at his actions and fear about the consequences she must now bear alone. Fighting to quell this clamour, Merry clenched her fists until her nails bit into her palms.

'Thank you, I can manage from here,' said Merry at last, in a flat tone, as if all natural feeling had been locked away.

'Do you have anyone else here with you?' asked Harry.

'No.'

'Where are your parents, child?'

'Both dead,' muttered Merry mechanically. 'Our father was killed six months ago.'

Harry's throat constricted with sympathy, and he regretted acutely his part in heaping further tragedy on this poor, orphaned boy, by failing to stop that infernal duel.

'Have you any relatives that might take you in?' he persisted.

'It is not your concern. If you could <u>please leave</u>,' insisted Merry, her voice breaking a little as she added: 'I need to lay out my brother.'

'Do you have anyone you can go to at all?' Harry would not be put off.

'No, but as I have said, it's <u>not</u> your concern,' those grey eyes now turning towards him in proud irritation.

THE RELUCTANT LADY

During these exchanges, Harbury had retreated awkwardly towards the door. Harry now turned to him and said: 'Thank you, Harbury. Go home, there's a good fellow. I will take care of things here.'

Harbury's eyebrows lifted in surprise at Harry's philanthropy, but he was only too happy to escape. He had not known the dead man and had no desire now to prolong his acquaintance with the poor brave brother. As he left, he hooked out the last two remaining guineas in his pocket, leaving one on the occasional table against the wall, a contribution to the interment, at least; the other was needed to get him home, if he could find a hackney in this godforsaken part of town.

Merry watched warily as Harry now walked to the door of the adjoining bedchamber and took a cursory glance inside. The ancient dressing table with its mottled mirror sported only a brush, a ewer and washbasin. On the table beside the bed lay a battered edition of *Waverley* and a copy of *Bailey's Guide to the Turf* with the remains of a tallow candle on a chipped saucer. A small leather trunk stood against the wall, on which a precious handful of books were heaped.

He seemed to derive no reassurance from this brief inspection, and looked back at Merry with a perplexed frown, as if she were a problem he now had to solve. He had a pleasant face and looked rather boyish as he raked a troubled hand through his blonde hair.

'Why do you remain, sir?' asked Merry, puzzled.

Harry sighed.

'Well, I can scarcely leave you here to fend for yourself, young man,' he replied. 'I don't wish to be blunt, but it's my guess you haven't two farthings to rub together, now that your brother has lost your savings … and I'll stake my hat that you owe rent, too.' Seeing Merry's dull red flush, he added: 'Aye! I thought as much. Well, if you think I'll walk away while you get taken up by the parish or thrown in debtor's prison, then you mistake your man.'

Though God alone knows what I'm to do with you, he thought to himself.

Merry's chin lifted defensively. The Griffith pride was a blessing and a curse. It stiffened her backbone when she longed to curl into a ball and weep. But it bristled at the thought of being the object of anyone's pity or charity. So, though this kindly gentleman was the only person in the world likely to assist her, she baulked at accepting his aid.

'Why would you care what happens to me?' she demanded.

'Well, I was your brother's second, for one thing, though I admit we were not acquainted,' he replied. 'But mainly it is that I am heartily ashamed that I did not do more to prevent the duel. At least allow me to atone by helping you now.'

Merry wavered. Worries harried her like crows on a gibbet. Though she tried to stifle it, rising panic made her strain to breathe. It was hard to say which she dreaded most – being flat broke, homeless or utterly alone in world - but facing all three at once, the future seemed impossibly bleak. Still, if this gentleman were prepared to make her a loan to escape her present difficulties, it would relieve one anxiety, at least. The thought steadied her a little, as did his kindly presence. He was clearly a gentleman, in the best sense, and Merry felt instinctively that she could trust him.

'Come!' said Harry, breaking her trance and taking command. 'Let us attend to your brother and get him out of that coat, for a start.'

Merry had been facing Harry much of the time, but now followed him to the bed and looked down at Bryn's ashen face. All the animation that had given those dear features life was utterly extinguished. Never again would he laugh. Never put his face up to the sunshine and smile at that simple pleasure. Never tease her out of a temper or put a comforting arm around her shoulder. Never. *He was gone ... gone!*

In a sharp twist of grief Merry felt acutely the lost comfort of his presence and the tragedy of his young life, which had once held such promise, now brutally cut short by a cold-hearted nobleman with a murderous aim.

Her throat raw and her lips pressed tight together to keep them from trembling, Merry helped Harry to remove Bryn's overcoat, but as they laid him back down, Merry saw the bloodstained hole in her brother's jacket and her slender frame shuddered violently. Clenching her fists, she fought to suppress the sobs that clutched convulsively at her aching chest. Harry reached out a comforting hand, but Merry shied away. In that instant, kindness would undo her fragile self-control. Amid her rage, dread and grief was a burning thirst for revenge, and Merry now channelled her storm of passion in this direction.

Oh, how she longed to have Bryn's callous killer at the end of a pistol barrel and blow a hole through his cold heart!

'Rothsea!' she ground out, naming her enemy.

Then she turned to Harry with murder in her eyes. 'Where will I find the cowardly blackguard who killed my brother?'

Startled by Merry's mercurial transformation from abject sorrow to implacable fury, Harry leapt to defend his friend.

'Rothsea is neither coward nor blackguard! Your brother offered him intolerable insults in the most uncompromising of terms' said Harry, trying to reason the boy out of his sudden rage. 'If he had done so to me, I should have been obliged to call him out. I'll admit my friend's temper is rather fiery,' he added. 'But your brother could not have found a more certain way to ignite it.'

'That other fellow said his reputation was no secret,' snarled Merry, her eyes pinning poor Harry like a lancet. 'Tell me the truth! Has he killed before?'

Harry's evasive look told all.

'I knew it! And yet he did not hang?'

'Good God! A gentleman does not hang for an affair of honour!'

Merry was incensed.

So the black-hearted villain clearly made a habit of killing! Bryn was merely his latest victim. And worse than everything, there would be no justice! That devil Rothsea would not hang!

'Gentleman, hah! We'll see that!' she spat, now determined to call Rothsea out herself. 'Give me his direction and let me be the judge of his character! If you will not oblige me in this, then be on your way! I will accept no other help from you.'

Harry was dismayed. Whatever happened, he could not in conscience allow the idiotic boy to face his predicament alone, but in the lad's present temper, an interview with Rafe would end in a brief and very one-sided mill. Yet there seemed no reasoning with the child.

'You would accept my aid once you'd spoken your piece to him?'

'Certainly,' Merry conceded, with an unholy light in her eye. *You can act as my second,* she thought.

'And if I do take you to him, do I have your word that you would not simply run off to fetch the constable?'

'Agreed,' said Merry. She wanted the scoundrel's blood more than she wanted the probable mockery of a trial.

Harry was still undecided, but Merry was already shrugging into her overcoat and reaching for her hat.

'Look here, er ...' began Harry, as Merry handed him his hat and nodded meaningfully towards the door. 'What's your name, by the way?' he demanded, realising that, in all the upheaval, they had not been introduced.

'Merion Griffith, sir, at your service,' said Merry, with a slight bow.

'Well, Griffith, I'm ... Wait a moment!' said Harry, an arrested look on his face. 'Merion? ... *Merry?*'

'Y-yes,' said Merry, momentarily distracted from her avenging schemes by the fact that this stranger had guessed her nickname.

'Oh Lord!' said Harry, who had witnessed her brother's dying words. 'That changes things. Yes, I suppose I must take you to Rafe ... but you'll mind your temper, my lad, or I'll dust your backside myself!'

Chapter Two
A Startling Discovery

Fog still confined the visible world, as Rafe strode blindly away from the debacle in Green Park. But he was disoriented less by the mists than by the revival of memories that he had fought hard to bury. Try as he might to block them out, they crowded his mind's eye … and now he had the stain of another boy's death on his soul.

As he stepped out to cross Piccadilly, he was nearly knocked down by a hackney bowling along from St James's.

'Damn it!' he said out loud, cursing his distraction. Then, he struck out more purposefully, heading for the Dover Street stable.

After speaking briefly with Needham, his groom, Rafe cut through Stafford Street, to reach the house in Albemarle Street that had been his home since he had won it in a card game eight years earlier.

Rather than walk up the front steps, Rafe ducked through a passageway that gave access to the rear of the property.

Rafe's long-suffering manservant Brooke was sitting in the servants' hall adjoining the kitchen. He was not alone, but was the only one sitting within sight of the back door. Rafe's valet Lain, who might otherwise have been sitting with him, was away for the week, winding up his late uncle's affairs.

Brooke had started out as a stable lad at Twelveoaks, the Wolvendens' country seat, but had thrown his lot in with Lord Rothsea when the viscount had been cast out by his father.

When he saw the bleak expression on his master's face as he came through the back door, Brooke's heart turned over.

Rafe caught his eye and gave a short beckoning nod, before disappearing up the back stairs towards the rooms on the first floor.

'I killed the man,' said Rafe, stumbling up the stair, as Brooke quickly caught up with him.

'So I guessed, my lord, when I saw you creeping in the back way.'

'Don't say it!'

'I wouldn't presume to comment, my lord,' said Brooke primly.

'Yes, you would, but I just don't want to hear it,' said Rafe bitterly. 'If it's any comfort, your dismay at my actions is matched only by my own.'

'It always is, sir,' observed Brooke. 'And it's not much of a comfort ... no.'

Rafe ground his teeth.

'The Watch heard the shots, but didn't see us. It was a pea-souper, but we didn't choose the most discreet of locations.'

'Hyde Park?'

'Green Park.'

Brooke gave a sharp intake of breath.

Green Park! They must have been mad! To kill his man in Green Park! This was extreme folly even for Rothsea.

'I see.'

'Don't say it,' repeated Rafe, and then after a long pause, during which they had made their way to the sitting room, he added: 'And don't think it so loudly either or give me that Friday face. You know what I am!'

'You are never less than fair, sir. You must have been provoked.'

'I was.'

Brooke stood awaiting orders.

'We'll have to bolt,' said Rafe. 'You take my coach and head along the Bath road to Bristol. Let them think I'm heading for the Sea Witch. It's a shame she's not closer. When you reach her, have them sail her to Porlock. We can embark there if we must. Take Needham to drive you. I've sent him to hire a chaise in the City. I'll head north and set another trail. Then we'll rendezvous at the

Fall and I'll decide what to do next. Perhaps it's time we saw Venice again, old friend.'

Brooke nodded ruefully, and hastened away to make the arrangements.

Rafe slumped in a chair, bone tired but harrowed to wakefulness by what he had done. He had killed a man, no more than a proud boy. His hands rose to his face, trying to block out the dreadful image of that beautiful youth dying in his arms.

Then, inevitably, the image of another dead boy rose up in its stead - an image that still had the power to evoke deep grief and remorse and make all that he had achieved seem hollow and worthless.

Rafe groaned. His self-contempt now had full rein. To silence this hateful inner voice, he turned to his customary remedy, a liberal glass of brandy. He dashed off the first with no apparent effect, but the second caused the voice to slur and become confused.

This was good.

Rafe filled the glass again and threw himself down on the large sofa, his shoulders leaning back against one arm and one foot resting against the other. He drank deeply again. The voice was indistinct now. All his other senses were swimming, too.

Finally, the brandy glass had fallen from his slackened grasp, the amber remains spilling from the rolling bowl onto the fine Persian carpet, as Rafe slipped into blessed oblivion.

Less than an hour later, Rafe was in the grip of a nightmarish re-enactment of the morning's events, helplessly watching the light slowly fade from his victim's grey eyes, when he was roughly awakened to find himself staring into those eyes once more.

Rafe started upright in dismay and for a fanciful, half-awake instant wondered if he were seeing a ghost. But Harry's next words sobered him.

'This is your victim's brother,' he said. 'His name is ...'

But Merry didn't wait for further introduction. She bent swiftly to pick up a glass from a tray of refreshments that Brooke had left and, before Harry could stop her, dashed its contents into Rafe's bleary face.

'There! Is that provocation enough for you?'

Rafe jumped up.

'Why, you puppy! I can do the job as well for you as for your damned brother!' he snarled, his face dripping.

'No, you can't …' said Harry firmly, but he was not attended to.

'Where and when, you damned cur?' ground out Merry, from between gritted teeth.

'I'll draw your cork first for that, you insolent …!'

Harry caught him as he lunged at Merry, holding him back with difficulty as Merry, too, took a furious step forward.

'Name your seconds!' snapped Merry.

'Name *yours*, damn your impudence!' Rafe spat back incredulously, adding with spite: 'If you can find an adult to squire you!'

'Why the sudden concern?' taunted Merry mockingly. 'You had no such qualms when you shot my brother and he was barely seventeen!'

Suddenly, there was a loud rapping at the door and shouts that indicated the authorities had been alerted much sooner than expected.

The fistfight was momentarily forgotten, as Brooke put his head round the saloon door, his face a question to which Rafe shook his head warningly. Brooke nodded with quick understanding before leaving to walk sedately down to the front door.

Merry turned with the unholy light of righteous wrath in her eye.

'I pray to God that I might see you hang for your crime *this* time! And then I'll be the first to pull on your legs and send you to hell, where you belong!' she flung at him in a low, throbbing voice.

As she heard the front door below being opened calmly by Brooke, Merry turned to call out and give Rafe away.

But the sound never left her lips.

A hand clamped over her mouth, as Rafe held her head painfully back against his shoulder, his other arm snaking around her throat.

'Not a sound, or I'll choke the life out of you here and now,' he said in a savage whisper, dragging her backwards through the connecting doors into his bed chamber and from thence via the dressing room to the back stairs.

Harry had remained upstairs, at Rafe's rapid instruction, to put off the authorities. He could only pray that he and the boy did not come to cuffs before he could join them.

As Rafe hauled her bodily down the final steps and into the small hallway by the rear door, Merry could hear the muffled sound of Harry's voice and the louder demands and thumping footfalls of the authorities as they searched his lordship's apartments. She struggled desperately to be free, but her captor's arms were like steel bands around her.

'So you'd like to see me hang, eh? Pull on my legs, would you?' he breathed in her ear, his arm suffocatingly tight against her throat. 'How does it feel to have a little pressure on your own neck, you impertinent little scrub?'

Writhing and kicking with all her strength, Merry felt his reaction when her heel met his shin with some force, and with grim satisfaction heard his suppressed grunt as her teeth connected with his palm. But she was obliged to stop struggling when Rafe's arm tightened about her throat. Merry felt the blood pounding painfully in her head and her eyes felt like they were exploding from within. Then everything went black.

Stunned that the lad had lost consciousness so quickly, Rafe frowned and lifted Merry's slender form in his arms. It was oddly light even for a youth. Looking intently at Merry's fine oval face, with its delicate features, long lashes fanned out against soft freckled cheeks and the pink, half-parted lips, Rafe was suddenly suspicious, not least because the freckles appeared to be dots of brown ink. With a cursory intimate inspection, achieved by a brief movement of his hands, Rafe made a startling discovery.

Suddenly, hearing voices emanating from the dressing room, he swiftly ducked into a large cupboard under the stairs and locked the door.

As he crouched in the dark, cradling Merry's slim body, there was something in the weight and the feel of it that brought back those lacerating memories he had tried to suppress. A tremor went through him as he relived the horror of holding his dying brother in the same way. With a groan, Rafe doubled up, crushing Merry's limp body to his own, as he had with Kit's, as if he could infuse it with his own living energy. But as his cheek pressed against Merry's, Rafe no longer scented the blood and dust of the past but fresh soap and an elusive essence that kindled other sensations and sent his demons flying back into the shadows.

With a grateful sigh, Rafe turned his face into her hair and breathed deeply.

A few minutes later, Brooke tapped on the cupboard door and said: 'All's bowman, m'lord.'

Rafe unlocked the cupboard and stepped out, thankful to escape all the unsettling emotions he had experienced in there. He shook his head as if to clear it and then looked down at Merry's unconscious face with a bemused frown, trying to account for the effect this changeling had had on him.

Brooke stared in dismay at this new casualty of his master's temper.

'What have you done to the lad?' he demanded.

'*Not* a lad,' grinned Rafe, enjoying Brooke's blink of surprise, before carrying Merry back upstairs.

Ignoring Harry's alarmed consternation, Rafe laid Merry on the nearest sofa. Now, it was his turn to dash water in *her* face.

Merry awoke choking, clutching her throat and cursing him roundly in a hoarse whisper. She struggled to her feet and squared up to him, ignoring Rafe's mocking look as she did so.

'You're no man!' said Rafe with asperity.

'WHAT!!' gaped Harry in utter disbelief. 'A girl! You're … a girl?!'

But Merry was too absorbed in her rage with Rafe to hear him.

'I'm man enough to teach you a lesson!' she barked in a roughened voice, her fists coming up in a surprisingly useful stance.

'Ridiculous!' scoffed Rafe, followed rapidly by: 'Ow! …Urgh!', as Merry took the offensive, punching him first on the nose and then very hard in his stomach.

Harry was agog, as Rafe furiously wiped the slight trickle of blood from his nose, while Merry nimbly bounced on her toes and then tapped her fists together, crowing: 'Hah! Drawn *your* cork! Aye! There's a taste of the home brewed for you, and plenty more where that came from, you craven!'

Rafe's eyes flamed with amazed ire and just a little reluctant respect, as he glanced briefly at the blood on his fingers and then back at Merry. Then his eyes narrowed dangerously as he swiftly analysed his opponent's many pugilistic weaknesses.

Harry, gathering his shattered wits, knew that look all too well, and hastily intervened, but was rebuked by both of them.

'Back off, Harry!' snapped Rafe at the same time as Merry growled: 'Keep out of this!'

'You're the only coward here, *madam*,' replied Rafe, watching Merry bristle. 'You know damn well I can't hit you back. No gentleman would fight a lady ... but I'm more than eager to give you the spanking you richly deserve, if you try that stunt again.'

'Huh! I'd like to see you try!' jeered Merry, adding with a meaningful nod: 'You'll be singing an octave higher if you do!'

Harry spluttered in shock, while Rafe gave a huff of incredulous amusement, and put his hands on his hips, as he eyed the bantam in fascination.

'Come on! What are you waiting for?' gibed Merry. 'It's a little late in the day to discover scruples. By God! If you had fought *me*, I would have killed you. I am by far a better shot. Well, will you accept my challenge or not?'

'No, I will not,' replied Rafe with maddening calm.

'Don't claim to be a gentleman again, you rogue!' goaded Merry in thwarted rage. 'My brother was a gentleman. You are no such thing!'

'*Such* a gentleman that he let his sister go about in this indecent get-up?' taunted Rafe, with a wave of his hand indicating her male attire.

'Hah! Who are you to talk of decency! That word is laughable coming from a cad like you.'

'Damnation!' snapped Rafe, all humour gone. 'You'll keep a civil tongue in your head, madam, or I'll school you myself!'

'Rafe! You lay another hand on this child, and you'll answer to me, do you understand!' roared Harry, drawing stunned looks from both protagonists.

'Then are you are willing to play me so that I may recoup what my brother lost?' demanded Merry, before Harry could say more.

'You are very confident,' Rafe remarked silkily, his eyes glinting. 'But what could you stake?'

'I have my mother's pearls,' she remembered, fishing the woefully thin necklet from beneath her mangled cravat.

'I swear there must be insanity in your family! This lust you have for gambling away your last groat!'

'Devil take you! Who says I'll lose?' snapped Merry. 'Well? Will you play me?'

'No, I thank you!' he said, adding provokingly. 'I have had my fill of fleecing little lambs today.'

'That's enough, the pair of you!' interjected Harry, pushing them apart in exasperation. 'Now, then, Merry ... er, I mean... '

'What?' interrupted Rafe, an arrested look on his face as he recalled that this same word had been her brother's last. '*YOU'RE Merry?*'

Merry watched in puzzlement as Harry turned to him and gave a nod pregnant with meaning

'Holy Hell!' groaned Rafe, sitting heavily on the arm of the sofa. Like Harry before him, he now looked at her as if she were a problem to be solved.

Merry ignored him pointedly and directed her conversation exclusively at Harry.

'What's my nickname got to do with anything?' she demanded.

Harry looked expectantly at Rafe, who sighed and raked a hand through his dishevelled hair. Harry knew his friend would do the right thing, though he guessed from his baleful look just how unhappy he was about the prospect.

'Parents?' asked Rafe of Harry.

Harry shook his head.

'Marvellous!' said Rafe, even less happy.

'Look here!' growled Merry impatiently. 'If you're not going to afford me satisfaction, then I might as well be off.'

Suddenly, Rafe surged to his feet and took a couple of steps towards Merry, so close he might have reached out and rested his hands on her shoulders.

'Not dressed like that, you won't!' he declared uncompromisingly.

Facing his broad chest and forced to look up to meet his eyes, Merry was forcibly reminded of the overwhelming strength she had felt when he had held her captive. Though she had lived amongst men all her life, it was the first time a sense of another's masculinity had unnerved her in such an odd way. Merry found the sensation threatening and took a wary step back.

'Why not? I'm damned if I'll take instruction from you!'

'If I guessed your sex, others may,' he replied.

'Stuff! *You* did not until … wait a moment! How *did* you discover it?'

'You are missing some essential equipment for the part,' he said with a significant glance at her breeches.

Harry's jaw dropped as Merry's hand unconsciously checked the wadding sewn into her drawers to supply the deficiency.

'You can't tell by looking,' growled Merry accusingly.

Rafe leaned towards her confidentially.

'I did more than look,' he confirmed, with a provoking glitter in his eyes.

'Rafe!' cried Harry, more shocked it seemed than Merry, who huffed in furious contempt and then nodded slowly, her narrowed eyes promising retribution for this new violation of her dignity.

'You disgust me!' hissed Merry.

'I disgust myself. What of it?' snapped Rafe.

Merry gaped, momentarily nonplussed by her adversary's self-contempt.

Harry watched in astonishment as the pair sized each other up like fighting cocks. He had never met anyone with a temper like Rafe's, but this volatile girl's seemed more than a match for it. Harry prepared to break the deadlock once more and cleared his throat, diverting Merry's attention from Rafe, with whom she had locked eyes for longer than she had realised.

'The fact remains that, though my friend's behaviour can leave somewhat to be desired,' said Harry, fixing Rafe with a disapproving glance. 'It was not he who instigated the duel …'

'I've not known him above fifteen minutes, and I want to shoot him!' interrupted Merry. 'It would not be the greatest wonder if Bryn had felt the same way!'

'Nevertheless, your brother had the opportunity to withdraw his insult or postpone the contest until tempers had cooled, but he did neither,' continued Harry. 'And now it is for us to address the unfortunate consequences.'

Harry's reasoning words had the desired effect. Merry's blinding wrath ebbed a little.

'You promised that I might help you,' said Harry.

Merry shifted awkwardly, wrestling with her pride once more.

'Well, if … if you would consider making me a small loan for a month or so, at reasonable interest,' she replied, with a grateful bow. 'Then I can shift for myself.'

'No! Damn it! You absurd chit! You cannot!' exclaimed Rafe, in a voice that brooked no dissent. 'And don't fire up at me again, you little termagant. You have no idea how comic all this posturing appears coming from a girl barely out of the schoolroom …'

'Schoolroom!' interrupted Merry, outraged. 'I am turned nineteen, and I've seen more of life than you have, you silk-wrapped popinjay!'

Rafe gritted his teeth, but continued inexorably.

'Nonetheless, I can scarcely go off with the thought of your trotting round town in that get up, trying to play the Captain Sharp … or worse, when your money runs out.'

'What business is it of yours what I do?' demanded Merry.

'Damnation! Your brother *made* it my business!' snapped Rafe. 'His dying words to me were: "Save Merry". Now that I realise what he meant, I must execute upon his last wish. There! Will that appease your foul temper?'

'Dastard!'

'Harpy!'

They glared furiously at one another and then fleetingly and most unexpectedly, each felt the flicker of an unfamiliar emotion that was not anger. For one suspended instant, it transformed the glare into a shared look of frowning mystification.

Harry's discreet cough broke the spell, and recalled Merry to the fact that Bryn had thought of her in his last moments.

Merry's eyes now flew to Harry's.

'Did Bryn really say that?' she asked Harry in a small voice.

Harry nodded.

'Truly,' he confirmed. 'Those were his last words as he expired in Rafe's arms,' said Harry.

Merry shot a glance at Rafe, her brow furrowed.

He held Bryn as he died, she thought, the idea jarring with her image of events.

'But ... but what did he mean?' she muttered in confusion. '*Help* me, makes sense ... but *save* me?' She shook her head uncomprehendingly. 'Save me from what?'

Both men looked at her in blank amazement.

'Yourself, perhaps?' suggested Rafe caustically.

Merry shot him a savage look.

'Shut up, Rafe!' snapped Harry.

Gently, he took Merry's shoulders and turned her to face him.

'Miss Griffith, surely ...' he began, but then paused as her eyes widened with a flash of stunned offence.

'What is it?' he said.

'N-nothing ... I had not been called that before, that's all.'

'God's teeth! How long have you been masquerading as a boy?' demanded Rafe, with an expression of dawning wonder.

'None of your business, confound you!' snarled Merry, her eyes flashing again and holding Rafe's in another contest of wills.

'How long, Miss Griffith, if you please?' insisted Harry, taking her hands to draw her attention from Rafe's provoking presence.

It worked. Merry gasped at this unfamiliar contact, and her candid grey eyes searched Harry's earnest blue ones. Though he gallantly tried to conceal it, she could see his shock at her imposture. Merry wished she had not pocketed her glasses - that missing piece of her armour - as she had made ready to fight. Somehow, more than Rothsea's domineering abuse, Harry's restrained disapproval made her feel discomfited.

'Since I was two years old,' she confessed.

Both men were staggered. Rafe sat heavily on the arm of the sofa once more and simply stared at her in undisguised fascination.

'Dear God! You poor child!' said Harry.

'No such thing!' Merry countered defensively, pulling her hands free. 'I have learnt more than I should have as a girl. I attended school with my brother, and was treated equally, as I would not have been as a female.'

'Did your tutors or fellow pupils never see through your disguise?' asked Harry in astonished disbelief.

'Not once,' she replied with touching pride, but then conceded: 'We moved around so frequently, that no bagwig had the leisure to notice that I was not growing as a lad might. I came off worst in a few fist fights and had to take care when I stripped for sports or a whipping…'

Merry faltered as she heard Harry gasp.

'I … I wore a padded vest, you know. We claimed I was bronchial to account for it … and Bryn was usually on hand to back me up, since we passed for twins for a good while. I was the better scholar, so I helped him with cramming.' Then she added wistfully: 'I should have liked to go up at Cambridge, but it was impossible, the cost was prohibitive … and I might have been discovered.'

'In a heartbeat,' said Rafe categorically.

'Why so? I have not been … u-until now.'

'You're too … beautiful,' said Rafe simply, drawing a choking sound and look of astonishment from Harry, who struggled to see beyond the warlike boy.

'Fustian!' cried Merry.

'Your face, your figure, your hands, your feet all give you away. They are much too slender and dainty for any nineteen-year-old man. You might pass for a boy of fourteen, but beyond that … impossible!'

Merry's chin had come up in tacit challenge, which masked a brief flutter of doubt.

'How did you come to begin the imposture? Surely your mother cannot have approved it?' enquired Harry in the soothing, politely inquiring tone that seemed to gentle her.

'What alternative had we? My mother died in childbed when Bryn was born.'

Harry glanced unconsciously at Rafe, but his friend's expression remained impassive.

'My father was a gentleman but had no income,' Merry continued. 'My grandfather had gambled away our estate, leaving only debts.' She twisted the cheap fob at her waist, looking down at it idly, veiling the expression in her eyes. 'Father disdained taking a paid position, so we lived off what he could win. We could not afford servants and we had no living relatives to whom I might go. I think he began it for expediency, but then it seemed to work so well …,' Merry shrugged. 'When I turned thirteen, my father made sure I had a room of my own and talked of ending the masquerade, but somehow we never did and well, … Faith! I never wanted it, so …' her voice trailed off.

'You mentioned that your father died last year?' recalled Harry.

'He was stabbed in a tavern in Southwark,' she responded, with quiet shame. 'A fine end for a "Griffith of Tal Hairn",' she said, as if quoting a phrase she had heard too often.

Despite the bitterness in her voice, a look of profound sadness ghosted across Merry's face. She looked away for a moment, staring blindly at the window and biting the inside of her lip to prevent it from trembling as she tried to master the unexpected surge of emotion which had arisen at the memory. That dreadful night, fetching their father's body on a handcart across cobbles and through mud; his burial in a pauper's grave at St Ann's and their disastrous decline in fortune that had followed. And now Bryn, too, was gone. Tears threatened to come, but she swallowed hard and suppressed them as she had done a hundred, hundred times before.

As they watched this inner struggle, the two men could only wonder at what the poor girl before them had suffered and marvel at the fortitude that she could muster even now. Casting a glance at Rafe, Harry was surprised by the strange, intent look in his friend's eyes, which were entirely focused on Merry, as she recovered her composure and her curious boyish stance of defensive bravado.

'Tal Hairn,' Rafe echoed, suddenly remembering his victim's other dying words.

'It was our family's home for three hundred years, until my grandfather lost it to Lord Northover in a card game.'

Harry's eyes met Rafe's in a quick look of comprehension.

'Did your brother not consider a paid position, when your father was no longer there to provide for you?' prompted Harry.

'He had no profession and was as proud as my father when it came to work. Nor would he allow me to seek a position, since the only one he could approve was as a governess, and never having been a girl, I could not instruct one in ladylike behaviour.'

This last caused both men to smile and inwardly concur, for Merry was now leaning her elbow on a chair back with her other thumb tucked into her breeches pocket in a unconsciously masculine pose.

'We had hopes of Bryn marrying into money when he courted the daughter of a cit a month or so ago. I think he grew quite attached to her. But her father found out about the circumstances of our father's death and that we were not in society, so he vetoed the match. Then we were back where we started.'

'So he thought he would try gambling? The poor fool,' remarked Harry

'So I told him. I am by far the better player, but because of what happened to father, he would only let me bet on the turf or on prize fights.'

'Dear God! Miss Griffith, I swear I feel my hair turning white ...' Harry had closed his eyes at the thought of the risk she might have run.

'I'd liefer you called me Merry or Merion, if it's all the same to you. I was born Marion, but I don't remember ever being called it.'

'Well, Merry, I'm Harry, then,' he said, reaching out to shake her hand, which she did in a truly boyish way.

'Hullo, Harry,' said Merry with the first smile he'd seen on her face since they met.

'Very affecting,' said Rafe dryly, inexplicably nettled by the sight of their camaraderie. 'But this isn't solving my problem of what to do with this little amazon.'

Merry's eyes flamed again at the offence.

'Damn you,' she hissed. 'You'll pay for these insults and for my brother's death. I shall see that you do!'

'Yes, I believe you will,' murmured Rafe, almost to himself.

'I am *not* your problem ... and I do *not* need saving,' she stated firmly. 'Harry will loan me a little money until I find employment, then ...'

'Over my dead body!' declared Rafe, with a stern glance at Harry.

'Those terms suit me!' countered Merry. 'And don't think to be throwing your glove at Harry, for you'll have to go through me to do it!'

Rafe gave a bark of laughter.

'Peawit! I shan't quarrel with Harry. He knows better than to go along with your mad scheme.'

Merry's heart sank as she saw confirmation of this on Harry's apologetic face.

'Besides, it would appear that your present fate lies doubly at the Wolvenden's door,' said Rafe. 'Northover is my father.'

Merry gasped and stared at him as if he had sprouted horns.

Rafe raked a hand through his hair and added wearily: 'Though I could have told your brother that my esteemed parent would have long since lost Tal Hairn in the same way that he won it.'

Merry now grasped the motive behind Bryn's wild gamble. To reclaim Tal Hairn had been their father's greatest dream.

'But this is all beside the point,' said Rafe. 'When your brother died he charged me to save you, and save you I shall … whether you like it or not!'

Merry would have entered battle once more, but was forestalled by Harry.

'Merry, we are *both* keen to honour your brother's last request. Indeed, I could not in all honour allow you to walk out of here without making provision for your future … and you gave me your word that you would accept my help,' he added. 'You will admit that, without your brother's protection, this masquerade puts you in danger of discovery, at the very least?'

Merry would admit nothing of the kind, but Harry's gentle tone disarmed her, undermining the angry heat of thwarted revenge and forcing her to look into her immediate future with a bitter sense of doom.

Breaking away, Merry walked past them into the space before the door. Rafe had taken a hasty step forward to prevent her from leaving, but was deterred by Harry's restraining arm across his chest. Harry was certain that Merry only needed space to think and he was proven right as she began to pace back and forth, a deep furrow between her brows. They watched in fascination as Merry's changing expressions unconsciously betrayed her inward struggle with her pride and her predicament.

Ordinarily, Rafe might have derived wry amusement from the fact that his company was being unfavourably weighed against penury and starvation. Instead, he held his breath, tensely awaiting her decision, as if it were of the greatest importance that this fiery tomboy, who hated him as much as he hated himself, stayed in his life.

Merry certainly longed to grind Rothsea's maddening face under her boot, but there was no getting away from the awful fact that Bryn's gamble had left her destitute with no obvious means of escaping this dreadful state. The Griffiths had known some very lean times, and often gone a little hungry, but this was the lowest ebb in their fortunes yet, and Merry had been left to face it alone.

Merry finally ceased pacing and stood unseeing at the window. The vengeful rage that had been a temporary sea wall, holding back the tide of her grief, was dissolving. Her shoulders sagged with the wave of misery that now rolled over her, making every breath a struggle. Her constant companion since his birth, Bryn was more than her brother – he was her only friend. His loss was eviscerating. Merry felt hollowed out, numb with shock and so alone that it was like swimming in a vast ocean with no sight of land.

Without their father's leadership, she and Bryn had been rudderless, drifting into deeper and deeper water. Rothsea was an arrogant menace, but there was something in his certainty, in his innate air of authority, that was so reminiscent of her father, that she keened to it even while she rebelled against it. At the same time, Harry's gentlemanly presence reminded her a little of Bryn, which was a comfort in this dark hour.

Merry cringed at her own weakness but, though she chafed at the plans of her erstwhile protectors, the alternative was unquestionably worse. So, her practical side triumphed over the Griffith pride.

Harry gave her a reassuring smile, which prompted an answering twist to Merry's lips, and Rafe relaxed as he saw reluctant capitulation in her eyes.

'Very well, I'll accept your help,' she conceded. 'But now I must return home to lay out my brother.'

Rafe winced and was about to veto this, when Harry surprised him.

'That's been taken care of, Merry,' said Harry, bracing himself for the storm. 'Brooke is there now, with my man Clayton. You may trust them to do all that is proper, and I will take you to see him when they are done.'

Merry stared at Harry in open-mouthed astonishment.

'Good work, Harry!' approved Rafe, clapping him on the back.

Merry found her voice, but perversely turned on Rafe not Harry.

'Well, I might have expected such a treacherous piece of high-handed interference from you!' Then she turned back with a hurt expression. 'But not you, Harry.'

'I thought you a thirteen year old boy! It seemed the least I could do to help you out,' he said. 'And frankly, now that I know your sex, I can tell you that it would be highly improper for you to execute such intimate offices.'

Merry coloured a little and kept to herself that she had laid out her father.

'Well, talking of her sex,' said Rafe, changing the subject. 'We need to dress the little monkey accordingly. I'm not yet sure what to do with her, but whatever the plan, this masquerade is at an end.'

'What! I'm _really_ to dress up as a _girl?_' gasped Merry, her outrage as keen as any boy's in the same situation.

Rafe ignored her.

'Harry, can you dash over to Curzon Street and borrow an outfit or two from your sister? Sprigged muslin or mourning dress, if she has any, and a scarf for her neck?'

Harry nodded, and began to make for the door.

'Wait a moment! Wait a moment!' cried Merry, feeling powerless as these plans were laid for her. 'I didn't ask to be turned into a woman, nor do I want it!'

'But you will accept it nonetheless, you ingrate!' said Rafe firmly.

Harry put a comforting arm round her shoulder, which Rafe didn't like at all, and said soothingly: 'It is the right thing to do, Merry, I assure you.'

'Well, bustle about, man! We're losing precious time,' snapped Rafe. Something about the way Merry was looking trustingly into Harry's eyes sparked an unsettling desire to throttle him.

'Before I go, Rafe,' said Harry sternly. 'I'll have your word there'll be no more fighting or arguing while I'm gone.'

Rafe rolled his eyes and Merry huffed her doubt.

'Aye, and yours, too, Merry,' he added, his arms folded, like a chiding parent.

Harry had to bite back a smile as the pair of them, looking like sulky children, nodded reluctantly.

'Shake hands on it,' he ventured, and then laughed when both their expressions told him he had now gone too far.

At the door, Harry cast an admonitory look at Rafe before leaving him and Merry alone together.

Chapter Three
Alone with Rafe

As the door closed, Merry turned to Rafe, who stood only a few feet away watching her, his face unreadable. Then, her own expression changed swiftly from mulish to wary.

Unshaven and dishevelled, Rafe emanated a different brand of masculinity to the brash bloods and debonair dandies that she had encountered at prize fights and horse races. His lazy self-assurance and lithe virility sparked an odd, unsettling frisson of sensation that Merry could not name and did not like. For the first time, she was palpably conscious of being alone with a man, and her pulse quickened. Now exposed as a woman, Merry felt unusually vulnerable and very much on her guard.

Rafe watched as Merry's chin came up a fraction, in what he now recognised as a telltale gesture of courage. When she fished out a pair of thick-framed glasses from her pocket and put them on, he couldn't resist a chuckle.

'Well, that makes *all* the difference,' he said with an odiously knowing grin that broadened as he saw Merry's fists clench with the longing to draw his claret once more.

'Come on, you little tigress,' he said, with a meaningful nod towards the door at the back of the room. 'My chamber is that way.'

'What?' gasped Merry, her eyes widened in shock.

Rafe laughed out loud at her expression, though for one mad instant the image of this willowy wildcat in his bed made his loins leap.

Looking at her now, he wondered how he could ever have been deceived for a second. Even with those ridiculous glasses, against the pale gold oval of her face, her clear grey eyes looked luminous and alluring, with their thick fringe of dark lashes. But it was the candid intelligence he saw in them that attracted him most. Like her brother's, Merry's short tawny hair fell into waves that would make a dandy weep with jealousy. He wondered what it would look like when it was longer, how it might feel between his fingers.

Despite the life she had led, Merry had not been awakened to any womanly thoughts of love or desire. She was untouched in the purest sense. Rafe knew a wild urge to take her in his arms and kiss her. It would be her first kiss, he was sure of it. Unconsciously, his gaze strayed to her lips, which parted in alarm, and he saw her tense for battle.

Rafe laughed again, but inwardly shook himself. He was now the child's erstwhile guardian. It was one thing to be a little intrigued by her, but quite another to entertain any other ideas. What the hell he *was* going to do with her, he had no idea, but if he didn't want another bloody nose, it was clear he was going to have to clarify his last remark.

'Come and help me pack, you idiot,' he said, the laughter still in his voice. 'This *"silk-wrapped popinjay"* will need a change of raiment on his travels.'

Merry had to suppress the tremor of a naughty grin at that.

There was something infectious about his laughter, not simply the way it changed his face but also that it seemed more at his own expense than hers.

'Just pack?' said Merry suspiciously.

'Certainly,' he replied. Then, in a masterful caricature of a coquette, he gave Merry's shoulder a playful prod and added: 'Why, Mr Griffith! Whatever did *you* have in mind?' fluttering his eyelashes in such a comical way that Merry stared in dazed amusement for a moment. Then she caught her breath, the smile dying from her eyes, to be replaced by a baffled expression.

'I *know* …,' he said sympathetically, reading her thoughts. 'You think you know someone and then they do something quite out of character …' he broke off, shaking his head in another comic gesture of mock-disbelief.

Merry's intelligent eyes narrowed, and there was a frown between her brows as she tried to make him out.

Rafe folded his arms patiently across his chest and returned her regard, with one eyebrow raised in polite enquiry.

'What are you doing?' asked Merry.

'Waiting for you to finish assimilating the fact that the monstrous Lord Rothsea has a sense of humour,' he said dryly. 'I wonder if you will place that information under my sins or my saving graces … the debit or the credit column?'

Against her will, Merry's lips twitched and her eyes flashed with reluctant fascination, which, unknown to her, had a disturbing effect on the monstrous lord.

'Come along. I meant what I said. I need to pack and you're going to help me.'

'Can't you do it yourself?'

'I could. But it will be quicker if you help … and frankly, if I leave you alone, I don't trust you not to bolt … and I would not be able to run after you, or the Watch will be running after me.'

Merry still vacilated, so he hastened her decision-making by taking her shoulders in a firm grasp from behind and steering her into the room.

'My traps are over there in the corner,' he said pointing to two leather bags stacked on top of a carved ottoman. 'And my shirts, linen and breeches are in the drawers behind you. Pack enough for three weeks.'

Rafe nerved himself for further wrangling, but it never came. Merry set to work, mechanically opening drawers and lifting out his neatly folded clothes.

In silent wonder, he watched as she handled his most intimate clothing without a blush, counting out and selecting the items to pack. She was clearly deep in thought, for her hands occasionally suspended mid-task as she wrestled with some new notion. Then he saw her fingers exploring the fine quality and transparency of his linen, and found, with surprise, that he had to make himself busy to overcome the unexpected but unmistakeable quickening of desire this kindled in him.

For her part, Merry was glad of the distraction of this mundane task. Grief was an abyss that threatened to drag her in, and her mind jangled with conflicting thoughts. She wanted a villain that she could punish for Bryn's death and her own predicament. But it now seemed that Rothsea was not as despicable or callous as she had imagined. He was merely arrogant, smug and very bad tempered. Now, he was dragooning her into changing her identity ... yet he had assumed responsibility for her welfare without question. He had taken her brother's dying wish as a solemn obligation ... and more than all this, the thought that dominated her mind, Rothsea had _held_ Bryn during his last moments. Somehow it meant more than she could say. Bryn had not simply been left to die on the cold turf. He had been lifted and held, even comforted, in those strong arms. Merry felt a surge of tangled emotions as she pictured it.

Her hands stilled and she looked across at Rafe as he laid a few waistcoats out on the bed. He sensed her gaze and glanced up.

'What is it?' he asked, as her expression made his gut lurch.

'It ..,' Merry swallowed hard, and continued in an unsteady voice. 'It should have been I who held him.'

Rafe knew precisely what she meant. A bolt of remorse shook him, and he covered his eyes with his hand then dragged it down his face.

'I know,' he said finally, his voice strangely intimate, as if he had known her all his life.

'But I'm ...' Merry faltered.

'You are glad that he was held, nonetheless?' supplied Rafe.

Merry blinked at his quick understanding, and then her expression softened in confirmation.

Rafe sighed.

'Would that I had shown such compassion sooner,' he muttered.

Then, he walked round the bed and stood before her.

'I don't expect you to forgive me, but allow me to apologise for taking your brother's life, Miss Griffith,' he said, then sighed and added. 'I cannot undo what I did, but I can regret it ... and I do, sincerely, regret it.'

Merry coloured a little. He was right, she would never forgive him, but at least his repentance seemed genuine.

They stood in awkward silence for a moment, then Rafe shifted the topic.

'I can't honestly undertake to keep my wretched temper in check in future,' he admitted. 'It tends to get the better of me when I'm drunk.'

'Then I infer you're still foxed?' said Merry, lifting her hand to her bruised throat to remind him.

Rafe's lips twitched in appreciation at her ready wit.

'Did I hurt you?' he said softly, with a rueful look.

'No, not at all,' she lied, and then nodded towards his nose. 'Did I hurt you?'

'Yes!' he said resentfully, making her naughty smile appear again.

'Good!' she said. 'Though I should have followed through with an upper cut when you doubled over.'

'Wretch! I don't suppose you can undertake to keep *your* temper in hand either?"

'I can't imagine what you mean,' replied Merry primly.

'Can't you, Miss I'll-pull-on-your-legs Griffith?' he responded dryly.

As Merry looked away and bit her lip to keep from smiling, Rafe glimpsed the reddened skin beneath her crumpled cravat.

He tutted, then reached for a small pot amongst the various items on the top of the chest of drawers. 'Arnica,' he explained.

One elegant hand then parted the shirt collar from her neck to inspect the damage. But as his fingers gently touched her skin, Merry gasped and stepped back, breaking the contact that had sent an unaccountable shiver of warmth through her. Rafe looked no less disturbed. He withdrew his hand as if burned and handed her the ointment, moving away.

'The packing,' he said swiftly changing the mood to Merry's great relief. The unsettling effect of his touch she put down to her troubled state.

'Packing,' she murmured absently, as if remembering why they were in the room together, and then turned to resume her task.

Rafe smiled, but his own brows dipped as he wondered at the strength of his physical attraction to this strange tomboy. Any liaison with her was out of the question, or Harry would have him marching down the aisle at the pistol point, and Rafe had absolutely no intention of getting leg-shackled.

Opening a wardrobe and pulling out some of his coats at random, Rafe remembered that he was still in his evening clothes. He knew he should repair to the dressing room to change, but a team of dray horses could not have dragged him from Merry's presence at that moment.

'Here, pass me one of those clean shirts!' he said, stripping off his waistcoat. '… er … if you please?'

Merry's back was momentarily to him, so he didn't see her lips twitch at this hesitant addition. She turned back to pass him a shirt and her eyes widened as he pulled his soiled one off over his head and then reached toward her for the clean one. Merry's lips parted and she found, unaccountably, that she was blushing at the sight of his well-muscled torso and broad shoulders. It was a long moment before she could drag her eyes away from it, only to find Rafe looking back at her, still reaching for his shirt, with a knowing smile on his face.

'If you're quite done taking in the magnificence of my manly form,' he said with that self-mocking tone, spreading his arms wide. 'Perhaps you'd be good enough to fish out a cravat for me too.'

Blushing furiously, Merry tossed a cravat towards him.

'We might make a woman of you yet,' he murmured, pulling on his clean shirt and chuckling at the strangled: 'Insufferable coxcomb!' that came from Merry's direction.

But there was something irresistible about his low laughter that dragged a reluctant smile onto Merry's lips despite her embarrassment. There was so much self-mockery in his manner that it was clear that his good looks were of little account. There was no vanity in him. Arrogance, yes, but not vanity. Merry had no idea why the sight of his body should have had such a singular effect on her, but his humour and his casual manner were certainly undermining her determination to despise him.

'I was only thinking that you strip to advantage and wishing that I myself had your physique,' muttered Merry. 'Then I should have no problem finding employment.'

Merry looked up to find Rafe staring at her open-mouthed.

'What?' demanded Merry.

'I literally don't know where to begin!'

'Praise God!' crowed Merry sarcastically. Then as Rafe opened his mouth to speak, Merry held up her hand. 'Pray! Let me cherish the moment a little longer!'

'Vixen!'

THE RELUCTANT LADY

'Ho! So much for giving Harry your word not to argue.'
'You started it!'

Glancing across to see him struggling with the row of small buttons at his cuffs, Merry walked over and took over the task.

'Spoilt to incompetence,' she said severely. 'You can't even dress yourself without assistance!'

'I rarely wear this shirt,' he found himself explaining. 'It's one of Lain's fancies.'

But Merry was not attending, her brow furrowed in thought once more.

'What are you thinking, my little valet?'

'"Puzzles the will".,' she murmured.

'Hamlet!' he replied, smiling at her look of surprised respect. 'We monsters are educated too, you know,' he said with a sardonic look. Then added, softly, looking down at her: '... and you would have loved Cambridge.'

A slight, proud smile twisted Merry's lips, and Rafe almost gasped at the echoing twist he felt in the unfamiliar region of his heart.

Merry saw the change in his expression and scanned his face appraisingly, looking for clues to make him out. Rafe nodded to his wrists to distract her.

'You're neglecting your duties,' he said.

Watching her downturned face as she did up the rest of the buttons, he mused: 'So are you finding your _will_ to strangle me _puzzled_ by my engaging manners and delightful ... er ... bedroom manner?'

Merry looked up, her intelligent eyes registering a respect for his acute interpretation.

'There!' she said, releasing his wrist. 'All done.'

'Would you like to help with my cravat?' he asked, with a disarming smile on his lips.

'Not unless it's made of hemp,' countered Merry smoothly, turning back to finish packing the traps.

'Oho! _NOT_ so puzzled, after all!' he responded appreciatively. 'Still, if that's your notion of tying a cravat, perhaps it's for the best,' he added, with a nod towards the sorry specimen around Merry's bruised throat.

'Well! I should like to see what your effort will look like after some thug has put his paws around your neck and dragged you up and down the back stairs by your throat!' replied Merry with asperity.

'Oho! "*a hit, a very palpable hit*",' quoted Rafe, thoroughly enjoying himself and unwilling for this unorthodox exchange it to end. 'You see! I can quote a little Shakespeare myself,' he quipped, with an insouciant wiggle of his head.

For a few moments, the intricacies of tying his cravat took up his attention, but then he glanced round to find Merry watching him thoughtfully.

'Trying to pick up tips?' he ventured. 'From a master?'

'Well, I would scarcely be watching *you*, if I were,' she replied, her caustic gibe undermined by the impish grin tugging at her lips.

'Oh! And there's another blow to my fragile self-esteem!'

Merry laughed out at that, but caught herself and shook her head, staring at Rafe, who was straightening his shirt points.

This man killed Bryn this morning! Yet, here I am laughing with him! What is wrong with me?

Merry looked back down at the traps, and carefully folded the coats he had selected on top of the other neatly packed things.

Rafe pulled off his Hessians with a carelessness that was the despair of his long-suffering valet.

'Pass me a pair of those buckskins,' said Rafe, breaking into Merry's train of thought.

Merry handed him a pair of riding breeches. Still a little distracted, she had not turned away. Rafe stood holding the garment in his hand and regarding her with a quizzical expression.

'What? Are they not the right ones?' asked Merry, confused.

Rafe did not answer, but his expressive eyebrow lifted a little higher. Then, as Merry continued to look uncomprehendingly at him, he lifted a finger to gesture that she should turn around.

Merry did so, but turned back unthinkingly as she scoffed at his prudery saying: 'Well! I wouldn't have guessed that you would be so shy …' then she gasped and flushed crimson as she glimpsed Rafe's bare thighs below his, thankfully long, shirt.

Her head whipped back round to face the wall as, to the sound of Rafe's wicked chuckle, she grasped that unlike Bryn and herself, Rafe did *not* wear drawers.

THE RELUCTANT LADY

'Well! You might have warned me!' said Merry in a choking voice.

'Why? What do you wear under *your* breeches, my fine fellow?' asked Rafe, genuinely interested.

'None of your business!!' croaked Merry blushing. Then realising that she was inviting unwelcome speculation, she muttered: 'If you must know, we all wore drawers!'

'Well, I suppose you would,' conceded Rafe. 'If it's any consolation, I sometimes wear the winter drawers that you so kindly packed for me when it's particularly cold. But – and I know you will call me a coxcomb again – I don't like to wear them, as they spoil the line of my skin-tight … er … inexpressibles.'

'Then, what …' Merry broke off in consternation, realising that her enquiries had entered very improper territory.

'My shirt,' said Rafe hastily, his hand across his eyes as he shook his head in disbelief at this most inappropriate discussion. 'I tuck my shirt in … er … thoroughly.'

'I see. What about Harry?' asked Merry, with irrepressible curiosity.

'What *about* Harry?' replied Rafe dryly, not at all happy that Merry's thoughts had so quickly strayed to what his friend wore underneath his trousers.

'Does he wear anything … underneath?' she whispered.

'I don't know! It's never come up in conversation!' responded Rafe sardonically. 'But I shall make certain to ask him the next time we're at cards! Are you sure you wouldn't like me to conduct a census at our club, just to satisfy your obvious curiosity on the topic?'

Merry couldn't help giggling at the incredulity in his tone and the ridiculous picture he conjured.

'You know, you could never discuss such things with me if I were a lady,' she said, thinking to illustrate the benefits of her masquerade.

'Well, by all that's holy!' cried Rafe in hard-done-by outrage. 'As if I wanted any part of *that* conversation anyway!'

Merry giggled again and once more reprimanded herself for laughing when she should be baying for his blood. But his sense of humour was so very much in concord with her own that it pierced through all her defences.

'You may turn around again,' said Rafe, now more decently attired. 'And I thank you for respecting *my* modesty, at least.'

Merry turned, but did not look at him. Rafe found himself wishing she would.

As he buttoned his straw-coloured waistcoat and put on a fresh dark blue coat, Rafe's eyes rarely left Merry's face. He had sensed the change in her mood and now he watched her intently. She was clearly thinking deeply about something. Good or bad, he longed to know what it was.

'The credit column,' she said unexpectedly, in a quiet, matter-of-fact voice, when she had finished fastening his traps, her hands resting on them for a moment.

Looking up, expecting to have to explain herself, she saw ready understanding in Rafe's face and a disturbing look that made her heart give an odd thump.

'Merry,' he murmured, in a strange, hoarse whisper. 'Come here.'

'Why?' she asked warily, his look and tone kindling the same unnerving sensation that his touch had done.

'Don't you know?' he asked in that altered voice, one hand on the bedpost as he tried to master this startling surge of unruly emotion.

'No, and I don't want to,' she said firmly. Whatever this unsettling feeling was, she wanted no part of it.

Merry picked up the traps and carried them towards the drawing room, as Rafe took a ragged breath, sobered by her rebuke. As she reached the door, Merry turned and nodded towards his face.

'You should have shaved when you had your shirt off,' she said, with a twinkle. 'You look like a pirate in his Sunday best.'

'Damn it!' he said, in vexation, the mirror confirming his hirsute state. 'Well you can't blame me for rushing! I was being ogled by a young man at the time! And when exactly did you meet that pirate?'

But, despite his quip, once she left, Rafe leaned heavily against the wall.

What the hell was that?

He had never experienced anything like it … just three words had knocked him sideways.

And what were you thinking, sapskull, calling her to you? She's out of bounds, you hound! God knows you don't need this complication! The sooner you see the back of her the better!

But even as he told himself this, and reviewed possible options for settling her future, he mentally rejected all that removed her entirely from his life.

Merry too was puzzling over the interlude with Rafe when the scamper of footsteps on the back stairs heralded the arrival of Harry with two bandboxes dangling from his hands.

'Dresses for the lady and all the unmentionables Sarah and I could think of,' said Harry triumphantly. 'I looked like a footman who'd misplaced his mistress … but anything for a lady in distress,' he added, with a chivalrous little bow to Merry.

Merry smiled, but looked at the bandboxes as if they harboured snakes.

'Well done, Harry!' said Rafe, emerging from the bedchamber and waving a very mulish looking Merry towards it.

Merry did not move and looked ready to open battle once more, but Rafe forestalled her.

'I'm perfectly ready to dress you myself, here, if you prefer?' he said, a glint of steel in his eyes.

'You wouldn't dare!' growled Merry.

'Would you care to wager your pearls on it?' he said silkily, 'You would lose, my dear.'

'Oh, very well, you damned bully!' she snapped churlishly, accepting the bandboxes from Harry. 'And I'm not your "*dear*", you patronising toad!'

'Need any help?' offered Rafe, as she passed him.

'Push off!' Merry replied crushingly, shutting the door in his face.

'Just wanted to return the favour,' he called.

'What favour?' she heard Harry demand from the other side of the door, as she emptied the various items of clothing onto the bed.

In the other room, a heated discussion was under way, as she quickly removed her familiar raiment and began to wrestle with the mysteries of female attire.

'I knew I shouldn't have left her alone with you! What favour, Rafe?' pursued Harry doggedly.

'Merry helped me pack and … er … dress,' confessed Rafe, enjoying the certain knowledge that Merry would be smiling and shaking her head at his baiting Harry.

She was in fact shaking her head at how to assemble the selection of items before her.

'She watched you dress!' bellowed Harry, aghast.

'Well, I could scarcely prevent her, dear boy. I'm a pretty well-put-together specimen. Besides, she's seen it all before …'

'All _WHAT_ before!' roared Harry.

The door to the bed chamber opened a crack and a bare arm emerged holding out one of the unmentionables that Harry had referred to.

'What's this?' asked Merry. 'And which way up does it go?'

Harry's hand shot to his mouth to stifle a crack of laughter, and Rafe passed an unsteady hand across his eyes, before reaching out and taking the garment from her hand.

'Stays,' he answered. 'And they go this way up, with the laces to the back. Are you _sure_ you don't want any help?'

The hand disappeared and the door closed with a snap in his face.

'Seriously … just eager to be of assistance,' said Rafe innocently through the door.

'Rafe!' shouted Merry and Harry in unison, and Rafe smiled to hear his given name so naturally on Merry's lips.

'So how exactly did Merry help you dress?' persisted Harry.

Rafe gave him a broad, provoking grin.

'Don't make me knock you down,' growled Harry.

'Do you honestly think you could, old man?' said Rafe in a mock-serious tone.

'Damn you! …'

The door opened a crack again.

'Do the stays go on over the shift or under it?' asked Merry.

'Over,' the two men replied as one.

The door closed again.

'How on earth is she going to do them up without assistance,' asked Rafe reasonably, watching the wrath kindle in Harry's eyes again, as he pretended to reach for the door.

'If anyone is going to help her dress, it will be I,' grated Harry.

'Why, Harry! You shock me!'

Harry couldn't help laughing at this comment, delivered with one of Rafe's quizzical looks.

'Well, at least I have a sister!'

'Whom you dress regularly?'

Harry laughed out loud at this outrageous suggestion, then the door opened once more.

'Harry!' came a furious whisper. 'I think you've forgotten something!'

'What?'

'Something *important*!' said Merry, in a rather suffocated voice.

Harry enumerated the items he had brought.

'Chemise, petticoat, stays, gown, stockings, garters, slippers, bonnet, spenser, gloves, scarf ... no, Merry, I don't think anything's missing,' he assured her.

'But, but ...' She couldn't continue. Then Rafe's ready understanding came to her rescue.

'No, Merry, I'm afraid there's nothing else to put on ... er... above the garters.'

There was a gasp and the door slammed shut.

'Drawers! I never thought ...' grinned Harry, shaking his head. 'M'mother won't have them in the house ... says they're *fast*.'

'What!' said Rafe, thinking of the array of bosom and damped petticoats he had seen when last at Almacks.

'Because they are made to be seen ... and should not be necessary, I suppose,' Harry clarified, uncomfortably.

Rafe rolled his eyes.

'Well, I suppose we'll have to buy her some if it makes her feel more comfortable,' he muttered.

'Well, I'm damned if I'm going to trot around the Pantheon Bazaar asking for them!'

Rafe gave a broad grin as he pictured that scene.

Five more minutes passed, and Rafe's patience snapped.

'Merry, you must be ready by now,' he called. 'Don't make me come in there and fetch you!'

There was a strangled cry of frustration, then the door flung open and Merry stomped out, looking like thunder.

Red-faced and awkward, her outfit all askew, and her bonnet held strategically over her privates, she looked every inch a boy forced to wear women's clothing.

'This ... is ... *indecent!*' she hissed in a mortified whisper, pointing down at the charming morning dress, which clung softly to her slender hips and revealed a glimpse of gently rounded bosom. 'I refuse to wear it outside this room! ... I can already feel a draught!' she gasped, trying to stuff the gown between her legs. 'It's obscene!'

This was too much for both men's self-control, and they burst out laughing, which only increased in volume when Merry turned on her dainty slippered heel, with what dignity she could muster, and stalked back into the bedroom, swiftly twitching her bonnet behind her to hide her bottom, as if it were somehow exposed by the thin muslin gown. The door slammed to renewed gales of laughter.

Rafe, recovering first, went to the door to open it and found it locked.

'Merry! Open this door!'

'No!'

'I'll break it down. You know I will.'

'Damn your eyes!' she swore, but the key turned in the lock.

He opened the door sharply and in two strides was standing over her, looking annoyed.

'Don't lock a door against me again, Merry. Do you hear?' he said in a stern, intense tone.

'I don't expect I shall ever have the opportunity!' she countered, defensively.

'Well, I still don't recommend it. Here! Turn around! You haven't buttoned this up properly, and what on earth is going on with your stays? They're all over the place!'

Under Harry's awed supervision, Rafe unbuttoned the back of Merry's frock, untied her petticoat and pulled both aside to position and retie her stays as professionally and matter-of-factly as any good lady's maid. This done, he turned her about firmly and retied her petticoat and tucker at the front and then he set her gown perfectly on her bust and shoulders, before turning her again in order to fasten it primly at the back. Then he picked up the black velvet spenser from the bed and fed her unresisting arms through its sleeves, before turning her about once more, like a child, to button it, finally arranging her scarf elegantly through her elbows. All these intimate offices were accompanied by a stream of ringing abuse from a crimson-faced Merry, who roundly denounced the character and morals of any man who could execute such tasks *so* knowingly and without the slightest shred of decency or delicacy.

'And all this,' replied Rafe, with maddening calm, placing the bonnet on her ruffled curls, teasing one or two out to frame her face. '... From a young lady who arrived dressed as a man!' He tied the bonnet ribbons at a jaunty angle beneath her chin and looked down at the results of his handiwork.

Merry was looking up at him, an indignant sparkle still in her lovely grey eyes, which unconsciously sought his approval and found it in the strange, hungry expression in his own.

Then he maddened her once more by snatching the glasses off her nose and trying them on himself in highly comic fashion, before pocketing them, lending a deaf ear to Merry's complaint.

Harry, reduced to a bystander, let out a low whistle.

'Why, Merry! Rafe was right. You're a beauty!' he said simply.

'Stuff!' replied Merry awkwardly. 'What's come over you, Harry? I'm still the same person I was ten minutes ago ... and I wasn't a beauty then.'

'Yes, you were,' replied Rafe, causing Merry to blush again. 'At least now you're properly ... wait a minute...' said Rafe, glancing down at Merry's skirt, his brows twitching together in a suspicious frown. After a swift glance at the bed, where Merry had folded her former raiment, he reached down and patted Merry's hips.

'Merry! Are you wearing those damned breeches of yours under this dress?'

Merry looked up at him in guilty consternation and then in panicked appeal to Harry, who was struggling manfully not to laugh.

'Take them off this instant!' said Rafe exasperated, and then seeing the mutinous look in Merry's eye, conceded: 'Oh, leave your drawers on, if it makes you feel better, but the breeches come off, now!'

Merry's face was a picture of flaming rage as she snapped, in a choking voice: 'You black-hearted devil! I should like to see how you would feel in my place, wearing women's clothes for the first time!'

Rafe merely grinned broadly, wondering why he delighted in provoking the poor child so much. Her candour was bracing. Most women courted and flattered him, whereas Merry delighted in puncturing his self-image as often and as brutally as she could, and yet, inexplicably, he was enjoying every moment of it.

Merry was now trying to push him out of the room, so that she could remove her breeches. He stood unmoved for a moment, despite her best efforts, smiling down at her in amusement, before yielding and allowing her to force him through the door, which she slammed behind him.

'Hellcat!' he called through the door.

'Bounder!' she shouted back, a reluctant smile once again tugging at her mouth. It was wonderfully liberating to abuse him so freely. *But how the devil does he make me smile even when I'm livid with him?*

After a few moments, Merry emerged looking a little more composed and in considerably better order thanks to Rafe's ministrations.

'So, now that you are *appropriately* dressed,' said Rafe pointedly. 'Let us sit down and discuss what's to be done.'

'I would much rather you loaned me a little money,' said Merry.

'And then what?' enquired Rafe.

'What do you mean?'

'How would you propose to keep yourself?'

'I'm not afraid to do honest work. Richardson's the saddlers are taking on.'

Rafe who was sitting, as before, on the arm of the sofa, snorted and jumped up, taking Merry's fine, white hands and turning them over in his strong, warm ones.

'They'd never have you,' he said dismissively. 'You would not last a day, and anyone with half an eye would know it. You can have no idea how hard it is to stitch leather, but any saddler could tell your fingers don't have the strength for it.'

Merry snatched her hands from Rafe's.

'Much you know about it,' she snapped. 'You've never stitched a saddle in your life.'

'Nor have you, but I, at least, have the strength to do it,' he replied sternly. 'In any case, you may give up any notions of working for a living. I have no intention of allowing it.' Then seeing angry pride kindle in Merry's eyes, he added with a short bow: 'In deference to your brother's last request, of course.'

'Then what *am* I to do to earn my keep?' she demanded.

'Learn how to comport yourself like a lady,' replied Rafe. 'That should be taxing enough.'

As he spoke, Merry was sitting back in her chair, in a very masculine pose, with her arms folded defiantly across her chest and a mulish look on her face. She shifted slightly and unthinkingly brought one leg up, to lay her ankle on the opposite knee, in her customary boyish pose, unconsciously presenting the gentlemen with an excellent view of her drawers.

'Merry!' they gasped, Harry extending his palms to block his view and Rafe covering his eyes with his right hand and laughingly shaking his head. At this, Merry blushed dark red, swiftly placed her feet on the ground and stuffed her skirt between her ankles.

Rafe and Harry then spent the next twenty minutes giving Merry a rapid grounding in the essentials of ladylike behaviour, which might have been highly amusing to them all, if less had depended upon it.

Rafe told her to practice walking around the room in her skirts, and drew Harry aside.

'I think she'll have to go to my stepmother,' said Rafe in an under-voice.

'Lady Northover?' whispered Harry in consternation. 'Can you trust her?'

'She can scarcely refuse me while I hold her purse-strings,' said Rafe.

'I don't like it,' said Harry.

'Nor do I, but I can't immediately think of a better alternative,' said Rafe. 'If I install her at the Fall, people will assume she's my mistress, and we can't put her up at an hotel while she has no notion how to behave. I don't suppose your mother will take her in during the season of your sister's debut?'

Harry shook his head regretfully.

'Before I leave the country, I'll try to hunt up a companion or a maiden aunt to teach her how to go along … somewhere in the country, away from the quizzes here in town.'

'Yes, that would be just the thing!' cried Harry.

'After that, we can think about what to do next,' said Rafe, with a half-smile at Merry, who had walked up to them and was now expressing tight-lipped distaste for these plans being made for her future as a woman.

The clock chimed. Rafe could put off his departure no longer.

'Will you put your trust in a monster?' he said, taking Merry's hands, and then as Harry cleared his throat with meaning behind him, he corrected. 'Well, one monster and one gentleman.'

Standing so close to Rafe with her hands still in his, Merry felt disconcertingly feminine. Then she saw him frown, as he put a finger under her chin, to tilt her head back a little. The gauzy tucker revealed the red marks on her throat, particularly where his arm had crushed her thin strand of pearls into the soft tissue there. The insubstantial feel of her fine muslin gown and the fact that her neck, normally bound thickly in collar and cravat, was now barely covered by filmy gauze, made Merry feel horribly exposed. Even this slight touch on her bare flesh made Merry's heart beat faster.

Rafe noted the rapid rise and fall of the well-filled bodice of her spenser with interest, but only remarked: 'Ah yes, my dastardly handiwork,' adding conversationally: 'But I console myself that you don't have a black eye to accompany it.'

'Not for want of trying!' said Harry dryly. 'What a pair of fire-eaters you both are!'

'Well, it won't do for my stepmother to spot *that* until she's given you house room.'

Rafe took the long slim scarf from her elbows, skilfully circled her neck with it once and arranged the long ends to dangle down in front as carefully as he might one of his own cravats.

This done, he stepped back to study the effect, and gave a nod of approval. Then he turned to Harry.

'Explain the situation to my stepmother and charge her to take care of Merry until I can make other provision,' he said.

'Although Rafe must leave,' said Harry reassuringly, seeing Merry's dubious look. 'I shall remain and would be honoured to assist you until we can find a more permanent solution to your future.'

What Rafe might have said to this, they would never know, as Brooke opened the door and in urgent tones, said: 'My Lord, the postillions can't keep their horses standing much longer and the Watch will be wondering what a hired chaise is doing waiting so long.'

'The other business?' asked Rafe.

'All done, sir,' he said. 'The lad's fit to meet his maker.'

'Thank you, Mr Brooke' said Merry.

Brooke blinked for a moment at the boy-turned-girl, but bowed, and then left the back way with the traps, shaking his head at this latest twist in the day's events.

'I must go,' said Rafe reluctantly. 'Don't believe everything my stepmother says of me. Remember, you credited me with one saving grace, at least.'

'I was momentarily caught off guard by discovering that they accept monsters at Cambridge,' quipped Merry. 'I've a mind to write a very stiff letter to the Dean about it.'

Rafe was still chuckling at this as he left the room, bringing an answering smile to Merry's face. It was astonishing that she had entered this house with the intention of killing Lord Rothsea, and had ended by placing her future in his hands. He was odiously overbearing, but now that he had gone, it was as though all the energy and humour that had charged the last hour or so had left with him. While Harry's kindly presence remained, Merry would have been lying if she did not admit that she missed Rafe's strength. He was pig-headed, provoking and had bullied her mercilessly, but a treacherous part of her admitted that it had been a blessing. He had entirely chased away the terror that her bleak situation had threatened.

Merry realised that she had to credit him with a second saving grace - he made her feel safe.

Stranger still, his humour and intelligence were so in tune with her own that it was like a connection between them, and in his company her grief had been momentarily suspended.

Perhaps it is as well that he has gone away, she thought, *and I can simply be thankful that my immediate problems are solved.*

As he followed Brooke through the back way to Dover Street, where the hired chaise awaited him, Rafe was undergoing a similar epiphany. Though she held him in the lowest possible opinion, Merry had sparked something to life in him. Her extraordinary upbringing and her wit and courage, had exercised a powerful effect on him. He looked forward more than anything to the next time he would see her, and before the chaise had reached Oxford Street, he was regretting not bringing her with him, and bedamned to Harry's prudery.

As soon as he had gone, Merry turned to Harry.

'So, tell me the truth. Why did you ask if Rafe could trust his stepmother? Why does she dislike him?'

Harry hesitated, but since Merry would no doubt find out soon enough, as Lady Northover would not scruple to tell her, he capitulated.

'Because Rafe caused the death of her only child, his half-brother Kit..

Chapter Four
Confronting the Countess

'D... did he?' gasped Merry.

Harry shifted uncomfortably.

'Yes, I'm afraid so,' he acknowledged reluctantly.

'What happened?' pressed Merry. Somehow it mattered more than she could readily explain.

Resigning himself to the fact that Merry would not let the subject rest until she had the truth, Harry sighed and proceeded to lay the whole sorry tale before her.

As he swayed in the hired chaise heading north out of London, Rafe, too, was reliving the past.

No doubt the countess would embrace Merry as a fellow victim, yet, looking blindly out of the window as the orderly cottages on the outskirts of town gave way to the scrubby wilderness of Hampstead Heath, it chafed him to think of the vile opinions his stepmother would pour into Merry's ears.

Rafe did not blame the countess for holding him culpable for Kit's death. He did so himself. It was the main reason why he had continued to provide financial support for his father and stepmother all these years, even though both reviled him.

Rafe was too much like his father for theirs ever to have been an easy relationship, but his birth had caused the death of his mother, Arianna - his father's childhood sweetheart, whom he had wed at sixteen and buried at seventeen. Rafe was a fine, lusty child, and his father could not bear the sight of him. Within an hour of burying Arianna, he left the house and did not return for three years. When he did, it was with a second wife, intended as a substitute mother for Rafe ... but in this and most other respects Lord Northover had chosen poorly.

Ellen Cavanaugh was a second-season debutante, who, despite her considerable fortune, had failed to 'take'. So it was considered a startling coup when her parents snared the widower of the season for her through a substantial settlement. But this coup cost them dearly, as thereafter they made him many financial accommodations until their own resources ran thin - for Lord Northover had discovered high-stakes gambling, his 'fatal tendency' as the countess termed it. At first, the thrill of it had been the only diversion that had pushed back Arianna's death from the forefront of his mind, but then it took on a life of its own. Only the birth of his second son had arrested the Wolvendens' certain decline into penury, for Rafe's father had the worst luck in Christendom.

Kit, or more properly Christopher Wolvenden 8th Baron Mumshall, had not been Ellen's firstborn, but had been preceded by a miscarriage and a stillbirth. So when the fine little boy not only survived, but grew up to be the most lovable little scamp imaginable, it was scarcely surprising that he was rather cherished by his parents.

Rafe had never been cherished. He had experienced only distant and disapproving coolness from his parents and had thought this the lot of all children.

Within days of Kit's birth, he knew better.

At just five years old, Rafe realised that his brother was beloved and that he was not. Constantly reinforced by his parents, his self-contempt originated here, and though he knew himself to be able and intelligent, it was never quite enough. For all his privileged existence, there was always a hollowness at the heart of his life. Unwanted and unloved, he was tolerated only because he was the heir.

But, though it might have been natural for Rafe to resent his little brother, Kit's winning ways were irresistible and from the first, the boy had hero-worshipped his big brother. Like everyone else, Rafe adored Kit and showed such patient forbearance and restraint with him, that his parents warmed to him a little, though his many attempts to gain attention still resulted in rebuffs or whippings.

By the time Rafe was despatched to Eton, his skin was elephant hide and he adjusted better to the challenging environment than did others his age. It was here that he had met Harry and Charles, both drawn to Rafe's tough courage and comic humour, which more than made up for his fearsome temper.

Thanks to his constant striving to impress his father, Rafe had become a truly excellent horseman. At a horse fair, during his last Lenten Half break, Rafe had bought an unruly pair of greys for a snip. They had flawless lines but foul temperaments. Though less experienced in carriage driving, Rafe was determined to tame them. After a term of bites and scraped paintwork, Rafe had managed to bring the brutes to drive up to the bit. When he took the pair home to Twelveoaks that summer, even his father was impressed and bought him a new curricle as a consequence.

But a few days later, delighting in his little brother's adulation, Rafe had taken Kit out for a drive with the greys on the back roads outside the estate. At first, they had maintained a sedate pace, but inevitably for two reckless boys delighting in a stolen adventure and driving a bang-up pair, this good sense had not lasted. Kit had wanted to take the ribbons. Rafe had refused but had driven faster to compensate.

Rafe drew a hand across his eyes as he remembered the elated expression on Kit's sunlit face as he had hung on to the side, laughing into the breeze as they had sped down the long, straight track towards that fateful corner.

Now, nothing could hold back the memories that followed: the sudden shift from exhilaration to alarm; his hands straining to rein in the careering greys; the awful instant when the first wheel lifted from the road; futilely flinging out an arm to protect Kit; his brother's piercing scream as the curricle began to turn over and over; and then worst of all, the image that still woke him in a sweat on occasion, holding Kit's bleeding and broken body as he passed away, in pain and terror, choking from a punctured lung.

Just as the blackness of that time threatened to claim him once again, the image of an angry, grey-eyed, golden-haired bantam, challenging him to fight or damning his eyes as she wrestled with her unaccustomed female attire chased away the darkness and filled the void with remembrances that twisted his handsome lips into a grin. Then he felt his pocket and fished out Merry's ridiculous glasses. Turning them over in his hand, he smiled wistfully and wished he had not left her behind with his all-too-handsome friend.

'Rafe carried Kit for over a mile to the nearest cottage, though he was badly injured himself,' recounted Harry, bringing the story to its close. 'It was Brooke's mother's cottage he reached, and Brooke was there on his afternoon off.' Harry broke off and sighed. 'Rafe passed out as he reached the door. Northover collected Kit's body himself, but left Rafe there unconscious on the settle. Didn't even send a surgeon, only a note telling him never to come home, if he recovered.'

'Good God! The villain!'

'He was distraught with grief ... but you are right: His behaviour was shameful,' concurred Harry, looking into the distance. 'Father and son both spent that summer going to the devil in their own ways.'

'Did his father disown him? However did he live?' asked Merry.

'Rafe had a legacy from an uncle but was otherwise left to fend for himself, though he was only sixteen.' Then Harry turned to his companion and smiled. 'I don't suppose that seems very extraordinary to you, given the challenges you have faced?'

'On the contrary,' said Merry with feeling. 'I have thought my life a little grim at times, but though Bryn and I must have been a burden to our father, we were both loved unconditionally. Even now that they are gone, I take strength from that. But to be alone and adrift ...' Merry broke off as she voiced her own secret dread, now thankfully averted.

'I think it was the guilt that weighed upon him the most ... and still does,' said Harry. 'He adored Kit – such an engaging little fellow. Rafe had to bear his grief alone and tore himself to shreds knowing he had been the cause of the little chap's death. For months he did his utmost, short of suicide, to destroy himself. He still wishes it was he who died.'

Merry began to understand some of Rafe's self-deprecating remarks: "I disgust myself," he had said, and Merry now knew that he had meant it.

'So his reputation as a rakehell began that summer, and he has never had reason to change.'

'I see,' said Merry.

Harry was already regretting giving away so much about his friend's private affairs, but Merry would certainly hear a less objective version from the countess. At least now that she had the facts, Merry might judge for herself.

'You're a good friend, Harry,' said Merry unexpectedly.

Harry coloured a little at the compliment.

'Well, I've done precious little to alleviate the burden of blame that he seems determined to carry,' Harry replied sadly.

'But you have stood by him while he carried it,' responded Merry. 'And if I were he, it would mean the world to me.'

Harry blushed and demurred.

'Should we leave now to meet this stepmother of his?' asked Merry.

'Heavens, no!' said Harry. 'She won't receive us before noon at the earliest.'

'Do we have time to return to Newport Street?'

'Not really, no,' said Harry hesitantly, thinking of the traffic that would now be choking the route. 'I thought we could return there in the morning, once we have settled your immediate welfare.'

'Tomorrow?' said Merry, a little shaken. 'But I should at least sit with Bryn tonight.'

'No,' said Harry hastily at that grisly image. 'You can do nothing for him now, Merry, except see him buried honourably. He would not have wished it. I would not, if you were my sister,' he added shuddering as he pictured Sarah in such a situation. 'I am certain he would have preferred to know you were safely tucked up in a fine room of your own.'

Merry thought of what Bryn would have made of such a turn of events. *Why, oh, why had it taken his death to effect this change in fortunes?*

She knew Harry was right. If their roles were reversed, Merry would have gone to heaven with a light heart if she could have known Bryn was taken care of. But, now, the thought of her sweet, hapless brother, lying cold, dead and alone on the other side of town, threatened to overset her again.

Harry saw the haunted look returning to her eyes and looked about for a way to distract her for the next hour.

'I could not help noticing that you had a collection of books in your room. Rafe has a splendid library downstairs. Perhaps you might like to take a look at it?' he ventured.

It was a good notion.

'Hmm,' said Merry nodding, taking her first proper look around the elegant drawing room, its walls hung with pale blue silk and decorated with several fine gilt-framed paintings of horses and landscapes. An Ormolu clock stood on the mantel above the fireplace, flanked by jade carvings and Sévres figures at the outer edges. In the alcoves on each side, an elegant table displayed a fine marble statuette of considerable antiquity. On the other tables and surfaces round the room were scattered an eclectic collection of treasures, clearly chosen for their beauty or interest, rather than how well they went with their fellows. And so a large hollow rock lined with stunning purple crystals, stood beside a detailed carving of a standing horse and a couple of exquisite snuffboxes with finely painted lids. Merry liked everything she saw and the taste it reflected.

Harry led her down the wide staircase to a door next to the morning room. He smiled in anticipation as he opened it, and was not disappointed as Merry stopped on the threshold and gasped.

If she could have imagined her perfect room, this would be it.

Only two sections of wall were visible, hung with dark red silk damask and exhibiting two extraordinary paintings that seemed to glow from within. The rest of the room was lined with bookcases filled with volumes of different shapes and sizes. Opposite the doors, with a window behind, was a large desk of burnished mahogany, strewn with ledgers, maps, papers and pamphlets.

A rather messy monster, thought Merry, shaking her head.

Two globes stood in a corner, one of geography and one painted dark blue with stars and constellations painted on it. A large leather sofa and matching chairs arranged around the fireplace invited the reader to curl up with one of the multitude of volumes within the room, and their well-worn seats indicated that this had been done countless times.

Harry smiled at Merry's rapturous gaze.

'Yes, I envy him this room too,' he said.

'It's wonderful,' said Merry, drawing her finger along the backs of the leather-bound books and savouring the distinctive smell of the room.

She was drawn to gaze at the two paintings, which both featured stunning skies and all in a style she had never seen before.

'The artist is a chap called Turner,' said Harry looking critically at the pictures. 'Rafe is a great admirer of his work.'

'Breathtaking,' said Merry, drowning in the burning, hazy colours and dreamlike composition.

If Merry might have had her choice, she would have happily stayed in that room until Rafe returned and the devil take his notions of turning her into a lady.

Leaving Merry amongst the books and treasures, Harry quickly returned home to shave and change in preparation for the forthcoming interview with the countess. He returned just as the clock on the mantel chimed noon, and practically had to drag Merry away.

'If Lady Northover will not receive us, we can return,' he promised. 'But I doubt that she will dare to disobey Rafe.'

As they travelled to see the countess, Merry and Harry quickly agreed to stick to the truth, but not to volunteer more information than was necessary.

If Merry had thought Rafe's house in Albemarle Street was grand, she had rapidly to revise that opinion as they pulled up outside Wolvenden House. It was half as wide again and faced with a fine pale stone. The broad front door was flanked by two columns crowned with a pediment, and Merry found herself rather intimidated when the door was opened by a very superior servant, who seemed to miss not one detail of Harry's nervous state and Merry's unladylike comportment. The footman seemed inclined to deny the countess, but Soames her butler, stepping up to see who was at the door, recognised Lord Stowe and bid him wait in a small saloon while he enquired if her ladyship was receiving. What Soames might think about Lord Stowe's arriving with an unattended female, no one could know, for his well-trained features betrayed not the slightest clue. When Harry asked him to impress upon the countess that he bore a message from Lord Rothsea, Soames merely bowed and said in an impassive voice:

'But, of course, m'lord,' as if he had known it all along, and then made his stately way towards the stairs.

Merry tried to remain seated demurely, but after a few minutes she began to pace the floor, her actions reflecting the agitation of her spirits. Everything about this house seemed forbiddingly grandiose and oppressive. Worse still, she despised Lady Northover and the thought of being dependent on her charity was pretty much intolerable.

It was fully forty minutes before Soames returned to show them upstairs, by which time, Merry's temper was pent lava. Harry, too, was annoyed, but he swallowed his vexation at the calculated spite he suspected was behind this needless delay, for he was the bearer of a message that was vital to Merry's welfare.

Harry later cursed himself for not better employing those forty minutes and, indeed, the hour that had preceded it, in rehearsing his role as emissary. For until that instant, when he was announced into the august presence of the countess and stood blasted by Lady Northover's arctic stare, Harry had not fully appreciated just how difficult it was going to be to request her assistance. Rafe would have done so with one smooth statement, dripping with the lightly veiled threat of withdrawing the finance on which her lifestyle depended. But Harry had neither his arrogance nor his audacity.

Harry was also knocked off-balance by the countess's freezing hauteur - the primary weapon by which ladies of quality depressed the pretensions of any who failed to live up to their exacting standards of behaviour, be they unctuous mushroom or clamouring mob.

Before Harry had even made his bow - and Merry had unthinkingly followed suit - the countess had absorbed the damning fact that Lord Stowe's companion was wearing a dress that had not been made for her and most certainly did _not_ have the deportment of a lady. From this scant information, Lady Northover began to draw her own conclusions.

When the countess had been apprised of the essentials of Rafe's duel, she had maliciously instructed her personal maid to give her stepson's direction in Albemarle Street to the nearest Watch. Now, her ladyship thought she was seeing the cause of this morning's deadly dispute in a borrowed dress that was at least an inch too short for her.

More than a little awed by the exquisitely appointed grandeur of Wolvenden House, Merry had forgotten all her earlier instruction and had unconsciously moved with the boyish swagger that was second nature when she felt a little intimidated. When she had glimpsed Harry begin to bend into his bow, she had automatically done the same, straightening up to colour at his swift glance of alarm. When they had then turned to observe Lady Northover's reaction to Merry's lapse, they were both momentarily abashed by the formidable power of the countess' raised eyebrow.

Harry tugged at his cravat and wished that Rafe were there.

Within moments of his opening his mouth to speak, so did Merry.

'Ah ... er ... Lady Northover, may I introduce Miss Griffith to you?' stumbled Harry with excruciating awkwardness.

Not by the slightest movement did the countess acknowledge Merry's existence.

'Er ... Miss Griffith,' said Harry turning to Merry in a misery of discomfort. 'This is Lady Northover.'

This time Merry executed a slightly wobbly curtsey, but was already taking the countess into even stronger dislike than she had when Harry had recounted Rafe's unhappy past. Had Rafe been present, he might have been a little more alert to the significance of the slight lifting of Merry's chin and the challenging glint kindling in her eyes.

Harry, however, was all too occupied with finding the right words with which to frame Rafe's request of his stepmother, to notice these warning signs.

'Er... I am sure your ladyship has been informed of this morning's unfortunate events?' opened Harry hopefully.

Lady Northover's relentless iciness gave him no encouragement.

'Yes, well ... ah, Miss Griffith here is the sister of the young man who most regrettably perished in that encounter. Er ... and as the poor fellow was Miss Griffith's only living relative, Rafe ... er ... Rothsea has undertaken to provide for her immediate future.'

Lady Northover's lips flattened into one disapproving line, but she said nothing.

'And ... and he wondered if ... er ... if you might oblige him by entertaining Miss Griffith as your guest ... er ... here ... until he is able to make other provision for her.'

The countess's eyes betrayed a flare of fury, before they were veiled once again with distant hauteur. There was a deathly silence for a minute or two.

'I see,' said the countess finally, in a voice that could have frozen brine. 'And where precisely is Rothsea?'

'He has departed London, Lady Northover,' said Harry.

Another flash of annoyance sparked in the countess's eyes.

'Where has he gone?' she asked

'Abroad or to Scotland, I am to understand,' lied Harry.

'And when does he mean to return and relieve me of my *guest*?' This last was delivered with caustic sarcasm.

'I'm afraid I don't know, but he spoke of finding a female relative who might be willing to act as companion to Miss Griffith in the country as soon as might be possible,' said Harry, fervently hoping that Rafe meant to make this a priority.

'No doubt,' spat the countess, raking Merry from head to foot, now certain that her suspicions about Miss Griffith were correct. Her mouth worked for a moment as she mastered her outrage.

'You may leave, Lord Stowe,' she said finally.

Harry hesitated, looking anxiously at the unpromising body language between the two ladies. He was reluctant to leave without some idea of what the countess planned to do.

'You may go, Lord Stowe!' repeated Lady Rothsea in chilling accents.

Harry was left with no choice but to depart.

'Miss Griffith, I must take my leave but I will call on you this evening,' he said, with emphasis, 'to make sure that you are settled.'

Merry thanked him warmly and shook his hand. 'You're the best of good fellows, Harry,' she said reassuringly, with much her old manner, although her heart was in her ill-fitting kid slippers.

Turning back towards Merry with a last encouraging look, Harry was almost unmanned by her valiant little smile of reassurance. The footman, who had been a silent but interested witness to the whole scene, opened the door and Harry had no option but to walk through it. A flick of the countess's finger sent this flunkey from the room with a bow, to escort his lordship to the front door.

Now that they were alone, the two women glared at each other with patent dislike.

Merry looked at this woman who might have been a mother to a deserted child, but had chosen instead to extend his mistreatment. This neglect had contributed to the tragedy that had visited such bitter punishment on all of them. But seeing this withered woman, her face soured by years of gnawing resentment and her eyes burning with malice, Merry knew she had never assumed her share of the blame for what had happened. Lady Northover sat upon a small damask sofa, in a very expensive, embroidered silk gown, surrounded by a stunning array of costly elegance, all of which was funded by the stepson she despised.

But Merry was not entirely correct. Lady Northover did not merely despise her stepson: She loathed him to the very core of her being.

Other than the cool exchange of a civil nod when encountering each other at social events, Rafe had had almost no contact with his stepmother in the decade that had passed since Kit's death. He provided the countess with a generous allowance and the use of Wolvenden House, for which he footed all the expenses, and so he had very reasonably expected her compliance, albeit reluctant, with his first ever request of her.

But what he had not reckoned with was her simmering desire for revenge, because for his stepmother the hurt ran even deeper than the loss of a son.

Since Ellen Cavanaugh had received no acceptable offers for her hand, Lord Northover had imagined she might simply be grateful to be offered a home of her own and would raise his son until he might be sent to school.

Having married his childhood sweetheart as soon as her parents would permit, Northover was unaware of his good looks and great charm. Despite his rather cool courtship of her, Ellen thought him a demi-god and dreamed of a romantic future as his loving wife, filling the void left by his lost wife.

When she first stepped across the threshold of Twelveoaks, she discovered her mistake – there was no void to fill, for Arianna was there still, as a vibrant and flawless memory, in a house that was all but a shrine to her. Ellen was obliged to live with so many paintings of her rival around the house that she had more than once bitterly remarked that Arianna must have spent her first and only year of marriage constantly striking a pose.

And she had another constant reminder of Arianna in those cobalt eyes of her stepson, who was the image of his father but for this one characteristic. So Ellen exacted her spite on Arianna's child. The little tot was crying out for a mother's love but received only cool reproofs and critical gibes.

Ellen had still been determined to win the affection of the handsome man she had married, and when she was delivered of a healthy son, Ellen truly felt some return of her love, as her husband doted on Kit and they became a family.

When Kit died, Ellen lost her beloved son and adored husband in one fell stroke. After the initial period of shared grief, their only common ground was gone and Northover could not bear her company. He returned to the gaming hells, eventually obliging Rafe to buy up the mortgages on Twelveoaks and Wolvenden House to prevent the banks foreclosing on his inheritance.

Today, Northover lived on a short leash at Twelveoaks, since Rafe refused to pay any more of his gambling debts. When his wife visited Twelveoaks, Northover would stay with friends until Ellen returned to London.

Lady Northover laid all these woes and slights at Rafe's door and had longed to be revenged for them. So she had waited like a venomous spider in her web, hoping for an opportunity to strike at him.

Regarding Merry with all the absolute certainty of the utterly mistaken, the countess thought she saw just that opportunity.

Rothsea clearly cared for this shameless chit, and the countess could not afford to disoblige him, but the slut would feel the lash of her tongue at very least.

But Lady Northover had not yet encountered the Griffith pride.

THE RELUCTANT LADY

After several minutes of standing in frosty silence, like an errant schoolboy in front of a schoolmaster, Merry's temper was at boiling point when the countess finally deigned to speak.

'Do you think I am stupid?' enquired the countess in an acid tone.

'I think you a great many things, but stupid is not the foremost among them,' said Merry her chin high.

'Insolence!' gasped the countess, shocked out of her superciliousness by the implicit challenge in Merry's voice and demeanour. 'Do you think because you lifted your skirt for Rothsea and got with child by him, you doxy, that I will take you in without so much as a word about your shameful conduct.'

'What!' cried Merry, outraged.

'Oh, don't think to dupe me with your affectation of innocence. I take it your brother died defending your honour? Hah! Poor fool! He might have saved himself the effort for anyone can see you are a fast piece. Well, if you hope for a wedding to legitimise the bastard you carry, you hope in vain. Rothsea knows his worth and means to do better for himself than to wed some lightskirt of low birth and no breeding and with a natural child growing in her belly. He will bury you in the country and forget you.'

'You think I carry Rafe's child? No wonder you are so brimful of spite. Well, your insinuations speak more to the tenor of your own vulgar mind than they do of me. But what can one expect of a woman who took out her jealousies on a boy and precipitated the death of her own child thereby? I was disposed to pity you a little, countess, but now that I have tasted the bile in which you wallow, I find I can only wish you a long life in which to contemplate how your own callous behaviour and the poison you spread brought this misery upon you and all about you.'

'How dare you speak so to me!'

'Oh ho! Does the truth smart?' jeered Merry. 'Well, I wish I might give you one fraction of the hurt you inflicted, and on a child who was little better than an orphan. You were a bully when you might have been a mother.'

'Well, now you have gone your length, my girl!' snapped the countess. 'You had better learn to mind your tongue while you reside under my roof or I shall see that you are whipped whether you carry Rothsea's babe or not!'

'I should not be so sanguine, madam,' snarled Merry. 'I did not want to come here, but I was persuaded to do so against my better judgement. Well, now I have acquitted my promise. Good day to you!' Merry finished, forgetting her female state and bestowing a curt bow on the fuming countess.

'Come back here, you impudent girl!' demanded her ladyship. 'I did not give you leave to go!'

But she spoke to empty space.

Chapter Five
Alone and Adrift

Merry strode away from the drawing room and down the stairs with such a furious expression on her face that the normally sedate footman fairly skipped to open the outer door, holding out her bandboxes in his other hand. Merry ripped these from his fingers with a snarl, descended the steps and had reached the corner of Grosvenor Square before she had even considered where she was heading.

Tugging at her skirts angrily as they impeded her mannish stride, Merry realised that she was drawing curious and disapproving glances from everyone she encountered. With some irritation, Merry felt one of her stockings slither down her calf and gather at her ankle. As she sat against a low, railed wall to retie her garter, as surreptitiously as she could, a passing couple paused to stare at her with ill-disguised shock.

'What are you staring at?' challenged Merry defensively. 'Have you never lost a damned stocking before?'

The couple started at this and swiftly walked away, only risking a scandalised backward glance when they were a safe distance from the lunatic.

But for all her bravado, Merry felt scared and exposed. People were staring because her borrowed feathers bespoke the well-dressed debutante, but she had no attendant and her boyish gait was far from the delicate, floating step of a young lady. A fish out of water – Merry was neither the boy she had grown up as nor the lady she was now dressed as, and she felt utterly disoriented.

Though she longed to change back into her boy's clothes, held in one of the bandboxes, there was nowhere to do so.

Turning sharp left, Merry ducked into the side entrance of a house on Audley Street to take stock.

Her cheeks still flamed at the memory of what the countess had said to her, and she felt annoyed with herself for falling in with Rafe's plans so trustingly. She had been encouraged to hope, but now felt foolish and forsaken. Now Rafe was gone and Harry had returned home, and she had no idea where he lived.

Had she been less upset, she might have thought to leave a message for the footman to pass to Harry when he visited later, but no part of her mind considered returning to the house where she had been so insulted.

Merry longed for the comfort of the familiar. Even the dismal house in Newport Street, where poor Bryn's body lay, seemed more inviting than all the hostile elegance around her.

Since she was a stranger to this part of town and could not bear to be stared at while she wandered around trying to find her way, Merry was obliged to squander precious money on a hackney to take her home.

As the cab bowled along Mount Street and through Berkeley Square on its way towards Piccadilly, Merry reviewed her situation. There was no point dwelling on the events of the morning or depending on any help from Rafe or Harry. Their well-intentioned intervention had left her in a rather worse case than before. With no means to meet her immediate financial needs, she felt that awful choking panic at the thought of being taken up for debt, or burying Bryn in the poor hole.

Then as the cabbie picked his way through the thronging traffic around Haymarket and Leicester Square, Merry saw a jeweller's and, with a relieved mind but a sinking heart, she remembered her necklet.

She bid the cabbie set her down in Lisle Street outside an establishment, whose sign indicated the option to pawn jewellery.

So less than an hour since she had seemed to be saved, Merry was now pawning her mother's pearls that she had so fiercely defended through all their troubled years. Her heart was weeping, but as she had so many times before, Merry put on a brave face and hid her feelings from the keen-eyed dealer. This wily character seemed to find a disparity in the lady's outfit, which was of the finest, and the sad little necklet, though the tiny pearls were real enough. He offered her a paltry sum, but after encountering a truly murderous look from the young lady, revised this sum upward to something a little nearer its value, which was still depressingly low.

Lisle Street led into Newport Street, so Merry was not obliged to walk far. In this part of town, her fine clothes drew glances of admiration, and most took her for a wealthy young matron.

As she approached their lodgings, Merry saw the landlord waiting for her outside, fearful that once the body of one brother had been collected, the other would depart without paying what was owed.

She turned before he looked her way, and stopped out of sight.

Jenkins was as grasping a lickpenny as any landlord could aspire to be, and he would certainly charge an extra month's rent if she remained overnight. Poor Bryn would have to be buried that day. So Merry headed off towards the church of St Ann's, just a few streets away.

Meeting with the chaplain and the sexton, she found the arrangements surprisingly straightforward, as there was an inscription grave in need of a second occupant. The sexton was keen to close it up that day lest the body-snatchers come in the night and take away the first. Both gentlemen took pity on the poor young lady and were respectful of her wish to give her brother the best send-off she could afford.

With the arrangements complete, Merry made her way back to Newport Street, collecting the traditional refreshments for the parish men on her way.

Mr Jenkins didn't recognise the boy he had barely seen in the finely dressed lady before him.

Merry paid him the back rent with ill-concealed resentment.

'When will the poor young man be laid to rest, ma'am?' enquired the landlord.

She saw through his specious sympathy.

'The parish men will come for the body at five o'clock. In the meantime, I will pack up my brothers' things and have them carried away. There is no need for you to remain. I will lock up the rooms when I leave and hand the key to the maid.'

Mr Jennings left reluctantly, for though he wished to see Merry and her brother's possessions off his property, he was not proof against Merry's haughtiest look of dismissal.

Entering their rooms at last, Merry found her brother laid out on his bed, washed and prepared for burial. His lifeless face had a sunken look. Even so, it was hard to believe his eyes would never open again or his lips curve in a sweet smile. She sank down beside him and took his hand, feeling its strange stiff weight and cool waxy skin. Unthinkingly, her soft voice roughened by emotion, Merry murmured soothing endearments, as though to a sleeping child. Her hand shook rather badly as she put her comb through his waving curls and kissed his brow, before finally pulling the sheet over his face and exhaling on a broken sigh. Her dear brother was gone and she was alone.

Gritting her teeth, Merry dragged herself to her feet. She could not give in to grief now, there was too much to do. Soon, soon, she would weep for Bryn.

Brooke had clearly called in a surgeon, as a certificate of death lay on the bed, and opening a note that had been pushed under the door, she read that both the constable and the coroner's man had called for <u>Mr</u> Griffith and would return at three, which was only forty minutes away.

Merry swiftly changed back into her boy's clothes, thankful that she had retained her boots and hat. Her overcoat, too bulky to fit in the bandboxes, had been left at Rafe's. Looking at her reflection as she tied her cravat, Merry found the familiarity comforting, as if she had regained a little of herself with her old outfit.

Working quickly, Merry packed their few things, together with her borrowed outfits, into the two battered trunks that had followed them since their childhood.

Picking up the blood-stained jacket that Bryn had been wearing when he was shot almost overset her. She tried to clear her throat, scalded and raw with unshed tears. Merry could not bear the thought of throwing away this signal memento of him, so she wrapped it in a thin linen towel and packed it on top of the trunk.

A knock at the outer door announced the arrival of Mr Kent the coroner's assistant. He was a harassed-looking man, who was clearly the over-worked instrument by which deaths in the parish were managed with admirable efficiency. It was implicit in his tone and manner that he and his employer the coroner were one, for he referred to the office in the collective.

'We,' by whom he clearly meant the coroner, 'have received your brother's certificate of death and we are content for the body to go for burial.'

Merry sighed her relief, since the arrangements had been made.

'There have been very few deaths in the parish this week,' he sounded faintly disappointed. 'So we will consider your case at the inquest to be held at three o'clock tomorrow afternoon in Grafton House. Do you require the direction?'

Merry shook her head. The building was a couple of streets away and well known in the area of Newport Market.

Mr Kent was taking his leave, when the loud rapping of a brass-topped stick on the outer door signalled the arrival of the constable.

The interview with this official was far more taxing than that with Mr Kent, and Merry had to choose her words with care to protect Harry.

'So you met the gentlemen involved?' asked the constable hopefully, when Merry explained how her brother's body had been returned to her.

'Yes, I believe they were the seconds in the affair,' replied Merry.

'Did you know them?'

'I had not seen them before and they did not introduce themselves when we met,' she responded carefully.

'Hah! No, I don't suppose they did, the rogues!' said the official. 'But at least they did not leave the body where it fell, so I must suppose them to be gentlemen.'

'Yes, that was my impression, sir.'

'Do you know who the other protagonist was?' he asked. 'You see a surgeon who attended a fatal duel in Green Park was apprehended by the Watch and gave Lord Rothsea as the surviving principal.'

'Yes,' said Merry. 'I understand it was the same affair. Both were intoxicated and my brother accused his lordship of cheating.'

'Ah! That was foolhardy,' said the constable. 'Well, it seems that his lordship has already left town and means to self-exile. So I can't even promise you much of a trial, I'm afraid.'

Once the constable had departed, Merry then left for Long Acre, to find a carrier's yard and arrange for the collection of their two trunks, since she could not carry them with her while she sought work on the morrow. Merry knew that if she found employment, then she might be able to redeem them; if not, their few possessions - her beloved books and what remained of their clothes – would be forfeit forever.

The Griffiths had few friends, even when her father was alive. They did not socialise with their neighbours, whom Mr Griffith had believed beneath their touch. This, together with Merry's masquerade and their fluctuating finances, had discouraged them from entertaining even after their father's death. There was no one that she could turn to for assistance, even in finding a job. But Merry had enough money left from the sale of her pearls and the guinea that Harry's friend had left to sustain her until she could secure employment.

Secretly, another tiny hope sustained her. If Harry had meant the things he had said, he might come looking for her when he found that she was not at Wolvenden House. So she penned a note for him, advising what had happened and the time of the inquest, and left it with Peggy the maid.

All this time, she had avoided looking at Bryn, but when the tinny clock in the parlour chimed the half hour past four, she realised that the parish men would soon come with the coffin and a cart to transport the body, and her time alone with Bryn was coming to an end. She sat beside her brother, her hand resting on the sheet above his own crossed hands. Her heart was too full to speak, so she prayed in her head – a jumble of wishes and memories, fears and appeals.

A clattering knock shattered the quiet: the parish men were early! Merry drew back the sheet from Bryn's cold peaceful face, stroked his cheek and kissed his forehead, then stood up like an automaton and answered the door.

At their father's funeral, the parish's communal coffin had been in use with another interment. So Merry and Bryn had watched his poor body joggled under a worn velvet cloth draped as the cart had negotiated the detritus, traffic and cobbles of the busy route to the church of St Ann's. Merry would have starved rather than have the same happen to Bryn, and so she had used ten shillings of her meagre funds to pay for a coffin, death knell and part-share of an inscription grave.

Merry offered the parish pallbearers and the ordinary a few refreshments, as tradition demanded, before they set out. She began to be cushioned from this awful experience by a sense of unreality as the men chatted and munched on two-penny cakes washed down by small beer around the empty coffin, before transferring the stiffening body to the black painted box.

Reaching in, she patted his hands and, for the last time, kissed the brow of his angelic face. The parish men had attended a thousand or more such sad events, but all were touched by this last brotherly salute and rendered speechless, lest the lumps in their throats betray them. The lid was fixed on the coffin and it was carried to the waiting cart. Merry donned Bryn's overcoat and tied the black armband she had worn at her father's burial around her arm, then followed them out.

With Merry as the only mourner, it was a pitiful procession that made its way down the crowded, foggy street, surrounded by the daily traffic of wagons, hackneys, coaches and handcarts. But the chaos of the busy street around her receded into a muffled blur as she walked behind her brother, numb with sorrow, holding back her grief like a dam and harried by her fears for the future.

A funeral party was all too familiar a sight to occasion much attention, apart from the respectful nods or lifted hats of pedestrians momentarily stilled as the low cart bearing the coffin draped in a faded black cloth passed by. But those that saw the face of the beautiful, bare-headed boy who followed the cart were stilled a little longer and would not easily forget those haunting grey eyes, too proud to cry.

In fact, as if protecting her from the grief that threatened to crush her, Merry's mind recalled the strange interlude with Harry and Rafe. They had meant well, she thought, but it had almost been worse to let her hope that they would help, for she felt more alone than ever now.

At the church gate, the cortege paused to read a rapid psalm over the coffin, which speeded up further as fat raindrops began to plosh down onto the open prayer book and the heads of the sorry party gathered around it. As soon as it was done, the pallbearers moved briskly to gather up the coffin and get it inside the church. With so few in the congregation, the parson kept the service to the barest minimum. Merry neither noticed nor cared, staring blindly ahead, her eyes straying occasionally to the coffin that now contained the remnants of the life that had run in tandem with her own for seventeen years. Images of that life played in her mind's eye: at school, when they had pretended to be twins; with their father learning how to tool a carriage; escaping from the excise men when they had attempted to run brandy; and the last time she had seen him alive, his eyes alight with excitement. A thousand pictures of that lost life and the knowledge that there would never be more. Suddenly, the pallbearers were rising to lift the coffin. The service was at an end. Merry mumbled 'Amen' and stumbled after them.

In the driving rain at the graveside, the poor parson skidded through the final prayers, in response to the pleading looks from the drenched parish men. It was only as the coffin was lowered to join the other that Merry felt her restraint crumbling. A moment of wild panic seized her, and she trembled with an urge to jump onto the coffin, rip the lid off, and shake Bryn awake.

But he could never, never awaken.

The parson had to place the dripping mud in her numb hand and make her drop this onto the coffin. He tried to draw her with them as they then made a dash for the cover of the church, but she would not be moved.

Slowly, her strength gave way and Merry dropped to her knees beside the grave, the rain ploughing down around her, the tears finally coming - in wrenching, racking sobs. She wept for them both, for Bryn's lost life and her own blighted one.

Chapter Six
The Comfort of Strangers

That evening, Harry dined with his mother and sister as planned, bending only a polite ear to their chatter about a fabulous heiress lately come to town, and sundry other topics. Having spent the afternoon buying mourning clothes for Merry, he was pondering how to hand them over without scandalising the countess.

So when he called at Upper Grosvenor Street at half past nine, he was appalled to discover that the 'young person' had left only a few minutes after he had.

With unaccustomed wrath, Harry demanded to speak with the countess, and was made to wait in the library for an agonising twenty minutes before he was admitted into her presence. As he entered the drawing room, Harry was angrier than he could ever remember being in his life. It was this to which he later ascribed his excoriating bluntness.

'So, I take it that you could not confine your wanton malice to Rafe, Countess, but saw fit to subject that poor child to a taste of it, too.'

'How dare you!' hissed Lady Northover. 'Or was she *your* doxy, too?'

'She was naught but the innocent victim of a senseless tragedy, and you have cast her out upon the world unprotected through some twisted quest for revenge!' said Harry. 'And if you think I dare too much in saying so, I welcome you to imagine what Rafe will dare when he finds out what you have done.'

Harry derived a little gritty pleasure from the flash of dismay that crossed her ladyship's face.

'She went of her own accord,' replied the countess, a little defensively.

'Aye, no doubt after you insulted her unpardonably with your vile insinuations?'

The countess coloured guiltily.

'Where did Miss Griffith go?' demanded Harry.

'I neither know nor care,' responded Lady Northover.

'I think Rafe will care and he won't be pleased to hear that you did not meet his request,' replied Harry. 'Of one thing I am certain, countess - you had better start looking for lodgings, if you mean to remain in London this season.'

With the curtest of nods, Harry turned on his heel and left, but not before he saw Lady Northover's hands close like claws on her chair arm and the blood drain from her face.

Harry questioned the servants, but none had even noted in which direction Merry had gone.

Annoyed but not yet overly concerned, Harry was certain that Merry would have either returned to Albemarle Street, which was his first stop, or back to her own home, where she might now be sitting in that dismal place, with only her dead brother for company. The thought wrung his heart, and he ordered his driver to make haste, as he picked his way to Newport Street as quickly as the evening traffic would allow.

But when he reached Merry's lodgings, Harry's nightmare truly began.

Beside the grave, drenched to the skin, Merry's storm of grief gradually abated.

Then, she heard a discreet cough a step away and a comforting hand was laid on her sodden shoulder.

'Ay, that's it, young sir. Better to let the pain out than keep it in.'

Merry turned to see a young man, not much older than herself. He was dressed in a well-worn, oil-skin coat and was holding his hat respectfully in his hand and getting a soaking for his trouble. Merry slowly rose out of the mud that was slipping in small torrents into the grave. As she did so, she pulled herself together a little, resuming her boyish persona.

'I'm sorry, sir,' she said with a polite, if soggy, bow. 'You have the advantage of me. I am Merion Griffith. This was my brother Bryn.'

'Ay, I know. I'm John Coley. It's my betrothed that shares your brother's grave and headstone,' replied the young man. 'If it's not an impertinence, Master Griffith, I'd like to know a little more of the man who will wake beside my dear Mary on the Last Day. May we talk in the church porch, out of this filthy weather?'

Merry nodded and followed him, casting a last wrenching glance at Bryn's coffin in the muddy grave as she walked away.

Since the porch of St Ann's offered them little protection, Merry and John repaired to the warmth of the nearest tavern for a hot coffee and a chance to dry off. Once there, they stripped off their overcoats and held their hands out to the welcome blaze. Merry kept her wet jacket on, to protect her identity, and was soon steaming as much as the coffee in the small stoneware tankard she held.

'I greatly respect your interest, Mr Coley,' she said. 'I had not even thought to ask who had the other share of my brother's gravesite.'

'Ah, I've had the advantage of time. My Mary passed five days ago of the typhus,' his voice constricted at the memory. 'We could only bear to let her go to burial this morning. Oh, it was a terrible thing to lose her! I don't think I'll ever get past it,' he finished in a hoarse whisper, holding back the emotion that had clearly been tearing at him for days.

Merry reached out, as he had done, and gripped his shoulder. It seemed to comfort and steady him, as sympathy from strangers often does.

'You need have no concerns about my brother as a grave companion for your betrothed, sir,' she reassured him. 'He was a true gentleman fallen on hard times. A kinder, sweeter man never lived and he will wait with your Mary until that day when we all shall rise.'

John met Merry's eyes with a brief thankful nod.

'I understand your brother died this very morning?' remarked John after a few minutes.

Merry nodded, still struggling to believe it herself.

'And you've buried him the same day?' he added wonderingly.

'I had to remove from our lodgings,' explained Merry. 'The landlord would have charged for another month had I delayed, and I couldn't afford it. I could barely afford the burial, but I couldn't let Bryn lie in the poor hole.'

'I felt the same way. The ten shillings wasn't easy to find but it was worth it to know Mary is not in the common grave, and that I might lay flowers at her headstone hereafter,' agreed John. 'But did you say you have no lodgings this night, sir? If so, you're welcome to a roof with us until you find your feet.'

'You are very kind, but I believe I must not trespass on such short acquaintance,' said Merry regretfully, since it was nearing seven o'clock and she had no idea of where to stay that night.

'Nonsense!' said John. 'It's a poor enough roof and your billet will be on the floor with the rest of us menfolk. Come! It is past dinnertime and you must be as hungry as I am.'

Merry had not eaten all day and the hot coffee had felt like it had run through to her feet. After a moment's hesitation, she accepted her new friend's offer gratefully.

It was a relatively short walk to Cranbourne Alley, where John and his family lodged in the rooms above his aunt's shop. The rain that had finally ceased had washed the pavements clear and had taken the smog with it.

As they walked in companionable silence, Merry remembered that Harry had planned to call on her at Wolvenden House that evening. If she wished, she could have returned there to wait for him and ask for his help. But their interaction now seemed like a dream or a distant pleasant memory. Rafe and Harry came from a glamorous world far above her own. Badly shaken by the day's events, Merry could not bear to have her hopes raised and dashed again. John Coley's help was real and certain.

Merry observed that John's accent was not local, and soon discovered that he and his family had sold up their business in Bicester to follow a dream of setting up a carrier's yard in London. But they had soon discovered that to compete with established yards would cost upwards of a thousand pounds – a staggering sum, far beyond their means.

Merry's heart went out to her new friend. But despite his family's misfortune and his own tragic loss, his faith was great and Merry could only wonder at it.

THE RELUCTANT LADY

Mr Coley shared two rooms with his mother, sister and three brothers; the men and boys sleeping on hay-filled palliasses on the floor of the room that also served as kitchen and sitting room.

The family were touchingly pleased to meet the brother of the poor fellow who shared Mary's grave. It was the first time any of these good people had sat in close company with someone of Merry's gentility, and they ascribed her slender white hands and delicate features to her gentlemanly blood.

The light from the small fire and the tallow candles was dim and they were not in the habit of staying up long after they had finished their broth. John read a few verses from the bible by the flickering candlelight and they thanked God for their many blessings.

Merry's heart was profoundly moved by how willingly they had shared what little they had with her and as she lay on her makeshift bed and pulled her benjamin over her, she felt she was amongst friends.

Mercifully, the men all slept in their shirts, and none seemed to think it out of the ordinary that she slept in her breeches. They were soon snoring gently, but it was long before Merry, as tired as she was, could find relief in sleep. She lay nearest the fire and watched the embers glow and fade as she turned over the events of the day. Many were too awful to think of and tomorrow was a daunting unknown. So despite the many things that had a greater right to her thoughts, it was the interlude with Rafe that danced before her mind's eye - his quick wit, his strength, that broad grin on his darkly handsome face, the low chuckle that met the rudest of her insults, and yet the odd, stern look on his face when she had locked the door on him, the disturbing way the sight of his bare chest had made her feel and yet the impersonal way he had re-dressed her. From that first bout of rage when he had almost choked the life from her, to the intent look he had given her when he had bid her farewell, it seemed as if every instant in his company was memorable. Harry was kinder and more gentlemanly by far, but it was Rafe who occupied her thoughts until exhaustion finally claimed her.

Swaying to the movement of the plain chaise that was carrying him along the Great North Road, Rafe would have been cheered to know this, for Merry was taking up _all_ of his thoughts. Try though he might to think of other things, images of her intruded until he finally gave up the struggle and reviewed every moment in her company from the instant he had awoken that morning to see her face, like an avenging angel's, looking down into his. He winced at the thought of how he had treated her at first, believing her to be an insolent young cub; chuckled at her scandalised reaction to demure female dress; and then frowned over the sensation that he'd felt when she had said "the credit column".

Telling himself that it was only natural to be intrigued by a young woman who had had Merry's most unusual upbringing, he laughed off the idea that he was actually forming a tendre for the maddening chit.

But as his journey increased the distance between them, Rafe found it hard to shake the nagging anxiety that the miles were stretching the connection between them to the snapping point, that somehow leaving Merry behind had been a mistake. These thoughts were more troubling than any fear that the Runners might be on his tail, and it was all he could do to keep himself from telling the postillions to turn the coach around.

In Newport Street, Peggy the maid showed Harry the empty rooms and told him that the boys' sister had paid up their arrears and left, she supposed, for it was just Master Merion who had followed the coffin to the church. Peggy began to weep again as she remembered the scene, and Harry knew an urge to join her, as he pictured it, too.

Dear God! he thought with gnawing remorse. *That Merry should have had to experience that alone! And now she might be anywhere in this wretched city, alone and destitute.*

He suddenly recalled that Merry had paid off the back rent.

'How much did they owe on the rooms?'

'Five pounds,' she replied. 'I saw the lady pay it myself.'

How in heaven's name had she found the money?

Merry could not have sold the fine clothes he had given her, for she had been wearing them when she paid the landlord. Somehow he also knew that she would probably starve before she sold them, since she would consider them as a loan not a gift. Then Harry remembered her mother's pearl necklet, and guessed that Merry must have pawned or sold it, since that was the only thing of value she seemed to possess. His jaw clenched as he felt the urge to howl like a dog.

What must she have suffered to let go of that last heirloom ... that last link with her lost mother?

Peggy then recollected the note Master Merion had left.

Harry scanned the brief lines anxiously, reading Merry's distrust in every word. Lady Northover had insulted her just as he'd thought. Merry did not give her new direction, which probably meant she did not have one, but at least the inquest tomorrow would be an opportunity to get her back in his safekeeping.

Had he known the fresh horrors the following day would bring, he would not have been so cheered.

Chapter Seven
Disaster at Seven Dials

The next morning, the Coleys rose early, as always, and Merry took her leave of them. Though they pressed her to stay, she had asked only one further favour of them. Since John worked at the same carrier's yard that held Merry's trunks, he readily agreed to redeem them with the shilling Merry gave him to cover this, and to store them until Merry could return to collect them.

'If you don't meet with success in looking for work, Master Merion, you come back and stay with us, won't you?' said Mrs Coley, watching the young gentleman depart.

Merry looked back, nodded her assent with a grateful smile and waved. No matter how dire things got, she knew she would never risk their discovering the scandalous truth about her masquerade. Such good, God-fearing people would be shocked to their core by such behaviour, and perhaps worry about her brother's character. Better by far to leave them with a happy false impression than to disturb their peace with the truth.

Despite the gnawing grief for Bryn, Merry's experience with the Coleys, together with the fresh hope that morning brings, had lifted her spirits. The bright sunny day had brought servants and shopkeepers out of doors early to clean windows and polish brass. So there was an extra glint and twinkle to everything as the streets began to bustle. She was not despairing of finding work. Though her hands were soft and she had little experience, she was young, strong and willing. Despite Rafe's pessimism, Merry set off towards the saddlers in Oxford Street, but took the precaution of asking around about other vacancies as she made her way there, and soon had several options, if Richardson's would not employ her.

But two hours later, Merry was beginning to see her life as Rafe had painted it, and it was a pretty lowering experience.

The saddlers would not have her. The foreman had taken just a cursory glance at her slender white hands and shaken his head.

'Come back when yer balls have dropped, lad, and I'll take another look at yer,' he had said, meaning it kindly. 'Or try Lardiner's, they're looking for a boy.'

But though she dodged swiftly through the Oxford Street traffic to reach the ironmongers he mentioned, the post was gone.

This was to be the pattern for her morning. One by one, all the promising prospects she had gathered in her enquiries came to the same end.

More than ever, she missed her brother. But loss and loneliness were bruises she dared not touch. Grief was a luxury Merry could not afford while she fought for survival. The knowledge that she no longer had somewhere to sleep that night and only enough money to keep her in food and board for a few weeks drove Merry on and pushed sorrow and self-pity to the back of her mind.

On her way to each opportunity, Merry ducked her head into several shops, as the role of shop boy seemed to offer her the best chance of success. This had proven more promising, as one or two had told her to return the following morning and one grocer had even tossed her an apple as she left.

The single hope that sustained Merry throughout that depressing morning was the belief that Harry might have read her note about the inquest. After all his assurances the previous day, it seemed unlikely even to Merry's sceptical mind, that Harry would abandon her entirely to her fate. Though she knew he could not risk attending personally, lest he be recognised by the witnesses, he might be watching for her nearby or might have someone pass her a message there. So, despite having walked for hours and enduring a steady stream of rejections, Merry's heart began to lift a little when she heard church bells chime one o'clock as she entered Stephenson's Brewery in Bainbridge Street on the recommendation of the grocer who had given her the apple.

It was another rejection, but as she was leaving, one of the draymen called her over.

'If you're good with your numbers, The Stone Cutter's Arms in Little Queen Street is looking for someone who can serve and help keep the books. You might be a touch young but it would be more up your street than humping barrels,' he said.

Merry thanked him and set off in that direction. With the streets and pavements so busy, it would be a good thirty-minute walk, but it was the best prospect she had had all day. If Harry did not appear at the inquest, she would need this job. Walking briskly, Merry calculated that she could reach the inn, enquire after the vacancy and still be back in Grafton House with time to spare.

But when Merry reached the hostelry, the landlord was out, though he was expected any moment. Merry waited anxiously, watching the precious minutes tick by on the large clock in the taproom. At a quarter past two, Merry dared wait no longer. So she scrawled a quick note for the landlord and left. She almost ran down King Street and, in her haste, decided to cut through Brokers Alley, a very narrow and rather squalid passageway that led directly to Castle Street, which though it skirted the dangerous Seven Dials rookery, was the quickest route to Grafton House.

As soon as Merry entered the alley, she knew she had made a mistake. She sensed, rather than saw, two men follow her into the passageway. Instinct made her pulses race in alarm and she broke into a run, but was not quick enough. Before she could reach the relative safety of the busy street, Merry felt a strong hand grab at her arm and she wheeled round to try and defend herself. The second thug had swung a knobkerrie, intending to strike her head, but it hit her shoulder a glancing blow as she was punching out at the first man. The pain was agonising, but Merry tried to pull free as she heard a shout and the distant clatter of the Watch's rattle.

'Here!' she cried, calling for help.

But then the first man landed a ringing punch to her cheek and Merry fell into a slimy mound of filth striking her head against the wall as she did so. The two villains cut her purse out of her pocket with a swift, practised slash of a blade and gave her unconscious body a couple of cruel kicks before racing off the way they had come, ducking into an open doorway before the Watch could see where they went.

THE RELUCTANT LADY

Waiting in a coffee house opposite Grafton House, Harry had hoped to spy Merry before she entered, but the throng of wagons, carriages, horsemen and pedestrians in a constant flow to and from the markets and shops to the south, made it impossible. He could only sit chafing while he waited for Clayton, his manservant, to return with her, and this could only happen when the inquest had concluded.

But thirty minutes later, Harry saw Clayton cross the street towards him alone, with a troubled expression furrowing his brow. Harry jumped up and met him outside the coffee house his face like thunder.

'Devil take you, man! Where is Miss Griffith? I told you to stay with her if she would not come to me!'

'My lord, she did not appear to give testimony, though she was called to do so ... as *Mister* Griffith, of course,' said Clayton defensively. 'The clerk called her name twice but no one stepped up. There were fewer than twenty people attending, my lord, so the young lady could not have been missed ...'

Clayton broke off as he saw his lordship's face blench with horror and his hand fly up to his forehead in distress.

Merry came round to a bustling hum around her - concerned voices, the clink of empty tankards, barked instructions – an inn or a coffee house, her jumbled senses told her. Hands were holding her upright on a hard bench and someone put a glass of brandy to her lips and poured a little into her mouth, forcing her to swallow it. Merry choked and gasped but began to revive. Then a female voice spoke offering something, and Merry was suddenly jolted by the pungent aroma of smelling salts waved beneath her nose.

'Aye! There you are, my lad!' encouraged a deep voice close by. 'He's coming round!' he added, addressing others around them.

'You were attacked, you poor boy,' said another voice. 'But the cowardly rogues ran off quick enough when they heard my rattle.'

Rattle? thought Merry, *that must be the Watch. Thank God someone had called him!*

'They took your purse, I'm afraid, but they were chased off before they could take your boots and coat,' he said.

My purse? Oh God!

'You're lucky they did not strip you, young man!' said another voice. 'They've done it before in that alley.'

Merry gave an ironic laugh that came out as a dazed grunt.

Yes, she was indeed lucky they had not stripped her, but without money or anything of value left to her name, she was in a pretty sad case nonetheless.

Thankfully, no one seemed to suspect she was a girl.

'You've a bad bruise on your face, son,' said the Watchman's voice. 'And it looks like you took a crack on the head, for there's quite a cut on your scalp.'

The racking pain in her head confirmed this, but her shoulder and ribs hurt just as much. She could remember nothing of what had happened but realised she must have been beaten.

'Scandalous! To be attacking children in broad daylight!' came the female voice who had proffered the smelling salts.

This opinion won universal agreement and several other voices around her commented on the wicked prevalence of pickpockets and villains in the neighbourhood, to the obvious discomfort of the Watchman.

'Took you for a young sprig up from the country, no doubt,' he said defensively.

Merry tried to get up but her head swam horribly and her hands were shaking with shock as she accepted the glass of brandy she was offered and took another sip. The fiery liquid helped to clear her senses a little, but she was still nauseous and dazed when she attempted speech in a thick voice.

'Must get to Grafton Street,' she mumbled. 'M'brother's inquest is at three.'

There was a wave of sympathy as her audience assimilated this.

'Not his day, is it?' muttered someone.

'Sorry, lad, but it's three now. Even if you took a cab you woun't be there afore half past in this traffic.'

Merry groaned as she felt despair crash over her, turning her insides to dust. She would never know if Harry had attended or not. Tearful and shaky, Merry seemed to hurt all over, but she swallowed hard and suppressed the tears that threatened.

With her purse gone, she was now utterly penniless. Panic roared, adding to the sick feeling that was turning her knees to jelly. If she could find no employment, it would be the workhouse, where she would have to admit her sex.

Merry covered her eyes, and the onlookers thought her faint again. But now that she had come round and seemed to be recovering, the novelty for her audience was likewise wearing off, and they first thinned and then disappeared. Even the Watch said apologetically that he had to get back to his post.

Merry got up unsteadily and began to make her way, rather drunkenly, towards Grafton Street, where the inquest was being held, often stopping to lean against a wall, when nausea or dizziness overwhelmed her. Merry remembered little of her journey, but her progress had been agonisingly slow, so that by the time she arrived at Grafton House, both inquests had long since finished.

When she enquired for the coroner or his assistant at the door of Grafton House, the servant looked her up and down – taking in her bruised face and filthy coat – and denied her. At full strength, Merry would have sent the horrid, little man running for his master, but she was weak, battered and utterly forlorn.

It was too much for even Merry's stoicism. Creeping into the open chapel beside Grafton House, Merry sank onto one of the wooden pews and wept.

As he entered his house in Half Moon Street, Harry was in despair.

The footman had news, but Harry pre-empted its delivery when he saw a neat-looking manservant mounting the stairs carrying a can of hot water.

'Fitch!' cried Harry. 'Is Lord Ventnor returned?'

'Yes, m'lord,' replied Fitch, Lord Ventnor's valet, permitting himself a slight smile. 'He is in his chamber …'

'The very man!' interrupted Harry, darting past him and sprinting upstairs.

Charles de Ferres had been his friend since before Eton. When he and Harry had left Cambridge for London, they had decided to share a house, and had done so ever since. Lately, Charles had ventured home to his family estate for the first time in years, and had been there for several weeks, but now it seemed he had finally returned.

'Come!' called Lord Ventnor, as Harry scratched on his door, and then cried: 'Harry! I thought you were Fitch with hot water for Rafe here.'

'Rafe!' gasped Harry, turning to see his friend, still booted and spurred, having only thrown off his overcoat before slumping exhausted into a chair in Charles' chamber.

Rafe rose lazily to shake his hand, with that glinting smile of his.

'I hadn't been threatened with mortal injury or had my eyes damned for at least a day, and so found myself unaccountably bored,' said Rafe. 'How is our grey-eyed bantam? Is my stepmother treating her well?'

But seeing Harry's drawn expression, the smile fell away from his face and he looked suddenly alert.

'Rafe … she's gone!' said Harry in a hoarse whisper, unmanned by the look in Rafe's face. 'We've lost her. She is dead or taken, I don't know which, but she was not at the inquest and no power on earth could have kept her from that.'

For one terrible moment, Rafe had the oddest impression that he had been hit in the chest by a hammer blow. It hurt so much he could not breathe. *Merry! Merry!* was all that he could think.

Charles watched this exchange in astonishment. Harry was near to tears and Rafe appeared turned to stone.

Who was this siren that had had such an effect on his friends?

'Of whom do you speak, Harry?' asked Charles.

'A girl we promised to help … the sister of that fellow who thrust a duel on Rafe. She was dressed as a boy … had been all her life. The bravest child … I fear she might have been killed …' Harry broke off, unable to say more, his throat choked by emotion.

'No!' Rafe finally spoke. 'Taken, perhaps, but not dead.'

'How do you know?' asked Harry and Charles in unison.

'Because I would know if she were dead,' said Rafe, causing Charles' eyebrows to lift in astonishment. 'She is alive somewhere, and I won't believe otherwise until I see her body.'

Suddenly, the grim image of Merry's body being fished out of the Thames came unbidden into his mind. Rafe covered his eyes as a sick feeling passed through him at the thought of it. They had all seen that sight. If you looked at the river long enough, you would see a corpse.

At this point, Fitch scratched on the door to deliver the hot water. No one moved or spoke until the door closed behind him.

'What happened?' said Rafe, turning sharply to Harry.

'I took her to your mother's – explained everything, but she was not in the best of humours. Just after I left, they fell out and Merry walked out and disappeared. I went to the house in Newport Street but she had cleared out,' Harry's voice grew hoarse again as he continued. 'She buried her brother alone and I think she sold those damned pearls of hers to pay for it and for their back rent,' he paused as Rafe cursed and kicked a footstool across the room to relieve his feelings at the thought. 'I enquired at every inn in the area, but no one had seen her. Naturally, I expected her to attend the inquest and sent Clayton in there to bring her back, but she did not come.'

'There are several reasons why she might not have attended,' reasoned Rafe. 'She might have found work that would not permit her to leave.'

'Yes, by God! You're right,' concurred Harry, hope dawning.

'But, Rafe, old man, why are you so determined to believe her alive?' enquired Charles.

'Because I ... because the alternative is unthinkable. So I will turn over every stone in this stinking metropolis until I find her!'

'I'm with you!' cried Harry, galvanised by Rafe's certainty. Merry could even now be praying for them to rescue her.

Indeed, as she wept in the chapel, Merry was badly in need of rescue.

'You poor fellow,' came a kindly voice after the first wave of Merry's misery had ebbed. 'You *have* been in the wars.'

Merry looked up into the sweet face of a well-dressed young lady, with blond hair and gentle, cornflower-blue eyes.

'My name is Lydia,' she volunteered. 'May I ask yours?'

'Merry.'

The blue eyes twinkled.

'Would you be offended if I observe that that seems a little ironic in your present state?'

Merry managed a watery smile and shook her head slowly.

'I'm not normally such a baby,' Merry said, shaking herself and grateful for the interruption of her self-pitying spiral. Nothing could serve her less well than to give in to despair.

'Looking at your wounds, I'm not surprised that you were shaken,' the young lady replied, her concerned look telling Merry how bad her bruised face and bloody scalp must look. 'Did you get into a fight with one of those market boys?'

'No,' sighed Merry wearily. 'I was set upon by robbers on the way to my brother's inquest.'

Had Merry the strength to laugh, she would have chuckled at Lydia's ludicrous change of expression, from gently teasing sympathy to horrified remorse, but she could only manage a wan smile.

'Heavens!' gasped Lydia. 'I ... I ...'

Merry raised a tired hand to stem the poor lady's embarrassment.

'I was a little downcast at having missed the inquest, as I have no idea how to discover the outcome.'

'Well,' said Lydia recovering herself. 'In that, at least, I may be of service, to make up for my earlier levity. The coroner is my uncle.'

Merry looked up at her and gave a relieved smile.

'Could you furnish me with his direction, ma'am?' asked Merry.

'I shall do better than that,' said Lydia. 'I shall take you to him myself.'

Lydia led Merry back to Grafton House and when the porter opened the door, her reception was very different to Merry's.

'Miss Dunwoody,' said the fellow, bowing ingratiatingly. 'Sir Hector is just finishing up, Miss. Would you care to wait for him in the carriage?'

'No, Harper, I must see him immediately. Please show us up.'

Mr Harper pursed his lips a fraction at Merry, who could not resist a rather triumphant look, but he did not dare to question the request of Sir Hector's favourite niece.

As Harper preceded them up the stairs, Lydia gave Merry a conspiratorial wink, winning a painfully lopsided grin from Merry, who was fast coming to see Lydia as a kindred spirit.

As they were shown into the smaller salon off the assembly room, where the inquest had been held, Sir Hector hailed his niece with delight.

'Lydia, my dear, are you done ministering to the poor? Your mother sent a carriage for you an hour ago. They've been walking the horses up and down the street looking for you.'

Lydia planted a kiss on her uncle's cheek.

'I will go directly, but you must promise me to help this poor young man in return. He has been most dreadfully set upon and injured and so missed his brother's inquest.'

'Dear me! Is this true?' said Sir Hector. 'Yes, you do look in sad shape, young man. Here, take a seat. You look sick as a frog.'

'Thank you, Sir Hector,' said Merry making her bow. 'I am Merion Griffith. My brother Bryn was killed yesterday and I should be grateful to know the outcome of his inquest, as only this dreadful attack would have kept me from the hearing.'

Merry sank gratefully into the proffered chair as Miss Dunwoody patted her shoulder before obeying her uncle's wave to depart.

Merry turned before she left.

'Thank you, Miss Dunwoody, from the bottom of my heart,' she said earnestly. 'I think you are the kindest lady I have ever met and I cannot thank you enough for taking pity on me earlier.'

Lydia blushed quite pink and demurred, wishing Merry as well as she might under the tragic circumstances, and then gave her uncle a look that bid him be kind to her new friend.

'So you were attacked on your way here?' said Sir Hector, shaking his head in dismay.

'Yes, sir,' responded Merry. 'It was pretty grim. I can't deny I'm still a little shaken, but I was determined to come and discover the decision of the inquest.'

'Well, we missed your testimony, young man,' said Sir Hector. 'Nevertheless, we had the constable's report of your statement, and sufficient evidence to rule the death an unlawful killing by the hand of Lord Rothsea. In light of the unequal contest - your brother being so young - the brazen location of the duel, and the fact that it was determined that Lord Rothsea had absconded abroad through guilt, the outcome was more severe than usual.

Lord Rothsea will be indicted, in his absence, with murder, rather than manslaughter.'

Sir Hector misinterpreted the flash of emotion in Merry's expression.

'I am afraid that I cannot promise you justice, Mr Griffith, I am sorry to say,' he said with an apologetic look. 'If his lordship were apprehended and contested the charge, he would likely be merely exiled, fined or even acquitted,' he remarked bitterly. 'There would be a rare scandal, but his lordship is no stranger to that!'

He expanded for a moment on the unequal treatment of the nobility under the law, which was clearly a hobby-horse of his.

Though she masked it, Merry brightened. Despite all that had happened, she did not wish for Rafe to hang. She was sure he had meant well towards her, even if his plans had come to naught.

'Were any of the seconds identified, sir?' asked Merry, hoping to discover if Harry's part in the duel had been revealed or if he had been spotted amongst the attendees.

'No, I am afraid not,' responded Sir Hector. 'The surgeon who attended the affair knew none of the protagonists and was very aggrieved at having been involved … though it is my view that they lined his pockets well enough.' He paused, then added: 'He said your brother did not suffer, if that is any comfort?'

Merry merely nodded dumbly, as a wave of sorrow washed over her again. *Poor dear Bryn! To have his life snuffed out over a gambling quarrel.*

'One of Bow Street's men attended to report that Lord Rothsea had departed the same morning, thought to be heading for his yacht moored in Bristol,' reported Sir Hector. 'Do you know of any other witnesses who should have been called? I understand two gentlemen restored your brother's body to you? You did not recognise them?'

'No, sir, I had never seen them before,' said Merry, with perfect honesty.

'Just as well! I recommend that you do not follow your brother's example, young man. Keep to your schoolbooks and follow a profession.'

'Yes, sir,' said Merry with a dismal look.

'You say you were robbed. Do you have the means to get home?'

'N...no sir, they left me with nothing.'

'Here, then,' said Sir Hector fishing a half-crown from his pocket as he stood to see her out. Merry rose and gratefully accepted the coin he pressed into her hand. 'I recommend you take a hackney home. You still look pretty sickly.'

'Thank you, sir. You are very kind.'

Merry bowed, asked Sir Hector to convey her thanks once more to Miss Dunwoody, and left. She did not ask if a message had been left for her, certain that Sir Hector would have mentioned if there had.

As she reached the street outside, Merry finally had to think about her immediate future.

So, Harry had not appeared, for good reason, of course, but Merry felt her heart sink through her boots. Perhaps he had reconsidered the wisdom of getting involved and had been relieved to find that she had left Lady Northover's.

Merry threaded her way through the bustle to the public pump on the street corner and sat down despondently on the low railing beside it. Her head and cheek still pounded and her shoulder hurt so badly that she could barely lift her arm. Gingerly, Merry touched her cheekbone and explored her bruised ribs to gauge the extent of her injuries. Her fingers came away bloody when she felt her scalp, and her coat was covered in drying filth from the alley where she had fallen. She received as many disapproving glances as sympathetic ones from people who thought she had been fighting and come off worst.

Merry worked the pump with her good arm and put her head under the cold water as it gushed out. It felt good. An urchin, shoeless and barely ten years old, came up and worked the pump for her, seeming to think it a very good joke. Merry smiled gratefully at the little boy and put her head back under the water teasing out the matted blood from her hair. The dirt on her coat and breeches would need to be brushed out when it was dry.

'You're gonna 'ave a proper shiner,' observed the urchin, and Merry nodded ruefully, before a coarse shout sent the lad running back to his master.

The cold water had brought her round fully and, dragging her fingers through her wet hair to tidy it, Merry thought about her options. She had meant to return to the Stone Cutters' Inn to enquire after the vacancy. But the prospect of walking there in her present state seemed a little overwhelming, and she quaked weakly at the thought of going near the place where she had been attacked. The half-crown in her pocket could buy her a hot meal and a bed for the night in a reasonable tavern and still leave her with a shilling or so. They might also lend her a brush to make herself more presentable for when she went looking for work the next day.

It was nearly five and Merry was famished, so she decided to find somewhere to stay and start her search for work early on the morrow. She and her brother had occasionally eaten at the Black Swan in St Martin's. It was cheap and clean, and now a bowl of their oyster soup followed by boiled beef and green beans, and then a wash and a night's sleep between clean sheets, seemed like heaven.

Sustained by this happy vision, Merry rose painfully to her feet and struck out towards St Martin's.

Chapter Eight
Descent into Hell

Back in Half Moon Street, Rafe had thrown orders at Fitch and Fuller, Charles's two trusted servants.

'Fitch, Lord Stowe and I need clothes more fitting to prosperous tradesmen than our own status. Oh, don't wince, man! I'm not asking you to wear them! We need them within the hour, so bustle about, there's a good fellow.'

'Fuller, we need a pair of hired hacks. Nothing showy, just serviceable, as befits those tradesmen I just mentioned.'

'You permit?' asked Rafe of Charles, as an afterthought.

Charles made a languid gesture as if he were helpless to prevent it, which won him the first grin he'd seen on Rafe's face since he'd received the fell news from Harry. He then listened as Rafe questioned Harry about his first meeting with Merry, the interview with the countess, and his search efforts so far. Then Rafe laid out his own plans.

'It's a little late, but I'll start at that saddler's that Merry mentioned. She would have loved to thumb her nose at me by getting a job there.'

'Harry, you talk to the coroner. I've no wish for that worthy to guess that you were a second at the duel, so you'll pose as a member of the family searching for the boy. I have a notion that if Merry were prevented from attending the inquest at the appointed time, she would have made every effort to discover the outcome when she was free to do so.'

'Yes! She might be there now! Damn Fitch! What can be taking him so long?'

'And, I have a passing interest in the outcome myself,' added Rafe lightly.

'Good God, yes! I hadn't thought of that!' said Harry. 'Clayton will know the verdict.' Harry left the room shouting for his valet.

'And am I to sit here while you two have all the fun?' enquired Charles, an edge to his tone of polite interest.

Rafe smiled his thanks at Charles' oblique offer of help.

'You, my dear Charles, could use that *Fatal Ventnor* charm of yours to persuade every tavern maid within a half-mile of Newport Street to keep her eyes peeled for our quarry?'

Charles's extremely handsome face displayed the dazzling smile that had broken hearts throughout the country.

'Done!' he said.

'You're to be indicted for murder, Rafe,' announced Harry, returning.

'Marvellous!'

'Murder! That's a touch heavy, isn't it?' exclaimed Charles. 'Heard the other fellow forced the quarrel on you.'

'Yes, but he was all of seventeen, and I could have just winged him, had he not fired me up,' acknowledged Rafe.

'Seems to me that he wanted to die, Rafe. Had you thought of that?' asked Harry.

'Yes, almost as soon as my blood had cooled,' replied Rafe.

'If we are to scour London for the fellow's sister, it will take more than the three of us,' reasoned Charles. 'I think we should enlist the services of a Mr Lyneham, formerly of Bow Street, who has turned his investigative talents to more lucrative use and has assisted me more than once when I needed to know when a certain lady's husband would be out of town.'

'Excellent!' approved Rafe.

'Pity Gil's not here,' said Harry. 'He's a good man in a crisis. Is your friend Cleve in town?'

Charles had walked over to the escritoire in the corner and was scratching a quick note to Mr Lyneham. He looked up and shook his head.

'Still in Derbyshire, I'm afraid.'

'What are you going to do about the countess?' asked Harry of Rafe.

'Yes, thank you for reminding me! I think my stepmother will benefit from an early retirement from society,' said Rafe grimly. 'She can join my father at Twelveoaks.'

He walked across to the escritoire as Charles was quitting it, and sat down to write three brief notes that would effect the end of Lady Northover's generous allowance, the closing of Wolvenden House and the swift removal of the countess to the dower house at Twelveoaks.

He had barely finished these notes when Fitch arrived with an assortment of clothes that fitted Lord Rothsea's request, and then wore a pained expression as he was obliged to assist their lordships to dress beneath their station.

It was remarkable what a difference a change of clothes could make. Charles shook his head and said that they looked like a pair of grocers. 'I've asked Lyneham to call at nine,' he said. 'So you can make plans for tomorrow.'

'It is nearly six now,' said Rafe. 'Let's meet back here just before nine and see what news we have between us.'

As the gentlemen set about searching for her, Merry was tucking into a second bowl of oyster soup. The landlord of the Black Swan had remembered her from past visits. Seeing Merry's battered face and hearing that she had been set upon on her way to her brother's inquest had squeezed even his flinty heart, and he had let her have a room and board for just a shilling. She retired straight after dinner, having brushed her clothes as clean as she could and washing herself thoroughly, thanks to an extra large can of hot water and piece of soap sent up by the landlord's wife.

As she finally laid her bruised face on the cool pillow and tried to achieve a sleeping position that did not further hurt her shoulder or ribs, Merry reflected on her turn in fortunes over the past two days. In that short time she had gone from having two hundred guineas and the prospect of buying a cottage and settling down to a safe and respectable life with her brother, to finding herself bereaved, alone, beaten and so poor that she was pleased to have saved a sixpence on her room. In the midst of this fall had been a false rise, which now seemed like a strange but vivid dream, where two peers of the realm had promised to care for her and turn her into a lady. Merry shook her head at that wonder and at her foolishness at having been taken in by it. They had meant well, but everyone knew the Quality were fickle and easily bored. Merry gave a stern sigh.

I was a flat to believe in such luck. The only one I can depend on in this world is myself, and it is I who must find a way forward now.

Yet, irrepressibly, an image of Rafe reading in his wonderful library filled her mind's eye. She imagined him turning and inviting her to join him with a book, and sighed at this happy dream. A few moments later, despite the awful events of the day, she fell fast asleep.

Harry had discovered the coroner's direction and was mentally rehearsing his role on the doorstep of Sir Hector's fine house in Soho Square, when the door was opened. The butler was disinclined to admit 'Mr Maitland', which was a novel but unwelcome experience for Lord Stowe.

'Look here,' said Harry in a vexed and rather haughty tone, entirely forgetting his role as a lowly tradesman. 'I am concerned about the welfare of my young nephew, Merry … I mean Merion, and …'

'Merry?' interrupted a lady's voice behind the butler. 'Oh, Piper, let the gentleman in at once!'

Harry was admitted and found himself bowing to a pretty young lady with neatly-arranged blonde curls and anxious blue eyes.

'I beg pardon, ma'am,' he said. 'Harry Maitland, at your service. Do I understand that you know my nephew?'

'Yes, I met him in the Grafton Street Chapel. He had been very badly beaten by thieves …' Lydia broke off when she saw the young man blench with horror.

'Beaten?' gasped Harry.

'Yes, I am sorry to say he was in a sad state. I think he had taken a blow or two to the face and head, and his left arm appeared injured too,' explained Lydia, and then she cried: 'Oh, I knew I should have taken him home myself! I regretted it the moment I left. My uncle gave him money for a hackney, but I should have stayed to see the poor boy home. I shall never forgive myself, if anything else befell him on his way there!'

'I'm afraid he had no home to go to, Miss … er …'

'Dunwoody,' furnished Lydia, dipping a slight curtsey as she looked properly at Mr Maitland for the first time.

THE RELUCTANT LADY

Suddenly, and most inappropriately, Lydia felt herself blushing. Merry's uncle was quite the handsomest and most personable young man Lydia had ever met. But a glance at his face showed that though Lydia saw Mr Maitland, he did not see *her*. His blue eyes were clouded with worry. His deep concern for his nephew was touching and only added to his charms… *but what was that he had just said?*

'No home?' repeated Lydia. 'Then where did he go after speaking to my uncle?'

'That is what I am trying to discover,' said Harry. 'Do you think Sir Hector would afford me a few minutes' conversation? Perhaps Merry said something that may help me find him.'

'Yes, he will be coming down for dinner at any moment,' said Lydia. 'Piper, please could you send for my uncle and ask him to join us in his study?' Then turning to Harry she asked: 'May I send for refreshments for you?'

'No, I thank you. You have already been more than kind.'

'Please follow me,' said Lydia, leading the way across the hallway and along a short corridor to her uncle's study.

'You live here with your uncle?' enquired Harry, making polite conversation while his mind was in turmoil at the news that poor Merry had been so brutally hurt. Instead of chatting with this nice young lady, he wished he were mobilising the militia to search for her and bring her to safety.

'No, I live with my mother in Henrietta Street, but we come to dine with my uncle once a week. My mother had another engagement this evening, so I came alone, in part because I wanted to know how my young friend Merry had fared.' Then, with a slight frown, she asked: 'Why does he have no home?'

'He and his brother lived a rather hand to mouth existence. Mr Griffith's unfortunate death left Merry alone in the world and without the means to pay for their accommodation.'

'How dreadful! But he is not alone, surely? Why did he not come straight to you?'

Harry felt himself sinking in the mire of his own lies.

'Pride,' he said, rather desperately. 'And he did not know that I was in London.' More lies.

'So you live outside London?'

'Yes,' Harry prevaricated weakly.

'Whereabouts? If you let me have your direction, I can let you know and, indeed, pass it on to Merry, if I should see him.'

Oh God! Thought Harry, dropping his hat on a chair and raking his fingers through his hair.

'This is intolerable!' he said out loud but to himself, making Lydia jump with surprise. Then he turned to her, his tone and manner suddenly altered.

'Miss Dunwoody, I cannot bear to deceive you further. I am Harry Maitland, Viscount Stowe, and I stood up for Merry's brother at that disastrous duel, though I had never met him before that day. When I went to return his body to his family, I discovered that he had one sibling – not a brother, but a sister. Merry is not a boy: She is a defenceless girl, brought up as a boy. I had thought her safely accommodated with Lady Northover, Lord Rothsea's stepmother. Lord Rothsea was the primary in that duel and, like myself, he, too, wishes to atone for his hand in that dreadful affair by providing for Merry's safety and future. But Lady Northover was… she misunderstood Merry's position. Merry was offended and left. I only found out when I went to call on her later that evening. I then found that she had buried her brother, all alone, and removed from her lodgings, without the means to long sustain new ones. I hoped to rescue her after the inquest, but she did not attend. Now, I know why. She is hurt and may have lost what little money she had … and I have no idea where she is. There! That is the truth. At least I won't have another lie on my conscience, and now I know you will appreciate my anxiety.'

'But he … she … was so brave, despite such dreadful injuries,' she murmured in astonishment, as Harry winced at the thought. 'And so … so gentlemanly.'

'I know,' said Harry. 'Unfathomable, isn't it?'

Lydia nodded in shared awe.

'Poor girl! How on earth can we find her and bring her to safety?'

'I'm hoping she might have given your uncle a clue. Ah! This is he, if I am not mistaken,' said Harry hearing a bustle in the hallway. 'Tell him what you will, Miss Dunwoody. I do not wish you to lie for me.'

Lydia met his eyes for one riveting instant before her uncle walked in asking why he had been sent for so close to dinnertime.

'Uncle, do you remember that poor battered boy who had missed his brother's inquest?' asked Lydia, taking her uncle's arm coaxingly and choosing her words carefully. 'Well, it seems that he did not reach home and Mr Maitland here is a friend of the family trying to find him and make sure he is safe.'

Lydia coloured only a little at the steady look she felt from Harry but was suddenly too shy to return it.

'Dear me!' said Sir Hector. 'How dreadful! The poor fellow! He was beaten and robbed, you know?'

'Yes, so I understand,' confirmed Harry grimly.

'The boy said they took everything, so I gave him a little something to get him home. I thought he would go straight there, but perhaps he succumbed to his injuries and rested somewhere?'

'He did not give you any clue where he might be heading?'

'Straight home, as far as I could gather,' replied Sir Hector. 'And you say he never reached it?'

'He did not return to the lodgings he had shared with his brother,' Harry responded carefully. 'Now his friends are concerned for his safety. I imagine he thinks to be brave and independent, but he is young and more vulnerable than he realises.'

'Ah, yes, young men can be very proud and stubborn. I hope he does not suffer by it,' said Sir Hector, shaking his head.

'Aye, sir, so do I,' concurred Harry. 'Well, I thank you for seeing me, Sir Hector, but I have kept you long enough and must take my leave to continue my search.'

'I wish you good fortune, Mr Maitland,' said Sir Hector, returning Harry's bow.

'Thank you, sir.'

'I will show you out,' said Lydia hastily, causing Sir Hector to raise his brows and take a second look at the handsome young man who was causing his favourite niece to colour up as she preceded him from the room. He would quiz her royally over the dinner to come.

'Thank you, Miss Dun...' began Harry as they left the study.

'Lord Stowe,' whispered Lydia forestalling him in the brief moment between leaving the study and coming into earshot of the footman attending the front door. 'If Merry would consent, I should very much like to have her stay with us in Henrietta Street. I think her a very brave young lady and would be honoured to be of service to her, if you would not consider it an impertinence?'

Harry was so moved by her kindness that he took Lydia's hand and kissed it, saying with fervent sincerity: 'Thank you! It would be the very thing! How can you imagine such a kind offer to be impertinent?'

Lydia was too overcome by the thrill of that kiss and the glowing look in Lord Stowe's eyes when he had bestowed it to do more than shake her head and demur.

The footman was already opening the door, so there was no chance to do more than exchange a bow and curtsey and wish each other well. As the door closed behind him, Lydia sighed and turned to see Sir Hector standing in the hallway, his arms folded across his chest and a wry look in his eye. At this sight, Lydia sighed again but rather differently.

When they met up again at Half Moon Street, Harry broke his news to Rafe, and watched as the horror played out on Rafe's features. He looked as if he were having his entrails drawn.

There it is again, thought Rafe, the crushing pain in his chest that choked the breath from his body at the thought of Merry being frightened, let alone being brutally attacked and injured. It made him feel physically sick and filled him with rage, all the more intense for being helpless.

'I swore to protect her,' he groaned, bracing his arms around his middle as if he were being eviscerated.

'We both did,' said Harry in a hoarse voice. 'And we failed her.'

Rafe groaned again clutching his ribs. He ached to hold Merry safe..

This strange feeling had been growing since he had left her. Before he had reached Grantham, he could bear it no longer and had abandoned his trip to the border, hiring a succession of hacks and riding each nearly into the ground trying to get back to London as quickly as he could. There had been no premonition of disaster, only the irresistible craving to see her face again. He had thought to find her safe but chafing at the constraints of skirts and polite behaviour. Instead, she was bruised, destitute and alone somewhere in London, prey to untold dangers. Rafe felt his insides wrench again at the thought.

Charles was sympathetic when he walked in a few moments later.

'But at least you know she is alive, which you did not three hours ago.'

It was at this ill-timed moment that Mytchett, the butler, entered with a silver salver bearing a letter edged in black, denoting notification of a death, and presented it to Harry, who froze as his eyes lifted to meet Rafe's.

'This was delivered by courier, my lord,' said Mytchett, wondering why his lordship wasn't reaching out to take it.

'Give it here,' said Lord Ventnor, taking the note and giving Mytchett a nod of dismissal. Turning it over, his brows twitched together in alarm as he read the name of the sender. 'It's from Gil!'

'Rip it open, man! Who has died?'

Charles's hand shook slightly as he broke the seal and scanned the opening line.

'Denny,' he whispered in shocked tones.

'Denny?' echoed Harry and Rafe together.

'Good God! How?' demanded Rafe.

'Hunting … this morning. Oh God! Poor Denny!' Charles handed the thick sheet of paper to Harry and sat heavily in a chair, his eyes unseeing as images of his lost friend played in his mind.

They were silent for a while, immersed in their own thoughts. Denny had been such an endearing character, very much a feature of so many of their memories.

'I'm afraid you'll have to search for your poor lost girl without me,' said Charles finally. 'I'm for Leicestershire to join Gil and Dev. No doubt they'll escort Denny's body to his family in Cheshire for interment. I'll explain what's toward here and organise empty carriages from you both.'

Rafe and Harry nodded and thanked him. It was awful to think of missing Denny's funeral, but Merry had to be found.

Charles wished them luck and left to make his arrangements.

A few minutes later, precisely at nine, Mr Lyneham was announced. Harry and Rafe had not agreed how much to reveal to the former Runner, but he surprised them both by turning to Rafe and saying:

'So, my lord, I hear that you and Lord Stowe here are lookin' fer the brother of that young sprig you killed a day or two ago.'

Rafe's eyes gleamed appreciatively at this demonstration of Mr Lyneham's ability.

'You're in the right of it, but what you don't know is that the brother is, in fact, a sister.'

My Lyneham sucked in his breath sharply, and then pulled out a map from his pocket. He laid it out on the nearest table and together they planned their search activities for the following day.

After Lyneham had left, Rafe and Harry had no stomach for dinner, so they rode around the streets until the early hours, before exhaustion drove them back to Harry's to sleep.

The following morning, Merry stretched and yawned, then winced sharply, rediscovering her injuries. For a moment, she tried to turn her head into the pillow and enjoy the luxury of a bed while she still could, but then the noises from the street outside reminded her that she had to find work, if she wanted to sleep in a bed again.

Her first call at the Stone Cutter's Inn was unsuccessful and set the tone for another depressing day of ceaseless rejection, by the end of which, she had walked miles in her threadbare boots, from the white lead factory in St Mary le Bone to the timber yards in Southwark. No shops would employ her with her face so badly bruised and none of the manufactories or yards would take her because she couldn't lift anything with her injured arm.

'If you come back when you're fit for work, I might have something for you,' some had said. Merry was too proud to say that she might have starved by then.

It was after seven as Merry made her way back across Blackfriars Bridge. Light-headed from hunger, she paused for a few minutes to rest, watching boatmen negotiating the busy Thames traffic in the golden light of the setting sun.

Then her eyes strayed westwards, where the spire of St Martin's stood out above the roofs and wharfs. Somewhere amongst the grand houses far beyond her sight, Harry would be getting ready for dinner. If she could not find work on the morrow, Merry knew she might have to swallow her pride and go looking for him. She cringed at the thought of his being embarrassed to see her turn up again.

But that would be tomorrow's pride-crushing experience, thought Merry, pushing away from the side of the bridge and continuing her journey. Her footsteps quickened as she made her way to Ludgate, where someone had said she might get a bowl of broth for a penny at the "Bell Savage".

This proved true, although the *Belle Sauvage's* offering was a pretty watery brew and she was hungry again by the time she had made the long trek back to St Ann's Church, where she planned to sleep on one of the stone benches inside the portico of the church where Bryn had been buried. It had seemed oddly comforting to be close to her brother; as if his spirit might afford her protection and company to assuage her loneliness. But when she reached the church at around ten o'clock, she found the benches, and the floor between, already occupied. Before Merry could try to join the other sleepers, they were all moved on by the Watch, checking that the burying ground gates were still locked.

Merry was exhausted, and she shuffled away to look for a doorway to curl up against. After a few moments, she was aware of being followed and turned to find that her pursuer was only a middle-aged lady in a cloak.

'I saw you turfed out of St Ann's,' said the woman. 'You in need of a roof tonight?'

'Er … yes,' replied Merry cautiously. 'But I should not wish to trouble you, ma'am.'

'It's no trouble, if you'll not turn your nose up at sleeping on the floor in the kitchen?'

'No, indeed,' said Merry, oddly relieved by this qualification of the offer.

'Follow me, then. I was on my way home and only live a step away,' said the woman, who led Merry across Compton Street and then down Milk Alley, where she stopped at the door of a large, rather grubby house. Once inside, she led Merry straight down into the kitchen, where a girl jumped up from the hearth. At a nod from her mistress, she hastened to lay a place at the table and to fill a bowl from the large pot that hung just to the side of the fire.

'However did you come by that bruise, dearie?' enquired the woman, as Merry took a seat at the table. 'Or find yourself on the street, for that matter?'

'I was robbed,' said Merry, keeping to the barest of facts. 'And my injuries have hampered my search for employment.'

'Dear me, you haven't had the luck, have you?' tutted the woman, taking in Merry's bruised face and stained clothes. She handed Merry a glass of wine as the girl placed the dish of stew in front of her. 'Here, drink this. It will put the colour back in your cheeks.'

Merry obliged before tucking ravenously into the steaming bowl.

'Well, I might have some work for you, if you're not too fussy,' said the woman, getting up and going to the door.

'Beggars can't be choosers, ma'am. I'm willing to work for food and board,' said Merry, finishing her bowl of stew and downing the last of the wine.

'Oh you'll work alright, my dear, but I won't be spoiling those pretty white hands of yours. Your work will be on your back,' she said with a leering wink, her arms folded across her withered bosom.

'Wh-what!' gasped Merry, uncertain of the harridan's meaning.

'Oh, I saw through your disguise straight off, dearie,' said the woman, opening the door to let in a burly man, who stood with his beefy arms crossed, looking Merry up and down as if she were naked.

'I was out looking for a new girl and 'aven't I found me a gem. You're a virgin, for all you're got up as a lad, and those fine hands tell me you're quality-born. Yes, you'll fetch in a pretty penny. A very good night's work, I'd say.'

'No!!' cried Merry, trying to bolt for the door, but caught by the bouncer. Merry tried to struggle, but every movement was an incredible effort and the room was swimming. The brothel keeper had drugged her wine.

When they convened again at nine that evening, Rafe, Harry and Lyneham had mixed news.

'I missed her by less than an hour at the timber mills in Southwark, damn it!' said Rafe, raking his hand through his hair. 'I followed her trail across Blackfriars Bridge, then lost all trace of her.'

'At least we know Merry is still well enough to be looking for work,' said Harry. 'She stayed at the Black Swan last night, but did not return there. She must be staying somewhere tonight.'

'Or sleeping rough more like, m'lord,' remarked Mr Lyneham. 'Still, if she is, my people should find her. I've a lot of old friends in that part of town, so I should know tomorrow, if she's holed up thereabouts.'

'I've bribed every Watch from here to Temple Bar,' reported Harry. 'We should hear something if she is spotted by one of them.'

'Well, we can do no more tonight, my lords,' said Lyneham. 'And beggin' y'r pardon, but the two of you look like you could stand a good night's sleep. Best you start tomorrow with fresh eyes, or you might miss your quarry while you're winking.'

Harry sighed and nodded but Rafe was not attending. He was wondering what new mischief might befall Merry before he had her safe. Harry showed Lyneham out and called for a late supper and baths for him and Rafe. But as he did so, Rafe came down the stairs, shrugging into the overcoat Fitch had found for him.

'One more hour?' said Rafe, holding out Harry's coat in invitation.

'Aye,' said Harry without hesitation.

Merry awoke in a seedy bedroom, dressed in a garish pink satin gown, cut obscenely low across the bosom. For a moment, she was terrified that she had been raped while unconscious, but, though her drawers had been removed, there was no other sign that she had been molested. As she struggled upright, still a little groggy, she looked around her squalid surroundings. It was hard to tell the hour from the dim light straining through the small, grimy window. The walls might once have been red, but were now a muted maroon. The bed creaked complainingly as she moved to get up. Its sheets were a dull grey and over it lay a thin coverlet of indeterminate pattern. A shabby dressing table against the far wall beside the tiny, empty fireplace, and a threadbare boudoir chair were the only other items in the room.

Merry was desperate to escape, but she found the window all but nailed shut. The panes were so small, she would have to smash out the whole window to climb out of it, and going by the sounds she could hear through the walls, she would be easily heard. Merry caught up a corner of the curtain and scrubbed the window to look out. The room was at the back of the house, with a two-storey drop to a closed courtyard, so Merry realised that she would still need to escape from there even if she got down to the ground, which seemed unlikely given the injury to her shoulder.

As Merry was crossing the room to check the door, the key turned in the lock on the other side and the maid from the kitchen came in bearing a glass of small beer and a little bread and cheese.

'Oh! You're awake, miss?' said the girl a little startled, coming into the room and closing the door quickly behind her. 'The missus will be up to check on you later,' she added with a scared, apologetic look.

'Does she have a … a customer … for me?' said Merry trying to hide her fear.

'No, miss,' the girl whispered. 'She put the word out about you today. It's been a while since she's found a real maiden, so she'll tout for the highest bidder … well, your first time, at least.'

'So I have a day or two's grace,' said Merry grimly.

'Well, a day, mebbe,' qualified the girl uncertainly. 'I heard her say she might get more if you wasn't so bashed up, so she might wait an extra day, but she's a sharp un, and if she's offered the right price ...'

'I see,' said Merry. 'Are you …?'

'No, miss,' said the girl quickly. 'I'm Miss Fulsome's niece. I maid for the girls, but my ma got Auntie Amy to promise not to … well, you know what I mean,' finished the girl miserably.

Merry nodded equally miserably.

'Here's a little something to keep your strength up. She won't give you much, so you won't 'ave much fight in you when you're done the first time. So eat whatever you can.'

Merry looked at the small beer warily.

'T'ain't drugged,' the girl assured her. 'She don't drug her new girls unless they struggle or try to escape. Then she drugs 'em or lets Dawlish have his way with 'em. He's a violent brute and hung like a bear. They say he takes them *all* ways,' she added in a low whisper. 'Unchristian, it is. So the girls are well ruined after he's had 'em and usually settle down to the business after that. Anything's better than Dawlish.' The girl shuddered eloquently.

Merry's stomach turned over. Dawlish was probably the lurching thug who had grabbed her in the kitchen. Merry remembered the lusting look in his eye as he had grabbed hold of her and she shivered sickeningly at the image the girl had conjured up.

Sometime later, Amy Fulsome came up to look at her new acquisition. She had stripped and redressed Merry herself, so that she could better inspect the merchandise, and though delighted by the slender white body and firm young breasts, Amy had pursed her lips at the livid disfiguring bruises on her face and body. Merry was the finest prize she had bagged for many a year and the bruises would affect the price Amy might hope to charge for her deflowering. Greed warred with avarice as she wondered whether to wait until the bruising had gone, or to take the best offer that came in the following day.

'I hope you're going to fall in with my plans for you and not give me no trouble,' said the besom, her ferrety eyes scanning Merry's mutinous stance. 'Face it, dearie, you'd only have starved out there on the street. Better to live and turn a little profit, that's what I say.'

'I'd sooner die.'

'Huh! They all say that, my dear, but they all open their legs in the end.'

Merry shuddered, nauseated by the prospect.

'I'll find you a nice gentleman for your first, don't you worry. And then when you have some regulars, you'll find it's not such a bad life. At least you'll eat, and if you work hard,' she said with a bawdy wink, 'you might make enough to retire before your looks have gone.'

Merry gave her a baleful look that concealed her inner terror. She knew would be held captive until her virtue had been stripped from her, but any man who tried it would be sorry.

Amy saw the martial look in Merry's eye.

'Don't you be thinkin' of laying a hand on my punters, or I'll have Dawlish put the fear of God into you, my girl!'

Awful images of violent rape, or worse, being drugged and unable to defend herself from that brute's violations, haunted Merry. She turned away from Amy, swearing at her and clenching her hands into fists, but her shoulders sagged a little.

'Hah! *Not* such a lady then?' remarked Amy, surprised by Merry's language. 'Oh, you'll fit in here all right!'

The old harridan seemed satisfied. Her niece had clearly told the girl about Dawlish, and that was usually all it took. She had only to threaten her girls with letting Dawlish have them for a night to bring them round her thumb sharpish. He might be hopeful of having a poke at her newest asset, but he could go hang himself. Amy was certain she could get upwards of thirty guineas for her first blood and maybe up to a guinea a pop thereafter, at least for a while. Dawlish could have her when she had the pox or her looks were shot, thought Amy as she left.

Merry sat dejectedly at the dressing table and looked at her reflection. The low-cut gown hung about her bare shoulders, all but exposing her breasts and revealing the purple-black bruising across her left shoulder.

So this was the destiny of the last Griffith of Tal Hairn? Forced by rape and penury to become a whore.

Suicide would be preferable, but that cowardly path would be her last resort.

Merry tried to think of a way to escape her fate, but none occurred. Sadly, she resigned herself to the necessity of giving up her virginity to the customer that the abbess procured for her. Better that than having it taken by force or while she was insensible. Perhaps if she appeared compliant, she might eventually secure an opportunity to get away from this dreadful place.

Merry tried to reason that her virtue was of no real import; that survival and escape were paramount. But deep inside, her heart broke.

Chapter Nine
A Dramatic Development

'Here you are, sir,' said Amy ingratiatingly as she entered Merry's room with a prospective customer the following evening. 'A real pearl, and you being the first to open her up, as you might say. You won't be disappointed, I promise you. She's a real lady and worth every penny of your forty guineas.'

Standing by the fireplace with her back to the door, Merry did not turn.

This was not the first man Amy had brought to her room that day, but the previous candidate, persuaded to pay over the odds for a high-class virgin, was instantly put off by Merry's aggressive stance and bruised state. The young merchant had simply wanted a clean girl for an hour of fun before dinner. He had no wish to partake in the rape of an unwilling maiden. Amy had slapped Merry across the face and simply whispered 'Dawlish' to her, but the client was already demanding his money back, his carnal desires entirely dampened by the whole experience.

As soon as he was gone, the brothel keeper had laid bare Merry's two choices: either accept the next customer willingly, or have Dawlish as her bedfellow that very night. Raging with helpless fury, Merry had agreed to the first only to avoid the second.

Now, she had no choice but to surrender to this degrading violation, but she was damned if she would pretend to enjoy it. Since she could not school her features into anything approaching a complaisant smile, Merry remained with her back to Amy, knowing that the abbess would take her lack of resistance as acquiescence.

'Well, I'll leave you to get acquainted. You have all night to enjoy her, as you requested, sir,' she said, before closing the door behind her.

Merry had pinned her arms tight to her sides to keep herself from fighting and was trying to hide the expression of sick disgust on her face when, suddenly, the man's strong arms turned her round and crushed her to his broad chest, as he buried his face in the curls on top of her head and kissed them.

Merry couldn't help herself. With a choking cry, she struggled to be free and forced her head up to glare murderously at her despoiler.

'*You!*' she gasped in a tone of utter astonishment, as she found she was looking into a familiar pair of cobalt eyes, and was so amazed that she was momentarily unsure whether Rafe was there to rescue or ravish her.

But then she was struck dumb not only by the look of fierce joy radiating his face but also by the warning finger he swiftly put to her lips.

'Here,' he whispered, placing a small, silver-mounted pistol into her numb hand. 'I have a plan, but just in case, put this in your pocket. It's loaded, so be careful.'

Merry blinked and wondered if she were dreaming.

It was too good to be true! Rafe was here, not in Scotland, and somehow he had found her and even had a plan to save her!

For a moment, Merry could only stare at him, and then she watched his lips curve into an understanding smile as he lifted his hand and gently brushed a finger down her bruised cheek.

'Did you really think I would not come for you?'

Merry bit her lip as it wobbled traitorously.

'Silly chit,' he said, chucking her chin, and then grinned as he saw her eyes flash indignantly.

'Well! I ...' started Merry, eager to give Rafe a short, sharp list of the many reasons why she had _not_ expected his aid and why she was most certainly _not_ a silly chit.

'Shh!' whispered Rafe, his finger on her lips again. 'That old witch will be listening. Now, put that pistol in your pocket, if that dreadful rag has one.'

'What about you?' she whispered back.

'I'm armed too,' he assured her, opening his greatcoat to give her a glimpse of the two sleek pistol butts peeping out of the large poacher pockets on each side.

'Why can't I have one of those instead of this little thing?'

He looked at her in laughing exasperation.

'God damn it, Merry! If you think I'm walking out of here with a duelling pistol in one hand and a lady's pistol in the other, you have bats in your attic. They'd all fall about laughing. Now stop arguing and follow my lead.'

'Mrs Fulsome!' he bellowed, causing Merry to clutch his arm in alarm. He briefly laid a reassuring hand on hers, before the door opened suspiciously quickly, and the surprised abbess came in.

'Is this some kind of a joke?' Rafe cried, with an outraged look. 'Are you trying to get us both hanged?'

'Wh-what do you mean, my lord?' babbled Mrs Fulsome, utterly baffled.

'This is Judge Griffith's girl … *Hanging* Judge Griffith. She's the sister of the lad I killed, and he has spies out everywhere looking for her!'

He noted with grim satisfaction the look of horror stretching the besom's painted face as she silently mouthed the word 'hanging'.

'What were you thinking!' he demanded. 'If he gets word of this, he'll stretch both our necks and all your girls along with us!'

Amy had left the door open in her surprise and there were half-screams from the girls eavesdropping outside.

'Is this true?' gasped Amy, shaking Merry's arm sharply.

Merry gave her an accomplished look of sullen guilt.

'So what if it is?' she muttered. 'All me and Bryn wanted was to see London. What's wrong with that? Papa kept us so close we never got farther than Ludlow.'

Masterful! thought Rafe with a surge of pride. *Clever girl!*

Mrs Fulsome was aghast.

'You silly little bitch!' she spat, boxing her ears, which Merry bore as one well used to a cuff or too, twisting Rafe's heart in a different way.

'Here, here! No need for violence!' he said, grabbing Amy's hand in a vice-like grip before she could hit Merry again. 'She's in for a whipping from her father, when she gets home, if I know him. Never knew such a vile-tempered man.'

'Well, it must be in the blood,' agreed Amy, with heat. 'She's been hitting out and cussing something vicious ever since she got here. Put off her last customer on sight.'

Rafe's gut lurched.

'I found the wicked hussy wandering around dressed as a man, if you please! Well, I'm glad your pa'll lay a rod across your back, my girl. I should have done it myself, but I never like to damage my goods.'

'Well, you've got to get her out of here,' snapped Rafe, struggling to keep the fury he was feeling out of his eyes. '… And that won't be an easy matter … though it might be to my advantage to help …' he added in a thoughtful tone. 'Here, if you could tell the judge that it was I who found you wandering the streets and dropped you off safely outside the hotel where he's staying, he might not be quite so blood-thirsty in my pursuit.'

'Very well, but I think I'd rather stay than go back and get a thrashing,' said Merry churlishly, like a recalcitrant runaway.

'Well, you can't!' snapped Amy. 'What's to be done, my lord? His spies could be outside now.'

'You said you found her wandering round in men's clothes?'

Amy nodded.

'Do you still have them?'

'Yes, surely. I never throw clothes away.'

Amy dashed off down the corridor to fetch them, scattering the girls in the corridor with a few sharp words. Rafe walked forward and kicked the door to.

'You've not been harmed?' he asked quickly, with a look of concern on his handsome face as his hand cupped her injured cheek and he frowned at the ghastly bruise on her shoulder.

'N…no,' replied Merry, suddenly undone by his warm, anxious tone. She felt unexpected tears prick her eyes, and then was startled when his arms closed strongly about her again and he pressed a kiss on her brow.

'My poor darling! My brave girl! Just a few more minutes, little one,' he murmured into her hair.

Merry was shaken in a dozen different ways by these words and actions, and found that tears were suddenly streaming down her face. No one had ever called her a 'darling'. In a lifetime of hard knocks and hard times, these were the sweetest words that had ever been said to her, and in such a sympathetic and vibrant tone that it kindled a strange jumble of unfamiliar emotions. Coming after the terrors of the past week, it was all too much and, to her shame, Merry burst into tears.

Finding Rafe with his arms around the girl brought a swift suspicious look to Amy's foxy eyes, but then he gave her an embarrassed, awkward look of a man who had been obliged to comfort a sobbing woman.

'She's fearing her beating,' he said, in a confidential tone, and Merry's genuine distress, as sobs wracked her slender body, allayed Amy's suspicions.

'Hmm ...' said Amy grimly. 'If she'd been beaten more often, we wouldn't be in this fix, I'm sure! Here are the clothes she came in.'

Rafe gave Merry's shoulders a little shake.

'Come on, Miss Griffith! Put on these clothes again, and we shall walk out of here like two merry debauchers ... er ... customers ... er ... guests of the establishment.'

'Oh, you've no need to mind your language around that one!' said Amy dryly. 'She's got a mouth like a sailor. Can't think where she heard such things!'

This, and the ghost of a smile in Rafe's eyes, steadied Merry. She picked up the clothes and ducked behind the door to change swiftly into her former raiment. Merry transferred the pistol to her coat pocket and then ground her boot heel on the hated pink dress as it lay on the floor, before stepping out. Rafe couldn't resist a small smile, as he saw her in boy's clothes again, but quickly masked this with an assumed look of horror.

'*That ... is ... indecent!*' he declared, mimicking Merry's first reaction to wearing a dress. A smile twitched Merry's lips, which Amy read as a shameless want of decency.

'That's what I thought, my lord!' concurred Amy. 'Indecent!'

Rafe dared not meet Merry's eye, or they might not have been able to suppress their appreciation of this encomium coming from a brothel-keeper.

He helped Merry into her greatcoat and pushed her out of the room. Some of Mrs Fulsome's girls were lurking in the corridor, despite her warnings, and glowered at Merry as she pushed her way through them to the stairs.

When they reached the outer door, He turned to Merry at the door, pulling her greatcoat around her, and clapping her hat down over her eyes.

'We'll leave like two happy revellers. Keep your head down, like you're foxed.'

He gave the doorman a nod to throw open the door to the street.

'Bon nuit, fair ladies!' he said with an unsteady, exaggerated bow. 'C'mon young man, s'pose I should get you home … you're three sheets to the wind, dear boy.'

With Merry's arm hauled around his neck and her body leaning drunkenly against him, he lurched off in a zig-zag down the narrow, dimly-lit street until he reached a waiting carriage, with Harry, in a frieze coat and muffler, sitting on the box. Merry was quickly bundled in.

'Spring 'em, Harry! We have her safe!' shouted Rafe.

Harry whooped, and the coach lurched forward, clattering along the cobbles in the direction of bustling Piccadilly.

As soon as they were off, Merry pulled off her hat and turned to Rafe in the darkness, her hand finding his in an unconsciously feminine gesture.

'Thank you,' she said, her voice shaking a little with emotion. 'Thank you for saving me.'

Rafe would never know how he kept from pulling Merry into his arms and kissing her until his own aching need and wild relief had subsided.

When he had entered that squalid room and seen Merry, it was as though his soul had reached out and embraced her and that his body had merely followed. Here in the intimate confines of the travelling coach, lit only intermittently by the streetlamps they passed, the touch of Merry's trembling fingers against his bare skin almost shattered his self-control. It sent a shock of physical desire through him that fused indivisibly with the connection that had dragged him back to London at the gallop just to see her again. Whatever this was, it overwhelmed and consumed him … and felt dangerously like drowning, leaving him out of his depth, helpless and vulnerable.

He had been so engrossed in trying to rescue Merry that he had not, until this moment, thought about what would happen when he did ... or if he had been motivated by more than duty.

With a sensation unpleasantly close to panic, he now accepted that his feelings for Merry were passionate, profound, irrevocable and entirely unreciprocated.

What divine comedy that he should fall in love, for the first time in his life, with this proud, strong-willed tomboy whose brother he had killed in a callous act of misguided pride!

Would she, could she, ever look past his crime and return his affection? And what was he to do if she could not?

Merry's emotions, too, were in turmoil. Rafe's earlier embrace had unsettled her. Feeling the strength and comfort of his arms around her and the throbbing emotion in his voice had made her feel oddly weak. Worse still, it had felt good.

But now that she was a 'boy' once more, Merry felt more herself and had no idea what to do if Rafe were to embrace her again. She felt his hand clasp around hers and heard him draw breath to speak

'Don't,' she whispered, surprising herself.

Hasty amorous words withered on Rafe's tongue.

'I ... I mean, don't say anything kind,' said Merry recovering herself. 'It might make me blubber again, and I'll wager you don't want a watering pot on your hands.'

'Well, that's rich!' said Rafe trying for a mock-indignant tone. 'When I'm unkind to you, you want to cut my heart out, and when I'm kind, you turn on the waterworks. I can't win.'

'Unkind!' snorted Merry, recovering her equilibrium. 'Do you mean when you choked me into unconsciousness!'

'Well, I was provoked,' he said meaningfully. 'And don't think I won't do it again if you leave my protection once more!' he added darkly, remembering that he had a bone to pick with his beloved. 'What the devil possessed you to stalk out of Wolvenden House on your own without at least leaving a message for Harry?'

'Your *protection*? Huh!' gasped Merry, firing up. 'You delegated that to your witch of a stepmother, who accused me of carrying your natural child! By God, if she had been a man!' Merry ground her teeth, fuming at the memory. 'Suffice it to say that my faith in you both was as strained as my temper at that moment.'

'Words, Merry! They were just words!' snapped Rafe, his own temper kindling as the jangling reaction to Merry's safe return fully set in. He found his hands were shaking and clenched his fists in surprise. 'That was no excuse to set yourself adrift in the world, selling your pearls, burying your brother alone …'

'What! Was I supposed to swallow her insults in return for a bed for the night…' gasped Merry.

'Yes! At least until Harry returned to …'

'And when my brother called you a cheat?' demanded Merry. 'Words, Rafe! *They were just words*!' she cried, mimicking him.

'That was different,' said Rafe hoarsely, his eyes holding hers with a rather haunted expression before he looked away, his body tensing as he pushed his head back into the shadowy corner of the carriage with a groan.

Merry instantly felt remorse for her lack of gratitude. Rafe had returned to find and rescue her, after all.

'I'm sorry,' she said, touching his arm. 'I'm being ungrateful. I know you meant well and I was ...'

But Rafe was in the grip of very strong emotion. The knowledge that he was the cause of all her suffering was eating him alive. Every privation, every fear, every blow she had sustained in the last week ultimately lay at his own door, and he could not bear it.

How could she ever forgive him if he could not forgive himself?

Yet, instead of abject apology, Rafe's torment vented in irrational anger.

'And when you had failed to find work? Or when you had been beaten and robbed?' grated Rafe. 'Why did you not return to my house and have my servants send for me?'

Rafe did not even mention Harry, who would have been Merry's more logical refuge. His friend was forgotten.

'Send for you!' Merry stared at Rafe in amazement, stunned by the hurt that she heard beneath his anger. 'I would not have dreamt of it!'

'Your damned pride!'

'No such thing! You are wholly unreasonable! As if your servants would even *admit* me, let alone summon you from God knew where! Rafe, I barely knew you, and...'

'*Barely knew me*!' said Rafe, as though he had been struck. 'Did our time together leave no impression on you at all? Good God, I abandoned my journey north just because I missed you and that damned grey-eyed glare of yours.'

'Y…you did?' Merry's heart fluttered and she felt that strange shaky feeling again that she had felt before in his company.

'And did you think so little of me that you believed I would not honour my debt to take care of you?'

'I … I…'

'No! I don't suppose you gave me a second thought,' said Rafe resentfully. 'Never considered that I would be frantic with worry, not knowing where you were, or what was happening to you and sick with dread that you might be dead.'

Rafe groaned again and dragged his fingers through his hair.

What's wrong with me? Why am I shouting at her? Why can't I just shut up?

'I did think of you,' whispered Merry.

Rafe spun round to look at her, suddenly intent, his heart thudding.

'In all my darkest moments, somehow remembering that time with you and Harry sustained me, though it was little more than a dream.'

Harry! thought Rafe, finally remembering his best friend, who was on the box, negotiating the crowded evening traffic along Piccadilly and no doubt wondering what was going on in the coach beneath him.

'My favourite dream was of reading with you in your beautiful library,' said Merry, looking at her hands. She was suddenly feeling hot and tingly and terribly aware of the man seated beside her, his eyes watching her intently. If she had looked up, she would have seen such a glow there that would have stopped her heart.

Instead, Merry looked out of the window beside her and, anxious to change the subject, asked: 'Are we heading there now?'

Rafe took a deep breath to calm the surge of unfamiliar sensation Merry's words had caused.

What is this? he wondered.

Oh, he realised, *it is hope*.

The connection was not entirely one-sided, even if his book room stood on an equal footing in her affections. Harry had said she had loved his book room. *But where,* he wondered, *did Harry stand?*

'No, my house is being watched, and now so is Harry's,' he said, searching Merry's face in the dim light. 'My stepmother was well served for her insult to you. I stopped her allowance and sent her home. But her Parthian shot was to lay information against Harry in retaliation for the trimming he gave her. Now he is a hunted man, too.'

'Damn that woman!' said Merry. 'I hope she rots in hell. I'll swear she was only vile to me in order to hurt you. She hates you.'

'She has cause.'

Merry heard the bitterness in his voice, and leapt to his defence.

'That's not fair! It was an accident! You were only a boy!' cried Merry, and then gasped, her hand flying to her reckless mouth.

Rafe pursed his lips and sighed.

'Harry, I suppose? Still fashioning a halo for me is he?'

'While you fashion horns and a pointy tail?' countered Merry.

Rafe shrugged.

'I thought you and my stepmother would have more common ground,' said Rafe sadly. 'You both lost the people you loved most at my hand.'

'Damn it, Rafe! Why must you be so idiotically eager to shoulder blame,' demanded Merry impatiently. 'I'll wager Kit encouraged you to drive faster,' she reasoned, and then added quietly: 'And it takes two to duel.'

Silence hung between them for a while.

'Merry ...' began Rafe hoarsely.

'Oh, stow it, if you're going to apologise again or find something else to blame yourself for!' snapped Merry. 'Yes! You killed Bryn! I can't say I forgive you. I don't even know how I feel about that right now because I'm so *very* grateful that you rescued me from that dreadful brothel and from destitution, too! When I went off on my own, you could have dusted your hands and thought well rid of me, but you did not. No, you found me and then risked yourself to save me!

'How *did* you find me, by the way?' she added, with an arrested expression on her face.

Rafe was still grappling with the glimpse Merry had given into her own mental turmoil, and it was a long moment before he answered

'Long story,' he said at last, recovering his balance. 'When you failed to appear at the inquest, Harry was in despair.'

'He came!'

'Yes, but I'll let him tell you all about that,' smiled Rafe, finally playing fair. 'When he returned to his rooms in Half Moon Street, he found me waiting for him.'

Rafe's expression darkened as he remembered the awful moment when Harry told him Merry was missing.

'We resolved to find you. By God, you led us on quite a chase! You always seemed to be just a step away from us. You can imagine how we felt when we discovered that you'd been attacked and when you just seemed to disappear. Thankfully, we'd enlisted the services of a former Bow Street Runner, who traced you. We formed a plan ... and the rest you know.'

'So now you are both wanted men?' said Merry.

'Yes, now I've put my best friend under the shadow of the noose. Quite a week's work, wouldn't you agree?'

Merry sighed impatiently at this resurfacing of Rafe's self-hate.

'Doing it much too brown, *my lord*,' she said in a dry tone. 'I heard that your fellow peers would never vote to convict you.'

Rafe looked at her in surprise.

'Harry and I are not peers, Merry,' he said. 'We're subject to the same laws and courts as you.'

'What!' cried Merry. 'But you're Lord Rothsea and he is Lord Stowe!'

'Courtesy titles ... our *fathers* are peers, and happily both are yet living,' he explained. 'As their eldest sons, we take our fathers' second highest titles, but we have none of the rights that go with them.'

'Good God! You mean that if you were captured, you could hang?' squeaked Merry.

Rafe's lips twitched at Merry's obvious alarm. She was clutching at his sleeve, her eyes wide with distress.

'Of course,' he confirmed. 'Though I hope it won't come to that ...'

'Oh, why, oh why, have you put yourselves in such danger for me?' said Merry, shaking Rafe's arm. 'Oh, this is worse than anything!'

'Hardly! Do you imagine either of us would leave unless you were safe? What a paltry pair of fellows you think us!'

'And do you imagine *I* would exchange your lives for my mine? What a paltry fellow you think me!' she replied.

Rafe stared at her enigmatically.

'Well,' he said after a moment. 'We both need to leave town for a spell, and stay out of the hands of the authorities, but Harry's father will smooth things out for him. He has a lot of influence, particularly with the Prince Regent, as should I given how much I've loaned him over the past few years! But it will be rustication and probably exile for me for a year or two. Then I'll write to Prinny begging for a pardon. It's worked before.'

'*That's* how you were spared in the past?'

'I was never indicted for murder before, so it is a little more serious this time,' said Rafe soberly. 'The first time, I was considered the victim, and the death accidental. The second, I paid a large fine and my sentence was respited in favour of self-exile. Then I wrote to Prinny and he was gracious enough to pardon me. I hope he will do me the honour once more.'

Merry was not entirely reassured, but she released her hold on his arm and sagged back against the squabs.

'You took a terrible risk,' she sighed disapprovingly.

'It was worth it,' said Rafe quietly.

It was probably as well for both of them that they felt the coach slowing to pass through the Hyde Park turnpike. There was a short pause, an exchange of voices, and the coach once again sprang forward, much faster this time. The surface beneath the iron-clad wheels had changed from clattering cobbles to crunching gravel. Inside the coach there was a charged silence, as they passed the villas and barracks of Knightsbridge. Once clear of the village, Harry pulled up the team beside the dark expanse of Hyde Park. He jumped down from the box and pulled open the door of the carriage.

'Well, is she all right?' his strained face lit by the carriage lamp.

'Yes, Harry, I'm fine!' said Merry, leaping down from the carriage to prove it and twirling round with her arms outstretched, luxuriating in the feeling of freedom.

'Thank God!' said Harry. Then as he saw her injuries by the light of the carriage lamp, he added: 'Holy hell! Look at the state of your face! You poor child, does it hurt very much?'

Merry shook her head, her eyes alight with the pleasure of seeing him again.

'Huh! You should see my shoulder, it's much worse ... but never mind that, you won't believe how we had to playact to get out of that vile place ...'

Watching them from the shadow of the carriage, Rafe felt a stabbing pain in his chest, and his hand went unconsciously to it. Harry was looking down at Merry's animated, upturned face, as she recounted the ingenious escape, with the same misty wonder that he felt himself. *Was Harry in love with her, too?*

He's a better man than I by a country mile, thought Rafe, *but he can't have her!*

They both turned as he stepped down from the carriage.

'That was a brilliant scheme, Rafe!' cried Harry.

'And masterfully executed,' said Merry. 'How lucky I am to have two such good friends. I thought I was pretty much in the suds, but you hadn't forgotten me, after all, and you both put yourselves in danger to rescue me and just in time, too! I had thought I was alone in the world, but I no longer feel that way. Even if we were to part now and I never saw you again, I should always be grateful for this moment.'

Merry had been looking shyly down at the ground as she spoke, so was unaware that her 'good friends' were not entirely attending to her, but were exchanging a steady look of deadly earnest.

Harry had guessed Rafe's feelings for Merry, but there was no earthly way he would allow his friend to force unwanted or improper attentions on the poor girl. His own feelings towards Merry were less clear, but the look he gave Rafe declared himself her protector, against Rafe if necessary.

'What is it?' Merry's ready intelligence could see that the mood had changed but was at a loss to account for it.

'I'm afraid you can't get rid of us that easily,' responded Harry, with a reassuring smile.

'We are just considering your future,' said Rafe.

'There's only one thing that will answer ... and that's marriage,' stated Harry, unequivocally, looking sternly at Rafe.

'Unquestionably,' replied Rafe, with a glinting challenge in his eyes. 'The sooner the better.'

'Marriage! For me?' gasped Merry goggling at them. 'Don't be ridiculous!'

Merry broke into incredulous laughter, which quickly abated when she saw the grim determination on both men's faces.

'But why?!' she demanded. 'Can't we remain as we are?'

'No!' replied both men in unison.

'Why not?'

There was a pregnant pause.

'Because I dread to contemplate what society will make of an intimate friendship between two men and an uncommonly beautiful boy, for one thing!' replied Rafe acidly.

'Merry, my dear,' said Harry, taking Merry's hands in his, ignoring as best he could the heat of Rafe's furious glare boring into his forehead. 'You're a young lady ... not a boy. It's the only proper solution. But I give you my word of honour that no husband will be forced upon you.' Harry looked straight at Rafe as he continued. 'You will be free to choose your bridegroom when you are ready to do so.'

'Well, that will be never!' said Merry.

'We'll see,' said Rafe. 'But first, you're going to have to learn how to be a lady,' he added firmly. 'But where to effect your education is the question. I expect all my properties will be watched for a week or two, as will your main residences now.'

'Miss Dunwoody offered to take her in, but she is fixed in town.'

'Lydia?' cried Merry. 'You met Lydia? Isn't she the most wonderful girl you ever met?'

'Yes, she was very kind,' he replied absently, watching as Rafe ground his teeth and folded his arms tightly across his chest.

'Absolutely not!' vetoed Rafe. 'I am not going to delegate my responsibilities for Merry's safekeeping to *anyone* ever again,' he said with emphasis.

THE RELUCTANT LADY

'You might not have the choice!' snapped Harry, with the nearest expression to bad temper Merry had ever seen on his affable face.

'But didn't you think her very pretty too?' pressed Merry.

'What?' said Harry, distracted by the sardonic grin on Rafe's face. 'Yes, yes, very pretty.'

'It doesn't matter how delightful she is, Merry. You are _not_ going to stay with her,' said Rafe categorically.

'But if I did, you could both get away. I wouldn't be a burden to you and there would be no more talk of marriage.'

'And have you put us through hell again, when you quarrel with this Lydia and go running off on your own once more? I think not!' said Rafe, glad to see the light of this possibility dawn in Harry's eyes.

'I would never quarrel with Lydia!' said Merry.

'Huh! You could quarrel with an empty room,' said Rafe. 'But that's beside the point. I am not letting you out of my sight again until you are safely settled and that is that!'

'I have a small hunting lodge near Quemerford,' suggested Harry. 'The hunting is terrible, so I'm hardly ever there. Just keep a couple of servants to take care of the place.'

'Excellent. Drive on,' said Rafe, pointing a finger to Harry's former place on the box with an unholy gleam in his eye.

'I'm damned if I'll leave Merry alone in a carriage with you!' hissed Harry in an angry under-voice audible to all.

'Well, I'm not going to leave her to your infernal hand-holding either,' snarled Rafe, not bothering to lower his voice.

'Then _I'll_ drive!' cried Merry, her arms folded across her chest, staring at them in disbelief now that she grasped that they were arguing about her. 'And you two can continue your idiotic argument in the carriage!

'I haven't driven four horses before, but I daresay I shall manage once I have them in hand,' said Merry, as she started to climb the box.

Rafe and Harry exchanged a speaking look, then in one easy movement Rafe plucked Merry off the step and tossed her, incontinent, into the carriage, whilst Harry wordlessly mounted the box.

'We'll exchange at Brentford, when we rest the horses,' said Rafe grimly. 'Then we should rack up for the night at Colnbrook.' Then he climbed into the carriage and closed the door with a snap. Harry pursed his lips tightly in vexation, but gave the horses the office to start.

Chapter Ten
The Unthinkable Option

As they rumbled off, there was silence in the dark carriage, but Rafe knew Merry was watching him intently.

'What?' he finally asked in an exasperated tone, as if her steady regard had been a persistent question.

'What was all that about?'

Rafe countered her question with one of his own.

'Why are you so opposed to the thought of marriage?'

'They call it leg-shackled for a reason, you know.'

'Well, a week ago, I would have agreed with you wholeheartedly,' said Rafe. 'But what aspect of the institution particularly irks you?'

'All of it,' replied Merry, throwing her hands up for emphasis. 'Having children, for example. The thought of something, a human being, growing inside *here*,' she patted the flat plane of her stomach under her waistcoat. 'It's creepy!'

Rafe's lips twitched and he had to bite them to keep from laughing.

'I mean, what if *you* had to grow the babies in *your* belly?'

Rafe bit harder.

'I hadn't looked at it that way,' he said, his eyes watering with suppressed amusement. 'Yes, I'd have to admit that that <u>would</u> be creepy.'

'There! You see!' said Merry righteously, glad to have made her point. 'We chaps think alike about these things.'

'But forgive me for pointing out that you're not a chap, Merry.'

'But I *think* like one! I *feel* like one! I've been a boy for seventeen years, and I *like* it!'

'What do you like about it?'

'The freedom. I can say what I like and do what I like and no one is shocked,' said Merry. 'You should have seen the way people stared at me when I had to retie my garter after I left your stepmother's house …'

'You … you … tied your garter in the middle of Upper Grosvenor Street?' asked Rafe, stifling his own scandalised humour. 'Yes, I can imagine that would have drawn some attention.'

'You would have thought my hair was on fire,' confirmed Merry. 'Besides, this is all irrelevant because no one would want to marry me, thank God!'

'I would,' said Rafe. 'In fact, I do, very much.'

'What? … Oh!' exhaled Merry, light dawning as she recalled his argument with Harry. 'But why?'

'Don't you know?'

'I can't imagine!' said Merry, racking her brains.

Rafe snorted and sat back against the squabs shaking his head in disbelief.

'Have you really no idea why I want to marry you, Merry?'

'Oh … I suppose it is because you feel guilty … about Bryn.'

'I do feel guilty, but no … not because of that,' said Rafe. 'And not because of any debt to your brother either.'

The dark carriage was quiet for a minute, with only the jingle of the harnesses and the rhythmic cludding of the horses' hooves to break the silence.

Rafe took a long breath and then gave a deep sigh.

'I want to marry you for the same reason that I came racing back from Grantham to see you,' said Rafe softly, the caress in his voice sending a frisson of warmth through Merry's veins.

'My "damned grey-eyed glare"?' she remembered.

Merry heard Rafe chuckle in the darkness.

'Amongst other things, yes.'

Merry could tell that he was smiling as he spoke. She now recollected other things that had disconcerted her.

'Harry said I was a … a beauty,' recalled Merry, suddenly shy, feeling that unsettling sensation again at the memory of Rafe's glowing expression as he had set the bonnet on her head in Albemarle Street.

THE RELUCTANT LADY

'You *are* beautiful, Merry,' confirmed Rafe. 'But beauty fades. A man who would marry for beauty is a fool. You have more important qualities.'

Since Merry did not think she was in the least bit beautiful, she was happy to concur.

'My education?' volunteered Merry.

'Your *intelligence*,' corrected Rafe, and then smiled as they passed by the lamps of the Kensington turnpike and he saw her nibbling her thumbnail in concentration. 'Any other thoughts?'

'Well, I've been a bit of a watering-pot lately, but I'm normally pluck to the backbone,' said Merry after a moment, putting forward the one quality in which she took true pride.

'You've been through enough to make a grown man despair, Merry,' said Rafe warmly. 'And you're one of the bravest people I know!'

Merry felt her throat constrict with emotion at this treasured praise, and then remembered the last time he had called her 'brave'.

'Umm ... and when you found me, you called me "darling".'

'I hope one day you'll give me permission to do so for the rest of our lives.'

Merry blushed as her heart gave an odd leap, but she said nothing, her mind in turmoil.

Fighting the urge to take her into his arms, Rafe also thought Merry incredibly desirable, but kept that information to himself.

'There's also the fact that I love you, Merry, and I have discovered the hard way that you are wholly material to my happiness.'

Rafe heard Merry gasp and wondered anxiously what she was thinking. Several moments passed, and Rafe's patience snapped under the intolerable suspense.

'Well, say something, for heaven's sake! I've just declared myself!'

'I don't know what to say.'

Say you love me, too! thought Rafe.

'Isn't there anything you like about *me*?' asked Rafe, sounding desperate even to his own ears.

Merry was silent for a few moments.

'I like everything about you,' she replied quietly. 'But I could never marry you, Rafe.'

Rafe felt his heart splitting.

'Because I killed your brother?'

'Yes,' said Merry. 'It would seem like betrayal … and yet …,' she groaned, her twisting fingers betraying the conflict of her thoughts, which came tumbling out. '… I enjoy your company so much. You're a shameless bully, but you make me laugh, even when I want to hate you, and you are never shocked, not really, even when you pretend to be, and you're as brave as anything, risking the drop to come and find me, and when you came into that awful room to save me when I thought I was going to be …' Merry saw Rafe's body tense. 'Well, there just aren't words. I'm so glad to be your friend that perhaps I am betraying Bryn already.'

'No,' said Rafe hoarsely, shaken by Merry's revelations. 'He committed you to my safekeeping.'

'But he didn't give me leave to enjoy it.'

'He would want you to be happy, would he not?'

'Yes,' said Merry after a moment, her guilt lifted by this thought.

'Then, stop worrying about whether we should be friends or not. I enjoy your company, too, Merry. More than I can say. And your wellbeing means more to me than my own. Surely your brother would have appreciated the irony of that turn of events, if nothing else?'

Merry smiled. There was a momentary pause as they both recovered a little from the disclosures of the last few minutes. Then Rafe employed his new knowledge.

'Of course,' he said in a plaintive tone, looking away in an exaggerated gesture of misuse. 'You abuse me mercilessly and utterly trample my self-esteem. I live in daily fear of your wanton violence and that volcanic temper of yours,' he achieved a creditable shudder. 'I vow you put me to the blush with your shameless ogling when I am in the *slightest* state of undress, and when I heroically offer - against my inclination and better judgement, you understand - to make an honest woman of you, you turn me down flat!'

Rafe's heart soared as Merry broke out laughing. It was an open, boyish sound, not at all feminine, but wholly infectious, and it made the enjoyment of the moment bubble up inside him and overflow into laughter too.

On that quiet stretch of road, Harry heard the sound, too, and his spirits were similarly lifted.

'Hey, what's the joke?' they heard him shout from the box.

Rafe dropped the window and leaned out.

'Merry's idea of turning me down gently,' he quipped, bringing a broad grin to Harry's face.

'Excellent!' said Harry, amusement fusing with relief. 'That's the ticket, Merry! Hah! That'll teach you for putting it to the touch so soon, Rafe, you bounder!'

'Drive on, cabbie!' shouted Rafe cheekily, putting the window back up.

Merry was still chuckling at this exchange as the lights of Hammersmith came into sight, and Rafe folded his arms across his chest and asked: 'So do you have anything else against marriage?'

'Yes, the way everyone treated me like a weakling or an imbecile when I was dressed as a woman. The landlord, the parson, even the pawnbroker tried to chouse me …'

'Ah! That reminds me,' interrupted Rafe, reaching into his breast pocket and fishing out Merry's pearls. He opened her unresisting palm and dropped them into it.

Merry couldn't trust her voice to speak for a moment.

'Oh, no,' said Rafe, nudging her shoulder playfully. 'Would this be one of those watering-pot moments? I thought you said you think like a boy.'

'Ratbag!' she said in an unsteady voice, nudging his shoulder back.

'Hah! That's more like my Merry.'

'Your kindness unmanned me, that's all,' said Merry, closing her hand around the precious little strand. 'How on earth can I ever repay you?'

'Well, you could marry me,' suggested Rafe conversationally.

'Rafe!' gasped Merry in a broken whisper.

'I'm teasing, you idiot,' said Rafe, nudging her shoulder again. 'To be fair to Harry, I think I only beat him to the shop because he was waylaid by the fair Lydia.'

This diversion was a happy one.

'Oh, she would be the very girl for him!'

'I concur,' said Rafe affably. 'Let's tell him together.'

'Rafe, you rogue! You've never even met her!'

'I defer to your judgement in these matters, my dear,' he replied unabashed and in the tone of a middle-aged husband.

Merry giggled.

'Well, I if I *were* a man, she's the girl I would want to marry!'

Rafe choked, but rallied.

'Aha! So you're not opposed to the institution then?' he reasoned. 'Only to being the wife and not the husband?'

'Well, can you blame me? The law says a wife belongs to her husband. Literally *belongs*, like a chattel.'

'But a husband belongs to his wife as much as the reverse is true.'

'Nonsense!' said Merry. 'The law doesn't allow a wife to beat her *husband* with a stick no thicker than her thumb!'

Merry was holding her thumb up in front of Rafe's face in illustration, when the coach was momentarily illuminated by another turnpike lamp. The light fell on Rafe's face, whose tender, indulgent gaze swiftly changed to such a comic expression of fearful trepidation as he looked at the thumb that Merry burst out laughing in her boyish way again.

'Do you honestly think I would beat you, Merry?'

'Well, you've already threatened me with strangulation,' she said dryly.

'Only if you leave me, minx,' said Rafe with a wry smile. 'And then you will have earned it.'

'And what if you left me?' asked Merry

'It could never happen.'

'You might fall in love with someone else.'

'The lovely Lydia?'

'I didn't mean that. I meant … husbands take mistresses,' said Merry darkly.

'And wives take lovers … but …' Rafe stopped abruptly.

'Not your wife?' supplied Merry.

'Precisely. Not you, Merry,' he said, his gut tightening at the thought. 'I would not allow it.'

'Would you take a mistress?'

'Not if I had you,' he said sincerely. 'I would keep myself only unto thee.'

'But I've already said I could never marry you.'

'Yes, that was a leveller,' he said grimly.

'But you still persist?'

'I'm a pretty determined fellow.'

'So am I, Rafe.'

'Then may the best *man* win!' he said, with a twinkle.

Merry huffed and shook her head uncomprehendingly.

There was another long silence as Merry looked out of the window, watching the villas of Chiswick and cottages of Turnham Green fly by, while she tried to digest all they had discussed. There was no question that Rafe and Harry had her welfare in mind, but now their schemes threatened to turn her world upside-down again. Merry wished she could think of some viable alternative, some way by which she might maintain her independence, but the last few days had shattered her confidence. Without the protection and company of her brother, Merry felt lost; and though it felt abominably faint-hearted, it also felt rather wonderful to be in the safekeeping of two such capable men.

Rafe leaned back into the corner, his face in shadow, watching Merry's troubled profile, lit by the pale moonlight and occasional streetlamps.

'Merry,' he said finally, even his gentle tone making her jump. 'As Harry said, you will never be forced to marry, so you have nothing to worry about on that account. All we ask for the moment is that you keep an open mind and just learn about being a lady for a little while. Is that too much to ask?'

'No, I suppose not,' conceded Merry, unable to banish entirely the churlish undertone to her acceptance. Merry had no relish whatsoever for donning those wretched skirts again.

'Now,' said Rafe, changing the subject as he saw the lights of Old Brentford ahead. 'Are you hungry?'

'Heavens, yes! I'm famished!' said Merry with feeling. 'Mrs Fulsome kept me on lean rations so that I'd … well, never mind that … I could eat a horse, that's all.'

Rafe felt his fists clench at the thought of what the abbess had planned for his beloved Merry. But his darling girl was safe now, and for the moment, that was enough.

Merry demonstrated just how hungry she had been by putting away a staggering amount of food, and then, under their disconcerted gaze, sitting back in her chair, her eyes closed with pleasure, letting out a satisfied belch and stroking her now-taut waistcoat, stretched over her full stomach.

'Ahh!' she said with a gusty sigh. 'Now, all I need is a pint and a pipe, and I will be in heaven.'

'A what??' snapped Rafe incredulously.

Harry was still boggled by the belch.

'A… a pint of ale and a pipe,' faltered Merry, sitting up and meeting Rafe's disapproving look.

'Are you telling me that you are in the habit of drinking ale and smoking?'

'When funds allow,' said Merry uncertainly, confused by Rafe's sudden sternness.

'Well, you can think again, Merry! You have downed your last pint and smoked your last pipe. A lady does neither of those things, nor does she approve her dinner in your singularly vulgar style,' said Rafe severely.

Merry jumped up at this and stood next to his chair glaring down at him.

'I knew it! *Quod erat demonstrandum*, Rafe!' cried Merry. 'This is just the high-handed, unequal treatment I was afraid of!'

'Sit down, you little termagant!' Unyielding blue eyes met furious grey once again.

'Really, Merry, it's not the conduct of a gentleman either,' said Harry with quiet reproof that seemed to take the wind entirely out of her sails. Merry coloured and looked down. 'Still less that of a lady or …'

'Or the fourteen-year-old boy you're aping, for that matter!' growled Rafe, irritated once more by Harry's ability to pacify Merry's starts. She gave him a fiery look. 'Don't try to tell me that your father approved such behaviour, because he was no gentleman if he did!'

Merry blushed crimson and looked away guiltily.

'I thought not,' said Rafe dryly. 'I can only assume your brother was too busy fighting with you to regulate your excesses.'

'My brother was the gentlest, sweetest-tempered man alive! He never once raised his voice to me. Never!' cried Merry, incensed, not least by the knowledge that she had, indeed, behaved badly. 'That's why I know he never forced a duel on you. You must have provoked him out of reason as you do me!'

'Sweet-tempered!' croaked Rafe. 'He had the same fire-breathing nature as you! I was all for waiting a day or so, but, no! he would …'

'Rafe!' barked Harry.

Rafe stopped in his tracks, stunned at himself.

He stood stiffly, looking down into Merry's angry, puzzled face. His account still made no sense to her.

'Forgive me,' said Rafe in a tight voice. Then he turned in disgust at himself and walked to the door, picking up Harry's hat, frieze coat, and muffler. 'I'll see the horses put to and await you both outside. We should leave soon, if we want to reach Colnbrook before midnight.'

He left without a backward look.

'Harry?' whispered Merry, turning her burning gaze on him.

'Leave it, there's a good fellow,' said Harry quietly. 'Better to remember your brother as you described. A man can behave out of character when he's badly dipped or in his cups.'

'I don't understand,' murmured Merry, turning away.

Harry glanced warily at her profile under his brows. It would not benefit Merry for her to share their suspicions about her brother's motives.

'Come! Rafe's right. We need to get on the road,' said Harry jumping up and tossing Merry her coat. 'And I think I should warn you that Rafe's driving is unlikely to be improved by his present mood.'

'I hope I keep hold of my dinner,' said Merry apprehensively.

'So do I!' replied Harry, with feeling.

Rafe did not look at either of them as they boarded the coach, seeming instead to be focused on arranging all four sets of reins in his left hand and then picking up the long whip in his right.

Merry and Harry exchanged a look and rolled their eyes. Within a moment, they both knew their trepidation was justified, as Rafe sprang the horses, leaving his passengers clinging onto the straps for dear life.

Harry's guess was correct. His friend was lashing himself inwardly for his thoughtless outburst. Thankfully Rafe got both his temper and his anxiety under control after the first mile and settled down to a brisk mix of canters and trots.

Inside, after laughing together at Rafe's prospects of ever being hired as a coachman should the need arise, they had both felt a little awkward. Harry's presence was much less disturbing than Rafe's, but unlike Rafe, Harry had, very properly, lit the internal lamps, which had somehow increased the embarrassment.

Merry prayed that Harry did not share Rafe's romantical notions towards her.

'If you should ever have need of employment, Harry,' said Merry, her lips twitching. 'I think you might make an excellent lion tamer, or keeper of tigers.'

Harry grinned.

'Aye, and my headstone would read *"mauled to death by his charges"*,' he said shaking his head.

'Rafe said you were outside the inquest waiting for me.'

Harry thankfully accepted this safe topic and together they filled the next forty minutes piecing together the activities of the past few days. As they came to the end, Merry sighed contentedly and leaned back, allowing her head to rock with the rhythmic sway of the coach. Harry watched as Merry's eyes flickered and then closed, as her large meal and the stress of the week's horrors took its toll, and the relief of truly being safe for the first time in a very long time swept her into a comfortable doze.

Putting his arm round her shoulders to keep her from falling, Harry was oddly relieved. There would be time enough to talk about the future. His own feelings towards Merry were a jumble. He was in awe of her fortitude, and would give his life to protect her, but was that love? For the first time, Harry was forced to look beyond his present way of life and consider what qualities he might look for in a wife.

An hour later, Rafe pulled the coach off the road into the stable yard of one of the less prestigious posting houses in Colnbrook. After a few clipped instructions to the ostlers, followed by the flash of tossed coins to each of them, the yard erupted into action, and Rafe walked into the posting house, calling for mine host.

Rafe's lips tightened as Harry walked in with an adorably tousled-looking Merry, her grey eyes blinking as they adjusted to the bright light of the inn. A smile tugged at Harry's lips, as Rafe shot him a murderous questioning look.

Merry defused the situation.

'Lord!' she said, the earlier argument long since forgotten. 'I must be tired if I could fall asleep while *you* were handling the reins, Rafe! You're a shocking driver!'

Rafe, a highly respected member of the Four-in-Hand Club, took this criticism on the chin, while Harry bit his lip and closely inspected a coaching print on the wall.

'Harry, you and I will have to share a room and they have no private parlour at present. I've ordered us all baths,' added Rafe.

'A bath!' said Merry, as if describing the highest luxury. 'This will be my first bath this year,' she confided as they made their way upstairs, causing her friends to share a look of consternation over her head.

'Our landlord started charging extra for each can of hot water,' she continued unthinkingly. 'So I had to make do with washing all over, standing on a towel.'

Both men shook their heads and blinked, as this mental picture danced before their eyes. This time there was no shared look.

Merry bid them good night and then stepped aside as the bath was brought into her room.

Fifteen minutes later, Merry sank into the warm water and revelled in the luxury of tilting her head back into the heavenly hot water to wash her hair, and then scrubbing all over with a piece of lavender scented soap, before lying back and just soaking until the water cooled. Then she tumbled into the warmed bed and sank into a deep sleep as all the terrors that she had endured during the past few days ebbed away, replaced by the certainty that her two knights errant would keep the dragons at bay.

The following day was bright and warm. It was Rafe's turn to join her in the carriage, but Merry was now rather wary of sharing that intimate space with him again.

Thankfully, Rafe declared that Merry had been cooped up long enough and suggested they both ride outside on the box, while Harry travelled inside, so that she could enjoy some fresh air.

After a couple of years of living in close proximity to the market, Merry had grown accustomed to the stale and unsavoury aromas of the area. Occasionally, she and Bryn had gone for a walk to Lincoln Inn Fields or out towards the village of Islington when the weather was fine. But here in the country, the air tasted positively sweet in comparison, and after the bitter cold of the winter, a warm March had brought an early flush of hawthorn and damson blossom. Merry watched as the fallen pink and white petals along the side of the road skittered with the light breeze and then lifted upward in swirls around them as they passed. They made her think of bridal blossoms … and this led her thoughts to marriage.

In their hand to mouth existence, Merry had rarely had the leisure to think about the future. Though they had tried to improve their fortunes by securing a bride for Bryn, the thought of Merry's ever being married had never once been considered. If she had dreamed of the future at all, it had been of settling down with her father and brother in a cottage somewhere and maintaining her male identity.

Now, she would be obliged to marry after all. For all the security it offered, Merry was genuinely appalled by the prospect. After the independence of her upbringing as a boy, marriage seemed like a prison sentence.

And to be a wife meant other things. Merry's eyes strayed involuntarily to Rafe's strong hands, easily holding the fresh horses under control. He emanated assurance and manly strength. Even in the guise of a coachman, his bearing and lazy grace betrayed his quality. The frieze coat that stretched across his broad shoulders lay open from the waist, revealing strong, buckskin-clad thighs. Merry then remembered seeing him undressed in his room. She blushed at the memory.

Suddenly, as if he read her mind, Rafe turned to look at her, a speculative glint in his eyes. Merry blushed again and he grinned broadly but said nothing.

As she sat beside him, Merry realised that somehow, even outside, the space between them always seemed charged by a strange energy that was never there when she was with Harry. This odd feeling hovered somewhere between fear and suppressed excitement and she could neither account for it nor ignore it.

When their bodies came together now and then through the swaying or jolting of the journey, the feeling was intensified. Merry wondered if it were just her imagination or if Rafe felt it too.

He did, and his faith in this magnetism had allowed him to put aside Merry's rejection and the turmoil of the last few days and look to the future with new hope. This had been bolstered unexpectedly by the sight of Merry unconsciously staring at his thighs and then blushing delightfully as their eyes had met.

Merry looked away pointedly at the passing countryside, and the rich, well-tended estates around Upton and Langley, trying to take her mind off the man sitting next to her. There was plenty to engage Merry's interest along the busy thoroughfare, as sluggish wagons, overladen carts, dashing tilburys, practical dogcarts and all shapes and sizes of horses and riders jockeyed for room as they journeyed to and from the metropolis.

Soon Merry began to appreciate the ease with which their own equipage seemed to negotiate the traffic, and she looked again at Rafe. He held all the reins in his left hand, whilst loosely grasping the whip in his right. He made it look effortless, but Merry saw the way his keen eyes measured the distance from the oncoming traffic, before lightly dropping his wrist, at which the team seemed to leap forward, easily overtaking the wagon ahead and then tucking neatly back onto the left side of the post road and resuming their former pace.

This manoeuvre accomplished, Rafe turned to Merry with a knowing grin. He had sensed her watching him, and his eyes now twinkled at her suspicious look.

'You're not a shocking driver at all!' she said accusingly.

'I never said I was,' said Rafe, and then sighed with an air of long-suffering. 'It was just another example of that shameless abuse to which I am learning to become accustomed.'

Merry chuckled, but was then diverted by the sight of a large group of spring lambs, startled by the carriage and running with the thrill of imagined fear along the line of the wooden fence until they reached the hedge at the end, where they bundled into each other in a confused huddle before one started running back the way they had come and the rest stampeded after him.

Merry laughed out loud like a child at their antics, turning to Rafe to share the fun. He gave such a boyish smile in return that it transformed his face. For a brief instant, they connected as they might have, if meeting for the first time under different circumstances. But then their remembered lives swept back like a returning tide. Merry was suddenly even more wary and defensive; and Rafe, though he studiously turned his attention back to the road, was watchful and intent. The more time he spent with Merry, the more possessive he felt of her – not just for his own sake, but because he believed that only with him would Merry find her true self – the woman within - who was still bound, like her chest, and caught up so long in a pretence that it was pretence no longer.

He was now convinced that if, just once, they could open up to one another, they might discover a love that would last a lifetime.

Since Rafe wanted to keep his match team with him, they made the journey in easy stages. Having stopped at Maidenhead at ten o'clock to rest the horses and have a coffee, they had planned to lunch at Reading, when they arrived at noon. But the busy town was full of people they knew, travelling to town for the season, so Harry pulled up his muffler, pushed down his hat and pressed on to the quieter Theale. Merry had continued to sit up on the box, happily watching the world go by in the warm Spring sunshine.

Rafe had taken up the reins once more after lunch and then they stopped in Thatcham, to allow Merry to purchase some essentials, including ladies' drawers. Rafe and Harry, banished from this particular shopping expedition, were obliged to kick their heels for twenty minutes before a crimson-faced Merry, with a discreetly wrapped package caught tightly under her arm, exited the emporium and gave Rafe a scorching look that forbade any conversation whatsoever on the topic. He was sorely tried, as he longed to know how Merry, in her guise as a young man, had managed to persuade the assistant to *show* her these unmentionables, let alone *buy* them.

Thankfully, Harry was her companion for the next stage, and his impeccable manners compelled him to crush his own curiosity and set himself to calming Merry's ruffled feathers.

By the time they exchanged again, after resting at the inn by the Halfway toll gate, it was already approaching five o'clock. Rafe and Harry discussed the next stages over tankards of ale, while Merry was handed a murky glass of ginger beer.

'It's late but we can still reach Quemerford tonight,' said Harry.

'The horses are tired, so we'll need to rest them again at Hungerford,' said Rafe. 'Then we could press on through Marlborough and stop for dinner at Beckhampton at eight.'

'I'm happy to take both stages after Hungerford, since I know the direction of the lodge,' said Harry.

They agreed to this plan and set out as the late afternoon light began to turn.

By the time they reached Savernake Forest less than a mile outside Marlborough, the sun was setting and the high trees arching over this stretch of road further obscured the waning light, as the bright day gave way to moonlit night. For the first time on the journey, even when they had passed through the inky gloom of Hounslow Heath, Merry felt a shiver of anxiety pass through her.

Then her heart gave a panicked lurch as three large horsemen, each brandishing ferocious-looking horse pistols, thundered out from the wood to block the road ahead, and bellowed:

'Hold!'

Chapter Eleven
The Stuff of Nightmares

Harry struggled to calm the careening horses. With Merry beside him so vulnerably exposed to their fire, and the way forward effectively blocked, he had had no option but to pull up.

Inside the coach, Rafe was forming a plan, but his stomach churned horribly at the thought of the risks. But in the few moments available to him, he could think of no alternative.

Though he appeared like any unhappy victim as he descended reluctantly from the coach, urged by the waving barrel of a horse pistol, Rafe's mind was racing. He noted that all three of their attackers were armed and two were unmasked. This did not simply denote a dangerous level of confidence: It suggested they did not plan to leave witnesses.

In his coachman's outfit, the robbers did not suspect that Harry might be a gentleman. They clearly assumed that Merry was a young groom, brought along to blow the yard of tin that still lay beneath the seat.

As he stepped down to join them, Rafe pretended to berate his coachmen, bitterly suggesting that they had put up no fight since he supposed they had nothing of value to lose.

'You, Griffith,' he grumbled in a voice that betokened a very disgruntled employer, but which electrified Merry and Harry. Both knew that Rafe would only draw attention to Merry, if he needed her to act. 'I don't suppose there is anything in *your* moth-filled pockets to interest these ruffians?'

Merry looked blank, then a glimmer of understanding flickered for the briefest second, before she shrugged and answered in a gruff Southwark accent.

'Don't suppose the contents of my pockets would do any of *them* much good, sir,' she said, and then to obscure any seeming significance, she added in an audible under-voice. 'It's not like you pays us handsome nor nothing.'

Well done, Merry! thought Rafe, while his heart wrenched with concern for her.

'Well,' he said out loud, with an almost imperceptible flick of his eyes indicating the ruffian still mounted. 'You'd better fish out what you have, before they do it for you.'

The highwaymen ayed and grunted in agreement, waving their pistols suggestively.

'Aye! And we'll have *all* your togs off, if you please, my fine fellows,' said the one nearest Rafe. 'We finds coves much less inclined to give chase when they're in the buff.'

Harry stiffened in alarm for Merry, but she was watching Rafe's movements from beneath her lowered lashes. As she saw Rafe's hands going for his pockets, Merry followed suit, her fingers closing around the small pistol he had given her in Milk Alley.

Harry had darted a swift and quickly veiled look of alarm at Rafe when he had first addressed Merry. Rafe was planning something and he heartily wished he knew what was toward, as he made a play of turning out his pockets.

One of the highwaymen lifted his own pistol to hurry Rafe along with handing over his money, saying: 'I hate cocky toffs like you. Might just pop your clogs for you, anyways,' adding threateningly: 'It's as easy to search a dead man as a live un.'

Rafe decided to take no chances and fired one pistol at the rogue through his coat pocket, withdrawing the second and swooping round to cover the other highwayman, who was momentarily goggling with shock, while Merry swiftly drew her pistol and, with arm outstretched, pointed it at the mounted villain, whose horse had reared at the report.

The first highwayman lay all but dead on the ground, and for an instant, it seemed his partners might accept the stand-off and depart, or allow their victims to do so. But then they exchanged a swift, furtive glance that gave away their intentions as much as the upward movements of their weapons.

Merry and Rafe had seen that exchange, but there wasn't even time to look at each other for confirmation. Both fired almost instantaneously at their respective targets, each watching as the dying men fell to the ground.

The mounted man fired as he tumbled from his horse, the bullet missing Merry by inches and embedding itself with a crunch of splintering wood somewhere under the box, to the alarm of the horses, which plunged forward twenty feet or more before Harry could run and catch their heads.

Merry had not moved an inch as the bullet had whistled past her. She was frozen with shock at having killed a man by her own hand. Her bullet had hit him under his chin, ploughing upward into his brain. His eyes had opened wide and he had coughed out a gobbet of blood, before tumbling from his frantic mount, his hands convulsing like claws. It was the most horrific thing Merry had ever witnessed in all her less-than-idyllic life, and she was its author.

Rafe plucked the pistol out of her stiff hand, put his strong arm around her shoulders and drew her firmly away from the scene towards the spot where Harry waited with the carriage.

Seeing the haunted look on Merry's face, Harry stepped quickly forward and would have hugged her or said something comforting, but, with a frowning look and a shake of his head, Rafe warned him off. Instead, Rafe gave her a gentle shake, which brought her back to the present.

'Good girl, pluck to the backbone, just as you said,' he said, matter-of-factly and then jerked his head towards the box. 'Now, back up there with you and show me your mettle. You'll tool the coach with me for the next stage.'

Merry seemed to shake herself and turned mechanically to climb back on the box but found her knees traitorously weak. Rafe saw her hesitation and lifted her easily onto the box.

'Pick up the reins, there's a good girl, and hold them steady. I need to speak to Harry for a moment,' said Rafe, unwilling to leave her, but obedient to Harry's tug on his arm.

They walked back to the site where the three men lay dead, their horses cropping the grass at the side of the road.

'The risk!' whispered Harry, still recovering from standing helplessly by as Merry had been forced to act. It had happened so quickly that there had been no time for him even to take over the pistol from Merry. Harry felt truly wretched about it.

'What choice had I? They meant to kill us.'

'Aye, so I thought when they unmasked. Blackguards!'

'And if they had made us disrobe ...'

They both cast a glance of remembered dread towards Merry's drooping figure on the box.

'What should we do with the bodies?' said Harry, looking at them with distaste. He had seen far too much of death in these past two weeks.

'Nothing,' said Rafe grimly. 'We can scarcely alert the constable. I expect the Mail Coach driver will spot them tomorrow as he leaves Marlborough. He will alert the authorities in Fyfield, I expect.'

'Come on,' said Rafe walking back to the coach. 'I don't want to leave Merry there to brood alone. I'm going to drive the next stage through Marlborough.'

'This is still my stage. I should be up there with her,' said Harry.

'You'll make a hash of it, Harry,' said Rafe soberly. 'You'll be kind and mawkish, with the best of intentions, and ... and that's not what she needs right now.'

'Oh, and I suppose you are?'

'Yes,' said Rafe, adding cordially: 'I won't be *at all* nice to her and will have her back on solid ground before we get to Beckhampton, you'll see.'

Rafe moved towards the front of the carriage. He and Harry traded looks – one from Rafe that was not quite a threat met with one from Harry that was not quite acceptance. Nevertheless, Harry found himself alone inside the carriage whilst Rafe took his place on the box.

But as he joined Merry, jogging his hip lightly against hers, quite unnecessarily, and settling in beside her, he could not resist one moment of weakness.

'There are only three people I would have trusted to read my mind and save our lives.,' he said, putting his arm round her shoulders and kissing her temple in a fatherly way that bespoke the great pride he felt. 'You're the cleverest and the bravest woman I have ever known.'

Merry didn't feel at all brave at that moment. Her hands were shaking quite dreadfully and she felt sick to her stomach every time she recalled the appalling experience. From the instant the three horsemen had ridden out to block their way, waving those giant pistols, Merry had been almost crippled with terror. Only Rafe's playacting the angry master and calling her surname had broken through the paralysing fear and galvanised her into action.

But she had had to kill a man. It seemed impossible to believe that that tiny pistol could wield such awful power. Her aim had not been as cool as Rafe's. She had panicked a little and her hand had jerked up higher than she had intended. To be shooting at a man in a hold-up was a very different thing to showing her prowess in targeting stones lined up on a plank, as she had with her father and Bryn.

Dear God, thought Merry, closing her eyes for a moment, *a very different thing!*

Rafe saw her gloomy, abstracted expression as she directed the horses forward, and once again set himself to restore her equilibrium.

'Good God, is that how Harry taught you to hold the ribbons? I can never let him drive my cattle again,' he remarked in such a comic tone of pained dismay, shaking his head with a suffering hand over his eyes, that she smiled despite herself.

'Well, if your driving yesterday evening was anything to go by, your poor team must welcome another hand on the reins!' she retorted.

Merry heard Rafe snort in appreciation, but he only said:

'Huh! We shall see! Whip them up, Merry, and let me show you how to catch the thong in your whip hand.'

'Coxcomb!' she bantered, without heat.

'Four-in-hand coxcomb, if you please,' he countered, with a comic preening look.

Merry smiled and shook her head, as though deploring his incorrigibility, but nudged his shoulder with hers – an odd gesture of gratitude for helping her past a moment of weakness. He nudged her back and then made her chuckle as, for a moment, it became a silly game of shoving shoulders, which she lost.

He had done it again, thought Merry, a few minutes later. *He had chased away the demons and made her forget them with humour.*

How did he seem to know just what she needed at such testing times?

'Well, since I am driving, you should blow up the tin,' she said, when the toll-gate outside Marlborough came into view. 'Are we going to tell the keeper about the highwaymen?'

'No,' said Rafe, giving a very accomplished tattoo on the horn.

Merry only nodded as they saw the keeper issue from the tollhouse and Rafe fished out the coins from his pocket.

Although, it seemed lighter now that they had left the forest, dusk was gathering and lamps had been lit along the broad High Street. Rafe took over the reins for a few moments, to Merry's initial annoyance, as they made their way through the town. But Merry was soon glad of the opportunity to look about the rather pleasing aspect of the main thoroughfare, with the many bow-fronted windows of the charming buildings on each side of the wide road glowing with soft light. As they passed by the prestigious Castle Inn and the buildings began to thin out, Rafe offered her the reins again, but Merry shook her head. Rafe looked a question.

'Did I offend you by taking the reins?'

'At first, perhaps, but then … I realised it was not because you didn't trust me.'

'No,' confirmed Rafe. 'I had told you already that I did trust you.'

'Who are the other two?' Merry asked, recalling that first glowing praise Rafe had given her when he had joined her on the box.

'Harry, of course, and Brooke. You met Brooke, didn't you,' said Rafe.

'Yes,' replied Merry. 'So you would trust your manservant so much?' she asked, watching his profile intently. 'That's unusual, surely?'

'Perhaps,' he said, looking down at her curiously. 'Do you think servants should be kept in their place, then?'

'Hah! Much I should know about that! I've never had a servant. I'm not quite sure what I'd do with one, since I am now so used to doing everything for myself,' said Merry. 'No, I was merely surprised that *you* should feel that way.'

'So you perceive me as some satrap, or one who lines up my staff up for a regular weekly whipping?' said Rafe dryly, one eyebrow raised quizzingly.

Merry chuckled.

'No, though I should not like to work for you,' said Merry, causing Rafe to blink in surprise. 'I meant that gentlemen like you seem to treat servants as though they were so much walking furniture.'

'And what gentlemen have you met that are like me?' enquired Rafe softly, turning towards her and holding her gaze for a long moment. Merry was the first to look away a little flustered. There had been something rather disturbing in that steady regard.

'None,' she answered, after a few moments of consideration, with a smile twisting her lips. 'I should have to say that you are unique in my limited experience.'

Rafe smiled at that and at the humorous tone in her voice.

'Now, that's a knife that might cut both ways!' he declared.

Merry laughed this time.

'Or it could be a very great compliment,' suggested Merry.

'I take leave to doubt that!' replied Rafe, and then changed the subject suddenly. 'Why should you dislike working for me?' he asked, looking intently at her again.

'You've a fearful temper,' she answered.

'Oh, and you're as meek as a lamb, I suppose?' he said with irony. 'If I were to ask *you* to bring me a glass of Madeira, I'd be as like to have it thrown at my head.'

His bantering tone of umbrage brought a grin dancing to Merry's lips. *Oh, how she enjoyed these exchanges with him!*

'Do you suppose that I visit my "fearful temper" on my staff?' he demanded.

'I imagine they certainly know when you are displeased,' she suggested, a challenging twinkle in her eye.

Rafe pursed his lips ruefully.

'Yes,' he acknowledged reluctantly. 'That they do.'

He turned to look at her.

'Now I suppose I must tolerate that gloating grin for the next mile?' he said with a laughing grimace.

Merry giggled and looked to see that Rafe was laughing too.

'Well, at least admit to having a pretty fearful temper yourself,' he demanded with comic outrage.

'I?' said Merry, a look of the most shameless wide-eyed innocence.

'Aye, you, minx! Miss I'll-pull-on-your-legs Griffith,' he replied.

They both laughed at this, but as they remembered that furious encounter, both wondered inwardly at the turn of events and at the profound connection they had forged over the past two days.

'It seems a lifetime ago,' said Merry.

'Yes,' agreed Rafe, wondering uneasily whither this subject might lead Merry's thoughts, but she surprised him entirely by asking where Brooke was now.

So, as they passed by the moonlit water meadows of the Kennet, through the undulating chalk downs of West Overton and the past the ancient earthworks of Silbury Hill, Rafe entertained Merry with several anecdotes that went to the heart of his great affection for his long-suffering manservant.

When they finally passed through the toll-gate and clattered into the yard of Beckhampton Inn just after nine o'clock, Rafe had kept his promise to Harry, and Merry sat down to dinner as though nothing untoward had happened.

While Rafe had seen to the disposal of a pair of his precious horses, Harry had sent an ostler to ride ahead to the lodge to warn his retainers to expect them. They set out an hour or so later, with a single pair, uncertain of the state of the stabling at the lodge, and Merry quickly appreciated the change in pace between a pair and four. Though it was barely six miles of good road, Merry heard the distant church bell toll eleven before they pulled into the short lane that led to the house.

Quemerford Lodge was a neat, square, stone-fronted building set back some way from the lane. A long, high beech hedge further obscured it from the public view, and a small cottage stood at the gate. In the moonlight, Merry could see a handful of sheep and lambs grazing the lawns around the building, as they followed the gravel drive round the back to the stable yard.

Although Harry had only visited the place twice in the past four years, the Copes had kept it in excellent order. Mr Cope was waiting ready with brushes, blankets, water and fodder in the stables, while his wife had rushed around lighting fires in the chambers and making the beds up with freshly pressed, lavender-scented sheets. Flustered but beaming, she appeared at the door as the party entered and showed them into the drawing room where a tray of refreshments had been laid on a table beside a welcoming fire.

All three of them had helped Cope to rub down and straw up the horses, so they sank gratefully into the chairs to rest and take a glass of wine while Cope took their bags to the rooms above. No one spoke.

Merry sat in a chair by the fire, her booted foot on the brass fender around the hearth, seemingly absorbed in watching the flames licking around the spitting and sizzling coal and sipping her glass of Madeira. Although she seemed to have recovered, both men watched her profile surreptitiously. It seemed unfathomable that she could have experienced such a traumatic event without a reaction, and yet Harry did not like to raise the topic and Rafe would not.

Merry *was* reacting, but she had grown rather good at concealing her fears. Deep inside, she was dreading the quiet darkness of her room, when the images that stood in the shadows of her mind would come forward to haunt her.

Sure enough, less than an hour after they had retired for the night, Rafe heard footsteps padding past his room and the faint creak of someone descending the stairs.

A few minutes later, Rafe stood in the doorway of the drawing room watching Merry, jacketless, looking down into the fire and occasionally kicking the log she had put on it, sending sparks flying up.

Lost in abstraction, Merry had not heard him approach.

Rafe finally walked toward the table and poured two glasses of brandy.

'Bad dream?' he said gently.

Merry jumped, turning her startled gaze towards him, but then nodded mutely and looked back at the fire.

'What are you doing?' he asked, as he approached her, seeing the flickering light playing across her face.

'Conjuring images in the fire – caves, faces, animals,' Merry murmured in reply. 'It helps to take my mind off things.'

Rafe put one of the glasses in her hand.

'You told me once that you disgusted yourself,' said Merry quietly.

'Did I?' said Rafe affably.

'I think I understand what you meant now,' she said sadly.

'Ah, so I disgust you, too, do I?'

'What?' gasped Merry, looking up at him swiftly in alarmed apology, and then seeing a lurking twinkle in his eye, she added darkly: 'No, you rogue. That's not what I meant, and you know it.'

'Drink,' he said, nodding towards her glass and tossing off the contents of his own.

Merry followed suit, shuddering with distaste as the bitter liquid burned her throat.

'There is no good to be had from brooding on the past, Merry,' said Rafe, shrugging out of his jacket and putting it around her shoulders.

Merry huddled into its welcome warmth and inhaled deeply that delicious scent that always clung to his clothes.

'I once saw an ant preserved in amber at the Royal Institute …' he began.

'*You* went to the Royal Institute?'

Rafe gave her a pained look.

'I can't think where you have acquired the impression that I am a frippery fellow, Merry…' he complained.

'*Can't* you?' she quizzed, with heavy irony.

'… but I assure you I am not,' he said. 'Now where was I?'

'Don't worry,' she smiled. 'The ant was in amber and going nowhere.'

'That is my point precisely, Merry,' said Rafe. 'The past is as locked and immutable as that ant. No matter how many times you revisit it in your mind, you cannot change one instant of it, and can only bring yourself pain by reliving it.'

'But I can't get it out of my mind,' she replied, shaking her head. 'The images are there every time I close my eyes.'

'Then we must put other images in their place,' he said, guiding her by the shoulders towards the sofa, and gently pushing her to sit. Merry eyed him apprehensively, as he picked up a folded rug and a cushion and then sat beside her, stretching his long legs out and putting his feet up on a footstool.

'Come here,' he said, laying the cushion on his lap.

Merry stiffened in alarm, but then he gave one of his disarming chuckles and pulled her down to rest her head on his lap, throwing the rug over her legs as she pulled them up onto the sofa.

'No funny business,' she warned.

'No funny business,' he assured her, a ripple of amusement in his warm voice.

But Merry felt her heart skip a beat as Rafe absently raked his fingers through her tangled hair to push it back off her face.

'Have you ever travelled?' he asked softly.

Merry had been facing away towards the fire, but, at this, she twisted and wriggled round to look up at his face.

'Do you mean abroad?' she asked.

'Mmm,' he said in assent, his own heart skipping a beat as he saw her lovely face so close, half glimmering in the firelight and half in shadow.

'Well, we went to Dublin once,' she said.

'One day, Merry, I should like to take you to Italy.'

'Italy!' breathed Merry, her eyes glowing. 'Have you been there yourself?'

'Many times,' he replied, and then proceeded to describe some of the places he had visited and sights he had seen. He recounted his adventures so vividly and with so many flashes of humour that Merry soon forgot the terrible image of the dead highwayman. She watched Rafe's expressive face as he talked, chuckling now and then at something he said or some comic expression he pulled.

He had continued to stroke her hair, as if unconsciously, while he spoke, and after a nonplussed look, which Rafe had ignored, Merry had accepted this and soon began to find it wonderfully soothing. His other arm lay lightly across her, his hand curled around her waist, lifting occasionally in a comic gesture or to draw his jacket more closely around her.

Although she lay in his arms, there was nothing lover-like in his voice or behaviour, so Merry relaxed and allowed herself to be transported by imagination to Rome, Florence and Sienna. When Rafe began to describe Venice, Merry heaved a deep, contented sigh and closed her eyes, picturing herself in that magical city.

Rafe continued to talk until Merry's breathing changed and her head gently lolled against his chest as she fell into a deep and peaceful sleep. At last, he put aside his mask of dispassionate friend, and looked down at his beloved girl with a look of such aching tenderness that Merry would have leapt off the sofa in panic had she seen it.

Rafe knew he should carry Merry back to her room, but holding her safe in his arms, his own demons seemed to recede. Merry sighed in her sleep, turning on her side towards him, her head snuggling into his chest and one arm snaking around his waist. Rafe closed his eyes at this sweet torment, a smile twisting his handsome lips. Then he leaned his head back and after a few minutes, dozed off into a sleep as peaceful as Merry's.

.

Chapter Twelve
A Difficult Pupil

The next morning, Merry awoke in her own bed with no remembrance of how she had got there.

As Merry recalled how she had fallen asleep and the extraordinary intimacy of the time leading up to it, her cheeks grew hot. They grew even hotter when she realised that her feet were bare. Rafe had not only put her to bed but must also have handled her legs to remove her boots and stockings. Merry closed her eyes in embarrassment and would have liked nothing better than to put off facing Rafe a little longer, but the irresistible aroma of bacon creeping up from the kitchen had her throwing back the covers and scrambling to get ready as fast as she could.

There was a little more of the defensive swagger in her stride as Merry entered the breakfast room.

'Good morning,' she said, with only the flicker of a wary glance at Rafe betraying her apprehension at what he might be thinking after she had fallen asleep in his arms.

But Rafe's expression was remarkably bland, as he looked up briefly from his breakfast and recommended the sausages.

As she stood before the chafing dishes, Merry shook her head and wondered for a wild moment if perhaps it had all been a dream. She piled her plate high and sat down at the table.

'Did you sleep well?' asked Harry, with a slightly anxious lift in his voice.

'Yes, thank you, very well,' replied Merry, her colour rising a little. This time she felt Rafe's eyes on her and steeled herself to ignore him, looking up at Harry instead and returning his smile. But she was not proof against that steady look, and as Harry looked down to continue his breakfast, Merry's eyes strayed to meet Rafe's.

'I'm glad to hear it,' said Rafe softly, as they exchanged a twinkling look, and then he added in a louder voice: 'I slept very well, too, Harry, before you ask.'

'What? Oh, as if I care if you sleep or not,' bantered Harry in response. 'Merry, you're a Trojan! You've the heart of a lion ..'

'And the temper, too!' threw in Rafe.

But Merry, having now sampled the sausages, was too preoccupied to rise to the bait.

'Mmm, delicious!' she said rather thickly.

To Harry's great relief, Merry refrained from belching after her gargantuan meal, but instead gave a satisfied sigh and leaned back in her chair.

'If you keep eating like that,' remarked Rafe with a wry smile. 'We shall have to let out your dresses.'

'You have no idea how good it is to eat and not still be hungry at the end,' said Merry, giving them both a new perspective on her appetite.

'So what is the plan for the day?' she asked.

'Well, we should first perhaps discuss our plan for your future,' said Rafe, glancing at Harry before his eyes returned to Merry's now-wary face.

'Have you been talking about me?'

'Well ...' began Harry uncomfortably.

'Yes,' said Rafe flatly.

'I see,' said Merry, her colour rising. 'Do you still think I have to be ... m...married.' She stumbled over that hated word.

'Yes,' they confirmed unanimously.

'Eventually,' added Harry.

Merry pursed her lips.

'What if I don't want to marry?' demanded Merry.

'We will cross that bridge when we come to it,' said Rafe. 'First, we will remain here for a month turning you from boy to girl.'

'And what if I don't want to do that?' asked Merry, her chin lifting in defiance.

'Ah, did I make that sound optional?' said Rafe affably. 'My mistake. Will you, nil you, Merry, we are going to turn you back into a girl and you'll find we can be just as determined as you.'

Merry gave him a look that challenged that last point, but it met one that confirmed it, and Merry was the first to look away.

'First, you need to learn how to walk like a lady,' said Rafe.

'I know how to walk like a lady,' grumbled Merry.

'Then why don't you demonstrate as you go upstairs and put on one of the delightful outfits that Harry purchased for you?' said Rafe sweetly, adding less sweetly: 'and give what you are currently wearing to Mrs Cope for cleaning, because you certainly don't smell like a lady.'

Merry glared at him.

'Unlike you, I have not had the advantage of a change of clothes or servants to keep my raiment clean!' she replied in tight-lipped annoyance.

'But now you do,' said Rafe pointedly, then he turned to Harry and said: 'Though you might want to explain to the Copes why our young man is suddenly dressing like a lady, before they get entirely the wrong impression.'

Harry, much struck, rose and headed off to the servants' hall.

Merry had risen too, but was looking mulishly at Rafe.

'Can't I just have a day or two of being comfortable before we begin?' she asked.

'Not in those clothes,' said Rafe categorically. 'And the sooner you begin the better. You have been living a masquerade, Merry. It is time for it to end. Now, show me how a lady walks back to her room to change.'

He waved a lazy finger towards the door but his eyes brooked no demur.

Merry, who was standing with her hands on her hips, hesitated but finally flung her arms up in a gesture of reluctant compliance and minced towards the door.

Rafe laughed.

'You look like a Macaroni, Merry!' he laughed. 'Clearly, you _are_ going to have to learn how to walk all over again.'

Merry gave an infuriated growl and stamped upstairs.

THE RELUCTANT LADY

There was no danger of the Copes getting the wrong impression as Merry finally appeared in one of the mourning gowns and handed Mrs Cope her boy's clothes with an embarrassed smile. The dark silk clung to her slender hips and set off her pale gold skin and gleaming tawny-blond hair to stunning advantage. The simple square neckline hinted discreetly at a well-rounded bosom, now liberated from the padded gilet that Merry had made to disguise her shape. Too conscious of her bare neck and bruises, Merry had snipped the black lace veil from one of the bonnets and now wore it as a tucker round the top of her shoulders and pinned at the front, so that only a small vee of bare skin at the base of her throat could be seen.

As she walked nervously into the morning room, Merry was feeling more of an impostor than she had disguised as a boy. Dressed as a woman, she felt stripped bare of her defences and her identity. Merry could see by the glowing looks that the men bestowed on her as they looked up that they both approved of the change, but this made her feel even less comfortable.

Standing just inside the room, framed by the doorway, Merry blushed attractively, her lovely eyes elusive, fleetingly catching theirs and looking quickly away. For a moment, she was the picture of a modest maiden, albeit one with the remnants of a black eye. Then, after a second, she determinedly crossed her arms tightly across her chest in a very boyish manner, leaned on one hip, and glared at them, dispelling the illusion entirely. Rafe grinned and Harry sighed; they had their work cut out for them, and Merry was a far from willing pupil.

'Well, at least you are dressed for the part,' said Rafe. 'But I think our first lesson will be how to stand, sit and move like a lady.'

For the next hour, Merry was made to parade around the room under Rafe's critical eye and ceaseless commands.

'You are not a sailor, Merry, so stop swaggering as if you are on deck! Try walking on the balls of your feet! That's it, light steps almost on tiptoes! Toe, heel, Merry! Toe, heel, not heel, toe! Hands, not fists, Merry! You are not a prizefighter! Turn them out slightly. Yes, I know it looks silly, but it might help cure you of making fists all the time.'

After this, there was another interminable hour of learning how to sit like a lady, which drove Merry equally demented.

'Sink gently onto the seat, Merry, don't drop like a sack of grain. Back straight! Don't slouch! No, don't lean back! For the most part, you should just perch delicately on the edge of the chair for the duration of the visit. Morning calls are not about being comfortable.'

'Then why pay them?' snapped Merry, her temper fraying for the thousandth time.

'You know very well why, Merry,' replied Rafe. 'You are a gentleman's daughter, so don't pretend to be ignorant of social etiquette.'

'I don't suppose you had much opportunity to pay calls in recent years?' said Harry the peacemaker, who was sitting next to Merry on the sofa, playing the part of the dowager duchess on whom Merry was paying her morning call.

Merry's kindling eyes calmed as they always did at Harry's sympathetic smile.

'None, except when we were trying to marry Bryn off to that poor cit,' she admitted with a rueful grin. 'Bryn was the one with all the social graces. I was the lout of the family.'

'I don't doubt it,' snapped Rafe, nettled by the intimate picture of Merry leaning confidingly towards Harry, who was looking down at her with fond humour lighting his all-too-handsome face. 'Now, try it again from the moment of being announced … and don't look so apologetic when you enter this time. You're a lady, not a servant.'

Merry jumped to her feet, glaring at Rafe balefully.

'Confound you, Rafe! I'm doing my best,' growled Merry, as she strode back to the doorway.

'Then heaven help us!' said Rafe, with feeling. 'And after that little outburst, young lady, our next lesson shall be how to address your elders and betters with proper respect.'

Merry stopped in her tracks and turned to face Rafe.

'Why certainly, my lord!' she intoned ironically, making a magnificent leg, worthy of an obeisance to the king himself.

Rafe stood with his arms folded and one eyebrow raised, a ghost of humour in his cobalt eyes. As Merry straightened up, her eyes glinting a challenge, Rafe merely raised his right hand and flicked a finger towards the door.

Merry's slender hands curled into angry fists as she turned and walked the last few feet to the door.

'Hands!' corrected Rafe.

Merry made a very rude gesture with them, making Harry's eyes widen in shock. Rafe's lips twitched, but he did not laugh.

'Not quite what I had in mind, Merry,' he said dryly. 'Now, let's try again. Your Grace, Miss Griffith.'

The rest of the day continued in much the same vein, and as they sat down to dinner that evening, they were all less than enthusiastic about the weeks to come.

The following day, all three stood in the paddock, looking at the big-boned roan gelding borrowed from the farmer. It was sporting an ancient side-saddle unearthed in the stables, and indicating his disgust in every line of his considerable bulk.

Harry had not had time to have riding dress made up for Merry, and there could be no question of attempting to ride in the confines of her round gowns. So Merry was permitted to wear her boy's clothes, but with a rug wrapped loosely around her legs and tucked into the waistband of her breeches. She already cut a rather comic character, but one look at the leather confection, perched like a tiny hat on the broad back of the roan, confirmed the potential for far greater humiliation. With its single pommel and stirrup, Merry could not fathom how she was meant to keep her seat.

Before Rafe or Harry could give her a boost, Merry put her foot in the stirrup and unthinkingly went to throw her leg over the horse's back but the rug prevented her from completing the movement so she ended up clinging to the pommel with one leg in the stirrup and the other lying along the roan's broad back.

"Well, that position might serve you well in Astley's but not in Hyde Park,' grinned Rafe, as he helped her down. 'This time, as I boost you up, try to turn so that you land sitting facing towards me. Then hook your right leg over the pommel in as ladylike a way as you can manage,' he said as he cupped his hand for her foot, and she sprang nimbly into place.

'That's it. Well done, Merry!' approved Harry.

'Now, tuck your left knee against the pommel while I tighten the stirrup leathers,' said Rafe as he did so. 'You might feel more secure if you tuck your right foot behind your left calf. Yes, like that.'

'How on earth do women manage to ride like this?' said Merry baffled.

'You're about to find out,' said Rafe.

'Here,' said Harry, handing Merry the riding crop. 'You'll need a whip as you only have one heel with which to control the poor brute.'

'Oh God!' croaked Merry, but she gamely gave the roan the office and began to walk him in a circle around the men. Although the position was still rather uncomfortable, Merry's confidence grew and she was eager to go a little faster. With a firm tap from the whip, the roan lurched into a bouncing trot that rapidly became a canter. This was Merry's undoing. Within a few strides, she was unhappily liberated from both pommel and stirrup, then had one ignominious bounce on the roan's rump, before hitting the ground with a thump that knocked the breath from her body.

Rafe and Harry came running up in a fret, expecting at very least to be scorched by a blast of Merry's quick temper, only to find her lying back in the grass laughing.

Rafe reached down a hand and hauled her to her feet.

'Ridiculous!' she said unexpectedly. 'Well, I shan't be beaten. If a woman can do it, *I* can do it. I can't conceive how women manage to ride to hounds on those things, but I'm not going to give up until I've mastered it.' Then rubbing her bruised bottom, she added: 'Though I think I shall regret it in the morning.'

Merry was unseated only once more, but was soon cantering around the paddock in a competent, if not quite elegant, fashion.

Merry was obliged to change back into a gown for luncheon, during which Rafe continued to point out improvements to her mannerisms until Merry was near to screaming.

Harry, as their host, sat at the head of the shortened dining table. As his guests faced each other, a martial glint in their eyes and the air fairly crackling with their clash of wills, Harry felt more than ever like an umpire. He tried valiantly to make polite conversation and prevent Rafe from further provoking Merry's swift temper, but failed in both goals.

Rafe kept needling Merry for the electric sensation he felt when her sparkling grey eyes were locked with his own. Other than those rare moments when they touched, Rafe never felt so alive as when he locked horns with Merry. If he could not hold her, he would spar with her.

Rafe believed it was their underlying attraction that made Merry feel uneasy and keep her distance. As a result, she keened towards Harry, for whom she felt no such stirrings. Only when her temper was ignited did she forget this resolve, and the distance between them evaporated. They were connected, if only as combatants.

After luncheon, Rafe announced that Merry was to practice her deportment once more, on a pretended shopping expedition in town.

'It seems like wanton affectation,' she complained. 'To have to tiptoe about like a fairy, instead of walking like a human being.'

'And how, pray, would you describe all your boyish mannerisms?' enquired Rafe pointedly.

'Second nature,' replied Merry defensively.

'Affectations,' said Rafe inexorably. 'Come along. We are wasting time. Now, Merry, show us how a lady should walk amongst the shops in Covent Garden or the Strand.'

Merry started walking round the room, trying to moderate her boyish gait, but still looked glaringly unladylike.

'Remember your arms, Merry! Tripping steps! Have you never seen ladies walking?' Rafe's criticisms seemed ceaseless.

Then, Merry's volatile temper ignited.

Suddenly, she flung her arms out, her hands waving limply at the ends, and skipped around the room like an effeminate lamb, looking from side to side with a vacuous expression on her face.

Harry doubled up with laughter, leaning back against the wall for support.

Rafe put his hands on his hips, watching her antics with a reluctant grin on his face.

Merry suddenly stopped in mid-skip, as if spying her prey, and gave Rafe an exaggeratedly arch look, her finger to her chin. Tripping up to Rafe, she plucked her handkerchief from her pocket, and dropped it artfully on the floor. Then, in a ludicrous caricature of the shamelessly scheming behaviour she had witnessed at Ackermanns, Merry gave an artificial trill of embarrassed laughter, deprecated her foolish weakness and rolled her eyes significantly in the direction of the lace-edged confection resting at Rafe's feet.

Her victim's eyebrow raised and his eyes glinted in appreciation, and then his smile broadened as he decided to treat Merry to a taste of her own medicine.

Dropping to one knee to retrieve the handkerchief, Rafe rose very, very slowly and suggestively, as if aware of every contour of Merry's body beneath the clinging silk gown. When he came to his feet looking down at her, he was suddenly very close, his left leg a little forward and the bent knee just touching her skirt. Merry's pretence fell away as she swallowed audibly, her cheeks quite pink.

Rafe then treated her to one of his most intensely seductive and devastating looks, emanating a kind of suppressed energy that held her in thrall, her eyes wide and her lips parted.

Rafe held the lacy scrap in his strong fingers. Merry lifted her hand to receive it, but Rafe, with a glowing gaze that never left her own dazed one, turned his face infinitesimally and held the handkerchief to his nose, subtly savouring its delicate scent, the gesture an intimate caress, before tucking it into the inside pocket over his heart.

Merry was spellbound, until she saw a wickedly triumphant grin spread over Rafe's face. This broke the spell, and Merry jumped away from him crying, in a slightly shaken voice: 'Here! Give that back!'

'Play and pay, Merry,' he said. 'Don't start a game you cannot win, little one.'

'You're a devil!'

'A charming devil, you must allow,' he murmured, with that glinting smile.

Over her head, Rafe saw Harry regarding him disapprovingly, all humour gone. Fortunately, Cope scratched at the door at that moment to announce that tea was served.

The rest of the day was largely uneventful. After that disturbing experience, Merry was more wary of Rafe than ever,

THE RELUCTANT LADY

and Harry stepped in to take a more active role in Merry's education.

That evening after dinner, they played cards for the first time and both men were forced to admit that Merry was a skilled opponent. Neither dared acknowledge it, however, for fear of reanimating Merry's notions of earning her own living.

'For God's sake, Merry, start wearing your damned skirts!' cried Rafe, his hands on his hips, as Merry skipped into breakfast the next morning once again wearing her breeches.

Merry scowled in response and then ignored him, trotting eagerly to the chafing dishes on the polished oak sideboard from which the most delicious smells were emanating.

She was never to see their contents.

Rafe's strong hands circled her waist and he flung her easily over his shoulder and stalked out of the room towards the stairs.

'Once again, minx, I have to teach you not to set your will against my own,' he said calmly, in response to the rich and colourful stream of invective hurled at him by his burden.

When he arrived at the door of her room, he set her down.

Crimson-faced, her eyes blazing, Merry tried to push past him, but with his arms either side of her and his body alarmingly close to hers, she was imprisoned against the door.

'How dare you!' she hissed.

'I will dare a great deal more, Merry, if you do not go into your room right now and put on one of your dresses,' he said.

Merry's eyes widened with outrage and she slid her hands up against his chest, meaning to push him away. But they stilled as Merry heard him gasp at the surge of emotion this unexpected contact sent through him. She looked up and froze as Rafe's head tilted a little and his gaze drifted to her lips in the most fascinated way.

Suddenly the sound of a step on the stairwell broke the spell and both pulled back in equal astonishment. Merry snatched her hands away and grasped the door handle, almost falling through the opening and closing the door as fast as she could.

Rafe rocked back on his heels for a moment, and then quickly mastered his expression as Harry appeared at the top of the stair.

'Thought I'd check you weren't *offering* to help her dress,' said Harry, still holding his napkin.

'Not this time, but don't put it past me, if she wears those breeches again.'

The chafing dishes had long since been removed before Rafe's determined attempt at patience crumbled. With a frown knitting his brows, he flung down the journal he was perusing and stalked off to find Merry. After a cursory glance into the two reception rooms, Rafe sighed and then took the stairs two at a time, skidding to a halt outside Merry's room and then standing for an instant with his hands on hips to take a breath and calm his mounting temper.

'Merry, what on earth is keeping you? You've missed breakfast, and I know you were hungry!'

'Go away!' Merry replied, in a tone more sad than angry.

'No,' he said, turning the handle and putting his head cautiously around the door.

Merry, clad becomingly in an elegant grey crepe gown with black velvet trimming, stood staring at herself in a long mirror. As she turned, her expression was more one of irritation rather than scandalized propriety.

'I told you to go away,' said Merry.

'Did you really think I would?' responded Rafe, walking towards her.

Merry gave a faint sigh of exasperation.

'You're not supposed to enter a lady's bedchamber,' she muttered in rather tired voice.

'Do you accept that you are a lady, then?' asked Rafe.

Merry looked back at her reflection for a long moment.

'Yes, no, … oh, I suppose so,' she said bitterly.

Rafe watched her inner turmoil and his heart went out to her. He longed to take her into his arms and kiss her and make her glad to be a woman.

'Let me guess,' he said walking up behind her and watching her expressive face reflected in the mirror. 'You feel that you are looking at a stranger.'

Her eyes flew to his reflected ones and she nodded.

'Who am I, Rafe, if I am not to be myself?'

THE RELUCTANT LADY

'You are still yourself, Merry.'

'No, I'm not,' said Merry, shaking her head, looking back at her reflection. 'I am lesser somehow.'

'Lesser?'

'Don't pretend that you don't know what I mean.'

'Very well,' replied Rafe. 'There is a difference, yes, but it need not be a negative one.'

'As a woman, I don't feel strong anymore. I feel dependent and weak!'

'Merry!' Rafe caught her shoulders and turned her to face him. 'You have been forced to be strong all your life. Now, it is time to let me ... to let men ... be strong for you.'

'Don't you understand? That's what makes me feel lesser. I don't like feeling weak!'

'Not being strong is not the same as being weak,' reasoned Rafe. 'You will need a different strength as a wife and a mother.'

'Huh! Strength enough to hang on a husband's sleeve, you mean!' replied Merry. 'Well? Do I not have to obey him and depend upon him utterly for my keep?'

'A marriage can mean partnership not ownership, Merry,' said Rafe, voicing for the first time his own hopes for their union. 'It is your husband's duty and privilege to protect you from harm and need. That is his role in the partnership. Yours is to provide him with a well-run household, and to bear him children, if you are both so blessed, and to see them brought up well. Being a good wife is not about pin money and pandering to your husband's vanity, though there are many ladies who think it is.

'And to my mind, there is also companionship,' he added. 'A husband and wife share so much, not least a bed, that they must be true friends as well ... able to laugh and dispute together ... and even cry together, if the need arises. That companionship must last a lifetime, so a friendship - which is a leveller you will agree? - is essential.'

'Perhaps,' responded Merry finally. 'But I still think I'd rather be the husband,' she added, with a mulish look.

Rafe grinned.

'Well, since we plan to marry off the lovely Lydia to Harry, your ideal bride is taken,' said Rafe with a wink. 'So you might as well resign yourself to being the bride and not the groom.'

Then as he reached the door, he bethought himself of something and turned back.

'Oh, and should a man enter your room again unbidden, you should call for a footman to turf him out,' said Rafe reprovingly. 'Or at least throw something at his head.'

He ducked out in time to hear one of Merry's boots hit the door.

After luncheon, Harry and Rafe were discussing whether to attempt to show her how to dance or to engage a dancing master later on.

As Merry contemplated the thousand potential pitfalls of actually having to attend a ball, she had a fan half-open and was absently nibbling a corner of it.

'Why, Merry!' she heard Rafe say, as he approached her. 'I should very much like to kiss you, too!'

From the corner of his eye, Rafe saw Harry's head snap up in shock, instantly distracted from his task of hunting for sheet music.

'What!' gasped Merry, her eyes wide.

'Putting a half-open fan to the corner of your mouth indicates that you wish to be kissed,' advised Rafe, his eyes glinting with amusement.

'You rogue! You're making it up!'

'No, indeed! But I rather think those who sell fans did so. Still, now, some gestures have been assigned a significance that may be misread.

'Here,' he said, taking the fan. 'All you need to remember is to fan yourself slowly, thus, and to carry it in your right hand, so. This indicates that you are engaged, which I hope you shall be before you need to use a fan in public.'

Merry blushed, and Rafe grinned as he turned the wafting fan towards her as though to cool her hot cheeks, before receiving a glare from her. This, together with the narrow-eyed frown he was receiving from Harry, made him laugh out loud, as he walked away fanning himself rather comically.

'My, my! Who knew that instructing young ladies could be such a perilous business,' he said, then turned and gave such a comic coquettish peep over the top of the fan that both Merry and Harry could not help but laugh.

Rafe chuckled and then tossed the offending fan onto a table and said: 'Come along then! Let us see if we can have you dancing like a lady.'

He took a seat at the piano and with careless skill, ran his fingers over the keys and played the opening bars of a minuet.

For the next hour, they took turns dancing with Merry. During one of the intricate moves of a dance with Rafe, Merry was reminded of something she had been meaning to ask him.

'What's that cologne you always wear, Rafe? It's very subtle but very nice.'

Rafe looked at her for a moment, then grinned.

'Ah ... something of my own concoction. Do you like it?'

'Yes, very much,' replied Merry, minding her steps. 'I should like to try it sometime.'

Rafe bit his lip, as his smile broadened.

'You're welcome to do so,' he said.

Merry smiled, but her eyes narrowed at Rafe's obvious amusement. She turned in the figure of the dance.

'I like your scent too, Merry,' said Rafe, as he stood while she promenaded around him.

'I don't wear any, silly,' she replied, as she moved to resume her starting position.

'Nor do I, Merry,' said Rafe, the humour evident in his voice.

Merry stopped in her tracks, and then slowly turned as realisation dawned, but Rafe was already bowing, as the music ended, his soft laughter still in the air.

'You should curtsey at the end, Merry,' said Harry, as he walked towards them. 'And I think you forgot your steps just at the last. What do you say to trying a waltz?'

Merry was glad of the change of subject, but her eyes strayed to Rafe's as he played a waltz for them, and from the knowing glow in their cobalt depths, she knew he was delighted by this new information.

Merry made such good progress over the fortnight that the gentlemen decided to test her new masquerade at a public assembly in Calne. It was a very spirited evening, with country dances made even livelier by the free-flowing local ales and ciders. Harry and Rafe tried to keep a low profile in their guises as merchants, but had underestimated their own attractions as two very handsome and unattached bachelors. Consequently, they were much sought after by the ladies, and so their vigilance over Merry was distracted at best.

Taking advantage of her new-found freedom, Merry drank liberally and then affably accepted a dance with a complete stranger. But her lusty young partner was soon to regret his choice as Merry, entering enthusiastically into the dance, soon forgot her feminine role and began to lead, finishing the figure, laughing and flushed on the gentleman's side and leaving her red-faced swain amongst the ladies, to everyone's great amusement.

Harry stepped in swiftly, offering apologies for his 'sister', as they all beat a hasty retreat. Poor Harry then heartily wished himself on the box with Cope, as Rafe and Merry bickered about the incident all the way home.

But though he later teased her out of the sullens, one unfortunate turn of events two days later would blight Rafe's chances of winning Merry's heart with dramatic consequences for them all.

Chapter Thirteen
Disastrous Decisions

The disastrous day began innocently enough.

They had agreed upon a morning of rest, while Harry ventured off to Chippenham in search of a London paper and to post letters. Rafe had been out to the paddock, where his bays had been reunited and were now grazing amongst the spring lambs. They were fully rested and very fresh. Rafe felt similarly invigorated and went in search of Merry, eager to tempt her out to enjoy the spring sunshine with him.

He found her sitting out of sight in a corner of a room reading. She was in her boy's clothes, sprawled comfortably in a very unladylike position.

Rafe sighed. As he walked forward, he picked up the footstool, then placed it in front of her and sat. Merry had sat up on his approach and looked every inch a guilty, but unrepentant, schoolboy.

Looking at her steadily for a moment, Rafe took her by surprise when he reached forward and caught her knees, held them together, then pulled her forward, so that her knees were resting between his own.

Merry went pink.

Rafe leaned forward a little.

'Is being a girl still so alien to you?' he said with remarkable calm.

'I hate it,' said Merry, a little flustered by Rafe's nearness.

'It's only been two weeks.'

'The longest two weeks of my life,' said Merry churlishly.

'I doubt that,' said Rafe, looking steadily into her eyes.

Suddenly, Merry leaned towards him, her eyes alight. Rafe's heart skipped a beat and he held his breath.

'Oh, Rafe!' she blurted impetuously. 'Can't we go out tonight to the tavern, for a pint and a pipe? My last, I promise! I'll do anything you say after that, but oh! I long for one last chance to be myself, before I have to be prissy and prim forever!'

Looking down at that beautiful eager face so close to his own, Rafe was shaken by a dozen thoughts and sensations a world away from the prosaic words he finally uttered.

'I don't think you could ever be prissy or prim, Merry.'

'Don't try to fob me off!' she responded impatiently, her gaze holding his. 'May we go to the tavern this evening?'

Rafe paused. It would be so easy to give in, and such a pleasure to see delight light up the dear face so close to his own.

'I'll let you kiss me,' she threw in as a clincher.

'What?' gasped Rafe, knocked completely off balance.

'I think that's what you want, isn't it?' she said, with an anxious look. 'Well, you may kiss me, if you'll let me go out for a pint and a pipe at the tavern tonight.'

Rafe's eyes drifted to Merry's lips. He longed to kiss her, and here was an opportunity. It should have delighted him, but contrarily he was annoyed.

'Trading kisses for favours, Merry? That's a slippery slope,' he said drily. 'You're more woman than you pretend.'

'Not at all!' said Merry defensively. 'It's all I have to trade.'

'Trade? Is that how cheap you hold your kisses?'

'You don't know the value I place on a jaunt to the tavern,' she countered. 'One little kiss means nothing to me.'

Rafe looked at her inscrutably for a moment then leaned forward slowly. Merry gulped as she felt a strange, breathless excitement shiver through her body. She closed her eyes and pouted her lips in anticipation of the light peck that she expected. But then she gasped as she felt the thrilling warmth of his cheek as it brushed against her own and the soft hush of his breath against her jaw and ear, as he whispered:

'When I do choose to kiss you, Merry, it should mean everything to you … and to me.'

Merry turned her head towards him in surprise, both at his words and at the effect they had on her. Their lips were almost touching, and Merry felt an aching wish that they would. But Rafe was looking stern and there was a ghost of hurt reproof in his eyes. He drew back and pushed her back by the knees, just as he had pulled her forward. Merry felt oddly bereft, as she watched him walk away.

Merry did not repeat her request when Harry returned. Whether the gentlemen liked it or not, Merry would have her last hurrah that evening.

Harry, looking only for signs that Rafe had taken advantage of his absence to advance his suit with Merry, was reassured by his coolness towards her as tea was served. Merry had changed back into her skirts, and enquired politely about Harry's trip.

Had Rafe been less preoccupied by their encounter that morning, Merry's model behaviour might have made him suspicious.

After tea, while the gentlemen were both engrossed in the newspapers that Harry had purchased in Chippenham, Merry excused herself murmuring something about wishing to finish her book. As she passed Cope in the hallway, Merry began her deception.

'It seems their lordships are both absorbed by the news from London. If they should ask for me, please let them know that I have gone to my room to read and then change for dinner.'

Cope bowed assent and Merry went to her room to change back into her boy's clothes. The thrill of tiptoeing down the stairs in sight of the open door to the sitting room, where Harry and Rafe could be heard discussing Napoleon's recent abdication, and then escaping through an open window all added to the illicit fun of her escapade. It was like bunking off school. Merry dismissed the nagging thought that her truancy was ungrateful and would cause her protectors anxiety. For this last evening, she would be the old Merry enjoying her former treat. Tomorrow, she would submit to their regime for her transformation once more.

Rafe noticed Merry's absence first, but Cope unwittingly played his part in delaying her discovery by reporting that Miss Griffith had gone upstairs earlier to change for dinner. It was only when Mrs Cope took hot water to Merry's room that her absence was detected.

Rafe cursed when Harry brought him the baffling news.

'Damn the minx! I thought I'd scotched that scheme!' fumed Rafe. 'Where's the nearest tavern? She was all for going off there tonight, and it seems she has done so, in spite of my disapproval.'

Harry was shocked, but relieved.

'I was afraid she had gone off to try and make her own way in the world again,' admitted Harry. 'We have been pushing her rather hard. I suppose we can scarcely blame her for kicking over the traces.'

'She's a wilful, stubborn, hot-tempered termagant,' said Rafe with asperity. 'And I shall have something to say on the topic when we find her.'

'I'll go and fetch her,' said Harry. 'You'll come to cuffs and we'll set tongues wagging even more than they are already.'

However, after what seemed like an interminable period, during which Rafe had taken up and thrown down his greatcoat a dozen times, he finally heard their voices in the hallway.

As they burst into the room, it seemed that they had been involved in violent altercation. Merry had a fine bruise forming on her cheek and Harry was sporting the remnants of a bloody nose. They were laughing like children as they entered the room, and this became hysterical when they spied Rafe's horrified and disapproving face.

'What the devil!!'

'You should have seen her, Rafe,' cried Harry, full of news. 'As neat a right as you could ever imagine on a girl. Hit the ruffian in the throat and he went down like a stone.'

'I can manage as long as I don't connect with bone,' conceded Merry, with a hint of simple pride, rubbing her bruised fist. 'Throat, stomach and crown jewels, that's what I aim for, if I am forced to fight.'

'Crown jewels!' repeated Harry, collapsing with fresh laughter.

But looking to Rafe for his reaction, Merry saw no answering humour in his eyes. He looked like murder, and Merry, who was standing only a couple of feet from him began to back away.

She was too late.

In one swift move, Rafe swept her up and then sat, throwing her downwards over his knee, and began to spank her, very hard, across the bottom.

'Ow! How dare you! Ow! That hurt, curse you! Ow! What on earth has got …! Ow! Harry, get him off me! Ow! Rafe! Stop it! Ow! *Please … Rafe!*' she gasped. His hand rose again, but was stayed by Harry's firm grasp on his arm.

'That's enough!' snapped Harry, suddenly sober.

Merry took the opportunity to jump up, rubbing her bottom and staring at Rafe as if he had entirely lost his mind.

'I'll serve you for that, you bully!' she cried.

'Be silent!' roared Rafe, with an expression on his face that she hadn't seen there since their very first encounter. 'One more word out of you and I'll take a whip to your back. Now go to your room and take those damned clothes off and put them outside your room. I'm going to burn them, once and for all!'

'No!' cried Merry, in furious outrage.

'Fine! I'll take them off you myself, here and now!'

'Rafe! For goodness sake!' interposed Harry, as Merry ducked behind him out of Rafe's reach. 'I won't let you …'

'Out of my way, Harry! You're lucky I don't knock you down for this! You should be ashamed of this night's work.'

'Don't blame Harry! It wasn't his fault …' cried Merry.

'I don't doubt it, madam,' ground out Rafe. 'But do you imagine for one moment that you would have remained in the tavern long enough to have got into a fight had I found you there? … Or that I should have let *anyone* lay a finger on you?'

Harry was looking a little struck by this and winced when Rafe, his eyes blazing, turned sharply and addressed him.

'And had you been the one waiting here, worried out of your mind about Merry's safety and I had strolled in laughing having let her get embroiled in a fist fight?'

Harry paused a moment, soberly imagining such a thing.

'I would have knocked you down.'

'Well, there's honesty at least!' conceded Rafe. Then turning to Merry: 'I have already told you, have I not, to go to your room and remove those clothes?'

'But I like these clothes! I don't want to be a girl!' cried Merry.

Rafe grasped her shoulders and shook her.

'Well you *are* a girl! There's no *wanting* about it. It is a fact!' he said.

Taking her hands, he held up her bruised knuckles to the light of the single chandelier above them.

'Is this something of which your future husband may be proud?'

'I don't want a husband. I don't want to be a wife ... trapped in a cage at home, stitching samplers and bored to tears! I have an educated mind, but you expect me strap it in a corset and confine my conversation to the weather and the opera and "yes, my lord, no, my lord"! Well, I'm *damned* if I will! ... and *you* can't make me!'

Merry's voice was shaking with emotion and tears of passion were slipping down her cheeks unheeded.

Rafe's emotions were no less in turmoil. He didn't know if he wanted to strangle or kiss her, chastise or comfort her. His arms ached to hold her, but this was a watershed and he could not let her have her way.

'And what would you be as you got older?' he asked harshly. 'Some quiz of an ageing lady, trotting around in boy's clothes, fooling no one and scandalising everyone? You can barely pull off the imposture now! And what occupation would you be good for? How would you earn your living? You might get a job in a playhouse, but even *they* would expect you to wear women's clothes once you left the stage!'

Merry was twisting her hands trying to escape his unyielding grasp, her face now ravaged by misery.

'Face it, Merry,' said Rafe, in a voice roughened by emotion. 'You are a woman ... no matter how you were raised ... a brave, beautiful, intelligent woman. It's time to put aside the boy and accept that marriage is the best and only future for you.'

Merry finally wrested her hands free of Rafe's, which had relaxed their grasp at the end. But it was to Harry's arms that she flew for comfort.

Rafe turned away at the sight and leaned his arm against the mantel, looking unseeing down at the fire and resenting every stroke of Harry's comforting hand on Merry's hair and every soothing word he was murmuring, as she sobbed out her grief for the life that she was having to let go.

Rafe knew with a crushing sense of desolation that Merry would not easily forgive him for what had just passed. The easy intimacy that had formed between them, despite his crimes against her, was shattered.

Rafe knew, as did Harry, who cast a sympathetic glance at his friend's back, that his fury at her behaviour that evening was more a reaction to the anxiety he had felt rather than disapproval of her dress or actions.

'Merry,' said Rafe finally, when he heard her tears abate. 'Go to your room and remove those clothes and leave them outside your door.'

Merry looked an appeal at Harry, but he only nodded in accord with Rafe.

'It is for the best, my dear.'

'I am going to Bath tomorrow,' added Rafe, surprising them all. 'I will obtain a wardrobe for you and return with a seamstress to make it up for you.'

Merry said nothing, but ran off to her room.

'How on earth will you persuade a seamstress to come here?' demanded Harry incredulously.

'Money, of course, Harry,' replied Rafe in a tired voice. 'You can obtain almost anything with money.'

Except the one thing I desire, he thought sadly.

'Perhaps I should go. You might be recognised.'

'Would you trust me here alone with Merry?' quizzed Rafe with a dry look.

'Yes, I think I should … now,' replied Harry quietly.

'Hmm … you're not going to start waxing lyrical are you?'

Harry gave a reluctant smile.

'Well …'

Rafe flung up a lazy hand.

'Spare me. You know I'm no saint,' he said dryly. 'No. I shall go. Merry will be glad not to see me for a few days after this little contretemps, I expect.'

When Rafe went upstairs later, he saw the small pile of folded clothes outside Merry's chamber. Merry, fearful that he would come into her room if she did not obey, had reluctantly complied, damning him to hell as she did so. Rafe picked up the sorry heap and took them to his room. Everything was there, bar her men's drawers, causing him to smile despite his heavy heart. Holding her shirt to his face and breathing in the scent of her on the much-darned linen that had lain next to her skin, he knew he would never burn the clothes that he had first met her in … the quaint outfit that suited her so well. He had noticed the carefully patched elbows earlier, when he had found her lounging with her book. Now, he could look at them more closely and his heart melted. They had been mended many times and the shirt cuffs turned and re-turned to extend the life of the shabby garment.

I shall buy you a wardrobe fit for a princess, Merry, he thought. *A trousseau for the bride-to-be, though you will not have me to groom.*

As he packed for his journey to Bath, he folded Merry's shirt into his bag. He would carry it with him always.

Early next morning, when Merry entered the breakfast parlour, with the haughty dignity of a wounded queen, Rafe had already departed. Despite herself, Merry felt his loss more than she dared admit.

Harry watched Merry's eyes stray towards the open doorway for the umpteenth time that morning, as he tried to teach her the order of precedence, and could not help commenting, with mild exasperation: 'Merry, you need not look for Rafe for at least a week'.

'L..look for Rafe? What do you mean?' she replied mortified.

As Harry gave her a meaningful look, he saw Merry shift uncomfortably as tell-tale colour crept into her cheeks, and he took pity.

'Now, back to your dinner table plan, Merry. Where are you going to seat the Bishop's wife?'

Merry took care not to look towards the door again.

As he journeyed along the Bath Road, Rafe knew only Merry could fill the deep void in his life, yet he was facing a lifetime of exile from her. How could he remain if the woman he loved chose to marry his best friend, as he was now certain she would?

Oh God! Never again to tease her quick wrath, or banter with her, or see those first signs of desire kindle in her eyes, or be the one she discovered her womanhood with - to find that it was a blessing not a curse.

Rafe was certain that, if Merry could once follow her instincts rather than fighting them, she would discover that he was her true mate ... and yet she would choose Harry.

Rafe groaned, dragging his hand through his hair.

'I should have kissed her when she gave me the chance,' he snarled to himself. 'Yes, by God, that would have put all thought of Harry out of her mind.'

But as he drew further away, the thought of losing her became increasingly intolerable. Life had had little appeal for him before he met Merry; it would have none at all if he lost her.

Merry's resentment about the spanking had not outlasted the day of Rafe's departure. She missed him, his presence, his smile, his quick understanding, his humour and something much deeper, that she tried to but could not name. She even missed arguing with him. But, she did _not_ miss the disturbing inner quaking that she felt at his touch, or in response to one of his steady looks. This nervous excitement was too close to the tension she had experienced when gambling or during the more dangerous exploits of her colourful past. It was not just the sensations themselves, but also the intuition that these were the shallows of a much deeper sea, one that might overwhelm her if she ventured in.

Harry's undemanding company was a soothing counterpoint to these feelings and a salve to the haunting experiences of her recent past. It was as though they had always been friends, and his companionship had gone a long way to helping her through the grief of losing Bryn. Merry still ached for her brother as though for a limb that had been removed, but Harry's gentle soul was so much like Bryn's that it was often like having him back.

In the evenings, she and Harry played cards for ludicrous stakes and laughed like children when they won or lost, especially when shameless and transparent cheating had been a factor.

'Oh, Harry!' she had cried one evening, laughing at his genuine expression of chagrin as she had laid out a royal flush and he had been forced to forfeit the miscellaneous assortment of objects that had signified their exotic stakes. 'How I wish I had met you years ago!'

'Huh! I should be poor as a church mouse by now, if we had!' replied Harry. 'How the devil did you get that king? I was sure I had palmed it myself earlier in the game!'

'You had, but I pinched it back when you rang for more wine,' chuckled Merry, dissolving into a fresh peal of laughter at Harry's outraged expression.

But their time together in Rafe's absence had not been spent wholly in such playful pursuits. Harry had continued Merry's lessons and without Rafe's incendiary presence, there were fewer altercations.

Despite the lacerating nature of their delivery, Rafe's home truths had sunk in. Merry no longer fought to retain her boyish identity, though she still reacted against some of the more irritating affectations practised by ladies of quality.

Harry was not proof against Merry's stubborn will, but Merry was not proof against Harry's quiet air of disapproval. So they had made excellent progress when the week was up.

Indeed, their rapport was so natural that neither had given a thought to the fact that they were, effectively and most improperly, alone together under the same roof. The topic of marriage had not arisen, but it came up, quite unexpectedly, the night before Rafe was due to return.

After dinner that evening, Harry had coaxed Merry into relating something of her history, and soon found himself struggling to conceal his shock at some of her revelations. When she related a particularly chilling anecdote about nearly getting shot by the excise men when they had attempted to run brandy, Harry could no longer hide his dismay.

'Good God!' he gasped.

'Yes, it was not one of our prettier experiments at making our fortune,' said Merry, watching Harry's horrified face with a mixture of curiosity and humour.

Idly, Merry wondered why Rafe never seemed to be scandalised, no matter what she told him, and then she had a momentary insight into the difference that Harry's stable upbringing in a loving home had wrought.

Merry felt a pang of envy, which swiftly turned to one of bitterness towards her father for the upbringing that his pride had forced upon them all. Though she loved him dearly, this one flaw had prevented him from taking up an honest trade or allowing his offspring to do so. It had kept them isolated from their neighbours and those who might have been their friends. Ultimately, it had caused his own death and, indirectly, poor Bryn's. Indeed, it had very nearly led to her own descent into prostitution.

'Pride,' she muttered, speaking her thoughts out loud.

'Whose pride?' asked Harry.

'My father's,' she replied. 'It blighted all our lives.'

'And what was it that prevented you from coming to find me when you left Upper Grosvenor Street?' countered Harry. 'Pride, Merry. The Griffith pride.'

Merry reluctantly accepted that she had same fault, differently expressed.

'There was no need for you to shoulder the grief of burying your brother on your own …' Harry continued. 'Or to act as if you were alone and friendless afterwards.'

'I didn't know you were looking for me,' replied Merry, in a small voice.

'You made it nigh impossible to find you!' he added, warming to his theme. 'Your wretched pride put me through the worst week of my life … And if you had seen Rafe's face when I told him I had lost you!'

'Angry?' suggested Merry.

'Bereft,' said Harry.

'Because he felt responsible for me?' asked Merry.

'Because he loves you,' he replied with irrepressible honesty.

'How do you know?' she pressed, seeking an answer to a question with which she herself was wrestling. 'What does love feel like?'

Harry looked across at her searching grey eyes, a little bemused. He had been struggling with the question himself. He admired Merry immensely. She was bright, beautiful and incredibly brave. For the most part, he enjoyed her company very much – so why did he feel that something was missing? A fleeting memory of Lydia's cornflower blue eyes, her gentler courage in protecting his identity and the extraordinary kindness of her offer to take in Merry came unexpectedly into his head.

'I need to know, Harry!' Merry's urgency brought him sharply back to the present. 'I have never been in love ... never even given it a thought. I don't know who else to talk to about it.'

'Well, I suspect Rafe might have a different answer, but I would say it's feeling profound esteem for someone – knowing that they are the best and kindest person you have ever met – in whose company you feel truly comfortable and happy, and wishing to stay that way with them forever.'

'But, that's how I feel about you, silly!' said Merry, unthinkingly. 'Good God, if marriage meant staying as we have been this past week, then it would be great fun ...' Then she gasped. 'Harry! Does that mean I love *you*?'

She can't know what she's just said, thought Harry, with a sinking heart.

Rafe could have batted away the obligation with a joke, but Harry was a true gentleman to his core. No matter how it had come about, they were alone together and Merry had formed a tendre for him. Harry's duty was clear.

'My dearest girl,' he said, reaching across and taking her hand. 'Would you do me the very great honour of becoming my wife?'

Merry was too poorly versed in the niceties of gentlemanly conduct to distinguish duty from desire, and Harry was far too well bred to give the slightest sign that this was not the greatest wish of his heart.

Oh no! thought Merry. *Harry loves me! I cannot break his heart. I suppose I have to marry someone, and I must love him ... because he is by far the best and kindest man I've ever met. Perhaps it won't be so bad. He's a great gun, after all.*

'I ... I would be honoured to, Harry, if you're sure you want to?'

Harry kissed her hand.

'You've made me the happiest of men,' he said, with every appearance of it.

They celebrated with hastily chilled champagne, and both drank deeply.

'Will Rafe be very angry, do you think?' asked Merry.

A cloud crossed Harry's face.

'I'm afraid he will take it hard,' said Harry darkly. 'You know he refused to believe you were dead, even though I despaired, I'm ashamed to say. He said he would know if you were dead.'

'He did?'

'Yes, odd thing to say, wasn't it?'

Merry's brow furrowed

'But that's Rafe all over,' he resumed. 'He's always been out of the common way, as my mother would say. It hasn't always been easy to be his friend, but it has been my privilege. I shall be sorry if our marriage causes a breach, as I fear it must.'

'Oh no!' said Merry, hating to be the cause of trouble between them. Remembering Rafe's proposal, and all their discussions on the topic, she could not pretend that he would not be hurt by this development. But she reasoned that she had made her sentiments clear. The inescapable and insurmountable fact that Rafe had killed Bryn meant every feeling must revolt at the thought of a marriage between them. If she must be married, as they both insisted, then surely there could be no better choice than dear Harry?

'We will all be abroad in exile for some time, after all,' reasoned Harry. 'But when things have settled down, I am sure he will come to visit with us, and perhaps bring his own wife to stay.'

Merry felt an inexplicable twinge of dissatisfaction at this notion, and that night, her dreams were disturbed by images of Rafe presenting a ravishing Italian contessa as his new bride.

Despite all the developments of the night before, Merry was astonished at how her heart soared when the sound of harness and hooves approaching up the drive announced Rafe's return. Abandoning all the precepts she had been taught, she jumped up, overturning her chair, and scampered off to meet him. It was she who opened the front door before Cope could reach it.

Rafe's heart, too, soared as he saw Merry's beaming face appear around the door. He flicked her cheek, a lazy smile curving his handsome lips, but as he glimpsed Harry's expressive face, Rafe knew in an instant that things had been settled between them and that he, Rafe, was to lose his love.

'Ah! So Harry has taught you how to be a footman in my absence,' he observed. 'Excellent progress!'

Merry giggled.

'Oh, Rafe, you beast! I've learned heaps of things,' declared Merry. 'You should see my curtsey! And I can walk and sit and everything! Though we just agreed,' she added with a wary glance towards Harry. 'That I need not chatter about gossip and fashion on morning calls, but could talk about books and politics, too.'

Rafe met Harry's wooden look with a ghost of a smile.

'Ah, so you _agreed_ that did you?' repeated Rafe, quizzing Merry until she coloured guiltily. 'Well, that should certainly make the calls shorter, at all events … and perhaps fewer in number, since you're unlikely to be invited back.'

'Oh, I should have known you'd side with Harry,' said Merry, unable to resist a chuckle at Rafe's comment, but she was too happy to have Rafe back in their midst to argue. It was as though he brought a new breath of life with him.

'Well, perhaps you will _want_ to talk about fashions when you have seen some of the ravishing new outfits that I've brought back. They're all the first stare in Bath this season,' he said. 'I think I hear the second coach carrying some of them arriving now, and it bears a young French seamstress who is to alter them to fit you. Why don't you go and see her installed in her room and the clothes carried to yours?'

'Alright, but you really didn't need to buy me anything, Rafe,' said Merry as she departed. 'I already have four gowns. I can't see why I would need any more.'

'Not quite converted into a lady yet, then?' Rafe said smilingly to Harry.

'No, but she has made good progress,' said Harry, then added with a smile. 'You really should see her curtsey.'

'Has it been bloody?' asked Rafe.

'Not at all. A few differences of opinion, perhaps, but I think your last words struck home. Merry seems to have resigned herself to being a lady.'

'Progress indeed!' said Rafe.

They were spared any further discussion by Mrs Cope's entry with refreshments, which was soon followed by Merry's return in wide-eyed horror at the many bandboxes that Cope was even now carrying up to her room.

'Rafe! You've gone completely mad!' she said, coming into the room at a run.

'You're welcome!' he said magnanimously, causing Merry to chuckle again.

'I'm serious! You've bought far too many things. It'll take me a lifetime to wear them all!'

'Or a *season*, as we like to call it,' countered Rafe. 'Trust me, Merry. You will need to replace most of it within the year, as you will think it soiled or out of fashion.'

Merry looked aghast.

'Never! What a scandalous waste that would be!' she declared. 'I just couldn't do it.'

Rafe and Harry exchanged another wry smile.

'Would you care to hazard your pearls on it?' said Rafe.

Merry's hand crept to her mother's necklet at her throat.

'Not those,' said Rafe, fishing a velvet box from his pocket. 'These.'

Lying on bed of deep blue satin was an elegant string of flawless pearls, much larger than her own but still discretely appropriate for a young matron.

'A betrothal gift,' he said, watching intently as Merry touched the beautiful necklace in utter wonder.

Merry blushed and her eyes unconsciously flashed towards Harry in a moment of alarm, confirming Rafe's earlier deduction.

'I shouldn't tease you,' he said, laughing to dispel the awkward moment. 'Here, take them. I need to speak to Cope and pay off the postillions.'

'I feel utterly wretched,' whispered Merry, as soon as Rafe had left the room.

'So do I,' agreed Harry.

'Do you think he knows?' she asked.

'I think he suspects,' said Harry grimly. His heart wept for his friend.

'Should I accept the pearls and all these clothes?' she asked anxiously. 'It seems iniquitous to do so!'

'I will reimburse him for the clothes, of course,' said Harry. 'But the pearls are more difficult. They are a gift. He would be offended if you returned them and insulted if I were to ask to repay him for them. I would in his place. You must accept them, there's nothing else for it.'

Merry groaned.

'I'm a cad,' she whispered.

'You're a darling,' said Harry.

But Merry just shook her head, feeling sick with duplicity and with trepidation at the thought of Rafe's reaction, whether he betrayed it or not, to the news that she was to marry Harry.

'Well, we must tell him after dinner,' said Merry. 'I can't and won't deceive him for another day.'

'Agreed,' said Harry, dreading that evening every bit as much as Merry.

In the end, the experience was not as traumatic as they had both expected. Rafe had carried the burden of conversation through dinner, regaling his friends with the latest news from Bath while he watched them both struggle to conjure up polite smiles that thinly concealed their inner torment. Towards the last remove, Merry's smile gave out altogether, though she seemed not to realise, and she simply stared at him, her face a picture of almost tearful fretfulness. Rafe gave her a steady, sympathetic look that made her lips part in a silent gasp.

In all the worry over how Rafe might react to being parted from them, Merry had not fully considered how she might feel being parted from Rafe. Suddenly, she remembered the word Harry had used yesterday – bereft.

Rafe flicked a glance at Cope, who left swiftly.

'I think you two have some news for me,' said Rafe, as the door closed.

'Oh, Rafe,' sobbed Merry, but could go no further.

'Don't cry, little one,' said Rafe, though his heart was breaking. 'I was fairly certain this would be the outcome when I left for Bath.'

'It was only decided yesterday,' said Harry hoarsely, his throat constricting at Rafe's kindly tone. 'It hadn't even been discussed until then.'

'I asked Harry how love felt, and … and, well, that's how I felt, so Harry kindly offered for me.' Merry finished with a helpless look.

'I see,' said Rafe with a swift glance taking in Harry's rather brittle smile. 'May I ask how you believe love feels?'

'Happy and comfortable,' said Merry. 'You must admit if we were together, we would probably fight all the time.'

'Not *all* the time,' said Rafe quietly. 'There have been times when we managed to get along pretty well.'

'Yes,' said Merry miserably. 'But there was an impossible obstacle.'

'The fact that I killed your brother?'

Merry nodded slowly and sadly.

'And to be fair, you told me that at the outset,' said Rafe bracingly, rising from the table. 'Well, come along, you two. Enough of the long faces. I shan't tease you any more on the subject. I have had a week to acclimatise to the idea, and now it seems that I knew before you did. I have some champagne awaiting us in the drawing room, and I intend to drink quite a quantity of it tonight!'

Rafe led the way to the drawing room and dismissed Cope with a nod of his head as they entered. A bottle stood chilling on the sideboard beside three flute glasses, and Rafe made his way across to them, while Merry and Harry exchanged glances of relief. They were both surprised at how well Rafe appeared to be handling losing the woman he loved. Clearly, he had mastered his emotions during the week, and was now surrendering graciously to Merry's decision. Harry knew that this apparent goodwill must mask an awful inner turmoil, but he could do nothing to assuage it.

Rafe handed them each a glass of champagne, then held up his own in a toast.

"To Merry and Harry, the two people I love best in the world. I wish you a lifetime of happiness,' said Rafe, noting the smiling but troubled expressions on their faces.

Harry's own joy was warring with his sympathy for his friend.

Merry appeared content with her choice, but betrayed none of the signs of being truly in love with her chosen groom. In fact, she was still experiencing some very unruly emotions as she stood looking at Rafe.

Harry tossed back the first glass and grimaced.

'Urgh! That's bitter.' he said.

Rafe appeared to savour it, taking another gulp, while Merry, too, drained her glass with a look of distaste on her face.

'Corked, I think,' said Rafe. 'Damn it! Yes, very sour. Damned if I'll buy from Farquar's again! Here, try the tawny port,' he said, cutting the thick wax seal with his pocket-knife and fishing three schooners from the cabinet.

'Hmm .. that's better,' said Harry. 'But I can still taste that nasty champagne.'

'There's only one answer to that,' replied Rafe with a wink. 'Drink more port. After all, it's a night for celebration!'

Harry laughed and drained his glass.

'Delicious port,' murmured Merry, finishing her glass and holding it out for a refill, like Harry.

Both Rafe and Harry laughed at this.

'Hmm ... Harry, I think you may have to keep your betrothed out of your wine cellars, or she may drink them dry.'

Merry rolled her eyes but then grinned as she sipped her fresh glass. This time both she and Harry commended the port.

But after a brief exchange of banter that seemed rather empty in the awkward situation in which they all found themselves, the conversation drew to a sluggish halt.

'Not feeling quite the thing,' said Harry, staggering a little and passing his hand across his eyes, as if to clear them.

'I'm sorry, Harry,' said Rafe, but his friend was already crumpling to the floor and Rafe had to move quickly to ease his fall.

There was only time for one shocked look from Merry before her knees folded beneath her but Rafe reached swiftly to prevent her from falling.

As he lifted Merry into in his arms, Rafe looked down into her face and drew a ragged breath.

'Ah, Merry! Pray God you forgive me!'

Chapter Fourteen
The Ice Bride

For a moment, Rafe's own legs felt weak at the enormity of what he had done and yet planned to do.

He sank into a chair, still holding Merry, and watched as her head lolled back in the crook of his elbow, her lips slightly parted.

Now, he looked at her face with a kind of baffled wonder.

Why should this face work such deep magic upon him? How had he fallen so profoundly in love with this one slip of a girl that he could betray the best friend he had ever had to secure her?

He had no measure for this, no comparator. Merry was the only woman he had ever loved and, like his father before him, the only one he ever truly would.

Lifting her against his chest and cradling her head like a child's so her face lay cheek to cheek with his own, Rafe rocked back and forth for a moment drinking in the scent of her hair and skin. When his eyes opened, the haunted look gave way to one of grim determination. He was committed now. It was a traitorous act, but Rafe was certain that he knew best and could only hope that he would be proven right.

Rafe placed Merry in a chair while he attended to Harry, who lay sprawled on his back in the middle of the floor. Rafe carried him to the sofa, placing a cushion under his head and drawing a rug over him. Looking down at that dear, trusting face, so innocent in repose, Rafe felt his throat constrict with emotion.

His best friend!

Rafe could not bear to contemplate what Harry would think of him when he awoke. The thought of their long friendship being turned into one of enmity was unbearable. Harry would never forgive him. How could he? Rafe could not have done so in his place.

Rafe bent and kissed his friend's brow.

'Forgive me, Harry.'

Rafe put the guard across the fire and took a letter addressed to Harry from his breast pocket and placed it on the mantel in front of the clock. Then he turned and went to the door. He needed to move fast, as Brooke had been instructed to arrive with the carriage at ten and Rafe needed to gather his and Merry's belongings. Although he had had some of Merry's new outfits brought in, the vast majority were on their way to Seaton Fall.

Chantal Sangat, the French seamstress he had hired, was standing in the hallway when Rafe strode out.

'Well?' he asked.

Chantal nodded.

'The Copes they sleep,' she confirmed.

'Come, let me see that they are comfortable,' said Rafe, heading towards the kitchen.

Rafe had planned everything from that moment on the Bath Road when he had faced the thought of Merry marrying Harry. It had been like looking into the abyss. Convinced that he knew what was best for Merry and himself, Rafe had decided on a different course of action and, from that moment, had pursued it with dread resolve.

If he had truly thought Merry and Harry were in love, he might have drawn back, accepted a life of exile and courted an early release from his mortal coil. But he was certain that they were mistaking abiding friendship for something deeper. Merry had unwittingly confirmed this in her guileless explanation of how the proposal had come about. Rafe had seen well-concealed strain behind Harry's smile. It was not the look of a man in love.

Had Merry unknowingly obliged Harry to offer for her?

There was certainly nothing remotely lover-like in their behaviour.

Or am I trying to excuse the inexcusable? He wondered.

Rafe had known that he would need an ally to prevent the Copes from interfering. The Frenchwoman, offered a sizable bribe, instead agreed to assist him if he employed her permanently as Merry's lady's maid.

'If I wanted to stitch until my eyes failed, I could have stayed in Paris,' she had said by way of explanation. 'As a lady's maid to a vicomptesse, there will be many opportunities for me, I think.'

Rafe thought the woman little understood the life of an English lady's maid, but simply shrugged and agreed willingly. It had solved the problem of recruiting a maid before he reached Seaton Fall.

But there would be one vital stop to be made before they continued to this haven.

Rafe and Chantal hurried to pack the last items and convey everything to the stables in readiness for Brooke's perfectly-timed arrival.

Brooke had already exchanged the carriage horses for Rafe's match bays, when Rafe emerged with Merry in his arms.

Like a parent with a child who had gone too far this time, Brooke gave Rafe one long accusing look, his lips pursed on the words he longed to speak. Rafe met this look with one of unshakable determination. But, as Brooke watched Rafe carry his precious cargo to the coach, he clearly saw something in Rafe's face or manner that changed his perspective entirely, because moments later Rafe was stunned to hear his disapproving retainer whistling cheerfully as he strapped the last bags into place.

Chantal, unsure of whether she was meant to travel inside the coach or on the box, gave Brooke a very Gallic shrug of enquiry. In response, he gave her a wink and nodded to the seat beside him.

At the gate, four armed outriders waited to accompany them. Rafe had no wish to repeat their encounter with highwaymen again, and had instructed Brooke to ensure they were protected on this journey.

Inside the carriage, Rafe did not lay Merry down on the opposite seat but continued to hold her in his arms throughout the journey. Sometimes he cradled her in the crook of his arm, gently stroking her hair. At others, when some demon of guilt or fear assailed him, he held her crushed to him, her head resting next to his own.

Brooke kept a fast pace, and they finally reached their destination a little over four hours later. It was a small but tidy inn, well off the beaten track. Rafe carried Merry up the stairs and laid her gently on the sofa in the larger of the bedchambers. With infinite tenderness, he brushed back some stray curls from her face and stood for a long moment looking down at her, so peaceful in this deep sleep. Straightening up, he surveyed the chamber, his eyes resting on the rather ancient bed that dominated the room, and then moving to a bottle of brandy standing on the small dressing table by the shuttered window. Rafe threw his greatcoat on the bed and poured himself a glass. Then he placed a chair a few feet away from Merry, sat back and waited for her to awaken.

Back in Quemerford, Harry finally roused in near darkness, the room lit only by the embers of the fire and one guttering candle outlasting its fellows in the chandelier above. For a moment he looked around dazedly and then his expression changed as he realised what must have happened. Harry sank his head into his hands for several minutes, overcome. After a while he looked up, his eyes not entirely dry.

Rising a little unsteadily, intending to see what had happened to the Copes, he made his way to light a candle on the mantle. His hand stilled as he spotted Rafe's note to him. Harry stared at it for a few seconds, before taking it and dropping it onto the embers unopened. He watched it sit there for a brief spell before a wisp of smoke and a flare of flame took hold and the words curled and blackened to ash.

There was nothing that Rafe could say to him that would mitigate what he had done this night.

Forty miles away, Merry, too, was rousing. As she regained her senses, Merry was conscious that her mouth was parched and she felt groggier than she normally did when waking. Blinking hard to clear her vision, Merry was surprised to see Rafe sitting very still, regarding her steadily with grim trepidation. Merry had been drunk before and this sluggish awakening felt a little similar to the aftermath of those rare occasions.

'Did I drink too much champagne?' she croaked groggily, puzzled by his stillness and the odd wary expression on his face.

Rafe slowly shook his head, his eyes never leaving hers.

'Then, how...?'

Rafe paused for a long moment.

'You were drugged.'

'Drugged!!' cried Merry, sitting up too rapidly for her recovering senses. Her hand lifted to cover her eyes as her head swam sickeningly. It was several seconds before she could continue, but lifting her head and looking toward Rafe, Merry grasped that she was no longer at Harry's hunting lodge. Her eyes sought Rafe, who had not moved and still watched her with a strange, suspenseful look.

'Rafe ... who drugged me?' she asked him slowly, knowing the answer but struggling to believe it.

'I did,' replied Rafe quietly.

Merry stared at him in slow-dawning horror. Dim memories of seeing Harry crumple moments before she lost consciousness began to come back to her.

'Where is Harry?'

'At Quemerford, I imagine.'

'And where are we?'

'Not in Quemerford, Merry.'

'Wh...what? Why? What have you done, Rafe?' gasped Merry.

Their eyes locked – Merry's accusing, Rafe's a kind of stern supplication.

'I have abducted you,' said Rafe finally, on a sigh, as if at last admitting it to himself as well as Merry.

'But, why?' asked Merry, puzzled. Then realisation dawned. 'Oh,' she added simply. 'You didn't want me to marry Harry?'

'No, Merry, I did not.'

'But he was my choice,' said Merry.

'Yes,' sighed Rafe. 'But, I think ... I believe you were mistaken.'

'Mistaken! What manner of choice is it that allows for only one outcome? Did you always mean to abduct me, if I chose another?'

'I never thought that eventuality would arise.'

'Arrogance!'

'Perhaps, but Merry, we had such moments of connection ... of attraction ... that I could not believe you were indifferent to me.'

Merry coloured, remembering those moments.

'I was not indifferent,' she faltered. 'but those moments were not ... comfortable. How could one live that way? I am always comfortable with Harry. He is my friend ... and yours, Rafe, or so I thought.'

'He's the best friend a man ever had,' said Rafe, with grim solemnity. 'But ...'

'Then how could you serve him such a trick?' cried Merry.

'And when you ask yourself that question, Merry, what answer occurs?' demanded Rafe. 'You're an intelligent woman. Does no cause spring to mind?'

'You could not bear to be bested,' said Merry, in a hollow voice that bespoke her low opinion of him.

'In *this*? No, I could not!' replied Rafe with asperity.

'I knew it!' cried Merry, jumping up, her head now clear. 'Pique! You have ruined everything because your pride was piqued!'

Rafe had risen too, and they now stood face to face, tempers flaming.

'Don't be ridiculous! Good God, do you think I would take such a step out of pride?'

'Yes!' cried Merry. 'Was it not for that ignoble cause that you took my brother's life?'

Rafe flinched as if she had hit him. He looked abashed.

'I've told you how sorry I am for that,' he said defensively. 'I have changed. You have changed me.'

'All evidence to the contrary, Rafe!' snapped Merry. 'For now you have become a cheat and an abductor in the name of pride.'

'No! Not pride. Love!' he said, his voice hoarse with emotion. 'I love you, Merry!'

'Love me? A week ago you threatened to whip me!'

'Did you really think I would ever do so?' asked Rafe, his cobalt eyes challenging her glistening grey ones.

It was Merry's turn to falter.

'I don't know. I don't know you at all.'

'Yes, you do Merry, though you choose to deny it.'

'The Rafe I knew would never have betrayed his friends in such a way.'

'And did you seriously believe that the Rafe you knew would meekly hand over the only woman he has ever loved to be another man's wife?' demanded Rafe.

Merry now realised that she and Harry had been pitifully naïve to imagine that Rafe's easy acquiescence was real.

'You clearly have no idea how I feel, Merry. Nor could Harry. Did you think that having discovered myself in love for the first time, having asked you to marry me, that I would happily hand you over to be Harry's bride? Don't you know me at all?'

Though he was the villain, Rafe felt a twisted anger towards his victims, the two people he loved best in the world and who knew him best, as the self-loathing that raged so wildly inside him spilled out unreasonably towards those he had sinned against.

'I've held you in my arms, Merry! I have *held* you!' he said, searching her eyes for understanding, and finding nothing but contempt, adding bitterly: 'I will <u>never</u> permit another to hold you, whether he were your legal husband or a lover you think of outside our marriage bed. I will kill any man who attempts it, and you know I mean it. I love Harry, better than a brother, but I knew, I *knew* that I could not bear to lose you, even to him. How long before I forced a quarrel on him ... or took some other desperate step that caused you both profound regrets?'

'"Our marriage bed"?' echoed Merry in astonishment. 'Do you seriously imagine that I will consent to marry you now?'

'This time I will not offer you a choice,' stated Rafe. His eyes flickered towards the bed.

Merry's eyes widened in horror momentarily, before the mask descended and her chin came up in that tell-tale way.

'This has gone far enough,' she said, in freezing tones and made to move past him to the door, saying: 'You will release me at once, and ...'

Rafe's hands came up and caught her shoulders.

'Take your hands off me!' hissed Merry.

'The door is locked, Merry, and you shall not leave this room until you agree to marry me.' Then, his quick intelligence interpreting the glint in her eye, he added: 'I have a parson waiting below with a Special Licence, so we may act immediately upon your promise.'

Merry glared at Rafe, as she tried to shrug his hands from her shoulders.

'You're a monster,' she said bitterly.

'I'm the monster you'll have to husband,' he responded.

'Never!' she cried, breaking free of him and assuming a pugnacious stance, rendered a little ridiculous by the elegant, though crumpled, grey silk evening dress she still wore.

Rafe was not complacent and watched Merry warily as she quickly scanned the room for escape routes or potential weapons. There were two small windows and only one door, but there were bottles, candlesticks and fire irons, so Merry did not despair.

Operating under the limitation that he would not willingly harm a hair on his beloved's head, while she would gleefully beat him to a gory pulp, Rafe decided to take the offensive and try to grab Merry before she could arm herself. He was quick and strong, and he knew Merry's preferred target areas. Keeping his chin down, he rushed her, parrying her blows, and though she boxed his ear once, he managed to grasp her arms and pin them behind her. As they stood struggling chest to chest, Merry brought her knee up sharply in the region she referred to as the "crown jewels".

'Urgh' groaned Rafe, and Merry felt his body cramp sharply in pain. He did not release her, so she made to repeat the clearly effective manoeuvre. But Rafe swiftly forestalled her by crushing her in a bear hug, lifting her off her feet, and hauling her to the bed, where he collapsed on top of her. Ensuring that his knees were safely positioned between her own, protecting the area of stomach-churning pain from further attack, he whispered roughly after a moment:

'Don't do that again.'

'Hah! I hope it kills you, you bully!' cried Merry, still struggling wildly to be free.

'Not quite that, Merry,' said Rafe, rapidly jerking his head back as Merry tried to break his nose with her forehead. 'You'll have to curb this passion for my destruction once we are married, my sweet,' he added, needling her, as he strained to grasp both her slender wrists in one hand so that he could free up the other to prevent her violent attempts to throw him off.

'I will stab you in your sleep!'

'So we *will* sleep together, then?' said Rafe, as if brightening. 'I had not dared to hope …'

'Never!' snarled Merry savagely. 'I mean I will creep in your room one night and do it.'

'What a delightful picture of wedded bliss you paint, my love! You make it quite irresistible,' his eyes glinted as he saw the ridiculousness of his situation. There were countless women in England who would fight for the opportunity to marry Lord Rothsea, yet here he was, wrestling with the only woman he wanted to call 'wife'.

Incensed both by his words and by the fact that Rafe seemed to be deriving amusement from this appalling episode, Merry called him all the worst names she had encountered in her colourful history, wiping the humour from her prospective husband's blue eyes.

'What you will, madam,' he said curtly, when she had exhausted her repertoire. 'But you will wed me and no other!'

Merry gave another infuriated snarl and renewed her efforts to be free of Rafe's inexorable grasp.

But, Merry had barely slept the night before and had eaten very little during the day. She was no weakling, but her strength was soon expended, and panting from her exertions, Merry channelled her energy instead into taunting abuse.

'I can't believe I was such a gull to be taken in by your kind words and easy charm. How you must have crowed at bringing me round your thumb so easily! My first reading of your character, if one can call it that, was correct. You are every low thing – you have murdered my brother, cheated your best friend and now you will practice rape upon me, whom you swore to protect.'

'It would not be rape Merry,' murmured Rafe, looking desperately into her eyes for that spark of attraction he had seen there so often, but it was not there now, only implacable enmity. 'If you would afford me one kiss, I could show you that your body cries out for mine as much as mine cries out for yours.'

'Never!' cried Merry icily. 'I shall never willingly permit you to kiss me, and I recommend, if you value your life, that you do not attempt it!'

'Make no mistake, Merry,' said Rafe with relentless determination. 'I will do whatever I must to secure you as my bride. Do you understand me?'

'You would not dare! Harry will kill you, if I do not!'

'Harry could never beat me in a duel, Merry. Would you want his death on your hands?'

'You are the devil!'

'Will you marry me?'

'No!'

Rafe had no intention at all of forcing himself on his darling girl, but he had to make her believe he would. He had freed his right hand and he now pushed the gown from her shoulder and held her jaw, so that he could kiss her neck and shoulder without risk of having his ear bitten off.

His ruse worked. Merry was genuinely alarmed.

'Stop!' she cried. 'Please stop!'

Rafe drew back and looked down at her, his eyes darkened with the rising passion that those few kisses had aroused in him.

'Well?' he said in a hoarse voice.

Merry saw the signs of ardour in his face and dared not provoke it further. She felt like weeping, as all her tangle of feelings for this man had turned as cold as a stone, yet she would have to submit to him, whether as a virgin bride or a ruined one. As Merry glared at him in helpless rage, she made a deadly vow – that she would make him rue this day, and if the opportunity presented itself she would be revenged both for herself and for Bryn … and for Harry too. Rafe would be made to pay for all his sins against them.

'Well?' repeated Rafe. 'Will you marry me, or shall I continue?' He began to bow his head as if to kiss her shoulder again.

'Very well!' cried Merry. 'As you offer me no option, I will marry you and shall make it my life's work to make you as miserable as you have made me. I shall not consummate it. My only hope is for an annulment. So be warned, if you come near me peddling your foul rake's charms I'll kill you, I swear it! But if such a bitter union is the price for leaving this room untouched, then so be it.'

'No tricks, Merry,' said Rafe in a stern voice. 'If you try to escape or fail to go through with the ceremony, you will find yourself back in this bed with me faster that you can say 'knife'. Do you understand?'

Merry simply looked at him disparagingly and said:

'Unlike you, I do not go back on my word.'

Rafe bit his lip and gave Merry a darkling look, but he pushed away from her and stood cautiously, watching her with a wary eye.

Merry stood quickly and tidied her clothing. She had no wish to incite a repeat of those hot kisses by appearing like a wanton.

'So you promise to go through with the ceremony now and remain with me as my wife?' enquired Rafe, unable to quite believe Merry's apparent acquiescence.

Merry fixed him with a cold look, and nodded.

'But in return you will promise me that there will be no wedding night until I come to you willingly,' said Merry. 'Not a kiss, nor a touch unless I invite it.'

They locked eyes for a long moment, but this time Rafe was the first to look away. Merry would become his wife. That was blessing enough for now. Let tomorrow take care of itself.

'Agreed,' he said, holding out his hand.

Merry looked at his hand, her lip curling in a sneer, to indicate what little faith she placed in his promises. Without meeting his eyes again, she walked past him in the haughtiest manner she could muster and stood by the door, waiting for him to unlock it.

The parson was waiting for them in the larger of the two taprooms. Brooke and Chantal, who were waiting with him, both looked up anxiously as the couple descended the stairs. Much though Brooke wanted his master to secure this bride, around whom his lordship's world now appeared to revolve, he would not have stood by if the young lady had screamed or had now seemed genuinely distressed. But Brooke did not know Merry's pride or her courage. He looked in vain for signs of tears or dismay, but saw only a hard resolve that did not bode well for a happy marriage. Rafe's face wore an expression of relief and a hint of elation. No matter how it had been brought about, this wedding was clearly a joyous event for one person in the room.

An ordinary man might greet with dismay the fact that his new bride despised him, but Rafe was simply too happy that the only woman he could love was to take his name, henceforth to be his and his alone. His heart felt like it would burst, and as the words 'man and wife together' were said, Rafe could not suppress an almost boyish look of sheer joy, that surprised even Merry, who looked like an effigy beside him.

My wife! he thought. *How wonderful that sounds. I never guessed what that word would mean to me one day or that I would treasure every word of my vows.*

Rafe shook hands delightedly with the parson and with Brooke, who wished him happy and meant it with all his heart. He'd seen this troubled young man encounter many far more suitable ladies, but wasn't it just like the boy to fall for the only one who would not have him? Still, it seemed that he had talked the lady round, or so he thought until he wished her happy too and she met his eye for an instant. In that moment, he thought he had glimpsed white-hot fury, but her ladyship's gaze was demurely downcast once more, and Brooke wondered if he had imagined it.

Merry accepted the good wishes of the others with the appearance of quiet calm, but in her mind the enormity of what she had done finally and forcibly struck home.

I am married to him! Married! No matter what promises were made, he has the power now to do what he will with me! What have I done? Oh, what have I done!

Merry's pride forced her to conceal her fears and regrets. Rafe kept looking at her, praying she would just once meet his eyes so that he might know how she was feeling. But she remained coolly elusive, never looking up, and responding in the briefest monotones to any remarks directed at her. Rafe would almost have preferred her temper to this unnatural quiet.

Brooke watched the strange couple with mixed feelings, half hope and half dread. His lordship seemed to gravitate to his bride, standing protectively at her shoulder and looking down at her with pride and a kind of mute appeal, as if willing her to look up at him. On the other hand, her ladyship seemed to be encased in ice, too still and silent for a bride. Brooke remembered the angry firebrand, unashamedly clad as a boy, that he had met in Albemarle Street. If she had been incensed by a duel then, how could she now accept her own abduction and forced marriage with such tame calm? Brooke, who has seen much in his master's service, knew in his bones that a bad storm was coming.

Merry's hand shook a little as she signed the licence. She had to suppress the urge to scrawl across it or rip it to shreds. Thoughts about how she might escape tangled up with ideas of exacting revenge, so that her head was soon genuinely pounding as she bid a cool farewell to the parson.

Dawn was already illuminating the sky. Though she had slept for several hours, in a drugged state, Merry was exhausted. They all were. Rafe had made Merry take a cup of tea before the service had begun, and he now nodded to Brooke to fetch a bowl of broth for his wife.

When it arrived, Merry declined it.

'I'm not hungry,' she said scowling.

'Eat,' he said. 'It will do you good.'

'I said I'm not hungry,' said Merry, in a tired voice.

'Eat,' repeated Rafe.

'So you are bullying me already?' snarled Merry. 'With the ink barely dry on the licence!'

Rafe tried to suppress the smile that tugged at his lips, but failed.

'How dare you laugh at me, you villain?' she gasped.

'How can I help it when you make idiotic remarks?' he said affably, gently pushing the bowl towards her.

'What else am I to call it when you force me to eat when I am so very tired?' she muttered churlishly.

'You may call it "*husbandly concern*", my love,' he said in a voice that would have undermined the resolve of any other woman. 'And the sooner you eat your broth, the sooner you may go to bed.'

'Alone?' asked Merry suspiciously.

'Are you inviting me to join you?' enquired Rafe.

'No, never!'

'Then, yes. Alone, it would seem,' he replied, with apparent equanimity, once more indicating the bowl.

Merry entertained the impish notion of throwing the broth in her husband's face, and the idea was writ large in the wickedly speculative glance she gave him. Reading this, Rafe's eyes gleamed first with incredulity and then with a mix of humour and righteous wrath as he silently dared her to even consider such a thing.

But Merry had caught the delicious scent of ham and vegetables and her stomach gave a groan of keen anticipation. With a final baleful look at her tormentor, Merry took up her spoon and ate with a comic balance between the frigid reluctance that her pride demanded and the eager delight that her body betrayed.

Rafe then escorted her upstairs to her room, adjacent to the one where she had awoken. Chantal was waiting for her with hot water and nightclothes.

At the door, Rafe bowed her goodnight.

'Thank you, Merry,' he said with an unfathomable expression on his face.

'For what?'

'For becoming my wife.'

'You gave me no choice.'

'I know.'

'I shall never forgive you.'

'I know that, too,' he said sadly, and walked away.

Chapter Fifteen
Heading for the Fall

When the company rose late the following morning, they were all a little jaded, except for Rafe, who was annoyingly bright.

From the moment he had stretched awake and had seen the gleaming gold band on his left hand, Rafe had had a smile on his face that neither Merry's surliness nor the thought of Harry's probable reaction could quite dispel. He had hurriedly shaved and dressed, and then spent more than ten minutes pacing back and forth in front of Merry's door, willing her to emerge, before he finally gave up and went to the private parlour, where breakfast had been laid out. At first, he had meant only to eat, but when the landlord's wife had entered with a plate of hot sausages, he had another idea.

Merry's reaction when she awoke and saw the ring on her finger was the complete opposite of Rafe's. Scowling, she wrested the ring from her finger and flung it across the room, where it hit the wall and then fell with a 'ting' on the uneven wooden floor. For several minutes, Merry lay back with a rebellious smirk on her face, which slowly faded before becoming an irascible frown. Finally, with a frustrated growl, she jumped out of bed to retrieve the wretched thing while she could still remember where it had fallen. Merry was still on all fours when she heard Rafe's familiar step outside her door, and her hand stilled. She watched the door in alarm, but when it did not open and no knock came, Merry crept a little closer, finding her ring with her knee in the process. After a moment or two, Merry realised that Rafe was pacing in his impatient way, waiting for her to wake up, and a look of unholy glee lit her eyes. It was a small act of mutiny, but Merry skipped back to the bed and climbed inside, intending to stay there as long as she could. As she lay enjoying the moment, it dawned on Merry that by not banging on the door or entering her room, Rafe was showing remarkable restraint. No doubt he was on his best behaviour, trying to demonstrate to her that he was in some respect a model husband.

This illusion was rapidly dispelled when she heard him return and call:

'Merry! Get up, for heaven's sake! Breakfast is laid out and there are the most delicious sausages!'

Then to prove his point, he took one of the sausages from the plate that he was wafting back and forth in front of her door, and took a bite, saying rather thickly:

'Mmmm ... delicious! Even better than Mrs Cope's!'

Merry could now detect the tantalising aroma, together with the smell of bacon that was also now emanating from outside her room. Merry's brows twitched together in suspicion and she scampered across the room to pull open the door. There stood Rafe with the sausages, and beside him a long-suffering Brooke, waving a plate of bacon around. Both looked so comic, caught in the act, that Merry could not help but smile, before rapidly schooling her features into a frown of dark disapproval. This was somewhat undermined when she picked up a sausage and proceeded to eat it while berating her husband.

'You wretched man! Can you not let me sleep? Are we all to jump to your tune?' she began, but they really were excellent sausages. 'Damn it! Are there any more? Don't wave them around like that, or they'll get cold. Can you keep them hot for a few minutes more? I can't eat in my nightgown.'

Rafe kept the triumphant smile from his lips, but not his eyes.

'Certainly, but hurry up, there's a good girl. We need to get on the road, if we are to reach the Fall in daylight.'

'You're an unscrupulous scoundrel to use sausages against me.'

'Yes, dear,' he said meekly, as the door slammed in his face. 'You know you shouldn't come to the door in your nightgown, don't you?' he called through the much-painted wood, and then grinned as something hit the door on the other side.

Merry had hurried to get dressed, but as she raked a comb through her tangled curls, her eyes met her reflection in the mirror and her hand halted. In an instant, she was transported back to the first time she had encountered Rafe. Then, as now, he had dissolved her wrath and undermined her thirst for revenge through his infectious humour, and something more ... something harder to place. He seemed to connect with her on a level that no one else did ... not even dear Harry. Merry wondered if it were this odd intimacy that had misled Rafe into thinking she was in love with him and he with her. Shocked and bemused at how easily Rafe's humour weakened her defences and the lowering notion that her frailty in this respect had brought them all to this sad pass, Merry resolved to be on her guard against it. If she could persuade him that there was no such connection, Rafe might consent to an annulment and they might be freed from this awful marriage.

Determined to harden her heart and bring home to Rafe that he had made a terrible mistake in marrying her, Merry walked into the parlour dressed all in black with an extremely frigid air, but her audience was not present. Rafe, anticipating a resurgence of Merry's wrath, had left to see the baggage loaded and the horses put to.

Merry decided to make a start on her campaign during their journey together. But though Rafe longed to spend time with his wife, he knew her likely stratagems, so Merry was disappointed to find that he had elected to ride and that her only companion would be her new maid. Merry had meant to keep this accomplice of Rafe's at a distance, but the Frenchwoman's obvious relish in travelling through a part of the country entirely new to her was infectious. After a little while, Merry thawed and invited the maid to join her on the forward-facing seat, and volunteered some historical insights about the places they passed through. Merry had never had a servant before or even a female friend, and she felt rather boyishly awkward at first, but Chantal did not seem to notice, so Merry was soon chatting away as she might have done with Harry.

They made a few stops, to change the horses and take a brief luncheon, but Rafe drove a relentless pace, and despite the traffic they made excellent time. It was just a quarter past three on the church clock when they pulled into the Red Lion in Mumshall to exchange the team for the final stage.

Up to this point, Rafe had foiled Merry's attempts to place a cool and impenetrable distance between them by failing to respond to her ploys. She was aloof; he kept his distance. She was taciturn; he elicited no responses. Far from being cast down by her coldness, Rafe himself seemed frustratingly elusive and uncommunicative. Merry was not only thwarted in her purpose to alienate him, but even found herself wondering how she might gain *his* attention. Her attempts to catch his eye failed. So mortifyingly, Merry was obliged to initiate conversation, only to be rebuffed with monosyllabic responses or brief non-sequiturs.

Merry began to wonder if, having achieved his goal, Rafe's ardour was now starting to cool. This notion ought to have filled her with delight but, perversely, she felt oddly hollow and a little anxious.

Would Rafe now abandon her at his country seat and leave for the continent without her? Would she be left alone again?

So it was with a rather contrary sense of relief that she greeted a change in the arrangements at Mumshall. As the jingle of harness and clatter of hooves signalled the switch of horses, Rafe pulled open the carriage door and addressed the maid.

'Mademoiselle, I believe Brooke would welcome your company for this last stage, if you would care to join him on the box,' he said, although it was implicit that it was not a matter of choice.

As Chantal stepped down, not unwillingly, for it was a bright, warm afternoon and the views were even better on the box, Rafe took her place beside his wife.

Merry was amazed at how his presence seemed to fill the carriage with a kind of masculine energy that was oddly exciting and yet, though he was the greatest threat to her present happiness, made her feel somehow safe.

Rafe noted the thoughtful frown furrowing his wife's brow and longed to know the cause, but he was playing a game at which he was rather adept, so he said nothing, but merely turned away from her to watch his hired saddle horse walked away towards the stables.

Merry was in a quandary. Unsettled by her earlier concerns that Rafe's interest in her was waning, yet still bent on securing her release from their marriage contract, she sought desperately for a conversational gambit that might address both needs.

'So you have recalled my existence then, my lord?' she said, aiming to sound haughty but instead sounding abominably petulant even to her own ears.

'Hm? What was that, my dear?' asked Rafe rather absently, as if his attention had been entirely elsewhere, rather than exclusively focused on the thrill of being alone at last with his new wife.

Merry was obliged to repeat her pathetic comment, in a flat tone, wishing heartily that she had not spoken.

'My apologies, Merry,' said Rafe, all solicitude. 'I had no notion that you might miss, or indeed even welcome, my company.'

Merry choked.

'That's not what I meant … I … I ..,' stammered Merry hotly.

'You..?' prompted Rafe gently, his eyes soft with apparent concern.

'I … oh, nothing,' she finished miserably. Her plan was not going well at all.

'Please tell me. I fear my absence from your side has offended you,' he said sympathetically. 'Not a very good start for a husband to neglect his new wife so?'

'No, … I mean … well, it didn't seem very …' stumbled Merry, then she reached for a little of her former mettle. 'But I didn't care a rush anyway.'

'But it seems that you did, Merry,' said Rafe with maddening tenacity.

Merry huffed in frustration as she tried to rally her wits.

'No. It was just that you seemed so very ardent before we were married, but today you seem … er … indifferent, and I wondered if this signified that you had thought better of our disastrous union?' Merry sighed with relieved satisfaction, certain that she had regained the conversational upper hand.

'So you would like me to be more ardent?' said Rafe eagerly, taking her hand in his and lifting it to his lips.

'What!!' cried Merry, feeling rock turn to quicksand beneath her feet. 'No, I didn't mean that at all!'

'But you said …' began Rafe, a confused frown clouding his cobalt eyes.

'I know what I said,' said Merry looking down in bemused consternation. 'But you seem to twist my words to ... Oh!'

Suddenly, Merry's head whipped round to look at him with an expression of incredulous accusation.

'You wretch!' she cried, eyeing Rafe with lively suspicion. 'You have been toying with me the whole time!'

Rafe's eyes glinted with appreciation. *His clever girl!* But he did not acknowledge it.

'But what do you mean? How have I toyed with you?' asked Rafe, with the air of a perplexed man.

'You avoided me at breakfast!'

'Did you miss me?'

'No, certainly not!'

'Then how did my absence displease you ... or "toy" with you, as you put it?'

'Because I ...' Merry ground to a vexed halt.

'You...?'

Merry stared at him, unholy comprehension beginning to dawn.

'Then you didn't travel with me, or speak to me for almost the whole journey!'

'Did you miss my company or conversation, Merry?'

'No, you devil! You know perfectly well why I am as mad as fire!' she snapped.

Her furious grey eyes locked with his innocent-looking blue ones, which slowly began to look much less innocent as the gleam of knowing humour began to kindle in their depths.

'But why, Merry? Pray enlighten me!' he said silkily, his face just inches away from his wife's.

'Because I wanted to punish you, you scoundrel!' she hissed. 'I wanted you to see that we are not so close in spirit as you seem to think!'

'But only see the consequence, Merry,' said Rafe, all pretence gone and an edge of steel in his voice. 'I have proven the opposite to be true. I know you! None better. So be warned! Do not attempt to play off your tricks on me, for I have some tricks of my own,' he said as Merry turned away from him in thwarted fury. 'Reconcile yourself to our union, my beloved. I am as ardent for you as ever and there is no danger - or hope, if that is how you wish to perceive it - of my love abating. There will be *no annulment*.'

'We shall see,' muttered Merry darkly. 'I shall never love you, Rafe. Never! How long before you tire of your unrequited passion, I wonder?'

It was Rafe's turn to look away.

'Merry, at least accept the benefits of your new position,' said Rafe finally. 'Look out of the window. We have been on our own land for the last mile.'

Merry's eyes opened wide at that, first flying to Rafe's face half turned towards her, and then to the window, taking in the cottages of the village they were passing through and the rich farmland beyond.

Villagers began to recognise Brooke and speculate that the coach might be bearing Lord Rothsea. They began to touch their caps smilingly and children broke into a run along the road cheering and waving to Rafe, despite their parents' admonishments.

Astonished, Merry could not help turning to see Rafe's reaction to this adulation. He was smiling and waving back at the children, to their obvious delight. Rafe was clearly a very popular landlord and Merry could not help but be curious and a little impressed, though she said nothing at first.

But as they passed through two more hamlets and then another village, the reaction was much the same and, her earlier anger long since cooled, Merry was moved to say:

'They truly like you! That is unusual, surely … I mean for tenants to be so fond of their landlord?'

'That rather depends on how bad the previous landlord was,' said Rafe.

'You have not always lived here,' Merry remembered.

'No, I was born at Twelveoaks, my father's estate,' he said. 'I won the Fall in a card game over four years ago. It was in a parlous state … the house, the farmland, and worst of all, the tenants' cottages,' he said. 'I suppose I could have sold it, but I decided instead to try to restore it to prosperity. I extended it quite a bit when some of the adjoining lands became available.'

He seemed a little shy talking about it, and Merry couldn't help warming to him for it.

'That must have been terribly expensive,' she said.

'Land is a long-term investment, Merry, as are people,' Rafe replied. 'I brought in a new steward to ensure the land was improved and farmed efficiently. Then we used the profits to repair the cottages. We have not completed them all, but after so many years of neglect, the tenants seem patient in the knowledge that their homes will be restored as soon as they can be.' Then he added with a wry smile: 'I suspect the fact that I reduced the rents, which were scandalous, and stipulated that tenants should not pay rent until their homes were fully repaired has rather encouraged their patience. But I must assume they are happier, as the farm yields have more than doubled in the last two years alone, and I have more applicants than I can give work or house.'

'I see,' said Merry quietly, looking into Rafe's eyes for a long moment, her brow furrowed a little. It was hard to reconcile this admirable conduct with Rafe's scandalous abduction of her, or of her notions of his character. It seemed that Rafe was not the irresponsible, aristocratic ne'er-do-well that she had imagined – almost the reverse, it seemed. Merry had considerable experience of landlords, and none had shown half the compassion for his tenants that Rafe had done. Most, like Mr Jenkins, bled their tenants as dry as they dare, and if they made improvements, it was only with a view to raising rents or evicting old tenants for new.

'Oh dear,' said Rafe ruefully, seeing Merry's slightly distracted expression. 'Am I talking too much? I'm sorry to bore you with such dull stuff.'

'No, no,' said Merry quickly. 'It is very interesting. Indeed, I should like to know more, really I would.'

Rafe waited, his steady regard forcing her to continue.

'Oh, I confess I was surprised at your actions, that's all,' explained Merry reluctantly.

Rafe sighed. Leaning forward, his elbows on his knees, he looked down at his clasped hands in silence for a moment.

Merry watched his handsome profile with a bemused expression, wondering what he was thinking. It was staggering to grasp that this enigmatic man was now her husband. Merry had only just, reluctantly, come to terms with being a female, and now she was *married* - bound forever to a man she didn't really know at all. Those carefree weeks of easy camaraderie at Quemerford had been one of the happiest times of her life, and now it was all at an end. Their relationship was altered. Heartsick, Merry wept inwardly for the loss of her wonderful, maddening friend Rafe.

He turned to look at her.

'I am not a complete monster, Merry,' he said quietly. 'You know that don't you?'

'Yes,' she whispered. 'Of course I do. But you *have* done monstrous things, Rafe … unforgivable things … and, … oh, I miss my friend!' Merry's voice broke a little as she finished gruffly.

'Harry?' sighed Rafe bitterly.

'No, *you*, you idiot!' she exclaimed, her voice hoarse with emotion.

'But I'm right here, Merry!' he said, taking her hand. 'I haven't changed.'

'*Everything* has changed, and you have changed it!' she cried, wresting her hand free.

Rafe bit his lip. It was torture to see his darling so tormented, and to know that he was her tormentor. He longed to reach out and wrap his arms around her.

'I know, my love. I know,' he murmured soothingly.

'Don't call me that!' she moaned as if in pain and twisting round to turn away from him. His caressing voice was seeping through her defences, 'puzzling her will' as it had all those weeks ago in Albemarle Street.

But Rafe continued doggedly.

'But some changes can be for the best,' he said.

'Not this one, Rafe. Not this one,' Merry whispered, her voice choked by emotion. 'You have broken us all apart.'

'We would have broken apart either way, Merry,' said Rafe. 'Would you have rejoiced to see *me* heartbroken? To see me tear myself apart or do my best to widow you? Would you?'

'No,' she admitted wretchedly. 'But you had no right to …'

'I know,' he interrupted. 'But what else could I do?'

'You could have put my wishes above your own,' said Merry, turning to glare reprovingly at Rafe.

'Well, I chose to put your *needs* above your wishes, Merry,' he replied, longing to kiss the lips that were parting in outrage so close to his own.

'*My* needs! *Your* needs, more like!' cried Merry, her eyes blazing once more.

'*Our* needs then, but not mine alone,' he ground out, clenching his fists to stop himself from reaching out and pulling her into his arms as he ached to do.

'So you presume to know my heart better than I do?' she demanded.

'Yes!' he said, turning to her, his eyes glowing in a way that made her heart lurch disturbingly. 'Don't tempt me to prove it, Merry, for I could in an instant. But I made you a promise, and I will keep it though it kills me.'

'What! Do you think that one kiss will turn me into a doting wife?' cried Merry incredulously. 'Huh! You are utterly deluded!'

Rafe turned towards her, his face just inches from hers.

'Would you care to put my theory to the test?' he murmured, with a sultry look at her lips.

'Absolutely not!' snapped Merry, turning away from him, alarmed at the way her heart was thumping. 'And not because I have any fears for myself, I assure you! It would simply be wrong to encourage a lunatic in his delusion.'

'Hah! Coward!'

'I am no such thing! I am merely holding you to your promise. I can perfectly understand why *that* might pinch you.'

Rafe gritted his teeth at that gibe, the more maddening for being deserved.

Suddenly, the coach slowed and then turned sharply left, pausing in front of a grand, wrought-iron gate. A beaming gatekeeper came dashing out to open them, and stood to the side waving his cap as the coach moved forward through a wooded area that shrouded the grounds from public view.

'Damn it!' said Rafe, sounding more frustrated than angry. Reaching up, he rapped on the roof of the carriage, which quickly drew to a halt.

Dropping the window, he called out to Brooke: 'We will walk for a spell.'

Brooke climbed down to open the door and let down the step. As Rafe put out his hand to help his wife down, his brows twitched together in concern.

'Will you be warm enough?' he asked.

'Yes, of course,' she said, looking past him to the wood for an explanation for his unexpected decision. It was rather pretty, dappled with spring sunshine and carpeted with a haze of budding bluebells, but there was no building in sight.

Rafe was giving instructions to Brooke.

'Go on to the house and have Frith muster the servants, then come back and meet us at the turn by the lake.'

The coach clattered away leaving them standing alone in the driveway, with trees arching cathedral-like high above their heads. Merry stood with her arms folded in an unconsciously boyish stance, an open look of curiosity on her face. Rafe seemed oddly ill at ease, almost embarrassed, and Merry was intrigued. *Why on earth had he decided they should walk?*

Rafe stood looking at his lovely wife, her skin almost luminous in the dappled light and her golden hair glowing like a halo against the severe black velvet of her soft, low-crowned bonnet. He wondered if he had made a terrible mistake bringing her here so soon after their forced marriage. Rafe was truly passionate about this place. He had put so much into reclaiming and restoring it that it felt as though he had almost created it, and despite the risk of arrest, he had wanted to share it with his beloved Merry as soon as he might. Laying it before her was like laying his heart at her feet, if she only knew it. If Merry hated it, she would effectively trample him.

The last thing he had wanted was to be locked in fierce argument with her when she first saw the house and grounds. Still less did he want her to meet the household, who were like family to him, with her eyes blazing with wrath.

Leaving the coach had certainly halted their quarrel, but now Rafe was momentarily at a loss.

After a few moments, Merry spoke with the hint of a puzzled smile trembling at the corner of her mouth.

'So you wish us to walk?' she prompted.

Rafe's brows twitched together as if he, too, was surprised.

'Yes,' he said hesitantly. 'I … I thought you might appreciate the fresh air,' he lied.

Merry's ironical smile surfaced. She didn't know why, but Rafe was lying and he was definitely ill at ease. Merry was starting to enjoy herself.

They still had not moved.

'Is it far?' she enquired politely.

'Ah, yes,' said Rafe, with a sudden glance down at Merry's dainty kid boots.

'Then had we not better get started?' she ventured, her eyebrows raised and her head leaning in mute invitation.

'Yes,' he said reluctantly, and then said suddenly: 'Merry, please don't let your dislike of me prejudice you against this place. It is your home. Please remember that. Anything may be changed if you do not like it, of course, but … well, I hope you like it, that's all.'

He turned to walk, but felt Merry catch his sleeve.

'Rafe,' she said in alarm. 'Why on earth did you marry me if you mean to abandon me here when you depart for exile?'

Rafe turned back to her in surprise.

'What? Wherever did you get that hare-brained notion? I love you, Merry! I will never leave you … here or anywhere else.'

'Then why have we come here?' she asked with a puzzled frown. 'Surely there is a risk that the Runners will come here looking for you.'

'Yes,' admitted Rafe. 'But some things are worth the risk. Come and see your new home,' he added, taking her unresisting hand and drawing her forward at last. 'We can leave in a couple of days. No one here or in our demesne will betray us, I promise.'

Merry allowed herself to be towed forward. She was curious to see the house, expecting something a little like the hunting box in Quemerford. It was clear that Rafe was much attached to the place, and remembering how much she had loved how he had decorated his London house, Merry now secretly longed to see what his country home looked like.

'This wood is called Iron Gates, not very originally,' he said with a grin. It extends for about a mile in each direction with a stone wall at its boundary with the road.'

Merry stopped in her tracks, dragging Rafe to a halt.

'Two miles!' she gasped. 'Two miles of woods, and still inside the property!'

'The parkland around the house is quite extensive,' said Rafe with a smile lurking behind his lowered lashes. 'Come on, let me show you!'

This time he was genuinely towing Merry, whose face now wore an expression of dawning alarm.

'In another week or so, the ground here will be a vision of bluebells,' he said, his heart lifting as he saw the edge of the wood up ahead, where the trees thinned out and gave the first vista of Seaton Fall.

Rafe turned to Merry his eyes alight with the giddy excitement bubbling up inside him.

'Race you!' he grinned and started to run.

Merry stared in astonishment for a moment, and then pelted full tilt after him, picking up her skirts in a scandalously unladylike way and shouting in laughing outrage at the head-start Rafe had given himself. She only gained on him when he slowed down as he reached the edge of the woods. Despite herself, Merry was elated by their madcap run and was about to berate Rafe for gaining an unfair advantage, when she suddenly saw the view open up before her, and gasped.

As with Rafe's library in Albemarle Street, if Merry were to frame her most perfect vision of a gentleman's country estate, this would be it. Her eyes pricked with tears. It was so beautiful she could not speak. Gently undulating grassland stretched into the distance to meet wooded parkland on the far horizon. The vast lawns were punctuated with occasional trees perfectly positioned, as if by divine hand, to lead the eye and frame flawless views. The sunshine picked out the dazzling fleeces of new lambs scampering playfully as their mothers grazed the lush spring grass, and in the distance, a few brave deer at the edge of a far wood were nibbling at the fresh new growth. To her right, was a long lake, sunlight skittering across its surface, where swans swam elegantly or shook out their feathers and pecked at the foliage by the folly at its edge. A boat lay tethered invitingly at the other end, gently swaying with the current. But then her eye was drawn to the house and Merry felt her heart squeeze with a strange tug of emotion, as if it called to her like a long-lost friend.

Though many times larger than the hunting lodge, it was not intimidating in appearance. It was built of warm straw-coloured stone and had beautiful curved wings, filled with long windows, that reached out from the main building as if inviting an embrace.

Below and to the sides of this lovely building, cultivated gardens radiated out and were already dotted with early colour.

Rafe saw awe illuminate Merry's expressive face and ached with grateful happiness. He moved to stand at her shoulder, wishing he could hold her tight as they shared this moment.

'You are mistress of all you survey, my darling,' he murmured in her ear, his voice a little unsteady.

Mistress!

Her still-glistening eyes flew to Rafe's in alarm.

If Merry had been in any doubt before that the role of Rafe's wife would demean or bore her, it evaporated in that instant. Merry had not seriously bent her imagination to what Rafe's country establishment might be like, nor what her role as Rafe's wife might entail, but now the responsibility of playing a leading role in the preservation of this heavenly place overwhelmed her.

'What is it?' asked Rafe anxiously, taking Merry's shoulders.

'I… I can't!' exclaimed Merry.

'What do you mean?' he demanded, his face a picture of hurt dismay.

'I've no idea what to do!' she cried, twisting her hands together and endangering the fine stitching of her black kid gloves. 'What if I make a mull of it?'

Rafe was so relieved that he did not resist as she pulled free of him and began pacing wretchedly before him.

'Oh, Rafe, you impossible man! You should have married a lady – one who could have done this place justice,' she moaned unhappily. 'How just like you, you contrary thing, to pick a little scrub like me, who has no clue at all about anything, and marry out of hand with no thought at all for the consequences. I feel about mouse-high, I can tell you!'

Merry's feverish rant was arrested by the sound of a chuckle from Rafe, who was watching her with a glow in his eyes and a slow smile curving his handsome mouth.

'Oh!' she exclaimed in righteous indignation. 'That's it, you irresponsible monkey! Make game of me, though I am the only one making the least push to do duty by this lovely place.'

'"Little scrub" indeed! You *are* a lady, Merry,' said Rafe. 'You are a gentleman's daughter, and the bravest, loveliest and most intelligent lady I have ever met, though you have by far the worst temper, I'll allow you that flaw!'

'Huh! Very funny!' countered Merry. 'I may be a gentleman's daughter, but I was raised as his son.'

'That's as may be, Merry, but you have held your own against highwaymen and the worst that London has to offer. You are equal to anything,' said Rafe warmly. 'Besides, what on earth do you think you will have to do that is so beyond you? You're not expected to scythe the lawns or clean the bedchambers, you know.'

'I don't know *what* is expected of me. That is the point.'

'Well, I will help you learn, of course,' said Rafe. 'But the household runs the place very well without us. I haven't been here since February. Has the estate fallen into ruin in my absence?'

'Don't try to fob me off,' she replied doggedly. 'Oh, Rafe, surely you must see that I am not at all the wife for you?'

'Merry!' snapped Rafe, his stern gaze compelling her attention as he raised an admonitory finger before her face. 'That is one thing I will *not* allow! You are not to speak of such things in the hearing of the servants. No talk of annulments, or the circumstances attending our marriage either. Abuse me in private, if you must, but I will not have our household upset by our personal bickering. Do you understand?'

Merry looked mulish but nodded curtly.

'You don't want them to think ill of you?' she remarked churlishly.

'I don't want them to be made uncomfortable,' he corrected. 'I have some experience of what it is to live in an unhappy household, and how discord can contaminate the lives of all within its orbit,' he explained. 'We set the tone, Merry. If we are publicly at odds, our staff will feel the brunt.'

Merry looked abashed and seeing her downturned gaze, Rafe softened.

'I may be an "irresponsible monkey" in a thousand other ways, my adorable "little scrub",' he quipped, seeing a naughty grin pull up Merry's mouth and a twinkle light her eyes. 'But in this respect, I hope I am not an entirely lost cause. One part of your role as mistress of the house will be to share my responsibility for the welfare of all the people who work for us or live on our land. They had a pretty torrid time of it with their last master. Now that their fortunes have turned around, I should like this happier trend to continue. Will you help me, Merry?'

Merry's brow furrowed slightly. Rafe made it all seem so reasonable, even beguiling, that she felt herself falling in with his plans.

'I will try, Rafe, publicly at least,' she said. 'But don't take this concession to mean that I am reconciled to our marriage, nor the way it was brought about, for I am not. I tell you in the spirit of fair play that I mean to do all I can to make you see that we are ill-matched and that you should release me from our marriage contract.'

Rafe sighed but nodded.

Time, he thought. *Time and the Fall will bring her to me.*

'Understood,' he said. 'But in the interests of fair play, Merry, I mean to do all that I can do to woo you and have you see that we were made for one another.'

The combatants exchanged a glinting, martial look.

'Now, come and meet your household, my lady,' said Rafe, holding out his arm to escort her. 'They will be agog to meet you.'

'They will think me a pretty poor thing,' sighed Merry dismally, absently placing her hand on Rafe's arm as he had taught her at Quemerford.

'They will adore you,' said Rafe. 'You are the lady who has made their master the happiest man on earth.'

'Oh, Rafe,' said Merry shaking her head. 'You do talk such fustian sometimes.'

Rafe merely smiled, and began pointing out places where trees had been removed to open up the views, or more had been planted to enhance the setting. Merry's boyish curiosity could not help but be engaged, and she was soon asking questions about the other improvements he had mentioned in the coach.

'I can show you the plans and accounts sometime, if you wish?' suggested Rafe.

'I should like that,' Merry replied.

'I am improving a couple of other properties in a similar way …' he began.

'Good God!' gasped Merry. 'How many properties do you own?'

THE RELUCTANT LADY

'Several ... and it's "we", Merry,' he said, as they reached the carriage.

'We?' she repeated, with a puzzled expression.

'_We_ own them,' he said, helping her into the carriage, as Brooke held the door open.

Merry looked a little dazed. She had once dreamed of buying a cottage, and now this veritable Eden and more besides were seemingly at her disposal. But then her brows twitched together as he took his seat beside her and the carriage moved forward.

'You know that is not true, Rafe,' she said sadly. 'As your wife, I am just another addition to your property.'

'Not to me, Merry,' said Rafe. 'I intend to have my man of business put all the unentailed properties into both our names, so that you will inherit, if anything should happen to me.'

Merry looked at him dumbfounded.

'Or will that only give you an even greater incentive to stab me in my sleep?' he said provocatively, nudging her shoulder with his.

Merry choked, remembering her threat of the night before. She had meant it at the time, but now it seemed ludicrous. How quickly he had undermined her wrath again. She looked at him with a kind of baffled wonder, as he met her gaze, biting his lip at his folly in reminding her of the night before.

'"_Puzzles the will_"?' he volunteered ruefully.

Merry only nodded, her eyes narrowed, trying to define how he worked this strange magic.

'I keep giving you reasons to thirst for my blood, then the next moment I tease you out of your vengeful purpose?'

'Yes,' gasped Merry. 'How do you _do_ that?'

'Have you ever asked yourself how that might be, Merry?' he asked quietly.

'Again and again,' she replied.

'And you can find no answer?' he prompted.

'None, except perhaps your sense of humour.'

'Which is so closely attuned with your own?'

'Yes.'

'Perhaps, Merry, you might consider that more than our humour is closely attuned?'

Merry was spared from answering as they began to approach the house and Rafe turned to inspect his bride, straightening her hat and scarf a little.

'How in heaven's name did you manage to lose a button?' he said.

Merry looked down in dismay at the empty buttonhole on her pelisse.

'I think it must have come off when we were running,' she said with a frown.

'Ah, yes. Sorry about that,' said Rafe, with an apologetic smile.

'Don't be. I enjoyed it,' she said twinkling. 'I haven't run for ages … well, not for fun, anyway.'

Rafe's eyes flickered closed for an instant, as he thought of the times she must have run out of fear. It made him want to hug her hard, but the carriage had pulled up in front of the house, and the steps were being let down..

Chapter Sixteen
An Uneasy Truce

Rafe quickly descended and proudly handed down his blushing bride in front of the outside staff, who were gathered on each side of the shallow steps at the front of the grand portico.

Though Merry was too dazed to appreciate it, the head groom and his stable hands stood to one side and the head gardener and his men to the other.

'Hello, everyone,' said Rafe, a broad grin on his face. 'This is Lady Rothsea.'

Rafe's delight was infectious, and though no one later knew how it happened, a cheer went up, which only ceased when Frith the butler walked forward, disapproval in every step. Merry smiled and lifted her hand in a nervous wave to acknowledge the enthusiastic welcome.

'Hallo, Frith,' said Rafe, shaking his butler's hand in a very informal way. 'My dear,' he said turning to Merry. 'May I introduce you to our excellent butler Frith?'

'Hallo Frith,' said Merry, who then surprised the poor fellow by shaking his hand just as firmly as her husband had done.

Frith bowed, bestowing a smile reserved exclusively for his lordship and now, too, for his lady.

'Welcome, Lady Rothsea. I hope you will find everything to your liking. I have taken the liberty of gathering the household staff in the rotunda, if you would care to follow me.'

'Thank you,' said Merry, wishing she could run in the opposite direction.

'Welcome to your new home, Merry,' murmured Rafe in her ear as he took her hand and laid it on his arm. But then, as they approached the large double doors, Rafe suddenly lifted Merry up in his arms.

'Rafe!' she gasped. 'What are you doing?'

'It is said to bring good luck, and I need all I can get,' he replied stepping over the threshold and placing his wife back on her feet.

'Well, don't rip up at me if I've lost another button,' she said, straightening her back and lifting her chin as she gathered her courage.

They were in a very large hallway with doors leading off on both sides and two elegant curved staircases on either side of a wide archway, through which Merry could spy a large, round room full of people. She fought a strong urge to bolt and was almost glad of the feel of Rafe's hand at the small of her back guiding her forward towards them.

The room alone was enough to make her gape. A huge space brightly lit from above by natural light streaming through a round domed glass roof.

'Oh!' she gasped with delight, seeing the blue spring sky above her head. This brought smiles to many of the faces lined up to meet her. The rotunda had been transformed from the grimy, puddled room, with water dripping through broken dirty glass, into a bright, glorious space, filled with fine statues and delicate palms, and which lifted the spirits of all who passed through it.

Merry was introduced to Mrs Dodd, the housekeeper, and the rest of the main staff, until her head was swimming in names. Rafe appeared to know everyone well enough to make personal references.

'Ah, Henry,' he said to one of the footmen. 'Did you get that tooth pulled in the end?'

'No, my lord,' he confessed. 'Cook ... Mrs Greaves, that is ... gave me some tincture of cloves, which settled it right down.'

'I'm glad to hear it,' Rafe replied, moving on.

At the end of the introductions, Rafe followed as Mrs Dodd led Merry to her room so that she could change for dinner, which had been put back until seven, just over an hour away.

Merry thanked the housekeeper and agreed to call for her in the morning to be shown around the house.

'That was terrifying,' she confessed in a whisper, when the housekeeper was out of sight.

'You did wonderfully,' said Rafe.

'Wretch!' she said, seeing him smile. 'Where is your room?'

'Next door,' he said. 'We have a connecting door, if you should ever feel inclined to use it.'

'Just be certain that *you* never feel inclined to use it!' she warned, waving her finger at him.

Rafe smiled again.

'How will I find the dining room?' demanded Merry, in a panic.

'I will escort you to the drawing room, and thence down to the dining room, when Frith comes to announce dinner.'

'Oh, right, then,' she said. 'I had better hop off and get changed.'

'Can you be ready in an hour?'

'I can be ready in ten minutes,' said Merry, with a frown.

'Take an hour,' recommended Rafe. 'I shall certainly do so.'

'Popinjay!' she called in a loud whisper to his back, as he walked off towards his room, and then seeing his shoulders shake as he chuckled, she entered her own room with a satisfied grin on her face.

Merry found Chantal waiting for her with cans of hot water, ready to draw her bath in her dressing room. Still delighting in the luxury of having baths whenever she wished, which had been her chief indulgence at Quemerford, Merry was now glad of the hour. It was only when she realised that Chantal meant to remain in the room while she was bathing that there was a departure from this happy state. After a few moments, Chantal found herself propelled out of the dressing room by her hotly blushing mistress and the door locked behind her.

'But my lady, who will wash your hair?' called Chantal.

'I will,' replied Merry categorically, but then she added magnanimously: 'But you can help me dry it, if you like?'

Of a certainty, thought Chantal with a smile, it would be a novel experience being lady's maid to such an unconventional lady.

Good as his word, Rafe tapped on Merry's door an hour later to escort his wife to dinner. His mouth went dry as he saw her standing in the doorway in a low-cut gown of glowing black velvet, the snug-fitting bodice glittering with delicate jet beading, echoed by the long black spangled scarf draped over her elbows. A shallow jet tiara sparkled amidst her slightly damp tawny curls and at her throat were the pearls he had bought as her betrothal gift. Rafe realised it was the first time he had seen Merry's creamy, pale-gold skin entirely free of bruises. His wife's grey eyes were wide with anxiety, but she looked perfectly radiant and utterly desirable.

Merry looked past him down the corridor, to check that no servants were about, before folding her black-gloved arms in frowning disapproval.

'I suppose you're responsible for this?' she said accusingly, her cheeks becomingly flushed as she nodded down indicatively at the tantalising display of cleavage revealed by the gown's design.

'I think Nature is responsible for that,' replied Rafe, mirroring her indicative nod with wry smile. 'And for that and your many other blessings I give heartfelt thanks.'

'Rafe, you rogue! Be serious for a moment!' said Merry, glaring at him. 'Did _you_ choose the design for this gown?'

'I did, yes.'

'Are they all as … as …'

'Delightful?' offered Rafe.

'Scandalous,' corrected Merry.

'Merry!' exclaimed Rafe, his expression one of offended innocence. 'That's not at all scandalous! Well, not compared to some I have seen, and in the best houses, at that!'

'Rafe Wolvenden, I should be very much surprised if you are even admitted into the _best_ houses,' said Merry sardonically, looking him in the eye, before turning to walk up the corridor, adding, in a smug undertone: 'Well, not by the _front_ door, at all events!'

'I heard that!' he said, his lips twitching as he strode behind her.

Dinner was a rather intimidating affair for Merry, though no one but Rafe could discern any sign of it in her manner.

They were seated at either end of a highly polished dining table, which had had most of its leaves removed to create an intimate surface a mere sixteen feet long. This was decorated with two branches of candles and a large silver epergne filled with early roses from the hot-house. Merry could only dimly make out through the bright haze of the candles that Rafe was still in the room.

When Rafe attempted to make conversation, Merry leaned over to the side and gave him an incredulous, quizzing look that eloquently expressed that she thought him a zany for trying to converse at such a distance. After the first remove, Merry leaned over and mouthed: 'This is ridiculous', and Rafe mimicked her earlier quizzing expression, making Merry giggle despite herself.

The household was quickly gathering that the new Lady Rothsea was not quite like the other ladies of quality that they had encountered. Though no one would dream of disparaging her, they could not help but note that she had a rather informal style, a very mannish walk and her behaviour towards her doting husband was far from adoring, or even affectionate. When Rafe dismissed all the staff from the dining room, with the barest flicker of a glance towards Frith, they all to a man longed to be invisible and remain, but they filed out obediently, as if they normally did so at this point in every meal.

Rafe got up and walked across to his wife, who watched his approach with trepidation.

'Did I do something wrong?' she whispered.

'No, and there's no need to whisper. We are alone,' he said, momentarily savouring the sight of his wife presiding at his table. 'Why don't you come and sit next to me, so that we can converse more easily.'

'Is that where I would normally sit, as mistress of the house?' asked Merry, knowing very well that her place would not have been laid at the end of the table if that had been the case.

Rafe bit the inside of his lip, as truth wrestled with his personal preference. Honesty won.

'No,' he admitted.

'Well, how the devil am I to learn how to go on, and maintain this pretence, if you keep breaking the rules?'

'I thought you might like to sit beside me,' he said quietly.

Given the odd feeling that stirred in her whenever he looked at her that way, Merry was very sure that she did *not* want to sit beside him.

'Huh! Acquit me!' she said, in as airy a voice as she could muster. 'I have no wish to promote this folly of yours by encouraging any kind of intimacy, or .. or offering you any opportunity to ogle my chest again for that matter.'

Rafe stood still for a moment looking down at her, reaching for a little patience in his impatient heart.

He leaned a little closer to his wife.

'The word is "bosom", Merry,' he said with an intense look that made Merry feel hot and flustered. 'Or "breasts" if you prefer,' he added, a glint in his eyes, as Merry clapped her hands to her ears and stared at him in scandalised alarm.

She glared at him as he walked across the room to reach for the bell pull.

'And don't say "devil",' he added, as he gave it a light tug.

'But then how am I to give you your proper name?' she countered saucily.

'You could try "my love" or "dearest",' suggested Rafe, returning her banter. 'I'd settle for "husband", if you could manage that,' he added, *sotto voce,* as he sat.

Merry popped up from her chair like a rabbit, with a ready insult on her lips, but Frith entered the room leading the footmen bearing dishes, so she sank demurely back into her seat.

At the end of dinner, as Frith stood holding a bottle of port, ready to serve his lordship, Merry remembered her training and stood to retire to the drawing room. She could not forbear a longing look at the ruby red liquid before she left, throwing Rafe a significant look eloquent of her sense of misuse. There was a lurking humour in his eyes as he bowed her out of the room.

Henry the footman was waiting to escort her to the drawing room, where Merry realised she was expected to sit in lone state, until her lord and master had finished enjoying his port.

Merry strolled about the room for a few minutes and rapidly appreciated that this was not a room regularly frequented by Rafe. It was elegantly furnished, in excellent taste, but had none of the fascinating *objets* or distinctive works of art that characterised his favourite rooms. After another few minutes of looking into empty drawers, walking her fingers along the wide marble mantel and plinking a few of the piano keys, Merry was heartily bored and decided to go exploring.

As she stepped out of the room, she was startled to find Henry, standing like a sentry to the side of the doorway.

'Good heavens!' said Merry, in her surprise. 'Whatever are you doing there?'

Henry blushed, stunned at being addressed so informally.

'Er ... er... awaiting your orders, my lady,' he stammered.

'Oh,' she said, thinking it a scandalous waste of a man's time. 'Then perhaps you could show me where the library is?' she suggested. 'Lord Rothsea does have a library here, doesn't he?'

'Yes, your ladyship,' said Henry, 'A very fine one. If you would follow me.' But then the poor footman was unnerved once more, when her ladyship fell into step beside him with a companionable smile.

When Rafe entered the drawing room some fifteen minutes later, having lingered over his port as long as he could bear, hoping that Merry might have learned to miss him and now be glad of his company, he found the room deserted.

His brows flew together in annoyance and he marched off to her bedchamber to drag her back by her hair if he had to, but Merry was not there either.

A pang of alarm went through him, and he cursed himself for leaving her alone so soon, while escape might still be at the forefront of her mind.

He almost ran to the stairs and startled Frith, though one would not know it, by descending them two at a time.

'Lady Rothsea ...' Rafe began.

'In the library, I believe, my lord,' said Frith.

Frith learned something, as he watched his lordship's body sag perceptibly with relief and the sharp lines of concern on his face relax. It confirmed his suspicions that there was a mystery attending his master's marriage.

'The library,' echoed Rafe. 'Of course.'

He then headed off towards this very predictable destination in search of his wife, a little vexed that while he had been missing her company intensely as he sat alone with his port, Merry had probably not missed him one whit as she rooted happily through his books. As he approached the room, he was a fair way towards to calming himself and restoring his determination to give Merry time to accept their marriage and eventually to cleave to him, as he fervently hoped she would. This resolve went up in flames when he heard voices through the half-open door. Merry's was saying, in the friendliest tone possible: 'Well, I'd recommend *Waverley* over *Rob Roy*, but I think you would enjoy either story. Shall I see if I can find them for you?'

Stepping into the room, his jealous temper flaring irrationally, Rafe saw that Henry was the object of Merry's kind attentiveness. Though elusive and fractious with her husband, with the footman it seemed his wife was all warmth and smiles. Rafe was about to give vent to his irritation, but when Henry turned towards him with the strained expression of a trapped man, his annoyance was dispelled by a sympathetic chuckle.

Taking his lordship's entrance as an opportunity to make his escape, Henry heard Lord Rothsea follow him to the door.

'Henry,' he murmured, as the footman turned to close the door behind him. 'Lady Rothsea is Welsh.'

'Ah! Yes, my lord,' said Henry, with a relieved bow, as if this now adequately explained any form of aberrant behaviour that her ladyship might display.

Turning back to his wife, who wore a rather forbidding frown of annoyance at having her charitable endeavour so rudely interrupted, Rafe's eyes narrowed in humorous speculation as he wondered how to handle this new situation.

'You scared him away!' said Merry.

'No, *you* scared him away,' corrected Rafe, walking towards a tray of decanters and glasses.

'We were getting on famously,' she protested. 'Until you walked in.'

'I doubt that he would see it quite that way.'

'What do you mean?' said Merry, a little hurt.

'They have their world and we have ours,' said Rafe. 'The two don't mix.'

'Snob!'

'I assure you the snobbery exists on both sides,' said Rafe. 'They no more want to us to try to be their particular friends than we want them to be ours. There is a distance, mutually respected, between our worlds. How can I be bosom bows with Alfred and then expect him to remove my chamber pot?'

'But I thought you said we were responsible for their welfare?' said Merry.

'Yes, but there was no need to buttonhole the poor fellow and foist your literary tastes upon him,' he said, his eyes twinkling with humour as he saw her expression darken with ire once again.

'I *"foisted"* nothing!' she exclaimed. 'I only asked him what books he enjoyed and ...'

'And what did he say?' interrupted Rafe, who was standing in front of her holding two glasses of port.

Merry's brow clouded.

'Well, I don't precisely recall ...' she said, thoughtfully. 'But we agreed that Scott was ...' Merry caught sight of Rafe's humorous quizzing look.

'Oh! You... you...'

'Don't say "devil",' he said, face glowing with humour as he held out a glass with a teasing smile.

Merry chuckled reluctantly, accepting the glass.

'Well, perhaps he didn't seem entirely comfortable,' she admitted.

'He was probably terrified,' said Rafe, guiding his wife to a chair by the fire and then sinking into the one opposite.

Merry chuckled again.

'Oh, Rafe,' said Merry leaning back comfortably against the leather back in a highly unladylike way and taking her first satisfying sip of port. 'You do talk some nonsense.'

Rafe merely grinned and watched her looking at the way the firelight illuminated the dark liquid. He couldn't drag his eyes from her.

Merry was lost in her own thoughts, and gazed absently at the fire, its glow reflected in the shimmering jet beads of her gown and headdress.

'Conjuring images in the fire?' Rafe ventured softly, after a few moments.

Merry's eyes flew to his and she coloured faintly as she remembered that night, when she had fallen asleep in his arms. Rafe returned her regard in that steady, compelling way that cut through all her defences. For an instant, their two worlds were one, as he too relived that memory, and they shared a momentary smile of shared recollection. Then Merry blinked and swiftly looked away in mild alarm, as she realised how much she had softened towards him in those moments.

When she looked back at him, his gaze was averted as he contemplated his wine, and Merry wondered if she had imagined that moment of connection.

Recalling his words *"I will do everything in my power to woo you"*, Merry mentally admonished herself for being so easily beguiled. Only a day ago, this man had drugged a glass of wine, much like the one she now held in her hand, and had forced her to marry him with the threat of rape. Yet here they now sat in companionable silence, drinking port in his library. Berating herself for such appalling weakness on her part, Merry determined to restart her own campaign to escape his clutches on the morrow.

As she sipped her wine and tried to formulate ways in which she could baffle her enemy, who was watching her expressive face surreptitiously, Merry's vengeful machinations became ever more tangled with images and memories of the day's events. As she closed her eyes, thinking to clear her head, the jumble conspired with the warmth of the fire and the inner glow from the port to make her drowse. It had been a long day, preceded by an exhausting night, and the drowse soon became a doze, and within a short spell Merry was fast asleep, her empty glass lying loosely grasped in her gloved hands.

Rafe reached forward and carefully plucked the glass from her fingers, and then sat back again. From the moment she had closed her eyes, he had watched intently her slow descent into deep sleep; the way her tense shoulders had gently rounded by degrees; the soft flutter of her eyelids; the rhythmic rise and fall of her breasts in that glittering bodice, as her breathing had deepened; the gradual uncurling of her fingers around the stem of her glass. Savouring every moment, Rafe thought he had never witnessed anything so achingly beautiful, and continued to gaze at his sleeping wife as he sipped his wine and the fire burned itself out.

He had noted her earlier transition from that thrilling moment of intimacy back to her wary, resistant stance. Merry would fight him all the way. If he could only be patient, there was hope, Rafe was sure of it. But patience was not his strong suit.

Eventually, Rafe moved to kneel before her, and could not resist kissing her forehead before gently shaking her upper arm to wake her … to no effect.

'Merry,' he said in her ear, his voice a caress. 'It's time you were in your bed.'

Merry did not stir.

Rafe sat back on his haunches, looking at his wife with a bemused grimace.

'Merry!' he called, so loud that Alfred, the footman standing outside the door for the past hour or more, jolted awake and scratched at the door, asking if his lordship needed anything.

Rafe smiled as he declined assistance. Merry was certainly the heaviest sleeper he had ever encountered. That night in Quemerford, he had been obliged to put her to bed, as he could not rouse her without waking Harry. Picking her up in his strong arms, he made ready to repeat the office. He looked down at her peaceful face, and wondered if he might be featuring in her dreams tonight. Rafe paused for a moment, remembering his promise, but then with a groan, he pressed his sensuous lips to her parted ones, in a tender, if one-sided, kiss.

'Dream of your husband, Merry, as he will dream of you,' he murmured, and then headed to the door.

Alfred betrayed his surprise, momentarily, at the sight of Lord Rothsea carrying her ladyship's lifeless body out of the library.

'It is possible that my conversation is not as scintillating as I thought,' remarked his lordship reflectively, causing the footman's lips to twitch. 'But I am choosing to believe my wife's state to be the result of a long and tiring day,'

'Yes, my lord,' said Alfred, as woodenly as he could.

As Rafe approached Merry's bedchamber, he was sorely tempted to keep walking and carry Merry to his own room. The thought of her waking up in his bed, in his arms, made his heart thump and his loins tighten. Merry had turned towards him, and curled against his chest, as once before, and the feel of it was enough to try the moral resolve of a saint … and Rafe was no saint. But he dared not give Merry any more reason to hate him or doubt his word.

Instead, he laid his wife on her bed, stood for a long moment looking down at her in a way that Chantal would never forget, and departed, leaving the maid to do what she could to undress her mistress.

Instead of returning to the library, Rafe went to his own bedchamber, throwing off his coat and unwinding his cravat as he looked balefully at the connecting door.

How long would it be before the torment of sleeping next door to his very desirable wife, whom he must not touch, overcame him?

He had occupied a chamber near hers at Quemerford without a qualm, but their marriage had changed everything. His body ached for the consummation that would complete their union and bind her to him for life.

Rafe threw himself on the bed, staring unseeing at the canopy above him and tried to distract himself by recalling the events of the past two days. The glow of treasured memories, from their first view of the parkland to the mesmerising delight of watching Merry sleep, lit his face and curved his handsome lips with a slow smile.

Tomorrow would be a new challenge, with Merry, no doubt, determined to annoy him and to pursue, with her customary dogged tenacity, some scheme to secure the annulment she craved. Praying that he would keep his temper and his passion in check for another day, he, too, fell asleep in his clothes.

His valet Lain arrived soon after, tutted at the sight, and began to remove his lordship's shoes and stockings. The knee breeches and waistcoat were a lost cause.

A little before six in the morning, Merry awoke in her chemise and drawers, with only a dim recollection of having fallen asleep by the fire in the library. Her cheeks burned with hot colour at the thought that Rafe might have undressed her once again, until she registered that her velvet gown and her other clothing had been removed and put away. Clearly, Chantal had put her to bed. Nevertheless, it was still worrying to think that Rafe had once again carried her to her bed without troubling himself to simply wake her. Merry knew that she generally slept well, but had no notion that, having grown up living in noisy taverns and boarding houses, she was able to sleep like the dead.

Though a sound sleeper, Merry was not one to lie abed once she had awoken. Merry jumped out of bed and walked across to open the shutters to look out at the view, which, if possible, was even better from this higher perspective than it had been from the driveway. Pushing open the casement and leaning her elbows on the stone mullion, Merry marvelled at the gardens, lawns and sparkling lake in the shallow valley beyond. After the many shades of hell she had experienced in her young life, this was surely the closest she had been to heaven. No sounds but riotous birdsong echoing near and far. No smells but sweet spring flowers and the deeper scent of the earth bursting into life around her. Merry swallowed hard and there was an unwelcome brightness in her eyes as a beguiling voice whispered in her ear.

All this could be yours if you just accept this marriage. There are worse things than being a viscountess … or Rafe's wife, for that matter. You have <u>done</u> worse things to earn your living before now. Accept what you have been given, no matter how it came to you. Be a part of all this beauty…

Long minutes passed before Merry could silence that inner voice and push away from the window and that all-too-enchanting view.

No matter how captivating his possessions, or appealing his humour, Rafe was the same man who had fleeced and killed her brother, cruelly cheated Harry of his bride, and abducted herself, forcing her into marriage with the threat of rape. He used 'love' as an excuse for the latter two sins, as if it placed him in a state of grace. But Merry was certain that Rafe had no more idea what that word meant than she did.

Pique and desire, certainly he knew those two states, but love? No.

And yet … and yet … there had been moments …

But it did no good to dwell on these. It was all part of his insinuating charm that dissolved her wrath and made her warm to him, despite herself.

At this point, Merry shook herself, walked over to the washstand, bowed over the basin and poured the remains of the cold water jug over her head, giving a gasp as the chill hit her skin and trickled down her back. As she stood dripping and shivering a little, Merry gave herself a very stern look in the mirror.

I'm on to you, Merion Griffith, you little worm! Her reflection seemed to say - her stronger self to the weaker one. *Don't you dare give in!*

Merry towelled her head roughly in disgust at herself for even contemplating surrendering her morality for the temptations that this wonderful estate offered. Nevertheless, she thought reasonably, as she changed her underclothes and dressed in one of the simpler and less revealing gowns that had clearly escaped Rafe's power of veto, there was no cause to upset the servants with a public show of defiance. Instead, she decided, dutifully, to get the dreaded interview with the housekeeper out of the way, sooner rather than later. That austere lady would know her for a noddy the minute Merry asked her first question about housekeeping, but worse still to have Rafe hovering about while she did so.

The house seemed deserted as Merry trotted downstairs in hopes of breakfast. She rather liked it this way and satisfied her curiosity by opening a couple of the doors to peep into the rooms beyond. As she passed silently through the great hallway, Merry noticed Henry still dozing in the porter's chair, his wig askew and his cheek pressed against one of the buttons in a way that was certain to leave an impression of it.

As she caught the distant hum of chatter, Merry followed the sound to the servant's hall. Only as she entered with a nervous smile, was she forcibly reminded of Rafe's assertion that *'they have their world and we have ours'*. The staff were sleepily assembling for breakfast, and crockery was being laid out amid a hubbub of idle chatter and sharp instructions that all ceased on a gasp as they saw their mistress standing in the doorway.

'My lady!' said Frith, mortified to be caught in his shirt sleeves, brushing his jacket free of lint. 'Did you ring? Has no one responded?'

'Ring,' echoed Merry, colouring in embarrassment. 'No, no … I'm so sorry to disturb you. Please don't stand on my account! I'm afraid I was just exploring. I shall ring if I need anything, I promise,' she added, backing out of the room.

Mrs Dodd asked if she wished breakfast to be served immediately, but though her stomach groaned in assent, Merry declined and assured them that the normal time would be quite all right, though she later cursed herself for not ascertaining precisely when that was.

Merry's embarrassment knew no bounds. It had been a stupid gaffe. She would never have ventured into the kitchens of a tavern, so what had possessed her to think she would be welcome in those of this grand house? Feeling the oppression of her lack of experience, Merry decided a walk outside would alleviate her misery more than kicking her heels in her room. The front door was still bolted and Henry still drowsed, so Merry opened one of the long windows in the dining room, and climbed out, feeling very much the naughty schoolboy. It was sunny but the air was still cool, so Merry set out briskly through the formal gardens, heading for the lake.

Rafe awoke with a sense of exhilaration. His left thumb rubbed against his third finger as the mists of sleep cleared, and a reassured smile softened his face.

They were married. It had not been a dream.

Sitting up, Rafe realised he was still in his clothes and remembered his truly remarkable restraint, which he now regretted, in carrying his wife to her room and not his own.

It was a little after seven. Merry might not be up for hours, but the thought of not seeing her for such a spell chafed him past bearing. He was tempted to peek into her room, but the thought of his wife all rumpled and sleepy against the soft lawn sheets, and himself sporting a monolithic 'morning glory' was a recipe for potential disaster. Instead, he resolved to bide his time, scratching his head and a number of other places, he threw open a shutter to enjoy his now second favourite view, while he hauled out a chamber pot for his morning pee. Looking across the park, as he struggled with the physics of transforming from his present state to the required one, he blinked as he spied a familiar, tawny-headed figure rowing across the lake. His blank surprise took care of the physics and within a few minutes, he had completed the task in hand, and was hauling on a pair of buckskins.

In the middle of the lake, Merry leaned back, propping her elbows on the seat behind her, and revelled in the sunshine. The row had warmed her wonderfully, and though she was certain she had heard more than one seam in her charcoal muslin gown give way, she did not regret her stolen trip one bit.

The swans eyed her warily, as if an oddity of nature, and she had no doubt Rafe's household now beheld her in the same light.

After all, that's exactly what I am, she thought miserably.

Merry lay back and flung an arm across her eyes, blaming their stinging on the sunshine rather than the inexplicable twisting sadness clawing at her throat.

No matter what her turmoil of feelings and choices, Merry knew she could never fit into the fabric of this beautifully ordered place, any more than she had when walking through Grosvenor Square in her borrowed dress. For all her father's heritage, she herself had grown up one step away from squalor, and as a man, not a lady born. But now that she had tasted the blessing of this other life, it was going to be very hard to go back to that world, when Rafe finally tired of this strange game and released her from their contract. Without Bryn's company, she would be adrift in a world in which she belonged nowhere and mattered to no one. Merry tried to tell herself it didn't matter, but it did. It really did.

The intensity of the events of the past few weeks had diverted her thoughts from the loss of her brother, and Harry's presence had been so reminiscent of Bryn's that it had filled the void for a while. Now, even that comfort was gone, and the grief she had held at bay suddenly swept in and overwhelmed her.

In her misery, so at odds with the bright May morning, Merry rolled on to her arm and tried manfully to steady her breathing and keep from weeping, but the harder she tried to suppress her anguish, the worse it fought to be free. Finally, Merry gave up the unequal struggle and broke down in racking, choking sobs.

At the water's edge, Rafe watched the lapping waves bring the boat closer to where he stood pacing anxiously, unshaven and dressed only in boots, buckskins and the shirt and waistcoat he had slept in. Seeing Merry cover her eyes and hunch over in distress, as he had run towards the lake, tore him within. This was not what Rafe wanted for his beloved girl. He had thought, given time, she might come to love this place, to love him, but it seemed only to make her even more miserable. Dragging his hands down his face, he asked himself if perhaps he had got it all wrong. That, like his father, Merry did not, nor ever could, love him.

If this were so, could he bear to let her go and seek her happiness with another?

THE RELUCTANT LADY

As the boat neared the shore, Rafe could tolerate the suspense no longer and waded into the water in his boots, to pull the vessel to a point where he could lift Merry up into his strong arms and carry her to a seat in the little Greek temple amongst the swans. He did not set her down but sat cradling her against his chest like a child.

Rafe expected Merry to fight him off, but she astonished him utterly when her arms crept around his neck and she curled into him for comfort, dragging her breath in long ragged gasps. Rafe's heart lurched and his arms closed around her in a hard hug.

In that instant, he knew that he would never let her go, for no one on God's good earth could ever love this woman as much as he did.

Merry didn't know why, against all her earlier resolve, she had weakened so pathetically. Why the reassurance of Rafe's strong arms around her at that moment had felt so very good. Was it a distant echo of parental comfort, or the raw truth that for all his bad deeds and impossible demands, Rafe was also her best friend? Even better, it seemed, than Harry, for whom she had barely spared a thought these past two days. And in this moment of grief and self-doubt, she needed her friend's solace and support.

Rafe rocked Merry gently back and forth, holding her tight while she strained to subdue her distress and force her breath to steady, as it fought its way past the aching lump in her throat.

As she calmed a little, Rafe stroked her hair soothingly, absently kissing it occasionally, as he might a child's, and murmuring endearments until Merry was no longer distraught, merely disconsolate, resting her chin on Rafe's shoulder and sighing brokenly.

Rafe's own voice was not quite steady when he finally mustered the courage to ask what he barely dared to hear.

'What has upset you, my darling?'

His breathing stilled as he waited for her answer.

'I miss Bryn ... and Harry,' she said. 'And ...'

'And?' prompted Rafe, his heart in his mouth as Merry faltered.

'And ... I made a fool of myself,' said Merry in small voice, despising her frailty.

There was a moment's pregnant silence.

'D…did you, love?' stuttered Rafe, at this unexpected answer. 'How so?'

He stroked her head and then gently rubbed her back in a wonderfully comforting way.

'Oh, it was stupid, so stupid…!' said Merry recounting her embarrassing incident.

'Think nothing of it,' said Rafe, biting back a smile, when Merry completed her tale of woe with her escape through the dining-room window.

'That's easy for you to say. You were born to all this,' said Merry, her chin still resting dejectedly on Rafe's shoulder. 'I don't belong here. I don't belong anywhere.'

'Well, I hate to contradict you, but you are precisely where you belong,' said Rafe categorically. 'Here, with me.'

In my arms, he added silently.

'I don't fit in here, and you know it,' whispered Merry quietly.

'Merry, the reason I brought you here was a certainty that has been growing in me, that I restored this place for you, and that we have both been waiting for you for four long years.'

Merry was silent, but Rafe felt her draw a ragged breath.

'Do you dislike it here?' he asked softly.

Merry gave a watery gulp and he felt her chin rub against his shoulder as she slowly shook her head.

'No,' she croaked. 'I love it.'

Merry felt Rafe give a deep sigh, and his arms tightened wonderfully for a moment, before relaxing once more into a firm but gentle hug. He stroked her hair and kissed it.

'Then nothing else matters,' he said.

Merry knew she should get up and put him at a distance in some way, but she was so comfortable and it was somehow easier to talk to Rafe when she was not distracted by those disturbing cobalt eyes.

'Some things matter,' she whispered.

'Ah, yes,' he sighed. 'Your fiendish plan to abandon me, to crush my heart under your little boot, and leave me alone and forlorn, while you scamper off to the altar with Harry!'

Merry choked and began to twist in his arms to protest, but Rafe gently held her in place and cradled her head back against his shoulder, rocking her tenderly once more.

'No, don't fire up!' he said softly, his voice an apology. 'I'm sorry.' Then after a moment, when she had relaxed against him, he murmured. 'You can't make me stop loving you, Merry, and I will never agree to release you, no matter how much you wish it.'

Merry was quiet for a moment.

'But I only love you as a friend, not as a wife,' she finally said awkwardly. 'I never will, Rafe.'

Rafe had his own views about what the future might hold. For right now, he could settle for friendship.

'That's no reason to leave.'

Merry sighed. Rafe wished he could see her face.

'Where would I go anyway?' she finally said sadly, giving voice to her other gnawing concern.

'You don't know?' asked Rafe, his breath suspended.

What of her love for Harry? Had she not intended to run to him?

He felt her shake her head. When Rafe had mentioned Harry earlier, Merry realised she no more wanted to be his wife than she did Rafe's. To go to him would only raise false hopes in Harry's heart, too.

'Then don't go,' he said hoarsely, trying to keep the joy from his voice.

Merry was quiet. She shifted a little but settled back, her arms still loosely draped about Rafe's neck, and her chin resting on his shoulder. Though she seemed deep in thought, Merry was idly thinking that she could not remember ever feeling so safe. If they could only remain as they were, as friends, and if he could only be trusted, it might be rather wonderful to stay.

Rafe had expected her to resist the suggestion, but her tacit thoughtfulness gave him hope.

'Your servants think I'm mad,' she said, dismally, causing Rafe to blink in hopeful speculation.

Was this an implicit agreement to stay?

'I shall turn them all off, without a character!' he said instantly. 'I think I can have them all off the premises within the hour. We can send their boxes on by carrier.'

Rafe felt Merry's shoulders shake as she giggled. He was free to smile at last.

'Oh, Rafe!' she gurgled, shaking her head at his incorrigible humour. 'You don't think that you might be overreacting a touch.'

'Well, … perhaps we'll let them stay on a little longer, then,' he conceded with seeming reluctance. 'On probation, of course.'

Merry chuckled again.

'I have no idea how to behave, you know,' she said.

'You are merely refreshingly unconventional,' remarked Rafe, as if it were high praise.

'Huh! You're trying to make a bad job sound good.'

'No such thing,' he said. 'Well, haven't you been telling me since we met that there are too many conventions, too many petty rules and constraints?'

'Ye-es,' she admitted hesitantly.

'So, is it such a bad thing if we dispense with a few?' he asked reasonably.

'Well … I suppose not,' said Merry, with a light frown.

'Then we are agreed,' he said. 'To be an unconventional couple?'

'Who live as friends?' qualified Merry.

'Until you discover that you are madly in love with me and have been from the first,' he added, in a comically extravagant voice, finally standing and setting his wife on her feet, before she could argue, and closing with the clincher: 'Now, let us go and get some breakfast, as I particularly requested sausages, bacon, muffins, and everything else you seem to like.'

'Oh, yes,' said Merry eagerly, suddenly famished. 'Do let's!'

For a moment, she felt a little shy as she stood in front of him straightening her gown. Then she took in his muddy, wet boots, his unshaven face, crumpled clothes and the absence of cravat and jacket.

'Huh! And I thought *I* looked rum! *You* look like a pirate! Are you not, at least, going to change your boots and shave before you sit down.'

'What, and have you empty the chafing dishes like a swarm of locust? Not a chance!' he retorted laughingly. 'I shall enjoy one of the benefits of our unconventionality, and breakfast just as I am.'

'Hmm,' said Merry speculatively, bouncing on her toes a little. 'Very well, then … race you!' she cried, tearing off towards the house.

This time it was Rafe who was left to charge after her in laughing protest.

Chapter Seventeen
A Battle of Wills

Fortified by a substantial breakfast, Merry decided that she could no longer put off her meeting with Mrs Dodd.

'Would you like me to accompany you?' asked Rafe, finishing his coffee and stretching.

'No,' said Merry, smiling at his dishevelled state. 'This is something I must do alone, even if I make a complete fool of myself.'

Rafe's words at the lake had given her the courage to take on the responsibilities of her role in the household, even if she had no idea what these were.

'Besides, you should probably get your feet out of those wet boots,' she said, looking at the damp still oozing out of the leather.

'Oh, I don't know,' he said, flexing his feet to make a squelching sound. 'I'm starting to get used to it now.'

Merry chuckled.

'Are you going to stay like that all day?' she asked, thinking that Rafe looked somehow different in this crumpled, unshaven state – less perfect, but more real – and for some reason, she liked it.

'Why? Would you like me to?' asked Rafe in a silky tone, his eyes quizzing her wickedly.

Merry blushed faintly, but parried him before he could explore that interesting development.

'I would not put poor Lain through such torture,' she said, turning to leave. 'I imagine he is suffering even as we speak.'

Rafe got up quickly and crossed the room so that he could open the door for his wife. He bowed his head a little towards her, and for an alarming moment Merry feared he was going to destroy their new peace by kissing her, but he merely whispered confidentially: 'Good luck.'

Merry sighed with nervous relief, and achieved a wink.

'I'll need it,' she said, then left for her sitting room to ring for Mrs Dodd.

Though it was fascinating to tour this marvellous house from the attics to the pantry, Merry's head was spinning by the end, as she had no notion what she was expected to remember.

Mrs Dodd then completed the tour by showing Merry into her own private room, which was something between an office and a sitting room, where a tea tray awaited them.

Then in an act that was clearly a wrench, though she tried hard to conceal this, Mrs Dodd removed the large set of keys from her belt and presented them to her mistress.

'Of course, m'lady, you'll be wanting the keys to the house and stores,' said Mrs Dodd in a formal voice.

Merry was very sure she wanted nothing of the kind, and the swiftly masked look of horror on her mistress's face brought a relieved twinkle to the housekeeper's face.

'Of course,' she ventured. 'If you would rather I took care of them for you, your ladyship, and continued to run things as I have been …'

'Oh, yes!' said Merry, with a gusty sigh of relief. 'Mrs Dodd …'

'Yes, my lady?'

'I … I have never even run a house before,' Merry confessed, colouring up. 'Let alone an establishment of this size.'

'My lady,' said the housekeeper reassuringly, with a motherly smile. 'We have all had to start somewhere. I should be honoured to help you, if you would like?'

'Yes, please, Mrs Dodd, if it would not be too much trouble?'

'It would be a pleasure, your ladyship,' said the housekeeper, beaming as Merry pressed the keys back into her hands. 'Now, would you care for a cup of my special tea?'

That evening, when they walked into dinner, Merry found that her place had been set next to Rafe's, on his right hand. She gave him a disapproving frown, but could not resist his grin, or his mimicking of the comic look she had given him across the table the night before. As she took her seat, though she tried to look severe, an unruly smile was tugging at her lips.

After dinner, they had both had a glass of port before withdrawing not to the drawing room, but to the library, where Rafe answered Merry's questions about improvements he had made to the house, and she told him all about her tour and meeting with Mrs Dodd.

As Rafe left Merry at the door of her chamber, he longed to kiss her so badly, that it was a physical effort to stop himself.

Lain was awaiting him in his room, and Rafe allowed himself to be divested of his clothes, which his valet took away for washing or brushing. Rafe stared for a long moment at the connecting door, before dragging himself to the bed and sitting up against the headboard. He picked up a pillow and hugged it to his chest, remembering every detail of the blissful feel of holding Merry's body in that same way, and having her arms willingly twined about his neck. One day, one day, they would be so again.

On the other side of the wall, Merry, too, was remembering the warm intimacy of that extraordinary moment. But although she had weakly abandoned her vengeful plans against Rafe and had even been baby enough to welcome a cuddle from him when her heart had been in her boots, Merry could not regret the decision to remain here at the Fall with him. The spirit of the place drew her in, as though echoing Rafe's notion that it had been waiting for her.

Merry saw nothing but smiling welcome in the faces of the servants she encountered, rather than the disdain she had feared, and her private pact with Mrs Dodd had done much to allay her concerns about her own role.

So Merry slept deep and long, awaking only to the smell of the hot chocolate that Chantal placed by her bed and the soft creak of the shutters being opened.

Rafe had been waiting impatiently in the breakfast room for over an hour, when Merry finally entered looking very trim in a grey linen riding dress the exact colour of her eyes.

'Yesterday, you were up with the lark,' he complained. 'And today, when I hope to anticipate you, you're a slug-a-bed.'

Merry grinned as she filled her plate and Rafe poured her a coffee.

'Chantal said we were going riding this morning,' said Merry sitting beside him. 'Is that true? Where are we going?'

'Well, yesterday, Mrs Dodd showed you the house,' he said, with a thinly suppressed eagerness. 'Today, I should like to show you the grounds.'

Merry's delighted expression did not disappoint, though Rafe had to recommend her not to bolt her food quite so rapidly, since they would be riding for much of the morning.

The expedition went as well as could be expected of two people with hot tempers – Merry bent on adventure and Rafe bent on preserving her from all harm. When, against Rafe's expressed wish to walk sedately through a gate some two hundred yards further on, Merry put her mount at the hedge … but travelled over it alone, her husband was incandescent.

Taking the hedge in one effortless bound, Rafe dismounted and anxiously began examining Merry, before folding her in a tight, relieved hug. He then commenced to read her a stinging lecture for most of their journey back.

With a surly glare in her eye, Merry feigned deafness for much of the time. Occasionally, she fired back, looking skyward in disgust when this served only to reanimate his efforts to bring her to a sense of her iniquity in defying his instructions and risking her neck.

By the time they rode into the stable yard, Merry was in a towering temper. She dismounted quickly, if a little stiffly, before Rafe could help her down and limped angrily off towards the house without a backward look.

When Rafe, with sudden concern, hurried to try and support her, Merry poked her crop at his chest and held him at bay.

'Go to the devil, you fussing old woman!' she hissed, between clenched teeth. 'If you're just going to turn into a regular jaw-me-dead every time I do the slightest thing you don't like, then I'm off!'

Rafe bit his lip. After a moment he looked pointedly down at the crop with the ghost of a smile in his eyes. Merry huffed and removed it, swishing it at her skirt as if she would very much like to hit him with it.

'May I not help you?' he asked, holding out his hand.

'No!' snapped Merry churlishly, marching painfully away to her room.

Merry had still not forgiven him by the time they sat down to luncheon. She responded tersely to his conversational sallies, until much goaded, he cried: 'Oh for heaven's sake, I'm sorry for lecturing you. Now, stop ignoring me, you impossible minx!'

'Do you promise never to do it again,' she challenged him, with a stern look.

Rafe pursed his lips tightly and returned her unrelenting stare with narrowed eyes.

'Damn it, Merry!' he said finally. 'You know I can't.'

Merry huffed again and turned her face away from him.

'Oh, don't try to give me the cut direct, Merry, you look ridiculous,' said Rafe, eyeing her averted profile with annoyance. 'I promise to *try* not to bore you with my husbandly concern. Will that appease you?'

'We're supposed to be friends, Rafe,' said Merry. 'So stuff all that "*husband*" nonsense! You wouldn't have read Harry a lecture, if he'd come a cropper, would you?'

'Merry, my feelings about you are very different to those I...'

'Well, they shouldn't be!' interrupted Merry, rising from her chair. 'We're just friends, Rafe. Isn't that what we agreed?'

Rafe did not answer, returning her regard steadily, as he rose out of courtesy. His jaw clenched for a moment.

'Well?' she demanded.

'You may regard me as your friend, Merry,' he said eventually, with obvious reluctance. 'But I can never regard you as anything less than my wife. You are dearer to me than any friend could be.'

Merry's lips parted in a soft 'oh' of consternation as she looked up at him. He was watching her face with an odd wary hopefulness.

'I was as clear about my sentiments yesterday as you were,' he said. 'You cannot love me, and I cannot *but* love you.'

Merry looked anxious.

'Still,' he said in a lighter tone, concerned that Merry might think once more of leaving him. 'If you can keep from killing yourself and I can keep from worrying that you might, we should rub along together pretty well, don't you think?' He smiled, and then changed the subject. 'So what do you have planned for this afternoon?'

'Mrs Dodd is going to show me how to draw up a menu,' responded Merry, still distracted by her rioting thoughts. 'Apparently, I choose what we eat each evening!' she said, as if this were an unexpected novelty.

Rafe smiled.

'So I may expect to have sausages for dinner as well as for breakfast?' mused Rafe.

'I suspect that is not what Mrs Dodd has in mind,' said Merry, turning for the door, which Rafe opened for her.

'I'll be in the library, if you want to come and join me later?' offered Rafe.

Merry gave a tight, uncomfortable smile in response, so Rafe resigned himself to waiting until dinner before he would see her again.

So, he was pleasantly surprised when Merry entered the library, a little consciously, just over an hour later.

Rafe stood with such a warm smile on his face that Merry relaxed a little.

'I thought I might read for a bit,' she said, with a diffident gesture towards the bookshelves on the wall opposite Rafe's desk.

Rafe gave an expansive wave of invitation, and pretended to return to his papers, though once she had passed, he simply watched her, his work forgotten.

When concentrating on other things, Merry still regularly forgot her lessons in femininity and reverted to her boyish stance.

Now, to Rafe's amused delight, as she looked up at books, Merry stood with feet apart, her hands on her hips and her elbows back, as if relishing the challenge.

Then spying some promising tomes, Merry pulled the stepladder over and climbed to reach them, pausing with her feet on different steps, unconsciously exposing one stockinged ankle and offering a tantalising glimpse of the lacy bottoms of her drawers.

Rafe took a steadying breath, and then came quickly over to hold the ladder, trying manfully not to look at the very tempting view.

'Rafe, you fusspot, I don't need your help,' grumbled Merry, climbing higher.

'Yes, and how should I feel if…' Rafe turned towards her and got an eyeful of stocking and garter, before looking swiftly away to continue. '…If you fell and broke your neck, while I sat and observed?'

Merry merely huffed in response.

'What are you looking for?' he asked, as she stretched precariously, scanning the spines.

'Oh, something by Scott or Sterne or Swift, if you have any.'

'Why don't you try something a little different?' he suggested. 'Here!'

To her annoyance, Rafe put his hands round her waist and lifted her easily to the floor. He picked up a book that he was clearly reading himself, for he pulled out a bookmark before handing it to her. Merry reluctantly accepted it, secretly curious to know what kind of books Rafe read for pleasure.

'This is an excellent new novel,' he said. 'By a lady.'

Merry looked her disbelief and turned it over in her hands with a look of distaste.

'I never thought you would be a fan of all that gothic nonsense,' she said, with genuine surprise.

Rafe laughed.

'Then you were correct. I'm not,' he confirmed. 'There's not so much as a cobweb in this, let alone a dungeon.'

'*Pride and Prejudice*,' groaned Merry, reading the spine. 'Sounds like a sermon to me.'

Rafe chuckled.

'Far from it,' he said. 'Trust me. It's already one of my favourites,' said Rafe.

Merry looked at him suspiciously.

'Really. It's witty, realistic and well-observed.'

Rafe turned away to return to his desk, hoping he had done enough. Any further advocacy, he thought, and Merry would put the book down to spite him.

His tactic worked, for Merry retained the book, and though he expected her to leave, she surprised him by curling up in one of the two window seats, surreptitiously watching him, as he did likewise with her. Rafe could not concentrate but nor did he want her to leave. Occasionally, their eyes would meet.

'What are you doing?' she finally asked, her curiosity piqued.

'Drainage plans and accounts for a property I bought in Devon.'

'May I see?'

'Please do,' said Rafe, waving his open palm above the papers invitingly.

'I am pretty good with numbers,' said Merry helpfully.

Rafe, who was outstandingly good with numbers, said: 'Excellent! I could use a little assistance,' stifling the smile in his heart.

Merry cast him a suspicious look, but Rafe managed to hide the surge of pleasure he was feeling at this détente and simply looked businesslike.

He pushed a ledger towards her.

'I am looking to develop a profitable crop rotation and need to calculate the most successful crops from the accounts.'

Merry's interest was piqued. She rubbed her hands together, in a way that brought a smile to Rafe's lips, and began to pore over the book, demanding pen, ink and paper after a minute or two. Rafe furnished these, unable to suppress the glow in his eyes. If Merry had seen it, she might have left.

Rafe accepted that, for him, any hope of useful work was now over. He shifted the maps in front of him now and then to keep up the pretence, but was in fact watching Merry intently.

In fascination, he observed as the black, feathered end of the raven quill moved from scanning the ledger to her face as Merry mentally weighed the information and then danced in the air as she scratched out her information, in a fine copperplate hand, onto the paper beside her.

If she cannot love me … If this is as close to heaven as I can get, then I'll take it, thought Rafe.

It was some thirty minutes later when Merry sighed with satisfaction and announced her findings. Rafe then showed her on the plans where those crops had been grown and how the existing drainage favoured them, and then other fields that might be adapted to provide the same favourable conditions. Merry was intrigued and inquisitive, and Rafe patiently answered all her questions. He was poignantly reminded of Kit, who had had a similarly enquiring mind and thirst for knowledge.

The next hour passed quickly as Merry explained her calculations and together they plotted out how to manage the land. They disagreed on a couple of points, and a lively discussion ensued, but both were surprised at how easy it was to dispute as equals – to each make their case and then to reason together on the most practical outcome.

They were standing side by side with the carefully hand-drawn maps of the land, with each tree, field and cottage diligently recorded. These were overlaid with scraps of paper on which they had written what they proposed, pinning these to the maps when they agreed.

As they worked, Merry seemed not to notice their physical proximity - their elbows or hands occasionally touching as they moved or scribbled on the scraps of paper. Even Rafe, absorbed in the conversation and enjoying this normally onerous chore more than he could imagine, found his desire for his wife subordinated to his enjoyment of working with her. But the spell was broken when leaning suddenly across the maps to tap her finger on a promising field marked only as sheep grazing, Merry's hair brushed lightly against Rafe's lips, as he was leaning forward in the other direction. Merry heard his soft gasp and turned her face to look at him. Rafe had moved back a little, but their lips were momentarily just inches apart. But it was not this that made her blush and look away in confusion, suddenly conscious of how close they stood. It was the expression in Rafe's eyes, a kind of hungry longing, that found an unexpected answering chord in her own traitorous frame.

'Merry,' said Rafe in a broken whisper, his hand unconsciously lifting to prevent her from breaking away from him.

But Merry was already moving to the end of the desk, her eyes carefully averted.

Merry was not upset with him, but with herself. For in that instant, she had wanted nothing more than to kiss him.

But what might happen if she succumbed to these disturbing promptings made Merry quake inwardly. Though he might talk of love, Merry knew that exactly what Rafe wanted to do to her. She knew how children were made, just as she had known what Mrs Fulsome had had in mind for her. Growing up in the company of men, there had been no escaping the bawdy banter, and Merry had often contributed to support her masquerade. Frequently, she had witnessed furtive couplings in shadowy alleys outside taverns, when a doxy would lift a leg for a drunken man with a handsome face or a few shillings. It had always seemed like a pretty awkward, beastly business, all grunting and shoving, with neither party emerging particularly happy. As a virgin, Merry knew it would hurt, at least the first time, but it was more the thought of succumbing to that degrading act, night after night, even with a friend, that appalled her.

It had been such an enjoyable couple of hours, working with Rafe on the plans, feeling useful and engaged. In one sense, it was how she imagined it might have been had she been a man and found employment where she could have put her education to use. But in another, it was so much more than that. It was a glimpse of how enjoyable it might be to work with Rafe as a partner, building a future together, during the day ... *but what of the nights?*

And did all this mean that Rafe's crimes against Bryn, Harry and herself were to be forgiven and forgotten? Every day Merry was finding it harder to hate Rafe. At this moment, she did not hate him at all.

Merry looked up at Rafe, who had not moved as he had watched with anxious intensity as her thoughts had been reflected in her expressive face. As her eyes met his, he longed to kiss her so much that he had to grasp the edge of the desk to stop himself from reaching out to her, certain that this would send her running from the room.

Merry misunderstood this, and the faint frown of concentration it brought to his cobalt-blue eyes, and thought perhaps he was annoyed with her.

'I should wash my fingers,' she said rather lamely, showing their inky tips, and turned to leave.

'Merry,' called Rafe as she reached the door. She paused but did not turn. 'I enjoyed working with you,' he said, sounding a little desperate to his own ears.

'So did I,' said Merry, without turning, and left.

Yes, thought Rafe. *I will settle for this, if I must.*

But in entertaining that idea, Rafe betrayed a parlous lack of self-awareness.

When Merry stepped out of her room to join him for dinner, Rafe sensed the change immediately. Though she talked lightly of the work they had done that afternoon, there seemed to be a distance between them that was not there earlier. Merry seemed unusually conscious of his regard, and he noted that she had altered her grey silk gown, which now sported a broad velvet ribbon trimming that concealed an extra two inches of her entire neckline.

Rafe pursed his lips.

'Was that entirely necessary?' he asked dryly, with a nod towards her gown.

Merry blushed faintly.

'It would appear so,' she replied pointedly.

Rafe was unsure whether to welcome Merry's new-found awareness of her femininity or to be irritated by it.

'But I am not lacking in imagination, Merry, my love,' said Rafe wickedly, raking her figure with his eyes as he opened the door for her to pass into the drawing room. 'I can clearly picture what I cannot see. Mmm, exquisite!'

Two flags of bright colour flew in her cheeks.

'Lecher!' she hissed.

'It is scarcely lechery, my darling wife, when "*with my body, I thee worship*",' said Rafe provokingly. He would rather have her grey-eyed glare than this prim distance. He followed Merry to where she stood, stiff with rage, beside the fire, and he stood so close she had to look up to speak to him.

'You wretched cheat! I should have known better than to trust you to behave like a gentleman!'

'And how am I a cheat, Merry?' demanded Rafe, a flame of anger in his own eye now. 'I never agreed that we should be merely friends. That was a concoction of your own. I simply behaved as a friend when you appeared to need one.'

'Well, I need one now!' she cried.

'Not as much as you need a husband, Merry!' snapped Rafe. 'In your arms… and in your bed.'

'You are obsessed!' she cried, her hands flying up in a gesture of madness. 'I suppose I could expect no more from an unprincipled and determined rake, such as you. You are incapable of …'

At that moment, Frith entered to announce that dinner was served.

Rafe and Merry maintained a tight-lipped silence through much of the meal, with only stilted attempts at conversation in front of the servants.

As the covers were removed, Merry stood up quickly.

'I think I shall retire early, my lord,' said Merry hastily, then added, as if delighted by her own ingenuity: 'I have the headache.'

'Then allow me to escort you to your room, my dear,' said Rafe, with disingenuous concern.

'There's no need. Please don't trouble yourself.'

'No trouble at all. It would be my pleasure,' he said smoothly, noting, with a gleam, his wife's barely suppressed vexation.

Merry walked briskly, though Rafe comfortably kept pace with her, so she was a little warm by the time she reached her door.

Instead, of opening the door for her, Rafe caught hold of the handle and then placed his other hand against the doorframe, so that Merry was trapped between his hard body and the even harder door. Though he was not quite touching her, it was as though he emanated some masculine energy that sent her own body trembling in response. He had not moved or spoken, but Merry was moved to gasp: 'Stop that!'

'What?'

'Whatever it is that you're doing!'

'I'm not doing anything!'

'You're standing too close. You're like a walking infection. Every time you come close to me, I feel feverish and shaky. Perhaps it is like hay fever. Oh, we should never have married!'

'Wrong! You're supposed to feel shaky when I'm close to you.'

'That simply <u>can't</u> be right!'

'I've worse news for you, my sweet,' he said, with a wickedly triumphant tone. 'The reason you feel feverish is because you want to… er… mate with me.'

Merry was aghast

'Mate? Like animals?'

'Well, I flatter myself that …' Rafe began, but he was interrupted by Merry's harsh, incredulous laughter.

'Impossible! I've no intention of doing *that* with anyone!'

'You must have done it with Harry, if you had married him.'

Merry was silent. She had never considered that, and had certainly never thought of Harry that way.

'Are you aware of what happens between a man and woman in the creation of their offspring?' asked Rafe, his warm breath hushing against her hair.

'Yes, of course,' replied Merry waspishly. 'And I've seen them do it in alleys, when they've had too much ale, too.'

Rafe winced at the thought that she had ever had to witness such things.

'Well, it doesn't have to be quite so vulgar or so base,' said Rafe tersely. 'And there's a reason why people do it for pleasure … because it's extremely pleasurable.'

'Well, it didn't look particularly pleasurable,' countered Merry. 'A lot of shoving and grunting. It was more like a bout of fevered ague.'

'*Quod erat demonstrandum*, Merry. You prove my point entirely.'

'What do you mean?'

'Well, you said I made you feel feverish …' began Rafe, letting the sentence hang in the air.

Merry gasped

'I assure you, no such thought has ever entered my mind!' she lied.

'But it has entered it *now*, has it not, my sweet?' responded Rafe with satisfaction.

Merry pushed him away from her, and he stepped back, grinning.

'Go to the devil, you wretch!' she snapped, as she slammed the door in his face.

'Already taken care of, my dear!' he said through the door, before sauntering off towards the library to enjoy his port.

He was right. The thought had now firmly entered Merry's head and refused to be dislodged.

That night, Merry's dreams were tormented by images of her and Rafe together in compromising positions, and more than once she awoke on a gasp, as the faces she recalled of couples copulating in alleyways were replaced in her fevered nightmares by Rafe's and her own!

Even when Merry finally awoke, unrefreshed, the next morning, she was haunted by intimate images that refused to be banished. Pacing her still-shuttered room, Merry determined to avoid Rafe until she could quell this flood of unwelcome sensations and unruly notions that made her too vulnerable to his approaches. Merry wondered if this were all part of his success as a rake.

If she stayed in the house, he would find her and resume his campaign, so Merry scrambled into her riding dress, grabbed her hat and crop, and crept out of her room, making for the back stairs.

Avoiding the kitchens and servants' hall, Merry nipped out of the back door to the stables, where Humphreys the head groom greeted her with a touch of his hat.

Her horse was saddled swiftly, but when she saw a second horse being prepared for an accompanying groom, she demurred.

'No, I shan't need a groom,' she said hastily.

'But his lordship will go spare, m'lady, if you go out without one,' said Humphreys in consternation.

'I just want to be alone for a little while,' said Merry, accepting a boost into the saddle. 'I will only ride within the grounds and I shan't be long.'

'That won't cut no mustard with 'im,' replied Humphreys with an anxious look, but he spoke to a cloud of dust and small stones.

The head groom was right. After a few moments wrestling with his dilemma, Humphreys went to find Mr Brooke, his sage counsellor in all matters concerning Lord Rothsea. He and Brooke exchanged a significant look, and Rafe's manservant sighed in exasperation.

'I'll let his lordship know when he wakes, but not before,' said Brooke rubbing his chin. 'Let's hope the missus gets back before he does.'

Brooke was not to get his wish.

Rafe, too, had had a troubled night. The knowledge that Merry was finally feeling some measure of the same physical desires that were damn near overpowering him, had sent his own into uproar. Like hers, his dreams had disturbed his sleep and left him exhausted and on edge. His thoughts and emotions were in turmoil and, with his typical impatience he had to know if Merry felt the same way.

Morning glory or no, Rafe threw on a dressing gown and opened the connecting door. In the half-light, with his heart pounding, Rafe looked towards Merry's bed.

Moving through the bluebell wood and looking up at the dappled canopy of bright, fresh-budding leaves, Merry felt a little of her former calm returning. She allowed her mare's head to drop and crop a little of the lush grass between the flowers, before walking on again to find somewhere to dismount and think for a while.

Back at the house, Rafe felt a pang of disappointment when he saw Merry's bed was empty and her nightgown lay in a heap on the floor.

Thwarted and irritated, Rafe went back to his room and rang for Lain, but was alarmed when Brooke arrived to wait on him instead.

'What is it?' demanded Rafe. 'Come on, man! I know you would not be here to dress me unless there was something wrong or Lain had broken his leg on the back stair.'

'Nothing like that, m'lord,' said Brooke matter-of-factly. 'Nor nothing to get yourself all het up about neither.'

'Then what?' said Rafe, as Brooke slowly put down the can of hot water he carried.

'I'll tell you all about it when I have you shaved, your lordship, and not before,' said Brooke with maddening calm, as he picked up the razor and drew it along the strop.

'You'll tell me now, be damned to you!'

Brooke simply folded his arms patiently and nodded towards the chair that he had placed for his master.

Rafe stared at him for one furious minute, before sitting with a grunt.

'Well, get on with it, then!' he said churlishly

Brooke wrung the hot water out of a linen cloth and laid it on his lordship's face, rubbing it firmly into his jaw.

'I take it Lain has not broken his leg,' came Lord Rothsea's muffled voice.

'That's right, sir,' confirmed Brooke. 'You'll be glad to hear that Mr Lain enjoys his customary good health, as you might say, and is below stairs weeping over them dark tops you went paddling in.'

'Tell him to throw them away,' said Rafe, as Brooke lathered his face and throat. There was something calming in this daily ritual.

'I think he's reading them the last rites, sir,' said Brooke. 'If the tops hadn't dried so crispy, one of the stable lads might have had them, though they'd have had to drag 'em from Mr Lain's tight paws, of course.'

Rafe's tension eased a little at this humorous image. He watched Brooke's impassive face as he drew the blade expertly around his master's face. Lain was good, but Brooke always gave him the best shaves.

As he rinsed his face in the remaining water and patted his throat dry, Rafe was almost philosophical when he said: 'Then I take it that my wife has done something I shall not like?'

'Well, as to that, m'lord,' said Brooke. 'Her ladyship hasn't done nothing that she shouldn't, as mistress of her own home. But knowing as how you're a mite protective and, lord knows, you're terrible hasty to judgement, I thought I'd best be the one to tell you, so you don't go off into one of your pelters.'

'Oh God! What has she done?' said Rafe ominously, pausing as he threw a fresh shirt over his head and accepted the buckskins from Brooke's hand.

'Her ladyship has gone for a little ride around the grounds, and will back shortly,' said Brooke in a voice he might have used with small children.

'Alone?'

'That's the rub, sir,' admitted Brooke. 'Not that she should need an escort on her own grounds, your lordship. I'll bet that's how her ladyship saw it.'

'And how do we know that she has remained on the grounds, and has not taken the opportunity to leave me?' snapped Rafe, suddenly galvanised into activity, reaching for his boots and ignoring the stockings that Brooke was holding out.

'Mr Humphreys said she couldn't have got nothing else under that neat little riding dress of hers,' said Brooke, by way of reassurance.

'Humphreys can keep his damned eyes in his head!' snarled Rafe. 'He might have been better employed in getting one of his lads to follow his mistress than in ogling my wife!'

'Now, there you go, m'lord,' said Brooke with a long-suffering sigh. 'Off on one of your starts and deaf to all reason! I've said it before and I'll say it again, it's always been all or nothing with you m'lord,'

Rafe was trying to fling on a cravat, but threw it down and turned for the door.

'Take a breath, your lordship, for pity's sake,' begged Brooke. 'Her ladyship might be sitting down to breakfast as we speak, and what kind of figure will you cut, dashing in half-dressed, like a bloomin' poet.'

This comment brought a reluctant twitch to Rafe's lips, and he allowed Brooke to place a fresh cravat around his neck. Brooke managed to get a waistcoat on his master, as Rafe made a better job of tying this one, whilst mentally rehearsing some very choice speeches for his wife's further education.

As he did so, Brooke took the opportunity to proffer some unwelcome advice.

'You've never been one to break a horse with the spur, m'lord,' he said carefully. 'I've always admired that about you. Gently does it, that's always been your way. Never lost that black temper of yours with an animal to my knowledge, I'll say that for you.'

'Are you likening my wife to an animal?' asked Rafe with an edge to his voice.

'Her ladyship's a very spirited young lady, to be sure,' replied Brooke cautiously. 'But it's *your* actions I was a'drawin' attention to, sir.'

Rafe frowned warningly, then walked briskly towards the door, when Brooke suddenly put his arms out to bar the way.

'No, sir,' he said. 'You're not to leave without a coat, for so I promised Mr Lain, and you wouldn't make a liar of me, would you, m'lord.'

'Oh, very well! Fetch one then!' cried Rafe in exasperation, then watched suspiciously as Brooke walked sedately across to the wardrobe.

His temper finally snapping, Rafe pulled open his bedroom door, and strode out.

'But, your coat, sir!' he heard Brooke shout.

'Keep it! And your damned lectures, too!'

'I thought I'd taught you not to cram your horse at a gate!' called Brooke after his master's retreating back.

Rafe only turned to give him a black look, before continuing his irate journey towards the breakfast room in long, purposeful strides.

It was more than two hours later, when Merry finally walked her mount serenely into the stable yard. The staff were all busying themselves suspiciously, and it was Humphreys himself, who stepped up rapidly, with an admonitory look, to take her horse's bridle.

Merry suddenly saw the cause of their consternation. Rafe, who had seen her approach from the prime vantage point of the drawing room window, where he had been watching for her, was now advancing towards her, his eyes blazing. Merry's wary expression now turned mulish as she prepared for battle.

Rafe put his hands up to help her down, but she ignored them and slipped elegantly to the ground unaided. This small but misguided act of defiance was all that was needed to set a torch to Rafe's fury. He caught her upper arm in a bruising grasp and began to drag her towards the house at such a pace that she almost tripped, only his unyielding grip holding her upright. When, almost instinctively, she moved to hit him with her crop, Rafe tore it from her fingers and threw it away across the yard.

THE RELUCTANT LADY

Rafe was utterly deaf to Merry's protests until he reached the library, where he flung her into the room and slammed the door so hard that it left a light spattering of dust and plaster around the frame. They heard the bang as far away as the kitchens.

A scorching row followed, which only two passionate people with such unprincipled temperaments and such deep underlying issues could achieve without killing one another. They roared and fenced for twenty minutes or more without drawing breath.

Having banished all the other servants out of earshot, Brooke stood outside, arms folded, leaning his back against the wall, ready in case violence should ensue.

Until now, Brooke had failed to see why his lordship had picked this odd girl for his bride, but he was forced to revise his opinion as he chuckled at her forceful delivery of some very sharp home truths, which his master found as unpalatable coming from his wife as he did from his manservant. By the time the blaze between them had burnt itself out to a cold, hard coke ash, Brooke was in accord with his lordship. This feisty little lady was the very woman for his difficult master, if she could be brought to see it, and heaven knew she liked him well enough when he wasn't setting her all on edge or putting her out of curl.

As he heard the shouting die down, Brooke scratched at the door and entered without waiting to be bid.

'Ah, Brooke!' said Rafe masterfully. 'You are to inform Humphreys that Lady Rothsea is not allowed to ride unless I am there to accompany her. Nor is she to be offered any kind of alternative transport without my express approval. I am to be informed of her whereabouts at all times....'

'Ho! So much for "you are mistress of all you survey", you wicked liar! I had more freedom in the sponging house!'

'If you want to give fool orders like that, you can give them yourself, m'lord,' said Brooke with a dry look, cutting through the argument like a knife.

Both combatants' spun round to look at him. Rafe furious and Merry alight with triumphant surprise.

'But I, myself, would be happy to escort her ladyship, if she wishes, whenever she cares to ride.'

'I shall be very glad of your company, Mr Brooke,' said Merry sweetly, her angelic stance somewhat marred by the crowing look she flashed at Rafe, who stood glaring incredulously at the pair of them. 'Shall we say nine o'clock tomorrow morning?'

'I'll have the horses ready, your ladyship,' said Brooke, with a slight bow. 'Now, begging your pardon, ma'am, but I think Mrs Dodd was a'lookin' for you a little while back, and cook was a'worritin' that you had missed your breakfast.'

'She can go hungry!' snapped Rafe petulantly, but was pointedly ignored.

'I believe she has a pan of eggs and bacon waiting for you whenever you are ready,' continued Brooke, as if he had heard nothing.

'God damn it!' cried Rafe. 'I don't suppose my cook has spared *me* a thought?'

'You may be right, m'lord,' said Brooke, as if giving this some thought. 'Mrs Greaves never mentioned you.'

Then, as Merry giggled at this and at Rafe's outraged expression, Brooke opened the door for his mistress.

'This way, your ladyship.'

'Thank you, Mr Brooke,' said Merry, as she passed him, the very model of demure acquiescence.

Brooke gave his master one last knowing look as he closed the door, grateful that his lordship had not yet had the notion to throw the inkpot at his departing back, as had happened once before.

Scowling in fascination at this brazen piece of insubordination, Rafe was left to pace out his annoyance on the library carpet, spying the inkpot all too late

Chapter Eighteen
In Vino Veritas

Rafe did not see Merry for the rest of the day.

Although he still felt righteous stirrings about the cause of his earlier loss of temper, he had long since begun to regret what he had said in its throes. Merry had a gift for making him mad as hell, but he missed her every minute she was out of his sight.

He was tying his cravat in preparation for dinner, when he heard a tap at the door of his bedchamber.

'Come!' he called with a light frown that turned into blank surprise when his wife peeped round the door, still in an afternoon dress.

With a swift nod to Lain, who rapidly disappeared into the dressing room, Rafe went across to meet her.

'Come in,' he said, with an inviting wave, watching her curious gaze skim around the room.

Merry noticed with interest that their headboards were positioned in the same place either side of the dividing wall. As they slept, their heads could be barely two feet apart.

'I... I wanted to talk to you...' began Merry.

'I wanted to talk to you, too,' said Rafe, intending to apologise for his earlier behaviour.

'... before you went down to dinner,' continued Merry, doggedly.

'Before *I* went down? Are you not dining tonight?'

'I would rather have a tray in my room,' said Merry tentatively.

'Are you unwell?' he demanded, a frown between his brows.

'No, I should just prefer to be alone a little longer. I need to think ...'

'I think you have been *alone* quite enough for one day!' growled Rafe, forgetting all his apologies.

'I don't mean to offend you,' said Merry as patiently as she could, her own irritation rising. It had seemed such a reasonable request when she had thought of it.

'How can I fail to be offended?' cried Rafe. 'When my wife chooses not to sit down to dine with me?'

'*"My wife! My wife"!*' parroted Merry, now as angry as her husband. 'I am heartily sick of hearing you bandy that term today! I am *not* your wife yet, my lord. We have not consummated this insane contract …'

'Well, I am more than ready to remedy that!' interrupted Rafe, waving his hand towards his bed.

'And we never will!' finished Merry.

'Don't be so certain of it, my dear *wife*!' snapped Rafe, taking a step closer to Merry murmuring: 'I know that you have imagined it … that you have pictured yourself, right there, in my arms, willingly taking me into your body!'

'Vile nightmares,' she snarled, blushing hotly, as she saw Rafe's eyes light up. 'Put into my head by your sneaky rake's tricks! I have no wish to subject myself to them any further over dinner. So you may rant all you like, but you will dine alone!'

Rafe took Merry's shoulders and guided her to the connecting door, where Merry noticed the key and cleverly managed to pocket it as Rafe was turning her about.

'You will go into your room and dress for dinner, or I will dress you myself.'

'I will not!'

'I hoped you'd say that!' said Rafe, pushing Merry through the door and following her into her room. He walked across to her wardrobe, wrenched out the black velvet dress and threw it on the bed. Then he advanced towards Merry, a determined look on his face.

'Don't you dare, you bully!' cried Merry.

'Then you know your other option,' he said ruthlessly.

'And then what do you intend?' she demanded. 'To drag me downstairs and force soup down my throat? There is more to dining with you than merely dressing for the *privilege*!' she spat sarcastically.

Rafe's lips flattened into one thin angry line. Merry had a point.

'Very well,' he said tightly. 'But if you won't dine with me, you won't dine at all!'

'Fine!' said Merry

'Fine!' snapped Rafe, walking to the door.

'Lucky that I filled up on cook's delicious bacon and eggs!' declared Merry victoriously, watching Rafe stop for moment, clench his fists, and then continue through the door, which he yanked closed behind him.

Unseen, Merry fished the key from her pocket and waved it triumphantly in his general direction.

Chantal had informed the staff that her ladyship was unwell and would not be dining, but cook sent up a tray, nonetheless.

Lord Rothsea looked like blue thunder as he dined in state, looking bitterly at Merry's empty seat, and drinking far more than he ate. Rafe remained at the table long after the covers had been removed, drinking his way through a fine bottle of cognac and slowly whipping himself up into a fury. The alcohol gradually had its customary effect of heightening a sense of grievance whilst diminishing any sense of accountability.

Upstairs, Merry had consumed her dinner, changed into her nightgown and then curled up in front of the fire, reading the book Rafe had recommended. She was already strangely charmed by his choice and how it reflected on her friend's character. Rafe might be driving her insane at present, but he had really excellent taste.

Though smaller in scope than her beloved adventures, there was something wonderfully entertaining in these finely drawn characters, many of whom she could recognise from her own life. One of her school tutors had been Mr Collins to the life, and Bingley … sweet natured, gentlemanly, biddable Bingley reminded her poignantly of Bryn, and Merry read his passages with a wistful melancholy. After a short while, she became immersed in the novel until she heard Rafe's footstep in the corridor come to a halt outside her door.

Merry saw the handle twist, but as she had wisely locked the door, it did not open. Rafe tapped on it.

'Merry, are you awake?' he called in a hoarse whisper, his face very close to the door, and then in a grumbling, drunken slur, he added: 'Damn it, Merry, why d'you have to sleep like the bloody dead?'

Merry had vast experience of various states of drunkenness, and grasped that Rafe fitted the description of 'well to live', and was very relieved when she heard him shamble off to his room. She skipped to the connecting door and listened, with a grin, to his poor valet's attempts to undress his master.

'Get off me, ye damned moth! I'm not so foxed that I can't take off my own necktie,' came Rafe's voice, followed rapidly by the unmistakeable sound of a chair crashing over and a body impacting the wooden floor.

'Let me help you up, m'lord,' Merry heard Lain say sympathetically, and she had to put her hand to her mouth to stifle a giggle.

'Don't need y'r help. Bloody chair fell over,' Rafe growled indistinctly, clearly struggling back to his feet with some difficulty.

'Yes, m'lord. If you say so,' said Lain, with a patience clearly born of long experience. 'Now, if you will just sit in it for a moment, I can have you ready for bed in a trice. Won't that be nice?'

'Oh, very well,' Rafe said, surrendering to his valet's ministrations.

'M'wife's asleep, Lain,' Rafe mumbled thickly.

'Well, that's a mercy, sir. You wouldn't want her ladyship to see you in this state.'

'Wisshh I was in there with her,' said Rafe.

'Just as well that you are not, m'lord,' said Lain. 'You may not know, sir, but you snore like a bear when you are in your cups.'

'Don't believe it,' said Rafe, shaking his head too fast. 'Ooh!'

'My lord, I'll need you to stand for a moment, so that I can remove your breeches.'

There was a momentary sound of struggle and then two bodies seemed to hit the floor. Merry stifled another giggle.

After a couple of moments, Lain's tired voice said: 'No matter, sir. I can as easily remove them with you lying there on the floor.'

Removing the key as quietly as she could, Merry peeped through the keyhole and spied Rafe lying naked on his bedroom floor rubbing his head and trying to get up, before Lain blocked her view returning with his nightshirt, which he threw on over his lordship's head. After some further effort to get his master upright, they both moved out of her range of sight, and she heard the creak of the bed as Rafe landed on it heavily.

Merry heaved a sigh of relief and returned to her heap of cushions by the fire, shaking her head. She had often had the dubious honour of putting her father and brother to bed in equally inebriated states. Bryn had always been particularly susceptible, but had been the sweetest drunk, continually apologising for causing trouble and calling her "the best sister in the world".

One of her candles guttered a little, so Merry took another from the sconce and replaced it, so that she could keep reading her book. In the distance, she heard Lain finally closing Rafe's door and padding away down the corridor.

A minute or two passed, then Merry was startled to hear the handle on the connecting door turning and then the door rattled in frustration as it was discovered to be locked.

'Merry, you witch! I know you're awake. Your candle is still alight.'

Merry kept silent and held her breath, hoping Rafe would assume she had fallen asleep with it lit and would give up.

'Open this door, Merry!' demanded Rafe, with a spark of annoyance. 'I can't believe you locked it. However did you get the key?'

Merry gave up the pretence.

'Go away, Rafe!' she said through the door. 'You're jug-bitten!'

Merry heard the clunk as his forehead came to rest heavily against the door.

'Merry, let me in,' he moaned plaintively.

Into your room. Into your body, he thought.

'No!' said Merry adamantly. 'Go to bed and sleep it off, you idiot!'

'Merry!' he growled. 'I told you never to lock a door against me.'

'Oh, do go away, Rafe!' said Merry impatiently, returning to her place by the fire. 'You're making an arse of yourself! Just go to bed, or I will call Brooke.'

Suddenly, her eyes wide with astonishment, Merry felt the jolt as Rafe put his shoulder to the door with surprising force. This was followed soon after by another jolt, and another, then the crack of splitting wood and Rafe came thumping into the room before stopping short, swaying unsteadily.

'Told you not to lock a door between us!' he said triumphantly, then rubbed his shoulder with a grimace.

Merry had jumped up and now stood ready to defend herself. Picking up the poker, she said with deadly quiet: 'Get out, Rafe.'

Her husband looked rather endearingly pathetic, standing in his nightshirt, with a confused, hungry look in his eyes, but Merry knew that drunken men were a deceptively dangerous breed.

'Go back to bed, Rafe!'

'Only if you come with me,' he said, holding onto the chair back to steady himself.

'Absolutely not!' said Merry.

'Just for a cuddle,' he said, his arms opening innocently. 'I just want to hold you … to feel you in my arms.'

'You want to do a lot more than cuddle, Rafe,' said Merry, testing the weight of the poker behind her nightgown.

Rafe ran his hands distractedly through his hair.

'Can't stop thinking about it,' he muttered, letting the truth slip out. 'Come to bed with me, Merry. You know you want to, really.'

'No, Rafe, I don't,' said Merry emphatically.

'Liar,' he whispered confidentially. 'Tell me you haven't imagined the touch of my hands and my lips on your skin, or feeling me between your legs, or waking up in my arms.'

Merry blushed. She had imagined all of those things, but to confess it now would precipitate disaster.

'I don't want to sleep with you, Rafe!' she cried. 'Can't you get that into your thick skull?'

'Why not?' he said shaking his head, trying to clear it. 'I don't understand. I know you want me. I *know* it. I've seen you look at me sometimes … and yesterday, you almost let me kiss you … I should have kissed you... Let me kiss you now!'

Merry brandished the poker.

'Confound you, Rafe! You promised me! Not a kiss or a touch unless I invite it! That was my condition of our marriage, and you agreed to it. You are not going to renege on that! I won't let you!'

'But why don't you want me to kiss you, Merry? Why don't you want to sleep with me and let me husband you?'

Rafe's plea forced Merry to search her heart for the last true obstacle to her accepting a marriage of convenience with Rafe, of submitting to his needs and taking what dark, heated pleasure she might from it. With the sweet-natured Mr Bingley fresh in her mind's eye, she knew it was Bryn's killing that would stand forever between them.

'You killed my brother,' she said implacably. 'No matter how sorry you say you are for it, you can never, never undo it. How can I submit myself to you when he lies between us?'

Rafe sat heavily on the end of her bed, rubbing the heels of his hands into his eyes. Behind him, Merry saw a rather dishevelled Brooke arrive in the broken doorway, having been summoned by the commotion of the door being battered. He was watching the scene warily and wondering how to extricate his master without violence.

'Huh! Your brother! Your saintly bloody brother!' Rafe groaned. 'Is that it? God, give me strength! Your brother, the damned fool! Why d'he have to pick _me_ to be the instrument of his suicide? Turned me into a murderer, too. Damned us both, the wretch! Could have put a period to his own existence easily enough... but, noooo... had to force a quarrel on me and make me do it, damn him! Called me a cheat ... knew I wouldn't swallow that ... and said "shoot to kill, for I will". And now you won't touch me, because I did as he bid. Well, that's rich!'

Rafe had been talking to himself, or to Fate, more than to Merry, so he had not seen the impact of his unguarded words on his wife. But Brooke had.

Her face had drained of colour as her expression had changed in an instant from exasperation to cold horror then bleakest disdain. Brooke then saw the colour flood back as she looked at Rafe with a truly murderous rage. Unconsciously, she lifted the poker and Brooke had to leap forward to wrest it from her hand, before she could strike Rafe with it. She released the poker but pulled herself free. As Rafe looked up in bewilderment, Merry slapped him so hard across the face that her own hand went numb.

'You unspeakable coward! You lily-livered little worm! You'll meet me for that!'

'Wh...what!' gasped Rafe, nursing his cheek.

'You cannot even take responsibility for murdering my brother in a duel, but must now foist *all* the blame on him! He who cannot defend himself! He who never hurt anyone in his life! You would blacken his soul in the cause of your base desires! Of all the cowardly, self-serving...! Ah!' Brooke had caught hold of Merry's arms, and she fought wildly to be free to claw at Rafe's dazed face. Thwarted, she spat at him instead. 'You are not fit to speak his name, you blackguard! But I can act for him! I should have done so from the start! Try your marksmanship against me, you dog, and we shall see who is left standing, if there is any justice in this world!'

'Don't be ridiculous!' said Rafe, sobering a little as he saw Merry's venomous expression. 'What's brought this on? What did I say?'

'Don't you dare ... *DARE*... try to deny it!' screamed Merry, making another frenzied attempt to free herself from Brooke's vice-like grip.

'You suggested her ladyship's brother intended to die at your hand, m'lord,' said Brooke in a matter-of-fact tone, hoping once again to bring this pair of fighting cocks to order.

Rafe frowned in annoyance at his slip, but was unrepentant.

'Well, so I think and what's more, you little harpy, Harry knew it, too!'

'Well, that's not going to help matters, is it m'lord?' sighed Brooke.

'Y'r a damned liar, Rafe!'

'No, I'm not! I'm finally telling you the truth, much though you can't stomach it! Harry was too nice to tell you.'

'Hah! So I have only *your* worthless opinion, my lord Rothsea? The word of a coward and a cheat!'

'Hey! Damn you! I'm no coward!' said Rafe defensively, and then adding more sheepishly: 'Even if I did cheat you and Harry a little.'

'Then accept my challenge, you cow-hearted rogue!'

'No!' said Rafe, rubbing his befuddled head and wishing it would clear. 'Can't fight my own wife. That's ridiculous. Not so drunk I don't know that.'

'I am not your wife!'

'Yes, you are!'

'No, my Lord Rothsea, I am not!' said Merry significantly. 'And as I made clear earlier, I shall never consent to be *made* your wife!'

Brooke's eyes widened at this illuminating news.

'Now, leave my room or *I will,* and you will never see me again!'

'Where will you go?'

'That is no longer your concern,' replied Merry coldly.

'You don't have any money,' Rafe said desperately, as Brooke began to manhandle him off the bed and towards the door.

'And whose fault is that?'

Brooke pushed Rafe through the door bodily, and they both heard a crash as another piece of furniture took the brunt of Rafe's unsteadiness, followed by a muffled: 'Please, don't leave me, Merry!'

Brooke sighed and shook his head. *What a mull the poor lad had made of this one!*

'My lady,' said Brooke earnestly. 'Don't go leaving in the night with nought but your cloak. If you still wish to leave tomorrow, I'll take you wherever you wish to go. I've a bit of money saved up, that can give you a start ... and his lordship will pay me back when he comes to his senses.'

Merry nodded and thanked him for his kindness, which made her suddenly tearful. The wild emotion of the past ten minutes was draining out of her and in its wake, Merry felt shaken and disoriented.

As Brooke pulled the door closed, as best he could, Merry sank onto her cushions, suddenly shivering and glad of the fire's warmth. A loyal sister, with a boyish code of honour, her unswerving belief in her brother's sense of duty towards her remained unshaken. Merry burned to avenge him, though she knew Rafe would not fight her.

So, she would have to leave. But Brooke was right: To do so in the heat of the moment, without a feather to fly with, would only spite herself.

I must think! Think! Merry said to herself.

After the disastrous events of the previous night, Brooke wondered if his mistress might think better of her wish to ride, but he had horses prepared, just in case.

When Merry appeared, neat as a pin, precisely at nine, he nursed a hope that she might be on the road to forgiving her husband. But the look in her eyes, as she bid him good morning with a bright, tight smile, soon told him otherwise. Only one other person had ever looked as determined on a course of action as she did now, and that was Lord Rothsea when he had carried her drugged body out of Quemerford Lodge.

Brooke sighed, but followed her, as he had promised Lord Rothsea he would, as she went about discovering the times and costs of stage journeys to different destinations.

They returned within a couple of hours, and Brooke was able to relieve Lain's vigil by his lordship's bed, lest the young man awaken and commit another rash act of folly to compensate for his last one.

Rafe did not stir until sometime after the mantel clock had struck eleven, and then he did so with a long groan, as the pain in his head made his return to consciousness an unwelcome one.

'Oh God!' Rafe said in a hoarse voice, once he had unstuck his tongue from the roof of his mouth.

Then his bleary eyes cracked open suddenly, as worrying recollections of his actions the night before came flooding back.

'*Oh God!*' he croaked in alarm.

'That's about the size of it, m'lord,' said Brooke, offering no solace.

'Is it as bad as I think it is?' asked Rafe bleakly.

'Can't see as how it could be *much* worse, sir, … if that's what you're thinking?'

Rafe's hands came up to cover his face.

'Oh, what have I done?' he groaned.

'I'd say you've outdone yourself this time, and no mistake,' said Brooke, shaking his head.

Rafe sat up with a wince, holding his head as if it might fall off without his support.

'You didn't let her leave?' Rafe demanded sharply.

'No, sir. But the lady's planning to leave you, right enough,' said Brooke frankly. 'You've a day, mebbe two, before she rubs off.'

'I won't let her go, Brooke,' said Rafe emphatically.

'Now, isn't that just the kind of talk that got us here in the first place, your lordship?'

'I love her,' he said simply. 'I know you've never understood… She's a hellcat, but she's the most wonderful woman I've ever met.'

'Oh, aye, m'lord. Mebbe I didn't see it at first, but I do now. The lady's a diamond, all right.' said Brooke. 'But she don't love you like you love her, and we both know what misery that brings you.'

Rafe groaned again and then was silent for a moment.

'Does she still want to kill me?' asked Rafe, hoping that a night's sleep might have diminished the bloodlust his wife had shown last night, if his memory served.

'Wants to run you through and through, m'lord, if I don't miss my guess.'

Rafe thought of the first time Merry had come into his life demanding satisfaction, and he smiled inwardly. She had challenged him again last night, he remembered.

'She'll come about. I'll tease her out of it, you'll see,' said Rafe optimistically. 'I make her laugh, … even when she doesn't want to.'

'I think you might find she's lost her sense of humour, your lordship,' said Brooke baldly. 'But I'd be happy to be proved wrong.'

'Where is she?'

'In with Mrs Dodd, trying to pretend that nothing's amiss, when the household's all a'buzz about you kicking in her ladyship's door.'

Rafe groaned again, putting his hand over his eyes once more.

'I've had Henry fit two stout bolts, so don't go putting your shoulder to it again, or you'll come off worst this time, sir.'

'I think we both know I came off worst the last time, one way or another.'

'Aye,' confirmed Brooke. 'You're right there.'

Rafe was silent, still piecing together what he remembered of last night. Now, he recalled the slap she had given him, but worse, the look in her eyes that held something resolute, something final.

'Her brother …' said Rafe suddenly, with a tortured moan of self-loathing, the heels of his hands going to his eyes again.

'Aye, that was the leveller,' said Brooke grimly. 'You all but called him a coward and a suicide.'

'Worse! I told her he had intentionally left her alone to face destitution … and damned himself into the bargain. Her so-gentlemanly brother.'

'You think it true, then?'

'Not a doubt of it.'

'Did you suspect it at the time,' asked Brooke.

Rafe nodded slowly.

'My saner self did.'

'Hm… we don't see so much of 'im as we'd like, do we, sir?' observed Brooke.

'He doesn't shout as loud as my other self,' said Rafe with a glimmer of humorous self-awareness.

'Nobody does, m'lord,' replied Brooke, with feeling.

Rafe sighed and tried to roll his eyes, but they hurt too much.

'So you really think she means to leave me?'

'Been plotting her escape all morning,' nodded Brooke. 'I've agreed to help her, and begging your lordship's pardon I will too, if she can't be talked into staying … with you making her laugh, and all,' he added with dry irony.

'Traitor,' said Rafe without heat.

'Knew you'd see the wisdom of it,' said Brooke, the ghost of a smile in his eyes. 'You'll want to know where the lady is and that she's safe, even if she can't stand the sight of you … that's my guess.'

Rafe felt his gut wrenching at the thought, and then threw back the covers impulsively.

'I've got to talk to her, man! Tell her I'm sorry!'

THE RELUCTANT LADY

'No!' said Brooke firmly. 'You'll not see her ladyship until you've had a bath and bite to eat. Leave her be to cool a little while longer. She ain't going nowhere… even heard her tell cook she would be dining this evening, and I don't think she'd knowingly mislead Mrs Greaves.'

Resigning himself reluctantly to the wisdom of Brooke's words, Rafe nodded and sagged back on the bed. Also, when his manservant was this determined, Rafe knew Brooke would likely mill him down, if he made a dash for the door. In his present fragile state, Rafe didn't like his odds.

Though Merry appeared to be attending to the housekeeper, who was demonstrating how the household accounts were laid out, Mrs Dodd could see that her ladyship's mind was elsewhere. Nor was she surprised when Lady Rothsea's eyes strayed beyond the ledger to rest unseeing on some unremarkable object, while her gaze was clouded by troubles that rumpled the poor young lady's brow. And no wonder. Everyone knew that Henry had been instructed to fix two big stable bolts to the connecting door, and Mr Timmins the carpenter was working to repair the damaged frame.

Mr Brooke hadn't given away by so much as a flicker of his eye, what had happened the night before, but gossip was rife. The most popular conceit was that his lordship had got steaming drunk, kicked in his wife's door and ravished her, with a titillating speculation that he'd had to be pulled bodily off the poor lady by Mr Brooke.

But there was her ladyship, having an early breakfast and looking fresh as a new-minted sixpence. There was a faint frown in her eyes now and then, but no other outward sign of distress or violence. She had gone for a ride with Mr Brooke, as arranged, and kept her appointment with Mrs Dodd. So no one now knew what to think.

Only when they finally saw husband and wife together did everyone know that something was terribly wrong.

Merry had not waited for Rafe to escort her to the drawing room before dinner; she awaited him there. Rafe paused as he reached for the handle, nervously wondering what his wife's mood might now be like after a day to reflect. Perhaps she had been tortured with doubts about her brother's behaviour and might want to talk them out. Or perhaps she would still be demanding pistols at dawn.

As he entered, he saw she was in a gown Harry had bought her and wearing her mother's pearls, instead of the ones he had given. It was not a promising sign.

Merry had her gloved wrist resting against the mantel and was gazing down into the fire. She did not move as Rafe entered, though her breathing seemed a little faster.

'Conjuring images?' said Rafe, with all the gentle, loving charm that his anxious heart could muster, as he began to walk towards her.

Then Merry, at last, looked round at him, and Rafe's world shattered. Unconsciously, he fell back a step as he reeled inwardly. Her expression held neither unhappy confusion nor murderous intent. It was much worse.

Every spark of life, of humour, even anger was gone, along with all the echoes of their shared memories. Marble-cold, deathly still … it was hard to trace his Merry in this cool stranger … though her hair, her skin, her figure were all the same.

She was a closed vault. He was excluded, unwelcome.

He was a child again, looking at a stone wall where love and warmth should be. Excluded. Unwelcome.

But he never remembered it hurting this much.

Merry had looked away again, without a word … as if he had not spoken … as if she did not know him. But in that instant he had glimpsed something else that froze him where he stood. Something resolute. Something final.

Rafe tried to speak, but his voice would not come. Fear, visceral and paralysing, strangled the words as they formed.

Hope was dying. There would be no forgiveness this time. Merry would leave him, and there could be no life without her.

And then the irony blazed in his mind, briefly illuminating the Greek chorus that laughed and wailed at his fate. The tragic irony that he was being punished not for the crime but for telling the truth about its cause!

Somehow, in that absurd moral code of hers, murdering her brother in a duel might be tolerated; disowning responsibility and calling it suicide was unforgivable.

Rafe was still standing, staring dumbstruck and desolated, when Frith scratched and entered to announce dinner. The butler took in this sad tableau and his own heart sank.

Lady Rothsea straightened and moved mechanically towards the door. His lordship seemed to falter and then held out his arm to escort his wife, with an expression that wrung his butler's withers.

Her ladyship froze and glanced towards the offered arm as though it were faintly offensive, but then her eyes flickered to Frith's worried face and, after a moment, she placed her gloved hand on her husband's arm and proceeded to dinner.

Only Rafe knew the hand never touched his sleeve, but hovered a quarter inch above it.

Who knew that so small a gesture could lacerate like a bullwhip?

As an extra twist of the knife, Rafe found that his wife's place setting had been restored to the far end of the table. His fury might have escaped at that, but it was too occupied lashing himself from within.

Dinner was excruciating. Rafe could not speak, and Merry would not.

When Rafe held the door open for her to depart, she gave a faint nod in his direction, without looking up, and drifted from the room like a ghost.

After a few minutes, Rafe left his port and almost ran to the library, but then sank into a chair hunched over, his face in his hands. Merry was not there awaiting him ...

... she was in her bedchamber, sobbing her heart out, stuffing her pillow into her mouth to stifle the sounds of her misery. If Rafe was distraught downstairs, his wife was inconsolable above them. Rafe would never know what it had taken to lock him out of her heart - the grinding will, the wrenching despair. To leave not one chink through which he might seep back in, to make her thaw with humour, to make her care with need, to draw her ever closer with that deepening bond for which she had not found a proper name.

A lifetime of conditioning, years of school beatings, dangerous gambles, life-threatening exploits, of concealing her sex day after day, year after year – it had taken everything she could muster to do what she had never had to do with Rafe … to hide her real self from him.

Even her wrath was a way in and had to be suppressed - compressed down to a cold, hard rock.

All day long, while she had maintained the façade of normality, she had been engaged in a savage business – killing her love for her friend Rafe. This glowing thing within her, which had so pervaded her mind and body that excising it had left her own self less than whole. In her mind, she had rolled this love into a tight ball and stabbed it repeatedly, only to feel it was her own heart that she slashed and left bleeding inwardly.

But no matter how much it hurt, she now knew the friend she had loved had been an illusion, a hollow man. *In vino veritas* – in that unguarded moment, he had revealed his true self – one who would tell an unforgivable lie, cast an unpardonable slur, merely so that he might sleep with her.

Yet, for all this, in the drawing room when Merry had first seen his face drain, like a man having his entrails drawn, her mask had almost slipped. She had wanted to rescue him even then. Merry now knew for certain that she could not trust herself to remain strong. Before long, she would begin falling towards him by inches once again.

I must leave this man, this place … and soon.

The thought brought on a fresh bout of uncontrollable weeping.

The next day followed a similar chilling pattern. Merry had packed a bag – only the few clothes Harry had bought her, and the two slim volumes of Pride and Prejudice, because she couldn't bear to part with this memento.

After a fruitless attempt to dissuade her, Brooke had finally agreed to help his mistress to leave that night. Merry could not bear to say goodbye to the household, to see their pitying, uneasy faces. She felt like she had brought a dark cloud to settle over this sunny, happy place. The sooner she disappeared, the sooner they might return to normal. In a little while, it would be as if she had never been.

Merry dressed for their last dinner together with particular care. As an odd concession, which she cursed as weakness, Merry dressed in the black velvet dress with the jet beading and the matching tiara. Merry would not wear Rafe's pearls, which lay on her dresser wrapped up in a short jumbled note of thanks and rejection. Her own pearls were packed away carefully in her bag.

Her mask firmly in place, they followed the same frigid ritual as the night before, but there was a profound underlying poignancy - both knew this was their last meal together.

Across the table, Rafe barely took his eyes from his wife. *She means to leave me tonight.*

Merry looked at him just once – fleeting, unreadable, but not stone cold.

Finally, Alfred and Henry moved forward to remove the covers, under Frith's watchful supervision, but Rafe dismissed them all with one slight gesture of his hand.

He had one last desperate hand to play and desired no witnesses.

Merry had not noticed the staff disappear. She was trying to stand on wobbly legs, trying to stiffen her backbone to leave the room, to leave Rafe, never to see him again.

Don't speak! You can't trust yourself! Just leave without a word or a look. If you look at him, you'll crumble.

Rafe was walking towards her, still holding a glass of the claret he had been drinking steadily throughout a dinner he had not touched.

Merry girded her loins, one last time, to hold her mask in place for a few minutes more.

Rafe looked down at that cold, forbidding face for a moment, and then dashed the contents of his glass full into it.

Chapter Nineteen:
A Deadly Gamble

'Is that enough provocation for you?' he snapped, as though goaded beyond the bounds of his temper.

'What?' gasped Merry, her face dripping, little rivulets of wine trickling down her neck and breast, her hands too stilled by shock to prevent the flow with her napkin.

'Let's have done with this! Do you wish to have satisfaction?' demanded Rafe. 'I don't care that you're a woman and my *wife*! If you want to put a bullet in me, you'll have to face me across twelve paces!'

Merry was dumbstruck.

'Well?' pressed Rafe. 'Or do I have to waste another glass of wine?'

At this, Merry finally jumped up, fury kindling her grey eyes at last.

'No, I'm for you!' she cried, her voice shaking with anger. 'Now, if you wish?'

'Oh, no. We are not savages, after all,' said Rafe, mockingly silky. 'Tomorrow morning, at five o'clock in the Home Wood. I'll bring the pistols.'

'Very well,' agreed Merry, trying to keep up the bravado, which was masking a disturbing tumult of emotions.

'What about seconds?' she asked.

'We won't need them,' he replied.

'… or a surgeon?'

'Why? He would be wasting his time,' said Rafe. 'We are not such poor shots as to miss our marks … are we?'

'N...no,' faltered Merry. The reality of what they planned hitting home.

THE RELUCTANT LADY

Tomorrow one or both of them would die at the other's hand. A husband and wife setting out to kill one another under the veneer of a duel.

'Very well then,' said Rafe in a voice stripped of emotion, reflecting the numbness he was feeling.

Merry had accepted the challenge. His beloved wife still wanted him dead.

'We are agreed. I shall knock to wake you in the morning. Now I must arrange to have our horses waiting. Good night, madam.'

He bowed slightly, without meeting her eyes, and left the room briskly.

Merry remained standing until Rafe was out of the room only by an extreme exercise of will. As the door closed, her knees gave way and she sank into her chair. Wine still trickled down her throat and into her bodice, but she didn't notice. She felt suffocated by panic and shock. But it was not fear for her life that choked her but something else, something she could not quite articulate.

Merry's train of thought was interrupted by the entry of the servants to clear the table, believing the room to be empty. Merry saw their expressions as they quickly assimilated the fact that his lordship had thrown wine in his wife's face, before they rapidly beat a hasty retreat and sought Frith's guidance on what to do next.

Merry rose, still numb yet steadier, but after a few steps she sobbed and ran to her room as fast as her skirts would allow.

Chantal arrived a few minutes later, clearly apprised of the news. Merry had already stripped off the soiled gown and kicked it into a corner, but she now sat at her dressing table in her stays and petticoats, her chemise stained at the top with the blood-red wine. She was staring at her reflection with wild, wide eyes.

Why am I so upset? Merry was asking herself. *Isn't this exactly what I wanted?*

Chantal broke the trance with a light cough.

'Milady, may I help you out of those clothes?' she prompted gently. 'I have taken the liberty to send for your bath. It is such a cool night that I thought perhaps you might appreciate the warmth.'

As she spoke, Chantal busied herself laying out her ladyship's nightrail.

These prosaic actions had their desired effect. Merry shook herself and responded.

'Thank you, Chantal. A bath is an excellent idea. I should like to wash my hair, too.' Merry thought that if she was to meet her Maker on the morrow, she would do so with clean hair.

Sometime later, she heard Rafe's bedroom door close and wondered if he was doing the same.

He wasn't.

Chantal continued her gentle ministrations in preparing her mistress for bed. She and the rest of the household burned to know what had actually happened.

'Is everything all right, milady?' she ventured.

'Perfectly,' said her ladyship, closing the door on the conversation.

Then, she looked up with a sudden notion and walked to her writing desk, pulling out a sheet of hot-pressed paper and scratching a note, which she carefully sealed.

'Please lay out my black riding habit, as I may go for an early ride, and deliver this note to Mr Brooke as soon as you have finished.'

Chantal demurred for a moment, pointing at the bath.

'You can have the bath water taken away in the morning. I would rather be alone for now, Chantal,' said Merry, wearily. Then as the maid opened the door, Merry called: 'Chantal, thank you … for your patience. I haven't been an easy mistress, but I am a grateful one.'

'Bon chance, milady!' said the maid, dipping a slight curtsey. 'I hope you find what you seek.' She added, believing that her mistress planned to leave tonight with Mr Brooke. After all, her ladyship had made no secret of packing her bag, which sat in the corner. Chantal sighed as she walked towards her own room. *Back to the sewing room for me then*, she thought unhappily.

Merry was sorry that she had no vails to leave Chantal. By the time she and the other servants rose in the morning, they would know the outcome of the Rothseas' deadly contest.

Chantal hoped to see the contents of the note she handed to Brooke, but he gave her a wry look of dismissal. He had been preparing the travelling coach to take his mistress where she wished to go to, and bedamned to her plan to ride the stage.

THE RELUCTANT LADY

Returning from the stables, he had heard the startling story about his lordship throwing wine in his wife's face, and was on his way to talk to his maddening master about it, when Chantal had intercepted him. By the light of the wall sconce, Brooke tore off the wafer and read the note.

Dear Mr Brooke,
Pray Cancel our plans to depart This night, if you Please. I am
Persuaded to remain Another night.
Yr humble servant,
Merion Griffith Esq

Merry had laboured over her choice of words, so as not to alert Brooke to the forthcoming duel, but then as her thoughts had wandered, she had dashed off her standard valediction and signature. Brooke smiled at her ladyship's unconscious lapse. It made him think of the first time he had seen her, dressed as boy and behaving so like one, in such a welter of vengeance and bravado, that he had not known the difference until he'd seen her all got up in sprig muslin. And all that talk of calling out his lordship, both then and two nights ago. Brooke stopped in his tracks and wondered just how long the lady had been pretending to be a lad, when he should instead have wondered if the *lad* had got his wish or not.

When Brooke found him, Rafe was well-prepared for his perspicacious manservant. He knew Brooke would put a stop to his scheme, no matter what rationale he put forward. His master's wild hope that his wife might see how sorry he was for hurting her, might choose to spare him, might somehow see that there was an indelible bond between them that made parting unthinkable, would carry no weight at all with Brooke. The notion that Rafe would sooner die than let his wife depart would carry less. If he lived or died, Rafe had made over the Fall to Merry. There would be no question of her going off to London and trying to make her own way in the world.

Rafe fobbed Brooke off.

'Don't start!' said Rafe, as Brooke opened the door. 'Her stony-faced silence would have driven a saint to murder! I had the wine in my hand. It was that or strangle her. At least it provoked her into speaking with me. Tomorrow, we are to go for a ride and discuss our affairs in private,' he lied. 'I have written to Purdue to put this property in my wife's name. She will not be leaving. I will.'

Brooke was suspicious, but this explanation seemed in accord with her ladyship's note. He did not think to ask at what hour they planned to depart for their discussion, and Rafe had instructed Humphreys not to tell him.

It was a wretched night for Merry, heartsick and straining to understand why.

Had she not always demanded this opportunity to avenge her brother? Now that her wish was granted, why was she in such turmoil?

It was not the risk of pain or death, though she relished neither.

Merry had fought two duels with swords when she was in school. Admittedly, they had been trivial affairs, under the watchful and disapproving eye of her brother. The only aim had been to be the first to pink the other. But before those encounters, Merry remembered being clear-headed and determined, fired with righteous certitude.

Tonight, she was consumed by doubt and tormented by elusive wraiths, which asked probing questions that she could not answer or that evoked memories she yearned to forget. Foremost amongst these was the feel of Rafe's strong arms holding her to his body, once in London and later by the lake. There had been such comfort there. It had made her feel small and weak, but so safe and cherished. In this dark hour, she longed for them again, but tomorrow she was to put a bullet through the chest that had offered such safe harbour.

Somewhere in the midst of all these thoughts Merry realised that she no longer wished she were a man. Perhaps it was the romantic charm of the novel she had been reading, as she found herself willing Mr Darcy and Lizzie Bennett to unite. Perhaps it was merely an acceptance of the realities Rafe had laid bare at Quemerford. But though she still felt gauche in her skirts, the thought of going back to her former masquerade now seemed absurd. Even more disturbing was the instinct, awakened by Rafe's wicked suggestions, that she might be ready to embrace her womanhood in other ways, to be a real wife, if she could find a man she could both respect and desire. Since this train of thought soon conjured up heated images of Rafe, Merry was obliged to jump out of bed and splash her face with cold water to try to dispel them.

Instead of these dangerous directions, Merry put her mind to whipping up her wrath. Every time a thought entered her mind that weakened her resolve, she would turn over. So, inevitably, she tossed and turned all night, finally falling into a fitful doze after three.

For Rafe, it was a long bleak night, dulled only by brandy. He slept in his chair and awoke aching in body and soul.

Well, perhaps this morning will finally see an end to it, he thought

It wanted only thirty minutes before they were due to meet, when Rafe walked across to the connecting door and knocked.

'Thirty minutes, Merry!'

Merry was already awake, heavy-eyed, groggy and sick to her stomach with dread.

'I shall be ready, never fear!' she called back.

Merry dressed quickly in her black riding habit, dragging her hair back from her face with two tortoiseshell combs. Looking at her reflection, it was that of a stranger. She tried to trace Bryn's features in her own, to fortify her resolve, but she saw only the haunted face of a troubled girl.

As Rafe quickly shaved by candlelight with cold water, he nicked himself. Seeing the blood creep out of the cut and a drop fall onto the linen cloth, his hand stilled for a moment and he felt a tremor pass through him. This was a terrible gamble. But then he thought, it was no gamble at all. He loved his wife. His heart and body ached for her, and she despised him.

Well, death was preferable to this slow torture, and perhaps it was justice after all.

Thinking back to that awful duel, he passed a hand over his eyes. He barely recognised the man who had then inhabited his skin.

How could he have taken that boy's life so coldly … and for nothing?

It made him sick to think of it.

'Yes, let's have done with it,' he said grimly to his reflection. 'Let me have peace at last.'

As he stepped out of his room, his heart lurched. Merry was walking down the corridor ahead of him, her slender figure turning to look back at him with wide eyes, deeply shadowed beneath.

Well, it was some dark comfort that her sleep had not been untroubled.

'I have the pistols,' he said quietly, as he joined her, and they walked silently down the stairs together.

Humphreys was waiting outside, walking their horses. He had received Lord Rothsea's message, to have the horses ready but not to inform Mr Brooke, as he was heading off to bed. Already intrigued, his eyebrows flew up when he was handed the box of duelling pistols, while his lordship helped his lady to mount, and then quickly did so himself, receiving the box back from his goggle-eyed head groom.

'Let Mr Brooke know that there are letters on my desk that must be delivered if I do not return.'

Those last words echoed round poor Humphreys' head like a death knell, as he watched the pair canter off towards the home wood. There was only one possible explanation, for everyone now knew that the master had dashed wine in his wife's face. Like others, he had struggled to believe that piece of gossip, but now he grasped that his lordship meant to have some kind of duel with his wife!

This outlandish idea seemed so incredible that Humphreys lost several minutes while he wrestled with it. At a loss to know what to do, he chose disobedience, dashing off for the house to rouse Mr Brooke and apprise him of what was toward.

Although they were hastening to a grim purpose, the familiar exhilaration of exercising fresh horses, the gentle thunder of their hooves on the dewy turf, the physical effort of holding them to a matched pace and the cool air against their faces, all these shared sensations seemed to be a bond between them. Each stole glances at the other, only once catching each other's eyes in an unreadable look, charged with emotion.

Slowing as they moved through the darkness of the home wood, they followed the bridle path until they reached the glade at the centre. The pale morning light was growing, although mist still clung to the hollows.

THE RELUCTANT LADY

Rafe dismounted first. He put the pistols down on the ground and reached up to help Merry down. For a moment, he held her waist, looking down at her inscrutably.

Merry felt his strength. She stood unresisting, a little awkward, within the span of his hands.

'It's a little unorthodox,' he said finally, in a voice not quite his own. 'But since it will be for the final time, would you object if I requested a kiss from my wife – our first and our last?'

Merry's heart gave a peculiar leap. Looking into his eyes, it was not lust or desire she saw, merely sadness and a kind of distant longing. Merry's thoughts were already in chaos. This odd, disturbing request was too much for her to parry, and, somewhere in her own dark thoughts, she did not want to die without having been kissed on her lips at least once in her life.

'I ... I ... er ... if you wish,' she stammered, suddenly noticing how attractive was the shape of his mouth.

Rafe wrenched off his gloves and threw them aside. For a long moment, he looked down at her without moving, before reaching up to trace his fingertips along her forehead and down from her temple to gently cup her cheek, then slowly burying his fingers in her hair, as his other hand settled in the small of her back. He bowed his head and brushed his lips softly against Merry's, which parted in surprise. Rafe felt the cool hush of her gasp, as she reacted to the delicious warmth of his breath on her mouth.

Suddenly, Merry felt his hands tremble slightly and it seemed as if a mask slipped from his face. He drew back to look at her, as if memorising her face with a kind of raw, agonised longing that caused her own heart to pang in response. Then, with a groan drawn from the depths of his being, he kissed her.

From the moment that his strong arms closed around her and his lips found hers, Merry's world tilted on its axis and threw everything she knew and believed into disarray. The warm pressure of his lips moving rhythmically over and over on her own, made her heart thud almost painfully against her ribs, and, unconsciously, she found herself inexpertly responding.

Rafe's body tensed and he gave another strange groan, his arms tightening, causing a surge of energy between them, and the kiss deepened, teasing her mouth further open. The touch of his tongue against her own, which ought to have repulsed her, instead awoke some wild thing within Merry that made her respond with a hunger equal to his own. When her tongue sought his, Rafe gave moan of desire and a shiver went through both their bodies, each pressed hard against the other's. Merry's hands had moved up from his chest and were now around his neck and tangling in his hair, her body arching traitorously, hungrily, against his. For several minutes, they were lost in each other, as if they couldn't get close enough.

Suddenly, the spell was broken. Rafe gasped and reluctantly dragged his lips from hers before the rising agonising ache in his loins threatened to overcome reason and scruples.

The kiss, intended to be the last supper of a condemned man, had been an awakening for them both.

'Merry,' he breathed, in a hoarse whisper, an expression of fierce wonder in his eyes as he looked down at her. 'You love me,' he said in an unsteady voice. 'Just as I love you.'

But the languid, mesmerised look in hers was rapidly fading to be replaced with one of shock and confused dismay.

'No! I don't! I don't!' she cried, stunned and disgusted at herself, for falling so shamelessly susceptible to a wild rake's kiss.

Though more horrified by her own actions than his, Merry was now also newly experiencing the acid burn of jealousy towards every other woman who had experienced that sinful euphoria in Rafe's arms.

Trying to wriggle out of his embrace as shamed reaction set in, Merry added bitterly 'I suppose you've used that technique on dozens of women? Very persuasive, I'm sure.'

Merry almost fell when Rafe's arms dropped suddenly from her sides and she felt an odd wrench when she saw a shadow of hurt cloud his eyes. He did not respond but turned coldly and walked away to fetch the pistols. Merry felt oddly bereft. She'd wanted him to respond to the bait, and realised she was craving a duel of words, not the deadly one they were about to commence.

Rafe came back to stand in front of her, his eyes now cool and distant. He opened the velvet-lined box, to reveal two elegant pistols, like deadly vipers resting in their niches.

'Choose!' he said starkly.

'Are they loaded?' Merry asked, trying to suppress the shaking in her voice.

'Of course,' he replied dryly. 'And be warned, they have hair-triggers and will fire at the slightest pressure.'

Merry gingerly removed her weapon. The weight felt familiar in her hand, although the balance of this was far superior to any other she had handled.

Merry followed Rafe to the centre of the clearing, her legs feeling heavy and numb, her head dizzy with nerves, and her breath coming in rapid pants.

Rafe took her shoulders and turned her about so that she faced away from him, moving her hand and arm to point the pistol upward in the correct manner for this form of duel, and then took his place with his back against hers.

'At my mark, walk six paces, turn, take aim and fire,' said Rafe sternly. 'Do you understand?'

'Yes,' she responded breathlessly, her pulse racing.

Merry's stomach was churning so much she thought she might be sick. A dozen thoughts raced through her mind in the space of a heartbeat.

We are going through with it! Dear God! I must shoot Rafe to avenge Bryn. I must fire quickly to get my shot in first. I hope his aim is true. I don't want to be wounded and left well enough to hang.

But, insidiously, other thoughts crowded in, all heightened by that staggering kiss.

How could the touch of his lips and the strength of his arms have such an effect on me? Why did he look so hurt when I sneered at it? He probably kisses women all the time. It probably meant nothing to him.

But, as if he read her thoughts, he said:

'I have kissed dozens of women, Merry, but I have only ever loved one.'

One?

'One!'

'Two!'

Merry stumbled forward. *It had begun!*

Her stride measured the lengthening distance between them, the train of her riding habit dragging over the damp grass. She was deaf to the riotous birdsong of the dawn chorus across the home wood; blind to the way the pearly light was bringing the colours of nature back to life around them. Her brain was in turmoil.

Why did he look so ... so ... overjoyed ... when he thought that I loved him? Could he be right? Or is he trying to put me off my shot?

'Three!'

Was <u>Love</u> the nameless feeling that bound her to him despite all he had done? Was this why the thought of leaving him, even of hurting him, had torn her apart?

'Four!'

There was now a gulf of difference between her feelings for Harry and Rafe.

Was <u>this</u> the difference? Was this what love really felt like? Not pleasant and comfortable, but confusing, disturbing and utterly overwhelming?

'Five!'

Merry was besieged by remembered sensations and images - of desire, comfort, humour, kindness, companionship and even exhilarating anger. Now, at this eleventh hour, she was forced to acknowledge that every moment she had spent with Rafe was more real and achingly precious than she dared admit.

And now I must put a bullet in him to avenge my brother!

'Six!'

Merry turned quickly, bringing her arm down to take aim and then gasped.

Rafe had not moved from the spot! He was standing just six paces away, facing her, his pistol down at his side, offering her a clear and utterly lethal shot at him.

Slowly, he deloped, drawing his arm wide and upward to his right and firing harmlessly into the sky, shattering the silent air with an ear-splitting crack, which seemed to ricochet amongst the surrounding trees, sending crows cawing noisily into the still air above the wood.

Merry flinched and her pistol wavered as she registered what he was doing. She saw Rafe take a sharp breath in, as if steadying himself for the bullet to come, but he did not move. He was looking at her with that same sad, steady look.

Merry's arm tensed, her finger cradled against the trigger, her face strained. Here was the chance to have justice for that terrible slur against Bryn and for his murder. To take revenge against the man she should despise for abducting her.

So why, oh why, couldn't she pull the trigger?

THE RELUCTANT LADY

A minute passed, an eternity. Along the length of the deadly barrel, she looked at the man facing her. The pistol wavered wildly again. Merry closed her eyes and turned her face upward in torment, as if seeking strength from above. Then she looked back at Rafe again, with a determined look on her face, levelling the pistol at his heart once more.

Just one moment of courage and things would be righted, she tried to tell herself. *I must harden my heart as he did when he blew a hole through Bryn's.*

Merry conjured up the awful image of that small dark hole in her brother's chest. That image should have strengthened her resolve, but suddenly the thought of a hole in the broad chest that faced her, turned her insides to water.

Why?
Because she would sooner die than cause it.
Why?
Not him! Not him!
Why?
Because ... because ...

Her hand wavered again.

The target was getting closer. Rafe was walking towards her ... five paces ... then four.

Now, the pistol was resting against that broad chest. Rafe was looking down at her, with an expression that mingled hope, wonder and a burning question.

'I can't do it,' said Merry helplessly, her hand dropping to her side.

'Why, Merry?' his voice was a charged whisper. He seemed to hold his breath for the response.

'Because ...' Her drowning eyes never left his and her expression almost caused Rafe's heart to leap out of his chest, as Merry slowly shook her head in disbelief. 'Because ... I think I *love* you,' she whispered.

Rafe's arms closed around her in a crushing grip as his mouth covered hers with an enraptured groan. They were lost in this wild kiss, when suddenly there was a deafening report.

Chapter Twenty
Flesh of One Flesh

'God damn it, Merry!' cried Rafe, clutching his calf. 'You've shot me!'

'I didn't mean to!' retorted Merry, horror suddenly giving way to hysterical laughter, as reaction to the duel set in and she watched Rafe hopping round with an incensed look.

'L..let that be a l..lesson to you,' she gasped. 'Not to kiss me when my finger is on a hair-trigger!'

'I shall keep the gun cupboards locked against you,' he said with asperity, wincing as he felt for the burning wound.

But Merry had already knelt beside him and was examining his leg. Looking up at him, she said:

'Well, if I couldn't shoot you in a fervour of revenge, when you were standing but twelve feet in front of me, I think your life is now safe.'

'It's not my life I'm worried about,' he snapped back. 'It's my other leg.'

But, ignoring the sharp agony of his injury, Rafe pulled Merry up to her feet, and his hands held her slender shoulders as he gazed at her in awe once more.

'I thought once or twice that you were going to blow a hole through my chest. What stopped you?'

'The thought of that hole in your chest,' she replied, wonderingly, as she looked into his now-dear face.

How on earth she had failed to notice how stunningly handsome he was before?

'I know what it looks like, you see. I couldn't do that … not to you. I'd sooner shoot myself.'

THE RELUCTANT LADY

Merry saw Rafe's eyes close as a wave of remorse and self-loathing swept through him. She felt his pain as if it were her own. This was another revelation: *hurting him was like hurting herself!*

Flesh of one flesh, bone of one bone, she thought.

'Oh God, Merry,' he groaned, kissing her brow, her eyes, her hair. 'You know that if I could undo any of the dreadful things I've done in my life, I would undo that … and the stupid things I said about it.'

'I know. I know. But, oh, Rafe! You took such a risk. I could have killed you!'

'Better that than live with my beloved wife despising me,' his voice broke a little as he said the word 'wife' and his arms closed even more tightly around her. 'I love you, sweet.'

'I … think I love you too,' said Merry hesitantly, still astonished at her own *volte face*, but resting her cheek thankfully against that broad chest.

'Love? Or *think* you love?' asked Rafe, with narrowed eyes, suddenly holding her off from him for a moment. 'Which is it?'

'Wretch!' she said, with a darkling look. 'I love you! I love you! There, does that satisfy your vanity?'

Rafe laughed. It was the freest, most joyous sound Merry had ever heard him make.

'Ah, such is the battered state of my self-esteem after the lashing you've given it over the past month,' he exclaimed, with a sparkling boyish look in his eyes. 'That I may need you to repeat that several times a day for the next fifty years or more, just to regain a little of my former confidence.'

Merry laughingly agreed to supply him with reassurances as often as was required. Rafe's eyes glowed with such an intense, joyous disbelief as he watched her smiling up at him, that it stilled her laughter with breathless wonder. She felt like the centre of his world, which she was.

'Ah, Merry! I had despaired that this day would ever come,' he said softly, his arms tightening around her again and his lips brushing hers. 'I can't believe my luck!'

'But what about your leg?' cried Merry, feeling him sway as he tried to keep the weight on his good leg without leaning too heavily on her.

'Damn my leg! I'll live,' he muttered, his lips finding hers again. 'I've waited five long weeks to kiss you, Merry, and I'm damned if I'll deny myself that luxury because of a scratch.'

So it was, as Brooke came thundering into the clearing, directed by the sound of the shots, he was greeted by the boggling sight of Lord Rothsea and his wife locked in a passionate embrace, a pair of pistols on the ground beside them. He tried to make a discreet exit, but Rafe looked up and shouted: 'Brooke! Call for a surgeon! My dear wife here has blown a hole through my leg!'

'He got off lightly,' she murmured provocatively, with half closed eyes, lifting her face for another kiss.

Brooke galloped off towards Mumshall to fetch the surgeon, shaking his head in puzzlement. He had never seen his lordship so happy in his life … and that with a bullet-hole in his leg!

Rafe and Merry rode back to the hall in a kind of wondering haze. Rafe was so happy that he barely felt his wounded leg until he jumped down from the horse and let out a sharp groan. Merry supported him into the house, where two of the footmen almost shooed her aside and assisted him to his room. Word had got around about the duelling pistols, and the household were now casting Merry some wary and accusatory looks. When his valet tried to bar her from his lordship's room, Merry's temper snapped.

'Good God, you imbecile! It was an accident! If I wanted to kill him, he would be dead! Now step aside and fetch a razor. We'll need to cut that boot.'

Lain pursed his lips but did as he was bid, disappearing into the dressing room to fetch his master's second best razor.

'Merry!' hissed Rafe. 'I'm going to have to take *all* my clothes off. Are you sure you want to remain for that particular revelation?'

Merry blushed adorably, and said: 'Perhaps I should change into something a little more appropriate to greet the surgeon?' and then dashed off to her own room.

The surgeon arrived some thirty minutes later, by which time her husband was in his nightshirt, his leg loosely bandaged and supported on a pillow.

Escorting Dr Brereton into the room, Merry experienced a strange thrill that set her blood tingling, when she saw her husband in his nightshirt, untied at the neck revealing a deep

THE RELUCTANT LADY

glimpse of the chest she had so much admired in Albemarle Street.

For a moment, Rafe's attention was divided between greeting the doctor and wondering what lay behind the very interesting look that had just crossed his wife's face.

Examining his wounded leg, the surgeon was a little confused.

'Most odd,' he said. 'It almost appears as if the shot was downward into your boot.'

'It was,' replied Rafe, with a conspiratorial look towards Merry. 'My wife's attention was otherwise engaged when her finger touched the trigger.'

'I see,' remarked the doctor.

He didn't.

'Well, thankfully it is just a deep graze. The ball has passed through a little superficial flesh and muscle. I must stitch you up, my lord, which will be no very pleasant experience, and you will need to remain off wine or other spirits for a day or two, until the risk of fever has passed.

Rafe endured the surgeon's ministrations stoically, more so than Merry, who winced and groaned with every stitch, as though it were her own flesh that the needle pierced. Over the surgeon's head, Rafe's gaze held hers, narrow eyed and promising retribution. Finally, the doctor cleaned the wound and Rafe jolted a little, dragging a squeak from Merry, when the surgeon ran a swab of brine across his work, having a strong belief in its restorative powers. After he had bound up the wound tightly in lint and gauze, the doctor turned to Merry.

'Perhaps a little broth and a capon for his dinner, your ladyship, but no wine,' he instructed, for all the world as if Rafe were not sitting there watching them both with a comic frown of disbelief. 'If his temperature remains normal, perhaps a small glass with dinner tomorrow,' added the doctor, before packing his things away in his bag and rolling down his sleeves.

'You should be back on your feet in a couple of days, Lord Rothsea, but no sooner, or you might burst your stitches and cause an infection,' he said to Rafe, in a louder voice.

Only a quelling look from Merry, giving him the novel experience of being momentarily under the cat's paw, prevented Rafe from informing the doctor, politely but firmly, that he intended to be back on his feet in a couple of minutes rather than a couple of days.

As Merry showed the surgeon out of the room ahead of her, Rafe got another fiery blast from those fine grey eyes accompanied by a gesture from her finger that he was to stay where he was until she returned. Merry had to bite her lip to keep from giggling when she saw Rafe fold his arms across his chest and give her a look of incredulous outrage.

But Rafe was already perceiving the clear advantages of remaining in his bed awaiting his very desirable wife's return. With a lift of his finger, he beckoned Lain, who was cleaning away the bloodied water and rags.

Merry saw the surgeon to the door and received his final instructions and his promise to return in a week to remove the stitches.

Almost as soon as the door closed behind him, Merry scampered up the stairs to check if Rafe had obeyed her request or was already pulling his boots on. She arrived at his door in time to intercept Lain bearing a bottle of claret to his lordship via the backstairs. She sent both the bottle and Lain to the rightabout.

'No wine for you, my dear,' she cooed, as she closed the door behind her. 'Doctor's orders.'

'Damn the man! If he'd ever had his own leg sewn up, he wouldn't deny a fellow a glass of wine to help him forget the wretched experience,' Rafe commented bitterly. 'Merry, for the love of God, one glass!'

Merry shook her head, but with such a misty smile, that Rafe suddenly forgot all about the wine and the stitching.

'Come here, Merry,' he said softly.

Merry walked to the edge of the bed and stood behind the bedpost at the end, her arm curved round its polished surface, looking across at him, with a sweet, shy, curious smile playing on her lovely lips.

'Aren't you going to tuck me in like a good wife should?' invited Rafe.

Merry shook her head. Her lovely eyes shone as her smile showed she was well aware of what her husband would do if she came within reach.

'Merry, my love, I swear that if you don't come here, I will come and get you, stitches or no stitches,' he said, sitting up and making as if to get up.

At this, Merry laughed in alarm, and came forward to push him back against his pillows, at which point her prediction came true, as Rafe caught her in his arms and drew her down onto the bed with him, rolling her under his upper body and looking lovingly down into her face, alight with laughter and suppressed excitement.

Rafe smiled broadly as she tilted her chin up inviting him to kiss her, and he was all too happy to oblige. This time he kissed her tenderly, reverently, brushing his mouth against hers, then deepening the caress, savouring the taste of her lips and often pulling back to look at her in a rather dazed way, as if he thought must be dreaming.

Merry reached up to cradle his cheek in her hand and tangle her fingers in his dark hair.

'How could I have been so blind?' she murmured, gazing up into his eyes. 'Have I always loved you this much? So much it almost hurts … but I just didn't know it?'

Rafe couldn't speak for a moment. His heart was too full.

'I felt such a strong connection between us almost from the first. I had to believe you would feel it too, eventually,' he said finally, his voice roughened by strong emotion. 'When do you think it began for you?'

Merry racked her memory. It had seemed like a jumble until he had asked that question, and then somehow it all fell into place. It had been a journey towards him from their first meeting.

'Albemarle Street,' she murmured. 'I see that now. When you first made me smile against my will.'

Rafe laughed and hugged her.

'Yes, so I hoped.'

'When did you first know you loved me?' she asked.

'I think it began a little earlier, when Harry called you "Miss Griffith" and you told us a little of your life. You seemed the oddest, bravest, truest girl I'd ever met, even when you wanted to cut out my liver,' he said laughing. 'But I knew it for certain when Harry said you were lost. I felt like he'd ripped the heart from my chest and kicked it out of the window. Later, when I thought I'd lost you to Harry, I really think I went a little mad.'

Merry hugged him impulsively, burying her face in his neck, and Rafe's arms tightened in response, almost crushing the air from her lungs in the most delightful way.

'Are you going to … um … _make_ me your wife?' whispered Merry in Rafe's ear.

'And have half your mind on my stitches? Not a chance!' he said, though he ached to make them one at last. 'When we consummate our union, my love, I will have your _undivided_ attention, if you please ... but if I may not leave this bed until then, nor shall you.'

So instead of making love to his wife, as he longed to do, he put his strong arms around her and folded her to him, with a sigh of deep contentment. His life had meaning at last. A smile curved his lips as he closed his eyes and he drifted into the best sleep he could remember.

Merry was still in his arms when Rafe awoke several hours later. His relief was palpable, as in those first moments of consciousness he'd feared their reconciliation had been a dream.

As usual, Merry was sleeping as one dead, draped deliciously across his upper body. Rafe smiled, his arms closing tight about her, as he bent his neck to kiss the top of her head in a long and grateful prayer. After a moment, he stroked the tumbled curls away from her face then lifted the slim hand that had crept across his chest, gazed wonderingly at its fine-boned beauty, before pressing it to his lips and holding it to his cheek.

Suddenly, his stomach gave an almighty rumble, bringing him back to reality with a chuckle. He was starving, and he longed to see his wife look at him with the same reassuring, starry-eyed wonder that he felt himself. Since there was nothing like the savoury scent of breakfast for dragging Merry from the arms of Lethe, Rafe perceived another advantage in ordering a tray to be brought up.

He leaned over to pull the bell-rope by his bed, dragging Merry with him rather inelegantly, but unwilling to let her go.

Brooke answered his call, with a disapproving expression eloquent of his view of his master's actions in duelling with Lady

Rothsea and keeping his intentions from his manservant. But, masking his surprise at seeing the lady, still fully clothed and fast asleep on top of the covers, Brooke's glance skidded back to his lordship's face and a slow, reluctant smile banished his frown.

This young man, who had always carried a part of his heart, as might a son, was beaming at him, utterly radiant with joy.

'Wish me happy, John,' said Rafe, using Brooke's given name for the first time, to signal this private moment out of time.

'Aye, I do, lad. With all my heart,' said Brooke with a slightly husky voice. 'You were right all along. The lady loves you fit to bust, after all. You've won yourself a diamond there.'

Rafe nodded and bent to kiss his wife's head, which he held cradled against his chest.

Then Brooke restored the natural order.

'Thought you was going to make the lady laugh, sir,' he commented dryly. 'Not let her take pot shots at you.'

'Hmm … I wondered when you'd get to that,' muttered Rafe darkly. 'Well, it worked didn't it? She couldn't do it. My wife couldn't shoot me dead when it came down to it,' he said, hugging her in thanks.

'Well, I suppose there are a mort o' husbands that can't make that claim,' said his manservant. 'Still, looks like she didn't miss you entirely, m'lord. The house is whisperin' of nothing else.'

Brooke had walked over to inspect the wound, and he retied the bandage, which had come loose while the couple slept.

'Tell 'em we were testing our marksmanship and Lady Rothsea failed to account for the hair trigger as I showed her the target,' said Rafe. 'She'll hate me for that,' he added, with the ghost of a laugh. 'But worse to admit that she shot me while we were kissing. I suppose I should have taken the pistol from her … but…'

'I know, sir,' said Brooke. 'That *saner* feller playing least-in-sight again, was he?'

Rafe twinkled in appreciation.

'Something like that,' said Rafe, with a rueful smile. 'Now, go and have Mrs Greaves send us up breakfast on a tray, you rogue! And it better smell delicious, or my wife will end up sleeping the day through.'

Merry did wake up at the arrival of the food, arching in a stretch before opening her eyes to find Rafe laughing down at her, while he waved a plate around.

'Ooh! Wonderful!' she said, looking a little conscious, lying on Rafe's bed, while he was wearing only a fine linen nightshirt, and looking very much like he wished they were both wearing even less. Merry blushed when she realised she would very much like that, too.

Rafe watched her fleeting expressions, and that exquisite blush, with interest, but Merry's attention had now turned, inevitably, to the food.

After their repast, they talked … and talked, until they were startled by Brooke, bringing in the tea tray and asking what they wanted for dinner. They spoke about the things they loved about one another, about their lives before they met, about things they liked and disliked. Their conversation was frequently suspended for kisses and caresses, but this verbal journey of discovery they were making was somehow even more enticing than their physical desires.

Rafe longed to know all about what had happened after they had parted in London, but dared not ask. However, as darkness fell, and Merry drank the wine Lain had cheekily placed on the dinner tray for his master, together with her own, under Rafe's disgruntled gaze, Merry told him of her own accord.

It was by way of telling him how much his intervention had meant, but as she regaled him with some of the traumatic events leading up to his appearance at the brothel, Merry saw the horror and torment in the back of Rafe's eyes and drew to a halt.

'Keep going,' he said hoarsely. 'I want to know everything.'

'No!' she said, her brows twitching together in a vexed frown. 'You're doing that damned thing again!'

'What thing?'

'Blaming yourself for every little bloody thing!' growled Merry. 'Well, I'm not going to abet you in it. I'm mum!'

'Merry, be reasonable. I *am* to blame! How can I not feel it?' said Rafe defensively.

'Oh, that's it! Not another word from me!'

'Merry …'

'No,' said Merry categorically, taking another generous swig of her wine.

'Merry!' cried Rafe in laughing exasperation, as his wife turned away from him pointedly. Then, he distracted her, by reaching for her glass. 'Here! Give me that wine, you minx! At least, let me have that last sip!'

'Aah! Rafe! Get off!' shrieked Merry, collapsing into outraged giggles, as she watched Rafe tip the last of the wine down his throat, then wiggle his face in front of her with a comic triumphant grin.

'You …! You…!' Merry struggled to find an epithet to express her outrage.

'Don't say "devil",' said Rafe laughingly, holding up a pillow as she moved to pummel him, then tossing it aside and swooping her into his arms as she tried not to giggle again.

'You're a shameless, thieving rogue! There! Is that ladylike enough for you, my darling devil?'

'It will have to do, minx, as there's clearly no hope that you will ever show me the proper respect,' said Rafe, on a long-suffering sigh, and then before Merry could respond, he kissed her hard and long, until she had forgotten her argument. Looking down at her, his eyes smouldering with desire, he said huskily:

'Now, my love, tell me what happened when you left the *Belle Sauvage* and I promise not to be an idiot.'

Nevertheless, when Merry finished, Rafe took a ragged breath, hugging her tight and kissing her until the horrors receded from both their minds.

There was one thing both very much wanted to do, but Merry refused to let him risk his stitches, and Rafe wanted her only to enjoy their first intimate encounter. So they played cards and filled that long evening with more anecdotes from their past, while the air crackled with charged desire between them.

It was after ten when Merry went to her own room to prepare for bed, and Lain came in to assist his master with his evening ablutions.

Thirty minutes later, when she heard Lain's footsteps on his way to the back stairs, Merry cautiously opened the connecting door with Rafe's room and peeped shyly around it towards the bed.

'Am I supposed to sleep here now?' she asked uncertainly. 'I mean, now that we are … er … friendly?'

Rafe's lips twitched.

'Absolutely! Every night, without fail,' he averred. 'The bed in your room is purely decorative.'

Merry's eyes narrowed suspiciously when she detected the ghost of a smile behind his tone of objective informant. But his information accorded so well with her wishes, that she chose to ignore her doubts and grinned.

As she padded towards him nervously in a nightgown he had bought her in Bath, he realised that sharing a bed with Merry without making love to her was going to be a near impossible challenge. But it was too late to send her back to her room. She would be hurt, he told himself, but the truth was that he had even missed her during those thirty minutes they had been apart.

Rafe held out his hand to encourage her, and Merry skipped forward to take it and then made him laugh out loud when she then climbed over him to get to the free side of the bed, rather than letting go and walking around it. Merry giggled, too, when she heard Rafe let out an 'oof!' as her knee caught his abdomen as she clambered across him, and then an 'mmmm' as she scrambled under the sheets and impulsively snuggled against him.

Rafe sighed deeply, his strong arms pulling her tightly against his side and drawing her arm across his chest. He lifted her hand to his lips before pressing it against his heart and stroking her head as it lay on his shoulder. After several blissful minutes lying thus, Merry wriggled to be free. Rafe released her immediately, a worried crease between his brows. But Merry had struggled up in order to lean on his chest and look into his face. She lifted her hand to smooth away his frown and then her fingers traced a line from his temple to the square strength of his jaw. Rafe felt the breath catch in his throat as his saw the look of loving wonder in her eyes as she did so. He felt truly loved.

'Rafe,' she whispered.

'Yes, my darling?'

'I'm your _wife_,' she said, with a kind of childlike awe.

'I know,' he replied confidentially, his eyes sparkling as an amused grin lit his face. 'I was at the wedding. Remember?'

Merry giggled.

'Idiot. I mean … it's amazing isn't it? How it feels to belong to someone you love, and have them belong to you?'

Rafe felt his heart give such a surge at these simple words that he couldn't respond for a moment.

'It's the most wonderful feeling in the world, my angel,' replied Rafe, his voice charged with emotion.

Cupping Merry's cheek in his hand and gazing into her wide grey eyes, he added reverently: 'I am so honoured to be your husband, Merry. I have no idea how you were able to return my love after all I've done. Almost from the moment you came into my life, I began to realise I couldn't live without you. Dear God! When I think of how it felt when I thought I'd lost you; first in London and then to Harry.' Rafe closed his eyes and passed his hand over them at the memory.

'I can't describe it. That's my only excuse for …' He halted, looking back up at her, concerned at reminding her of the abduction.

'For scouring London to rescue me from a life of prostitution or penury?' prompted Merry. 'Or preventing me from making a terrible mistake in marrying my good friend, rather than my true love, little though I knew it at the time?'

'All, minx,' replied Rafe softly, returning to his point. 'Whatever lies in the past, I mean to make it my life's work to make you happy. You are all that matters to me now.'

Merry smiled mistily down at him, before wriggling up against his chest so that she could kiss him. This, and the delicious movement of her breasts against his chest, sorely tried Rafe's restraint.

There was something heady about having Rafe's powerful body beneath her and controlling the kiss. Though as Rafe's hands wandered over her upper body and his long fingers plundered her hair, so that he could deepen the kiss, Merry felt no sense of control at all. It was as though some hungry thing within her had taken over and she moaned with nameless need as Rafe's tongue tangled with her own.

Merry's leg lifted across his body as Rafe's hand slid down to caress her bottom. Suddenly, Merry seemed to tense a little and was momentarily distracted from their kiss. Her inner thigh lay across his arousal, and she moved her leg back and forth in tentative exploration, as if trying to ascertain what it was that she was feeling. Rafe stilled, but then gasped out loud as he felt her hand feeling experimentally along its shaft through the linen of his nightshirt.

It was Merry's turn to gasp.

'Is that you?' she whispered.

Rafe manfully stifled the laughter that bubbled up inside him at this question and at the very intimate inspection he had just undergone.

'Yes, Merry,' he whispered tightly. 'Who else would it be?'

'I mean …'

'I know what you mean, and, yes, that's all me,' he said, adding, 'and your exploration isn't helping matters.'

'So they get a *lot* bigger then?' she asked. 'Like horses'?'

'Well I can't promise quite those dimensions …' he chuckled.

'Rafe!'

'Well, you started it!' he retorted, still laughing.

'I was just curious, that's all. I mean, I've seen indications, of course,' she whispered. 'Bulges in men's breeches when tavern girls flirted with them, but I've never … well, not actually seen …'

'I'm glad to hear it!'

'Bryn called them "*stiffies*",' she informed him, confidingly.

'Dear God! I don't wish to appear prudish, my love,' said Rafe plaintively, as he passed a hand over his eyes and his shoulders shook as he tried to suppress his laughter. 'But this is not how I imagined this moment playing out.'

Merry's surreptitious exploration of his manhood had continued while they spoke, and Rafe now had an almighty and agonising erection to will away, unless he cast aside his plans for a perfect first experience for Merry.

But that elusive 'saner self' that Brooke felt they saw too little of surfaced at last, and Rafe caught hold of Merry's hand and laid it over his heart, once more. He gently guided her leg down to his side and said: 'Sleep, my love. There is time enough for lovemaking tomorrow.'

Merry sighed and curled into him. Rafe closed his eyes and waited for the ache in his groin to pass. Well, at least it had taken his mind off the burning pain of his stitched leg.

THE RELUCTANT LADY

When Rafe awoke in the morning and reached across for Merry, the bed was empty.

An irrational sense of panic made him first sit bolt upright to see if she was in the room and then to jump out of bed with a wince, and limp to the connecting door to check if she was in her own bedchamber. The room was cold and empty.

Rafe almost yanked the bell rope from the ceiling as he rang for Lain. By the time his valet arrived with a copper full of hot water for his master, Rafe was already in his riding breeches and shirt and was starting to tie his cravat with a speed and lack of attention that almost unmanned his fastidious manservant.

'Where is my wife?' demanded his lordship.

'I believe she is in the kitchen, m'lord, having a tray prepared for you' replied Lain. 'Would your lordship not care to shave before her ladyship returns?'

Rafe sighed quietly with relief. His tense body relaxed as his groundless anxiety ebbed, and his hands paused and then stripped off the offending cravat.

'Yes,' he conceded. 'Lady Rothsea has a horror of pirates,' he added, in a laughing under-voice. But, though he sat for Lain to shave him, he chafed at the time it took. Rafe could not relax entirely until he saw Merry. Their happiness was too new, too perfect to be believed or trusted. The only thing that confirmed that it was real was the mirror of his own joy in her eyes. But at the heart of his fear was a lifelong belief that he did not merit love or deserve happiness.

Merry soon arrived, flushed and very pleased with herself, accompanied by Henry, bearing a tray of food, and Alfred, carrying a steaming coffee pot and a little silver jug of cream. Both men were trying to keep their obvious amusement from their expressions.

Merry's face fell with dismay when she discovered her husband dressed in all but boots and coat, but Rafe grinned and waved them in, saying:

'Lain, I find I am not yet ready to leave my bed after all ... and it doesn't do to disobey a doctor's orders.'

He was rewarded by a sparkling look from Merry, who was finally embarking on the adventure of being a young bride, some four days after her wedding.

Rafe watched his wife with a proud loving smile, as she directed the footmen to set everything down on a table, hastily cleared for the purpose. Unable to resist kissing his beloved girl any longer, Rafe then waved all but she from the room, closing the door firmly behind them and leaning his back against it.

'Merry, come here,' said Rafe softly, as he had done twice before, now awed and misty-eyed, with a hopeful smile twisting his lips.

This time Merry came to him instantly, to find herself enveloped in the miracle of his strong embrace. Nothing in life compared to the delight of being in Rafe's arms … except perhaps the touch of his lips, as now, when he kissed her with such fathomless love in his every caress.

After a long, dizzying kiss, Rafe raised his head reluctantly, when he felt Merry wriggle as she recalled her mission.

'So you have brought me breakfast, have you, my love?' he said with a grin, an adoring glow in his eyes.

'Yes,' said Merry, dragging him to his bed. 'And trust you to spoil the surprise! Now, back to bed, you wretch, so that we can do this properly!'

Rafe laughed at the unexpected pleasure of being ordered about by his wife. But, obediently, he climbed on the bed, and helped Merry to lift the tray to straddle his lap, before she climbed on after him, sitting beside his legs.

Though he appeared to be inspecting the tray, Rafe was watching Merry. She was smiling down at his stockinged toes in odd fascination, before she reached unconsciously to close her hand around his foot. This small act sent an arc of electricity through him, like one of Mr Farraday's machines, and as this had its inevitable effect on his loins he was glad of the position of the tray.

Merry had no idea why her hand had been compelled to touch his foot. Despite the fine white stocking, it was so large and strong and …male. Somehow it seemed to emphasise the physical difference between them. A difference she was now starting to rejoice in, and one that was making her mouth go dry in an unsettling, but not unwelcome, way.

Feeling suddenly a little shy, knowing that Rafe was watching her intently, Merry peeped up to meet his gaze, blushed and looked down again rapidly.

She bit her lip, wondering if he could read her thoughts.

When she did so, Rafe absolutely could, and the *"stiffy"* beneath the tray became as hard as a poker. Merry's hands trembled faintly as she poured a cup of coffee and buttered one of the warm rolls for him. But as she handed it to him, the hunger in his speaking look was not for food. Merry looked away again blushing, as embarrassed by the overwhelming desire she felt to climb back into that bed with him as the sight of the same desire in *his* eyes.

Suddenly, Merry noticed the stain of blood, sluggishly oozing into his stocking from his aggravated injury.

'You should not have disturbed your wound so soon!'

'Don't worry about it,' replied Rafe hoarsely, with barely suppressed passion.

'There speaks a man who has never had to remove bloodstains from silk,' she replied reprovingly.

Rafe then tensed with another pang of raw desire when Merry coolly unbuttoned the leg of his breeches at the knee and he watched her long fingers carefully roll down his stocking and touch his bare leg as she examined the dressing beneath.

He now knew, as he knew his own name, that there was no way that he was going to be able to wait until nightfall to make love to his wife.

'I need to bind this up more firmly.'

'Yes, do!' he said, with meaning. '*Very* firmly.'

Merry coloured but did not pretend to misunderstand. A secret smile played about her lips that was, Rafe thought, one of the most exquisitely provocative things he'd ever seen. He twisted to put the untouched breakfast down on the floor beside the bed, and grunted as the movement chafed his wound.

'Rafe! For goodness sake keep still!'

'Merry, just so that we may be very clear,' said Rafe in a tone that brooked no demur. 'I have no intention of keeping still, or quite frankly putting off my marital duties any longer. Keeping my hands off you last night was torment enough. I'm not a paragon of restraint …' he was interrupted by a crack of laughter from Merry.

'No, you are not that, my love,' said Merry, looking down at him ruefully as she bound his leg, very firmly, watching him both wince and nod approval as she did so.

'Well, I had the most diverting schedule of romantic entertainments planned,' he replied primly. 'Until you practically forced me into bed and began disrobing me in the boldest manner imaginable.' This was accompanied by one of Rafe's comic expressions of offended propriety.

Merry giggled, climbing back onto the bed by his feet.

'Like this?' she said teasingly, undoing the buttons of the other leg of his breeches and pulling down the other stocking, which pooled at his ankle.

Merry watched his response in fascination, his eyes flickering closed for a second as he seemed to surge from within with a wave of strong emotion. Then in a husky voice, all trace of the comic gone, he whispered: 'Merry, come here.'

Merry obeyed, crawling across the bed like a prowling cat, an expression of suppressed excitement and nervousness playing on her face. His hands found her shoulders and he drew her bodily towards him, firmly laying her against the pillow before his lips closed on hers in a hard, hungry kiss, unlike any that had gone before. Merry felt the difference in his mouth and in the unconscious urgings of his body and her own. They held a kind of physical promise of imminent fulfilment that made her senses roar with need. The rhythmic movement of his mouth and tongue as they plundered her own, and the languorous undulating grind of his hips against hers, heightened the growing throbbing sensation between her legs. Merry could feel his huge, hard length pressing against that same place, as if in answer to a mute appeal she herself was making. She ached for him. Ached to feel him against her skin, inside her body, and devil take the pain.

When Rafe reached to rip off his cravat, she broke off from the kiss for a moment.

'Are we going to …' Merry finished her whispered sentence with a meaningful lifting of her eyebrows and tilt of her head.

'Yes, my darling, that's exactly what we're going to do,' he said, his hungry lips tracing a line down her neck and back up to her mouth again. 'Do you object?'

'No,' she replied, but then stunned Rafe by breaking free and jumping off the bed. She was running towards the window when Rafe called in a husky voice:

'Merry! Where are you going?'

'I'm going to close the shutters, of course,' said Merry, resuming her task.

'But I want to *see* you!' complained Rafe.

Merry stopped dead and spun around, a little shocked.

'What!? When we…?' once again resorting to the meaningful nod she had used earlier.

'*Particularly* when we…,' stressed Rafe, using the same meaningful nod.

Merry hesitated, looking apprehensive.

'But, you'll see …' Merry ground to a halt, blushing profusely.

'Good God! *Now* you're shy?!' he remonstrated. 'After laying bare all the mysteries of my body last night in the most humiliating detail.'

'You didn't like my touching you,' gasped Merry, dismayed.

'I absolutely *loved* your touching me. I will spend most of my waking hours thinking about it and wishing to repeat the experience.'

'You're sure?'

This was too much for Rafe, and he burst out laughing.

'Yes,' he choked. 'Very sure! I simply crave a little equality of the privilege and liberty.'

Rafe watched in fascination as Merry's thighs clenched involuntarily as a throb of anticipated pleasure pulsed through her. Enjoying an answering pulse in the same region of his own body, Rafe got up and walked towards her.

'I think I'd like that too,' Merry confessed, her eyes straying to the bulging mass in her husband's breeches as he approached.

Without hesitation, Rafe swept his wife up in his arms and carried her to the bed, ignoring his wound's complaint. As a sop to Merry's wishes, he yanked the bed curtains loose from their cords and they fell partway together, leaving them both bathed in alluring half-light.

He sat at the foot of the bed for a moment to remove first her slippers and then her stockings, his hand sliding underneath her drawers to untie the garters, with telling deftness. Merry now entirely understood Rafe's reaction to her own touch on his bare legs, as she gasped and tensed with the pleasure of his touch on hers. Then she shivered with delight as he crept along the bed towards her, and resumed that hard, hungry kissing that had driven her so wild a little earlier.

Rafe kissed and caressed his wife continually while he undressed her as expertly as he had once dressed her. A groan of delight escaped him as he felt Merry pull his shirt free of his breeches and begin to push it upwards to relieve him of it. He broke off their kiss to take it off. Merry's breathing was ragged and she stared drowningly into his eyes, as she helped undo the buttons at the cuffs, both remembering a time she had once done them up for him.

Rafe reached for her and gently began to lift her chemise, his expression almost a question, which she answered by swiftly raising her arms above her head so that he could remove it. At first, she raised her hands to cover her exposed breasts, but Rafe gently caught her wrists and pulled her against him, skin to skin, which dragged a deep sigh of pleasure from her. His arms closed about her and he kissed her passionately, parting her lips and touching his tongue to hers, before they tangled eagerly once again. Merry's legs, still clad in her drawers, seemed to arc themselves around Rafe's and her body arched desperately against his, demanding a deeper connection.

Merry now wore only her drawers and Rafe his breeches. In the dim light, Rafe's monumental arousal was unmistakable and clearly struggling to be free of its constraint.

Over the roar of desire, which impelled him to be inside her as soon as was humanly possible, Rafe heard the quiet voice of restraint. He wanted Merry's first sexual experience, this first consummation of their love, to be special, to set the tone for all that would follow it.

With an almost Herculean effort, he dragged his lips from hers and rolled away from her, pulling her sideways so that they each lay on their sides facing each other. Merry looked momentarily bereft, until she saw the look in Rafe's eyes, blurring with love and desire. His hand reached out and he traced the line of her breast, his fingers cupping it gently before teasing the proud nipple in a way that made Merry's thighs clench deliciously again. He lifted her hand and laid it suggestively on his own chest. Merry's wide eyes showed quick comprehension and soon became languorous as she traced the lines and planes of his muscles, circled his taut nipples and teased the dark tangle of hair between them. She watched his body's response in his eyes, his breathing, the way the muscles tightened under her touch and in the way his erection jerked against the fall of his breeches. Merry understood what he was doing, what he wanted. Rafe was offering himself to her as an equal in this intimate act. He wanted her to comprehend that, to him, her touch was as powerful on his body as his was on her own. Nothing would happen that she did not wish, and she could freely ask him to do anything that might give her pleasure as he might freely ask her. This was what marriage meant. Their bodies were one: No embarrassment, no barriers.

They shared a gaze of perfect union, as Rafe saw that she understood his intentions completely. It was a moment he would remember forever.

Then a teasing smile tugged at Merry's kiss-bruised lips, as she trailed her fingers lower, down the bunched muscles of Rafe's abdomen, circling his navel playfully before drawing the line along the edge of his breeches. His groan of pleasure became a tight gasp of delight as her fingers once again traced the outline of his erection against the buckskin, and then closed around it, feeling its strength in wide-eyed fascination, her thighs clenching again in sensuous anticipation. Rafe's body arched as a sharp wave of raw desire coursed through him, and he strained against his need to bury himself within in her.

This was sweet torture, but he could inflict such exquisite torment too.

His lips took Merry's in a drugging kiss before drifting lower, caressing her neck, her shoulder, then gently pushing her onto her back so that he could kiss her breast and take her nipple into his hot mouth. Merry startled herself with the loud moan of pleasure this dragged from her. Her legs twisted with the throbbing heat of desire that was building between them. As he turned his attention to her other breast, he stroked his hand down her waist, across her hips and then between her legs, drawing a soft gasp of approval from Merry. Involuntarily, her hips moved against his hand as it rhythmically teased and explored her. Then, as his fingers delved deeper into the warm, wet depths, Merry gave herself up to the wild instincts that consumed her. Her hand splayed against Rafe's erection, craving union, while her mind was consumed by the tension building within her like a coiling spring.

As his skilled fingers found the exact point of greatest sensitivity and the motion that drove her most fervent reaction, Rafe felt Merry's body slowly tensing as she began to reach for climax. Her hand was now tugging at the buttons of his breeches, while her other wrenched at the ties of her drawers, thinking on some primal level that his presence inside her was what her body was straining for.

He had intended to draw out her pleasure for much longer, but Merry's clever fingers had already undone his fall and were closing around his hard, heavy length, sending him beyond reach of that quiet voice of reason. He hauled his breeches over his hips, where Merry's feet unconsciously took over and pushed them down to his ankles. It dragged a delighted laugh from him, as he finished the job and kicked them off, the pain in his leg numbed entirely by the wild, wondrous throb of passion.

His wife's curious fingers, exploring this solid staff that was to enter her and join them forever, were almost Rafe's undoing. He strained to hold himself together, not helped by the feel of Merry's other hand firmly gripping one of his taut buttocks.

Taking Merry's lips again in a passionate kiss, Rafe lifted her hips a little to pull off her drawers and part her legs. They both groaned in unison as Rafe inched his erection inside her wet warmth in rhythm with the spontaneous movement of her hips against him, until he could go no further without force.

'My love,' he murmured hoarsely in a voice not his own. 'This might hurt a little.'

'Yes, yes! Please! More! I want you ... inside me!' she gasped, her hands sliding down to the tensed muscles at the small of his back.'

Her words, driven by a primitive need that consumed them both, broke his self-control. His hips lurched forward, impaling her on a cry, dragged from them both. He shook palpably from the effort not to drive into her again, but to pause for her sake.

'Are you all right?' he whispered tightly, his jaw clenching as he suppressed the rampant demands of his loins.

'The veriest scratch,' she panted, her eyes lustrous with desire. 'Pain's passed already. Hurt more when you spanked me.'

Rafe gave a half-laugh, and Merry felt him move inside her, a strange marvel – *flesh of one flesh*.

'How do you feel?' he asked hoarsely.

'Full!' she gasped as she felt her insides move apart to accommodate him. She felt him laugh again. 'I can't believe you fitted inside me, but I feel… like a part of you. How do you feel?'

'Complete,' he said, kissing her forehead.

'What does it feel like inside me?' she asked, moving slightly around that hard, hot, male presence. It burned a little, but Merry had felt more pain barking her shins. *Trust women to make a big fuss about a little pain!*

'There aren't words,' murmured Rafe, moving slowly within her body. 'It's not just the sensation. With you there is so much more. You are my soul's mate, Merry.'

Merry kissed him for that, but her hips pressed against his as if begging for more.

'So is that it?' she asked, trying not to sound disappointed. 'Isn't there a lot more pushing?'

Rafe laughed out loud at that, and Merry wriggled deliciously against the movement within her.

'Yes, my darling,' he gasped. 'There is a lot more pushing, if it will not pain you to continue.'

'Oh, thank God!' she murmured thankfully. 'Because I was just starting to feel something wonderful.'

'Let's find out just how wonderful, shall we?' said Rafe, pulling back and gently sliding into her again, a few times, trembling with the exquisite sensation of the friction of her smooth, tight flesh sucking at his own.

Merry watched him disappearing into her body with a kind of awe, and saw the expression on his face in fascination. His eyes were dark with some profound emotion, while his hips began to move with an animal need that found an answering drive in her own. A tremor shuddered through him, as with a groan he increased the pace, and her legs curled and tightened about his. Rafe's fingers found that sensitive spot, teasing it rhythmically until Merry's moans were almost screams and her hips writhed desperately as she strained for climax. When it came, it broke over them both as one, the clutching muscles inside her springing his own orgasm and releasing them both with cries ripped from the depths of their bodies, and then bathing them in a drugging wave of ecstasy, while they clung together trembling with tiny aftershocks.

Rafe, shattered by this climactic union of love and passion, could only wrap his arms tightly about his beloved wife, drawing her with him so that he remained within her as he rolled over and, like her, surrendered to the blissful sleep of kings..

Chapter Twenty-One
Unfortunate Discoveries

Rafe was the first to awaken, an hour or more later. They had not moved as they had slept and, tantalisingly, they were still intimately connected. Rolling carefully onto his back, his strong hands holding her close so that they remained joined, Rafe felt himself growing inside her. He tensed his muscles, hardening his arousal, which strained exquisitely against the sleek walls that constrained it. Rafe groaned with the pleasure of it, pushing deeper to seat himself firmly within his beloved wife's body.

She was his now completely. Merry's love made the broken pieces in his life whole at last and seemed to wash away the bitterness and self-contempt that had polluted his world. If Merry could love him so freely, after all his mistakes, perhaps he was not so unworthy after all. Perhaps his time in Purgatory was finally over.

Rafe's hands caressed her slender body, the sensuous curve of her back and the firm rounding of her buttocks, as his erection grew hard and full inside her. Gently, he slid out just for the pleasure of gliding inside again.

'Mmm,' sighed Merry. Rafe had discovered something else that could awaken his wife.

Drowsily, Merry writhed slowly, with unconscious sensuality, against the warm strength of her husband's body. Merry nuzzled and kissed his neck, his jaw and finally his beautiful mouth.

'May we do it again?' she whispered, looking down at him lovingly, moving her hips suggestively.

'Whenever you wish, my love,' he said against her lips. 'If it will not pain you?'

Merry huffed her scorn at the question, and felt the thrill of his movement inside her as Rafe laughed

'Try this,' he said, his strong well-muscled arms flexing as he lifted her to sit astride him. Merry shyly hid her breasts, until smiling, Rafe drew her hands away, kissing each palm, and took their place with his own. His long warm fingers teased them to hard points, as gently and slowly at first Rafe began a deep rhythmic motion with his hips.

Rafe watched as Merry's intrigued smile swiftly gave way to mounting desire as his rhythm gradually quickened, until with a gasp, her head fell back and she moaned: 'Oh! Oh! That's… that's…'

Words failed her, and Merry arched back, gripping his thighs with abandon as the new stimulation fired a fierce craving at the core of her body. Merry sensed that irresistible tension growing inside her once more, much more intense than before, as she felt his hard length pressing against a new source of delight deep within her. Rafe increased his pace in response to her sharp groans of keening need and wild enjoyment, pleased to have found another way to pleasure his wife.

Merry was near to screaming, when she finally felt her entire body tauten like a bowstring and then snap as she cramped forward with a cry of ecstasy, jolting again and again as pounding waves of hot drugging bliss crashed through her over and over.

Rafe swiftly rolled them over and thrust deeply into Merry's shuddering body with a hoarse cry of joy, as his seed shot into Merry's convulsing inner depths. Rafe's lips found hers and he crushed her to him with the last of his strength, before collapsing beside her in blissful exhaustion.

Another hour later, Brooke knocked several times, and hearing no response, he peeped into the room. Catching a brief glimpse of sleeping nakedness on the bed, he left swiftly, with a broad grin. Well, the feisty little lady had been _made_ a wife now! At least his lordship might be less resty now that they were truly husband and wife.

It was nearly one in the afternoon when Rafe awoke to the touch of his wife's slender hand slipping into his own as she lay flat on her back beside him, wonderfully and unashamedly uncovered.

'Is it always like that?' she whispered, no longer surprised that people did that for pleasure.

Rafe shook his head slowly, his eyes still closed.

'Never been like that for me,' he croaked. 'And I'm no novice.'

'Good!' said Merry.

Rafe laughed.

'Which pleases you most?' he enquired, raising her hand to his lips.

Merry chuckled

'Rogue! I'm glad it was … unique … for you, too,' said Merry, then added wistfully. 'I wish it had been your first time, as well.'

'Hah! It was worlds better than my first time!' said Rafe, with feeling. Then he rolled onto his side to look down at her, his eyes twinkling. 'And if it *had* been my first, I suspect I would not have lasted a minute. I would have shot my bolt the moment you rolled down my stocking, you glorious baggage.'

They both laughed at that.

'Well, I hate every woman with whom you've ever done that,' said Merry, her eyes glinting with jealousy.

'And I suppose you'll call me a coxcomb when I say … I think they'll hate you more,' he said, with a meaningful look. 'As you have done what no other could.'

'Cured the rake?' suggested Merry hopefully.

'That, and made me happy, minx,' said Rafe. 'And in one respect, we are equally innocent.'

Merry looked her question.

'I have only ever *made love* twice, too,' said Rafe huskily, bending to brush his lips against her smiling ones.

The power of their attraction astounded Merry. She could barely look at Rafe without wanting to feel him inside her, to savour that profound intimacy that went beyond words. 'Making love' was the right term. That was how it felt. When Rafe reached for her, when his lips found hers and his warm, sleepy body tautened at her touch and then pressed against her own in shared need, any distance between them that their minds preserved evaporated. When their limbs and tongues entwined and Rafe entered her body, where he left off and she began were blurred. It was primitive, heavenly union.

For the next two days, the couple barely left Rafe's room, other than to bathe and change. It was an intense honeymoon of talking, eating and making love. In between, they read to each other and played cards and chess, although both found it nearly impossible to concentrate. It seemed that almost every pursuit ended with lovemaking, sometimes passionate and spirited, sometimes leisurely and intimate.

On one such occasion, as Merry watched with a kind of fascination as Rafe's substantial length slid in and out of her body with delicious ease, Rafe smiled at her and said: 'So you don't think this is "creepy"?'

Merry looked at him in puzzlement, and then laughed as she remembered her words in the coach as they had left London. Blushing a little, she gazed down at the timeless wonder of this rhythmic, physical interlock, and shook her head.

'I think it's amazing,' she said huskily.

'And how do you feel about the idea that we might be making a child, in here,' he laid a tender palm against her stomach. 'Even now.'

'I think that's pretty amazing, too,' said Merry, her eyes glowing, and a shy smile trembling on her lips.

Rafe groaned with a wave of love, his arms closing tightly around her.

'So, not creepy?' he murmured hoarsely in her ear, as his strong hands angled Merry's hips in the way they had discovered, through much experimentation, gave his darling the greatest pleasure and the surest route to climax.

Merry gasped, her eyes closing as the throbbing thrilling wave began to build. She shook her head.

'No, … wonderful," she moaned tightly, and then cried: 'Oh! WONDERFUL!' Before losing the capacity of speech altogether.

During these two days, Brooke brought their meals and redressed Rafe's wounded leg, which was healing surprisingly well despite his master's exertions.

Rafe had scarcely given it a thought. Love was a most effective palliative.

It was Brooke who, opening the windows on the morning of the third day, while her ladyship was bathing, suggested to his lordship, that he might like to go out in the sunshine and take the air.

'You ought to get walking on that leg, sir' said Brooke. 'Before it forgets its purpose.'

Rafe frowned. He had just had the best two days of his life, and was unwilling to change the pattern.

'Mr Lain is drawing you a bath next door, and I'll be here to give you a shave when he's done,' said Brooke, laying out the plan, and ignoring his master's irritated look. 'I'll let Mr Lain pick out your clothes, and he's been stretching a boot, so it won't chafe your wound. Though it went against the grain, as you'll guess from his long face.'

'I see,' said Rafe. 'So it's a conspiracy?'

'Well, I believe Mrs Dodd would like to change your bed linen and spruce up the room a mite.'

Rafe coloured a little. His chamber smelled a tad unsavoury and the sheets bore the evidence of their insatiable lovemaking. Merry had revelled in every aspect, frequently initiating the action with soft kisses or teasing explorations. She had discovered her womanhood, together with her power over him in just two days. It was all an astonishing revelation for them both. He had not dared dream it could be like this, and just the thought made him want to stride off into her dressing room, lift her out of her bath and make love to her all over again. But, instead, he groaned: 'Oh, very well!'

'Also, been meaning to ask when you might be thinking of departing for the continent, m'lord,' said Brooke, with a serious look. 'Heard there was a fella came to the village from London, near on a month ago, asking how often you came to the Fall. Everyone was mum, of course, but Barnet the innkeeper said the cove said he would return... and it don't do to tempt fate, now you've found your diamond, and all.'

Rafe dragged his hands over his face to dispel the traces of sleep and then raked his fingers back through his hair, nodding with a frown between his brows. He had forgotten that he was a hunted man still under charge of murder. It was true. They would have to leave or risk discovery and the misery for them both of his arrest and trial. But it was such a joy to be at his favourite house with his beloved wife.

'So, when shall I organise the departure for, sir?' said Brooke, surprised at having got over heavy ground so light.

'The surgeon will be here in a couple of days to remove the stitches,' said Rafe. 'We'll leave the day after that.'

'*Sea Witch* to Rome, sir?'

'No, we'll travel via France, since we may, now that Bonaparte is at *point non plus*,' said Rafe. 'I should like Lady Rothsea to see Paris. Purdue will already have made banking arrangements, I believe.'

'Yes, sir,' confirmed Brooke.

Rafe got up and stretched, gloriously naked and erect, then reached for his robe. Brooke grinned as he turned away to put out his lordship's shaving things. Never been coy about his body, had his lordship.

If Rafe thought he would regret leaving the room, where he and Merry might act instantly upon their physical impulses, he was wrong. After a lifetime of inner solitude, it was a stunning sweetness to find every mundane activity deeply enriched by simply sharing it with someone he loved and who loved him.

Merry, too, had been reluctant, almost mutinous, about surrendering the intimate enclosed world they had made during those two days. But, like Rafe, was soon awed by how that love expanded to recolour vividly the world around them, and how a warm look, a caressing touch or a soft word could invest a moment with blissful magic.

Riding together around the park, walking in the gardens to exercise Rafe's leg, rowing across the lake, they presented onlookers with the perfect picture of a couple profoundly in love. The staff, who had been tense and edgy during the days before the duel, now collectively relaxed and shared secret smiles when they passed one another. It was rather wonderful to witness such happiness and to see their much-loved master so well matched and contented at last.

As Frith, escorted the couple into dinner, Rafe was like a proud king presenting his beloved queen to his court. Merry looked down, blushing a little and with a shy smile on her lips, well aware that everyone in the household must know how she and Rafe had spent the past couple of days. But Rafe's low chuckle as he seated her beside him and a glimpse of his humorous knowing look, quickly replaced her embarrassed look with one of kindling ire.

'Have you no shame?' she whispered, as he sat, a lurking smile in her own eyes.

Rafe grinned broadly, with a laughing rueful look, and then swiftly, and most improperly, he leaned across and kissed her lips, still parted in surprise.

'None at all!' he said, then taking her hand and holding it to his lips, while his twinkling eyes quizzed hers wickedly. 'I thought we had firmly established that these past days.'

Merry gave him a scandalised look of admonishment, somewhat undermined by the fact that she was trying not to laugh as she did so.

Then Rafe laughed out loud, that joyous sound, which made everyone smile, including Frith, who could scarcely disapprove the footmen for looking like grinning fools, while he himself could not stop the corners of his mouth turning upward nor strip the glow from his own eyes.

After dinner, Rafe and Merry sat together on the sofa in the library, sipping port in front of the fire.

'What would you like as a bride gift? I've already arranged your settlements and allowance with Purdue, but I should like to give you something special, something that you wish for.'

Merry was about to say that she had everything she could have ever have dreamed of and more, but then something occurred to her that she would very much like. She turned in his arms to look at him.

'Are you very rich?' she asked earnestly.

Rafe looked a little surprised at Merry's sudden seriousness, but then smiled.

'Well, I'm no Croesus, but, yes, I think I can say that _we_ are fairly rich.'

'Then I should like money,' she replied.

'I think you'll find your allowance is very generous,' he replied, smiling.

'Oh, no,' Merry replied. 'Not for me, but for a man I know.'
'What man?' said Rafe, no longer smiling.
'John Coley.'
'Who?'
'The man I met at Bryn's funeral,' replied Merry, watching in fascination as Rafe's frown deepened and his eyes kindled. 'He invited me to stay with him that first night I was alone.'

'I'll bet he did! I'm glad you declined the rogue,' growled Rafe.

'I accepted. Didn't I tell you?'

'What!' That kindling look had become a flame.

Merry was already enjoying this glimpse of his jealousy and could not resist playing with the fire a little.

'I was grateful for his offer of shelter and for the dinner we shared together …,' began Merry innocently.

Rafe's expression was thunder and had John been within reach, the poor man might have joined his beloved Mary much sooner than Nature intended.

'… with his three brothers, his mother and sister,' concluded Merry, now giggling. 'Though I flatter myself that at least one of them had a very promising tendre for me before I left the next day.'

Rafe was slightly mollified by the presence of others during her stay, and he now knew Merry was baiting him, but the comment about the tendre turned his lips to a thin disapproving line.

'Unfortunately, it was the *sister* who fell in love with me,' lamented Merry, her eyes sparkling with suppressed laughter.

'She had a narrow escape,' Rafe commented dryly. 'I only wish I had been as fortunate.'

'Oh, Rafe! How ungallant of you!'

'So, that's where you were that first night!' said Rafe. 'But I don't recall your mentioning this John in your account. Was he an older fellow?'

'No, I would guess he was not much more than twenty,' said Merry, stunned that Rafe was not ready to dismiss the topic until he was certain that John was not a rival.

'Callow, then?' suggested Rafe.

'No, he was a "well-put-together specimen", as you might say, with a wise head and a kind heart,' she replied, trying to appear dispassionate but smiling crookedly as she tried to conceal the enormous fun she was having at Rafe's expense.

'Hmm ... Not handsome though?' he said, his arms folded across his chest and his eyes narrowed in suspicion. 'I think you would have mentioned that sooner ... as it would be certain to vex me even more.'

Merry laughed out at that, reaching out to shake him.

'Well, one might have called him <u>*very*</u> handsome,' she said, her eyes brimming with love. 'If one had not first seen you, my dear husband!'

Rafe's lips twitched with pleasure despite himself, though his stance remained stern. He allowed his naughty wife to wriggle back into his arms, commenting: 'Damn it, Merry. Sometimes I can't tell if you are an angel sent from heaven or a devil sent to torment me.'

'I am your wife, my sweet, ...so a little of both, I conjecture,' replied Merry, kissing the strong hand that lay closest to her face, and then sighing as her husband's arms tightened around her and she felt his lips caress and then kiss the top of her head.

The next morning, Rafe wrote to Purdue, his man of business, to make out a draft to John Coley for five thousand pounds, ten times the amount that Merry had tentatively requested. It was to convey the compliments of Merion Griffith Esq. with his thanks for their hospitality at his time of need and with his hope that since his own dreams had been realised, the enclosed might make theirs manifest too.

When Rafe had secured from Merry the full story of her meeting with Coley at the graveside, of his family's sharing unquestioningly their meagre fare and roof with a stranger, and of their great plans gone awry, his heart had gone out to the Coleys every bit as much as Merry's had. But more than that ... Rafe owed Coley a huge debt for comforting and sheltering his beloved girl in her darkest hour. Money was a small compensation for this great gift, but the sum would enable the Coleys to buy a thriving carrier business and provide the daughter with a respectable dowry ... *for the next time she falls in love*, thought Rafe with a smile.

When Rafe told her of what he had done, Merry blenched, gasped, and then threw her arms round her husband, bursting into tears.

'Here! Here!' he said, hugging her tight. 'It was supposed to make you happy!'

Between sobs, Merry squeaked: 'I *am* happy, you idiot!' causing Rafe to laugh, then press his lips to the top of her head, before he lifted her off her feet and sat on the nearest sofa, cradling and patting her as he had done just a week earlier by the lake. Between ragged breaths, Merry sighed with the remembered bliss of that first experience, a foretaste of the comfort that was here in Rafe's arms whenever she needed it. She slid her arms around his neck and rested her head on his shoulder, as she had done that day.

'You're remembering?' he murmured.

Merry nodded, then kissed the side of Rafe's head. His arms tightened.

'I, too,' he said.

'Thank you for my bride gift,' whispered Merry, when she could talk more easily. 'May I ask why you gave them so much?'

Merry felt Rafe's mood darken.

'I owe them all a great debt,' he said austerely. 'I'll never forgive myself for leaving without you and putting you through that awful time alone.'

Rafe expected to feel his wife's body stiffen in denial or to wriggle in impatience at this surfacing of his self-contempt, so he was surprised instead to hear what sounded like a giggle.

He pulled Merry away from him so that he could see her expression. Merry gave an odd smile, and then pulled herself back against him to rest her head against his once more, reaching back to guide his arms back round her. Rafe complied with her wishes, with a puzzled but uncomplaining look on his face.

'You find that amusing?' he enquired.

'No... but when you told me that day, when you obliged me to wear skirts for the second time, that someone could be strong for me, protect me,' murmured Merry in explanation. 'I never realised how ... nice ... that might feel.'

The arms tightened deliciously, and then Merry found herself scooped up in those arms as Rafe started to carry her towards the door.

'What are you doing?!' cried Merry, in consternation.

'Taking you back to bed where I can more eloquently express my delight at that piece of news,' replied Rafe, looking down at his wife's blushing response with that broad misty smile that he now wore much of the time.

'Rafe!' protested Merry. 'We only got up an hour ago and it's nearly lunchtime! We missed breakfast completely.'

'Of course, you're hungry,' he responded, reluctantly starting to loosen his hold, to let her down. 'You'd rather eat.'

Merry abruptly tightened her arms around Rafe's neck.

'No, not really,' she said, kissing his surprised lips.

Rafe needed no further encouragement, carrying Merry rapidly along the corridor from the sitting room towards his bedchamber, pausing only to call down to the footman by the front door, as they passed the stairwell: 'Henry, tell Frith to put back luncheon … by an hour!'

Henry's well-trained mask only slipped for a second, and a twinkle peeped through.

'Yes, my lord,' he replied, but the couple were long gone, their laughter echoing from the corridor to their rooms. Barely a single meal had been served on time since her ladyship had shot her husband, and the household were delighted about it. Henry swiftly trotted off to alert cook.

Over the next two days, Lord and Lady Rothsea remained inseparable, except for an hour a day after breakfast, when Merry went about with Mrs Dodd, learning more about running a household, and Rafe visited the estates office or attended to his correspondence. After that, they worked together in the library, with Merry in her element, looking at accounts or property plans. Then after a nuncheon, they would ride around the estate, where Rafe would show her the kind of features they had discussed on the maps. When he showed her some of the land improvements and the repairs to cottages and villages he had set in motion four years earlier, Merry fairly swelled with pride in him, and he smiled with delighted embarrassment when he saw it.

On the third day, the surgeon arrived to remove the stitches, and this time Rafe tried to banish Merry from the room, saying that the discomfort was as nothing compared with the mirror of it in her face. But Merry refused to budge, so Rafe was once again obliged once again to live through her grimaces and groans, as she watched intently as the sutures were snipped and pulled through the flesh, though this time with significantly less pain associated with them, until the surgeon applied the brine once more.

When the doctor had left, Rafe told Merry they would be leaving the day after tomorrow. Merry was as sad as Rafe at departing from this idyll they had made, but also excited about the opportunity to visit dreamed-of places in the company of the man she loved.

But the next morning, a well-intentioned delivery would bring the annihilation of both their idyll and their plans.

It arrived just after Merry had joined Mrs Dodd in one of the guest bedchambers to discuss its redecoration and whether any of the furniture should be kept. Henry scratched at the open door and informed her ladyship that two small trunks had arrived from London, together with a note by the carrier's own hand, all addressed, care of his lordship, to a Merion Griffith Esq.

'My books!' cried Merry, and then swiftly added: 'Did the carrier remain?'

'No, my lady,' said Henry. 'That's what his lordship asked. The fellow didn't ask for payment neither, and when he was offered an ale in the kitchen, he said he wouldn't presume, but only said he was glad young Master Griffith had found his family as he supposed. No one let on about … er …'

'Thank God!' said Merry, saving Henry further elucidation.

'Frith told him that Mr Merion was safe in the bosom of a family what loved him, and that he was set for life. The carrier seemed very pleased to hear it and said Mr Griffith had friends in Long Acre who wished him more than well and so he would know from the letter, if he might kindly trouble himself to read it,' reported Henry. 'Seemed quite overcome, my lady, and left in a hurry then, so as not to let us see it. Fine fellow, we all thought.'

'Yes,' said Merry. 'He is a very good man, from a good family, too'

'His lordship had us take the trunks to your room, my lady,' added Henry. 'Would have come himself, but Jim Sutterley's broke his leg, falling out of the lime tree he was pollarding, and has been taken home on a hurdle. His lordship's sent for the doctor and gone to see the break for himself. Said he would join you as soon as he might.'

'Thank you,' said Merry, turning to the housekeeper to make her excuses and scamper off to her room to be reunited with the remnants of her old life.

The laboriously written letter from the Coleys, which ran over three pages and was signed by each one of them, made her cry with happiness all over again. Rafe's generosity had truly transformed their lives overnight. They could not understand how their small gesture towards a scion of his house, as they supposed Mr Griffith to be, had warranted such a fantastical gift from Lord Rothsea, but they assured both their benefactors that their magnanimity had been heaven sent, for the eldest Coley had broken his hand and been dismissed, and they had not known how they would manage, until a Mr Purdue had visited them that very evening in Cranbourne Alley.

Merry dried her eyes and sighed with profound contentment that her own good fortune had been shared by such deserving people. Then she sat on the floor by the trunks, broke the carriers' seal and opened the nearest.

Rafe, a glowing smile pulling at his lips as he anticipated Merry's joy in the gift he had secured for her that morning, before he had been called away, took the stairs two at a time, eager to share his news with his beloved wife. Finding the door to her chamber wide open, he moved stealthily to lean against the doorjamb and catch her unawares. He was about to try to mask the delight clearly apparent on his face, lest it give away the surprise, when all the happiness fell away from him as he grasped what he was seeing.

Merry was kneeling bent double on the floor, her back to the door, grasping her brother's bloodstained jacket in her hand so tightly that her knuckles stood out white against her skin. Clearly in excruciating distress, her body jerked with dry sobs. Rafe was horrified and began to move forward to comfort her, when her next words froze him where he stood.

'*Bryn! Bryn! Oh, God! Rafe!*' she rasped in hoarse barking sobs. 'What a blind fool I've been! Blinded by love! How could he *do* this to you! How *could* he? The villain! The wicked coward!' she cried, her voice shaking with a passionate loathing. 'I loved you, I trusted you, now I damn you to hell. I will never, never forgive you! *Never!*'

Rafe did not stay to hear more. He backed out of the room swiftly, silently, dreading to the depths of his being seeing the face he loved, the mirror of his soul, turn towards him in hate.

Stumbling blindly along the corridor, he felt as though he were being crushed. He could scarcely drag breath into his body. Masonry should be crashing around him, wood splintering, plaster cracking.

How could his universe crumble to nothingness about him and leave no mark on the physical world?

Somewhere deep within there was a crack as his heart broke. It sounded as if continents were splitting apart, fracturing the fabric of the earth, and yet the paintings on the walls did not move an inch; the glass in the windows behind him did not shatter into a thousand shards.

Go back, you fool! cried a voice in his head. *Tell her you're sorry! Tell her you love her! You just bought Tal Hairn, her father's ancestral home, for her! Wrap your arms around her until she has cried herself out! She loves you! She loves you!*

But Rafe lurched onward. He could not bear to see Merry's face with all the new-found love drained away from it, replaced by that expression of implacable loathing that she had worn when he first beheld her or the ice-cold mask she had worn before their duel. A mask that his father's face, too, had worn.

Somehow this seemed just – a restoration of the balance in the world. Rafe Wolvenden was not destined to be loved. He did not deserve it. He had caused the death of his mother and brother, and three other men besides. The last was his own wife's brother. How could he possibly expect Merry to forgive and forget such a sin? That she had done so for a week, and astonishingly for that short time had returned his love, was a miracle and more than he had any right to expect. In that time, he had experienced such happiness that he should have known better than to believe that it could last.

But he *had* believed it. For a brief spell he had dared to trust that he was actually loved and had loved freely in return – holding nothing of himself back, nothing to protect himself now.

It was not that women had not loved him before Merry, but he had not loved them. Something had been missing, lacking. From the moment he had met Merry, he had felt himself connecting with her in different ways as if threads were intertwining. The fabric of his life was now threadbare without her. Merry *was* his life.

Merry's upbringing had forced her to be courageous and strong, but from the first, Rafe had seen the fragile dignity wrapped about a yawning vulnerability that made him ache to protect her.

Her mind was keen, educated and resourceful. When they had worked together, she had rapidly grasped the salient details and applied them easily as well as he. They had been equals.

Merry's wit and humour – a memory flashed into his head and made him wince it was so precious – two of her greatest charms. Humour had been a saving grace in his life and she not only appreciated his jesting, but she extended it with her own.

All this came together in the most extraordinary way when combined with their miraculous physical alchemy. He had been attracted to Merry even when he thought her a boy! And she had been drawn to him even when she wished him to hang. When they made love, they were one person – complete and indivisible.

For one brief, dreamlike week, he had thought that they were made for each other and that they might have the rest of their lives to grow even closer over the years, as their understanding deepened with shared experience. When they had walked by the lake, he had imagined for an instant what it might be like when they were old and might bring their grandchildren down to see the ducklings.

Now, Rafe knew how it felt to feel loved by the one he loved. Rafe had tasted heaven. To return to earth now would be like hell.

Rafe's step faltered on the stairs as the awful realisation dawned that he would never hold his wife's soft face in his hands again and see that wondering glow light her beautiful grey eyes, never kiss her, never hold her in his arms, never feel her body rise to meet his own as they consummated their love for one another. It was too much to bear.

Remembered hurts and grief from his youth added to his sense of loss. Somewhere deep within, he was thrown back twenty-two years to the moment when he discovered what being loved looked like, and knew that such a blessing was not his lot.

"Better to have loved and lost ..." he thought bitterly. *What a foul lie!*

But then as every joyous moment with Merry since their insane duel played across his mind's eye, crushing his shattered heart to pieces, he accepted on some level that he would not have sacrificed one second of it to alleviate the agony he now felt.

'My lord?' It was Frith.

Somewhere, in some compartment of his brain, where a pattern for normality was still preserved, Rafe registered that his butler might be bemused by the expression on his master's face. Perhaps he thought there must have been a death in the family, not realising that he was looking at little more than a walking corpse.

'My lord?' Frith said again.

'It's alright, Frith,' said Rafe, hearing his own voice as if from far away. 'I'm alright.'

'My lord, the constable is here, with an officer from Bow Street,' came Frith's anxious voice. 'They say they have a warrant to arrest you.'

There was a moment of silence, and then Rafe gave a loud crack of harsh laughter.

'Perhaps there is a God, after all, Frith,' replied Rafe, coming back to the present and registering the presence of his two visitors.

'Gentlemen! I believe I am as eager to go to the gallows as you are to escort me there.'

The constable and the Runner exchanged sharp glances of alarm and disbelief.

'Well, as to that, my lord,' said the Runner, 'you will have your trial before there'll be any talk of gallows.'

'Pity,' said Rafe, as he stepped out of the front door, leaving his escorts, still gaping like landed fish, to follow him incontinent.

THE RELUCTANT LADY

As the constable turned the wagon, Rafe stood, his arms folded tightly across his chest, bracing against the agony in the region of his heart. He tried to stop himself glancing back at the house where he had been truly happy for the first time in his life. He failed. His gaze raked over the gardens where they had walked, the parkland where they had ridden together and then swiftly, painfully, up to the windows of their adjoining rooms. At least now Merry would have revenge for her murdered brother, justice at last, now that the need for it had been brought back to her so forcibly by the gruesome remnants of that awful day's work.

Frith had abandoned a lifetime of discipline and staggered across the gravel driveway to his master, who seemed to have run mad.

'My lord?' was all he could say in his disbelief.

'Don't worry, old fellow. My wife will take care of you all,' said Rafe in a constricted voice. 'Tell her … tell her …'. But he could not continue.

It was some time later that a rather forlorn looking Merry, her face still ravaged by her first reaction to what she had found in the trunk, came downstairs looking for Rafe. She wanted the comfort of her husband's arms, to talk to him and have those wise, smiling eyes and his beloved voice tell her that she was overreacting, that she was wrong.

Descending the stairs, she saw Frith uncharacteristically pacing the hallway, his normally impassive face distorted with anxiety.

'Frith, are you all right?' she enquired.

Frith's head spun round to face her and his expression told her instantly that something terrible had occurred.

'Frith! What has happened?' she cried, tripping rapidly down the stairs to join him.

'It's his lordship, my lady,' said Frith, manfully attempting to regain his customary self-control. 'He has been taken up by the constable and a Runner from Bow Street.'

'What!' gasped Merry, the colour draining from her face. 'But, when? Why did he not call for me?'

'Thirty minutes ago, my lady,' replied Frith, unsure of how to explain what had happened. 'His lordship seemed eager to accompany them.'

'What!' cried Merry in response to this incomprehensible news.

'I can't account for it, my lady. He came downstairs, looking like he had seen a ghost. In pieces, he seemed, if I may say so,' said Frith. 'The constable and the Runner were waiting here with a warrant. Then his lordship said he was *"eager to go to the gallows"*, your ladyship! And when the Runner said he would receive a trial first, he said *"Pity"*!'

It was a long moment before Merry could speak as she slowly processed this improbable account.

'But what had happened to upset him so?' she asked, in a baffled voice.

'That's what I can't fathom, my lady,' said Frith. 'Henry said he looked very happy when he went upstairs to find you.'

'But wait a moment,' she said, confused, her voice shaking. 'Lord Rothsea did not come to see me.'

'Beg pardon, but he did, my lady,' replied Frith. 'He asked where you were, and Alfred told him that you were in your room unpacking the trunks that had arrived from London. He was only upstairs for a few moments before he came back down.'

'But why did he not ...' murmured Merry, racking her brains.

When she had smoothed out Bryn's jacket on the floor, Merry had heard the faint crackle of paper and, exploring, had found his note concealed in an inner pocket. It read:

Dearest Merry, I thought I could Win back Tal Hairn, but All is Lost. I am a Coward, I know, but I cannot Bear it nor this Miserable life we lead. I have Forced a Quarrel on Lord Rothsea. I think it will be Quick. Do not hate me, I Beg you, for I will Love you Always. B

It had been a catastrophic revelation.

Horrified by her brother's cowardice, his suicide, his knowingly leaving her alone, defenceless and in utter penury, to deal with the consequences ... and to have forced the stain of his death on another man - her own dear Rafe! To think what she had said and done to Rafe when he had only told her the truth, and all because she had believed unswervingly in Bryn's honour and love for her! Even now the blood pounded in her head at the thought. Bryn had been the source of her woes, not Rafe, though it was he who lashed himself constantly for them ...

Suddenly, Merry saw with terrifying clarity the interpretation that Rafe, with his habitual penchant for self-blame, might have put on some of her impassioned words in the first storm of her distress. If Rafe had thought her bitter rage had been directed at him and not at Bryn ...

'Frith! Send for Brooke!' said Merry, her low, breathless voice freezing his blood with renewed anxiety, before she put any further action out of the question by fainting clean away for the first time in her life.

Chapter Twenty-Two
Desperate Measures

George Lawson was feeling pretty miserable as he drove the closed wagon out of the gates of Seaton Fall, under the horrified gaze of his cousin the gate-keeper. As constable of the parish, it was his duty to assist in the execution of the warrant that Mr Worton, the Runner, had produced. The fellow had followed the carrier all the way from London, he had said, hearing a rumour that Coley had come into a large sum of money from Lord Rothsea and, inexplicably, his victim's brother.

Lawson had heard about his lordship's trouble in London, and had known that Lord Rothsea was back in residence. No one in his lordship's household would be buying his mother's quails eggs for themselves. But, like others in the area, he would not have given up Lord Rothsea of his own accord. Lawson was feeling even more wretched because his parents lived in one of his lordship's cottages and now had a new thatched roof, mended walls and a water pump just outside the kitchen door. If that Worton fellow had not been with him every minute since he had arrived that morning, Lawson might even have tried to get a message to the Fall to warn his lordship.

But, unfathomably, it seemed as if Lord Rothsea <u>wanted</u> to be arrested. Worse … he said he wanted to <u>hang!</u> This had caused Mr Worton, with a perplexed look at his prisoner, to elect to travel inside the wagon with him, in case he did himself a mischief.

Worton watched Lord Rothsea's face intently as they rocked along the road to Mumshall. He had seen some desperate expressions in his career, but never in all his puff would he forget this one. Toff or no toff, his was the face of a man roasting in hellfire.

THE RELUCTANT LADY

It seemed so incongruous with his crime and with all he had heard about his lordship's character during his enquiries that Worton wondered if he might be guilty of some more heinous act of which the authorities were as yet unaware.

Lord Rothsea seemed not to see him at all. When his eyes were open, they were focused on some other scene, playing in his mind's eye. But more often they were closed, and his face grimacing as if he were in acute pain. For the entire journey, his lordship clutched his arms tightly about his ribs, as if they would fall all to pieces if he let go.

Worton shook his head wonderingly. This was a new one on him.

Back at Seaton Fall, Merry caught the pungent scent of smelling salts. As she began to regain consciousness, she felt herself being carried in a pair of strong arms. For an instant, before opening her eyes, she thought it was Rafe, and that Frith's words had been a mistake. But the arms felt different, and she awoke to find Brooke bending to lay her on a sofa in the morning room.

'Brooke,' she whispered weakly.

'Aye, it's true, my lady,' he said grimly, adding severely. 'Now, don't you be going off in another swoon, ma'am, as I need some answers from you. Did you two have another of your dust-ups while I was seeing to Sutterley?'

Brooke was standing with his hands on his hips, looking down at her very sternly. Merry struggled upright, realising that both Mrs Dodd and Chantal were now fussing around her with salts and damp cloths. She accepted the cloth, as her head pounded like the devil, but waved the ladies away, just as Rafe might have done.

'No, I swear! I didn't even see him, Brooke,' she said. 'It's much worse than that. I think he overheard me say something ... Oh, Brooke! He totally misunderstood! He will be torturing himself and for nothing! For nothing! It's so stupid! And now he's been arrested and wants to die ...'

Merry burst into tears, and the two ladies rushed forward to comfort her, but jumped back in alarm as Merry leapt to her feet, exclaiming passionately through her tears in a low throbbing voice:

'We have to save him, Brooke! We must overtake them! Do we have any pistols? We will need to be armed!'

Brooke shook his head in exasperation, and shooed Mrs Dodd and Chantal from the room like a pair of hens, closing the door firmly on their outrage.

'Right,' he said, taking charge. 'Before we start waving pistols at the King's men, how about you explain to me what you think his lordship heard to make him go off courting the noose?'

As he spoke, he had taken Merry's shoulders and gently forced her to sit back down. As he dashed some brandy into a glass, and put it into her nerveless hand, he added: 'And no roundaboutation or hysterics, now. Tell me, man to man, if you take my meaning.'

Merry did take his meaning. She had behaved appallingly like the very women she despised most. Shaking her head as if to clear it of feminine nonsense, Merry recounted what had happened when she had found her brother's note.

'But you never saw him, nor spoke to him?'

'No,' admitted Merry. 'But I was in an awful taking.'

Since Brooke had had the dubious privilege of witnessing at least one of those takings, he had no difficulty in imagining that the lady might not notice her husband in the doorway, or the effect on the poor lad if he thought he were the object of her misery and rage.

'But I can't understand why Rafe didn't come in and speak to me, when he saw I was upset,' said Merry, at a loss.

'No,' said Brooke after a long moment. 'Not when he's been so happy. First time he's felt his own love returned. Suspect he didn't want to see it die there in front of him. He'd probably sooner die himself.'

I s'pose I should be glad he didn't get to the gunroom, he added to himself. *No good sharing that thought with the missus.*

'Oh God!' cried Merry. 'Then we have to find him and tell him that I *do* love him, with all my heart.'

'Might not be easy to convince him, if he's in one of his dark moods, which I think he must be,' said Brooke with grim foreboding. 'And now he's been taken up for murder ... and has admitted as much. I dunno as how we *can* save him even if he wanted to be saved.'

THE RELUCTANT LADY

'But I have my brother's note that proves he meant to die by Rafe's hand. It was suicide not murder!'

'Aye, m'lady. But his lordship done the killing – that's what the law will say, but we need help, that's for sure. Do you have any influential friends, ma'am?'

'Not a one,' said Merry bleakly, and then thought of her only other high-born friend. 'Well, there's Harry …'

Brooke gave her an ironic look.

'No, you are right,' said Merry sadly. 'He would have no cause to sympathise, and he has had to leave the country after the countess laid information against him.'

'The constable told Frith that they were taking his lordship to Newgate.'

'Newgate!' gasped Merry. She had seen hangings outside those forbidding grey walls. The threat of seeing a noose being tightened around Rafe's beautiful strong neck, or the horror that she knew followed - whether the neck broke cleanly or did not - came sharply into focus in her mind.

'Aye,' said Brooke, with similar images playing in his own imagination. 'So we can do no good for him here. We need to get to London … and if we make haste, we might get there before they do.'

Merry jumped up, galvanised into action.

'Yes, let us leave immediately!' she cried.

Brooke sighed. *Aye, she's Rothea's rib all right … damn resty!*

'You'll need to pack, m'lady,' he said, and when Merry made an impatient gesture, he added: 'You'll need to make a case to some important people, ma'am, and do his lordship proud. It won't do to be looking like you slept in your gown.'

Merry took a steadying breath. She wanted to do nothing more than throw her leg over Rafe's fastest horse, gallop after them and save him at the pistol point if she had to, but Brooke's wisdom prevailed. There was no way that Rafe would be tried and sentenced within a day, so there was a little time. But the thought of Rafe's suffering one second longer than was necessary, or being interned in that dread place, was almost more than she could bear.

'Very well,' she said reluctantly. 'But we leave within the hour, and anything that cannot be packed in that time will have to follow later.'

Brooke nodded.

'I'll see to his lordship's things and will have Miss Sangat do for yours,' he said. 'Now, get Frith to gather the household and then you give them a talk as will steady them down, like his lordship would, if he'd been in his proper mind when he were took. They're all sick with worry.'

Merry closed her eyes for a moment, and when she opened them again and looked at Brooke, he gave an odd, proud sigh.

'Aye, there's my Lady Rothsea! There's why he married thee, lass!'

Merry gave him a smile, straightening her back and taking another steadying breath.

'First, I must apologise to Frith. What a scare I must have given him,' said Merry. 'I've no idea what came over me. I've never fainted before in my life.'

Brooke nodded, but said nothing.

They set forward within the hour. There was not a soul that heard her ladyship's short, reassuring speech, that did not love her almost as much as their beloved master when she finished, nor a soul that doubted that she would do all in her power to bring his lordship and all of them through this dark hour, if she had to carry them all herself.

The whole household waved them off, from Frith to the gardener's boy.

Though she was dressed in a smart, travelling dress of grey silk twill with Russian frogging, with a grey astrakhan Cossack bonnet and matching muff, Merry felt like a knight going off to war. Though she was still in full mourning for her brother, she no longer felt the same level of respect for him as she had and she was damned if she would dress like a widow while her husband's life lay in the balance. It seemed too much like tempting fate.

Brooke had harnessed the same quartet of horses that had brought them from London to Quemerford, and Merry had high hopes of overtaking the lumbering constable's wagon before they left the county, only to see it approaching in the other direction when they had scarcely been on the road for an hour.

It was driven by Lawson, looking very downcast.

Brooke waved him down and they discovered that Worton had used his warrant to secure passage on the mail coach for him and his lordship, at Lord Rothsea's insistence. His lordship had even paid their passage.

Brooke groaned. There was no way they could catch up with the mail coach.

Lawson explained that his lordship was being taken to the rotation office at Bow Street, where the warrant had been issued.

'What happens there?' asked Brooke.

Lawson scratched his head.

'Well, if the justice thinks there's a case to be answered, then his lordship will be held in custody while a sessions clerk writes up the charge and the grand jury approves it.'

'That sounds like a lengthy process,' sad Merry hopefully.

Lawson looked less sanguine.

'Well, I dunno about that, m'lady,' he said glumly. 'Since a warrant's been issued, they may already have done their bit in his lordship's absence.'

Merry twisted her hands anxiously.

'Then if it has, what would happen?' she said.

'He would be arraigned, then, depending on how Lord Rothsea pleaded, there might be a preliminary hearing in the same office, or perhaps in the magistrate's home, as his lordship is a gentleman. The rotation office is public, see?' said Lawson.

'And what will happen if he pleads guilty?' demanded Brooke.

'Well,' said Lawson miserably. 'He would be held for sentencing ... and it being a capital offence ...'

Lawson looked down and sighed, his heart in his boots.

'How much time do we have?' asked Merry, with a hunted look.

'Well, if he pleads not guilty ...' began Lawson, more hopefully.

'No,' interrupted Brooke. 'If it goes the other way. How soon could sentence be passed.'

Lawson sighed despondently.

'Well, that would be the worst case,' said Lawson, still baffled that Lord Rothsea should have such a deathwish upon him. 'Because if he pleads guilty, there's no option but the gallows.'

'But how soon, man!' said Brooke.

'Could be as little as a week,' said Lawson. 'If they already have a hanging planned. They like to do them in batches, so ...'

'A week!' cried Merry. 'Oh God!'

'But I can't think it will come to that, m'lady,' said Lawson. 'A dozen things might happen to save him before he's sentenced. He might change his plea or... or...' Lawson was clearly racking his brains but could think of nothing more.

'But once he is sentenced?' said Merry.

Lawson paused, then shook his head, with an expression of doom.

The three of them stood in the road for a moment, each lost in their own unhappy thoughts.

'And he'll be held in Newgate while all this is happening?' said Brooke.

Lawson nodded gloomily.

'Thank you, Mr Lawson,' said Merry, holding out her hand. 'You have been a great help.'

Lawson bowed.

'Thank you, my lady,' said Lawson, feeling very low. 'We'll be praying for him ... for you both. I hope you can bring him home to us.'

Merry gave him a tight reassuring smile that wobbled a little, before she turned swiftly and climbed back into the carriage, where Chantal was waiting, her eyes wide with alarm at all she had overheard.

Brooke was already climbing back on the box beside the groom, and they were bowling off towards the London road within a moment.

Despite the two other passengers in the mail coach, Rafe had put Worton through a similar line of questioning.

'So, how soon after I plead guilty may I be hanged?' he had demanded.

The lady passenger gave a muffled shriek and pressed her handkerchief to her lips, her horrified eyes the size of saucers.

'Well, there will be a sentencing session, but that will likely be quick,' said Worton, a deep frown wrinkling his brow as he stared at his prisoner's face in ghoulish fascination. He had seen men wriggle like worms to avoid the hook, but never seen one throw himself on it. 'Then the law says you must hang within two days of sentencing.'

This time the lady passenger gave a sob, and buried her face in the handkerchief, whilst her companion put his arm about her and gave Rafe and Worton a very severe, disapproving look.

Rafe did not see this. He had sighed with bitter relief, his head falling back onto the squabs, and holding his sides tightly again.

This agony could be over within the week.

Once they arrived in London, the procedure went much as Lawson predicted. Justice Sir Henry Willards, learning that the prisoner was Lord Rothsea, opted to hold the preliminary hearing in his own house in Portman Square.

When Mr Worton the principal officer had rapidly outlined his experiences of the preceding four and twenty hours in his lordship's company, Sir Henry was aghast.

'Means to plead guilty!' he declared. 'But he cannot! I never heard of such a thing! There must be some mistake, Worton. Does he understand that he might hang?'

'He does, your honour,' confirmed Worton. 'Seems to be banking on it, if you were to ask me.'

'He... he *wishes* to die?'

'Think he'd hang himself, if we don't do the job for him,' averred Worton.

'Good God!' gasped Sir Henry. 'Is he in his right mind?'

'Well, if you mean is he a candidate for the Bethlehem, then I'd say no, your honour, for he seems as sane as you or me,' said Worton. 'But I never seen a soul in such torment, and that's a fact. I've a notion that there may be more to it than that duel.'

'What do you mean?'

'Well, no one ever saw the brother again,' said Worton. 'The boy was called at the inquest, but did not attend, though he was the key witness for connecting the body with Lord Rothsea's duel. Sir Hector Parfitt said the lad called on him later, much beaten about, saying he had been attacked and robbed. But what's to say Lord Rothsea did not arrange it, meaning it to be fatal?' said Worton, with a knowing nod. 'The day after the lad spoke with Sir Hector, he vanished. And then Lord Rothsea ups and gives five thousand pounds to a carrier as helped the lad … and did it in the name of the boy.'

'*Five thousand pounds!*' squawked Sir Henry at this staggering sum. 'Was the carrier in on it, do you think?'

'No, your honour,' said Worton, shaking his head consideringly. 'You never met such an honest fellow. He was as perplexed by the gift as I was, and thought the boy must have been Lord Rothsea's long lost heir or something, but I knew they were not related.'

'So it was guilt money, you think?' said Sir Henry, still disbelieving.

'I can't otherwise account for it, your honour,' said Worton. 'A Mr Maitland, who I believe was really my Lord Stowe, an intimate of Lord Rothsea's, was very worried about the boy's disappearance and made substantial enquiries himself before he left town after information was laid against him. Of course, that turned out to be a hum, as the only witness, the surgeon at the duel, said Lord Stowe was not present at the affray.'

Worton did not mention that a man answering Lord Rothsea's description had also enquired, thinking it a ruse by his lordship to cover his crime.

Sir Henry continued to shake his head at the outrageous notion that Lord Rothsea had, for some inexplicable reason, done away with the brother of his victim, to the apparent consternation of his own friends.

'And I can't find any trace of the sister, neither.'

'The boy had a sister?'

'Yes, sir,' confirmed Worton. 'She arranged the burial and paid off the landlord, but no one has seen *her* since, and she wasn't at the funeral. The ordinary confirmed that. Just the boy alone, and very forlorn.'

'But there's nothing in that! Ladies of quality rarely attend such sad affairs. It is too much for their fragile constitutions,' said Sir Henry. 'But look here, man. Rothsea may have felt guilty at depriving the child of his brother, and may have asked his friend to find the boy to make his amends. There's no cause to think the worst. And perhaps he was found and given some kind of home by his lordship?'

'Then why would he be so keen to plead guilty, your honour?' asked Worton reasonably. 'Or be courting the three-legged mare so readily?'

Sir Henry had no answer, but like Pontius Pilate, he heartily wished he might wash his hands of this one.

'Very well. Show the prisoner in, and you better not have shackled him!'

'There was no need, your honour,' said Worton. 'Never had such a willing prisoner.'

To Sir Henry's continued dismay, Worton's assurance proved to be true. Lord Rothsea seemed eager to hang and chafed at the necessary delay.

Sir Henry was baffled. He sent the others from the room and remonstrated with his lordship.

'I beg you will reconsider, Rothsea. Damn it, sir! It was a duel. Perhaps it was not precisely in the proper form, and the location was very ill-advised, but there was nothing havey-cavey in it. You are entitled to a trial and legal representation. Think of your family, sir. What will your father think of your actions?'

'He will not be surprised,' said Rafe dryly.

'But he will not be happy, sir,' said Sir Henry. 'You are his only son, are you not?'

Rafe's head jerked upward, as if a lash had curled across his back, but he uttered only a dry, humourless laugh.

Sir Henry regarded Lord Rothsea's harrowed expression, and reluctantly entertained Worton's lurid speculation.

'Is there some other reason why you wish so ardently to hang, my lord?'

'What?' said Rafe with suspicious alacrity.

'Is there perhaps another crime weighing upon your conscience, sir?'

Rafe frowned enquiringly.

'What do you mean?' he asked, momentarily intrigued.

'I see I must ask you bluntly, my lord,' said Sir Henry uncomfortably. 'Did you have a hand in the disappearance of Mr Griffith's younger brother?'

Rafe stared at him incredulously for a moment, before a broad smile of genuine humour banished the haunted mask.

'Yes, Sir Henry,' said Rafe, his eyes alight with the unholy glow of a great private joke. 'Yes, you may hold me responsible for the de… *demise* of *Mr* Merion Griffith.'

'Good God, sir! You admit it?'

'I am proud of it!' said Rafe, watching Sir Henry's face turn apoplectic, while his own glinted with the divine comedy that was playing out here.

'Where is the body?' gasped Sir Henry.

Rafe choked back a laugh.

'You will never find it,' he said, again with a smile twisting his lips and his shoulders shaking.

'But will you not reveal it, so that he might have a Christian burial?' demanded Sir Henry aghast. 'It might help to clear your conscience a little.'

Rafe paused, and Sir Henry saw the humour turn into a more wistful glow.

'No, Sir Henry,' murmured Lord Rothsea. 'Where the disappearance of *Master* Griffith is concerned, my conscience is clear. I never did a better thing in my life.'

He heard the magistrate gasp.

'And the sister?' asked Sir Henry, since Lord Rothsea seemed willing to make a clean breast of his crimes.

Rafe's odd smile appeared again.

'Oh, I married the sister,' he responded with the ghost of a laugh. 'And never did a better thing than that, too.'

'You married your victims' sister?' cried Sir Henry, utterly boggled. 'She consented to such a thing?'

Rafe paused, looking down.

'Eventually.'

'Oh, dear God! Did you compromise her, you… you fiend?'

'No, but I confess I threatened it,' said Rafe. 'However, my wife was reconciled to our union and it was willingly consummated a week since. We are legally married. That is incontestable.'

'You are newly married? Will you leave your poor bride a widow?' said Sir Henry. 'Or is it she who wishes you dead, for her poor young brother.'

The secret smile appeared again.

THE RELUCTANT LADY

'No, I think she does not resent the demise of the boy.' But then the humour evaporated and the haunted look returned. 'But she will certainly never forgive my murdering the elder brother... for I intended him to die, Sir Henry, before we took up our weapons. So will you arraign me and play this farce to its end?'

Sir Henry looked at the young man before him in exasperated frustration. Lord Rothsea's words left him no choice but to endorse the charge. The issue of the younger brother was perplexing, but there was no body and no accuser, other than his lordship himself. Sir Henry resolved to write to Lady Rothsea for clarification, but on the issue of the duel, for which the warrant and the charges had been drawn up, the path was clear.

'Then, regrettably, I must rule that there is sufficient evidence for a charge against you.'

'I plead guilty,' said Rafe swiftly.

'You may do that at your arraignment, sir! I shall not hear your plea here.'

'Oh, God! More delay!' groaned Rafe. 'When will the arraignment be?'

'Not before tomorrow,' said Sir Henry categorically. 'I will have you spend tonight in a condemned cell in the hope that it might bring you to your senses.'

'You will not change my plea, Sir Henry,' said Rafe darkly.

'Perhaps not,' said Sir Henry. 'But I will, in conscience, have done what I might to do so.'

As the door closed behind him, Sir Henry sat heavily down in his chair, pulled off his wig and threw it on the floor in frustration. Then after a moment or two, he huffed and reached down to pick it up and put it back on his head, slightly askew. Then, his brows lifting as recalled the earlier conversation, he pulled across a piece of paper and began to pen a note to Lady Rothsea.

When they arrived in Albemarle Street late that afternoon, Merry dashed upstairs to Rafe's bedroom to change her travelling dress, while Brooke took the horses round to Dover Street to see them safely bestowed.

The sight of that familiar room and the poignant memories associated with it lacerated Merry's strained nerves. This is where it had truly begun for her. The strange, intricate, uneasy dance that had brought her finally into the arms of the man she loved.

When Brooke returned to find her ladyship pacing the sitting room in her pelisse and hat, ready to depart, he had news.

'Lord Stowe's been exonerated,' he announced, as he closed the door behind him. 'His lordship's pa squared it with the witness. Anyhow, he's here at his house in Half Moon Street. His groom at the Dover Street yard told me. Been here for a week or so.'

'Harry,' murmured Merry thoughtfully. 'Well, I don't know why, but that's good to know,'

'Felt the same way myself, m'lady,' said Brooke. 'Never been a finer gentleman than Lord Stowe. He might hate his lordship's guts right now, but I can't think he would watch him hang, if he could help it.'

'No,' said Merry. 'Well, let's not trouble him until we have to. Let us go and find Rafe and see if we can't talk some sense into him, first.'

Some hours earlier, Rafe had been through all the pride-crushing process of being imprisoned in Newgate as if in a trance. Mechanically, he subjected to a body search and shackling before being led to a small, dank, dimly lit cell. Nothing touched him. He was far gone in a dark depression. He longed only for release. Every memory of Merry was both a heaven and a hell. Finally, the door clanged shut and he was at last alone in the darkness with the pervading smell of damp, urine and bad drains. The cell boasted only a rudimentary bed near the window, and in the corner, just out of sight of the door, a slops bucket with a wooden lid. Rafe sat on the hard bed, alone with his thoughts, his misery complete.

Merry and Brooke had a frustrating afternoon. Discovering that Rafe was being held for arraignment in Newgate, they had hastened there to visit him, only to be denied. Sir Henry had stipulated that Lord Rothsea was to be treated as a condemned man for the night, so he was not permitted visitors and would be on bread and water until the arraignment.

THE RELUCTANT LADY

Lady Rothsea had gone off like one of Whinyate's rockets at that, but the guards would not budge, other than to accept a fee for easement, so that his lordship might have his shackles removed.

The lady had then demanded to see this 'Sir Henry' and had been told that he was in session.

When Merry finally tracked him down, she was only able to have a note passed to him, announcing that she was desirous of speaking with him, only to have one in return saying that Sir Henry would be equally grateful for an interview with her, and begging her ladyship to wait on him at his house in Portman Square at eleven the following morning.

Merry was then left with nothing to do but pace around Rafe's sitting room, or to sit hugging one of his jackets to her face, because it still carried his wonderful scent, and trying not to cry. Downstairs was his beautiful library, but Merry was certain that entering that sanctum would overset her completely.

While Merry paced, Brooke hung about the prison making enquiries and trying to find a guard open to a little friendly bribery.

The following morning, as Merry was preparing for her interview with Sir Henry, Rafe's arraignment had been unexpectedly brought forward.

Lord Justice Bracton, was surprised to see the heir to a peer of the realm appear before him, and became more surprised as the clerk of the court read the charge. *A murder charge for a duel? Why the devil had the fellow not left the country, like any other blighter might?*

But this was as nothing to his shock when the clerk stated: 'Rafael Alexander James Wolvenden, how say you? Are you guilty or not guilty?' and Rothsea replied: 'Guilty!'

'What's that?' said Lord Bracton, thinking that he had misheard the plea.

'The accused pleaded guilty, my lord,' said the clerk, leaning toward the judge as he spoke.

'What! Put the question again!'

The clerk did so.

'Guilty!' repeated Rafe exasperated.

'My lord Rothsea,' said the judge. 'Perhaps you do not fully appreciate that this is a capital charge?'

'I do understand it,' replied Rafe tersely.

'But by a plea of guilty you place a sentence of death upon your head, and there will be nothing I may do to respite it.'

'I understand.'

'But you will hang, sir!'

'Yes,' said Rafe impatiently, adding under his breath. 'Though it seems to be taking a damnably long time to get there.'

'But Lord Rothsea,' said the judge uncomprehendingly. 'It was a duel. Were there not mitigating circumstances that might reduce the charge?'

'None. Are you able to pronounce sentence or not?'

'No, sir,' snapped Lord Bracton in irritation. 'That will occur at your sentencing session.'

'And when, in heaven's name, will that be?' demanded Rafe.

But though Lord Bracton's own temper was shortening, he was an ambitious man. Not for the world was he going to accelerate the pronouncement of a death sentence against the Earl of Northover's only son. Northover was a spent force, but he had run with the Prince Regent's set for several years and still had powerful friends.

'I will not advance you to sentencing, sir, until I have seen the witnesses identify you in person at very least.'

'Then bustle about, my lord,' cried Rafe, a man in torment. 'Have them brought in today, for pity's sake, and let's have an end to this!'

'Do you mean to contest the charge in any way, my lord Rothsea?'

'No!'

'Have you taken legal counsel of any kind?'

'No.'

'Will you at least engage it?'

'No.'

Lord Bracton looked at him nonplussed and finally spoke.

'Very well, but I wish to take advice on this matter. I will have you before me again tomorrow morning. Take the prisoner down!'

Welcoming Merry into his study, Sir Henry said:

THE RELUCTANT LADY

'Lady Rothsea! I can't think how you received my note so soon.'

'Your note?'

Sir Henry showed her ladyship to a chair and then proceeded to explain the extraordinary revelations made by her husband the previous day.

Merry sighed.

'I can explain, Sir Henry, but you may be a little shocked,' said Merry. 'I am both the sister and the brother of the man who died in the duel. I was brought up as a boy. We had not the resources to bring me up as a gentleman's daughter, you see. When Lord Rothsea discovered this fact, he decided to try to fulfil my brother's dying charge on him to take care of me by restoring me to my rightful sex and to provide for me in some way. He … he…'

'He forced you to marry him?' supplied Sir Henry.

'Yes, sir, though not with violence …'

'Only the threat of it?'

'Yes, but I should have known he did not mean it. He would never have done me the slightest harm, he only loved me… too well to let me make the mistake of leaving him… and he was proved right, for I love him more than I can possibly say.'

'So that is why he was proud of the demise of <u>Master</u> Griffith?' said Sir Henry, seeing the light.

'Yes, I put off the boy when I became his wife, and could not have been happier, until this occurred.'

'But if he loves you and you love him…?'

'A misunderstanding,' said Merry. 'I found this note from my brother. His last. I was very upset, and my husband thought my rage was against him.'

Sir Henry's reaction to the note was not what Merry expected. He scanned it and then patted her hand in the most patronising fashion.

Sir Henry was touched by Lady Rothsea's rather simple attempt to clear her husband. *Lilac paper*, he thought, certain that it was her ladyship's own, smiling inwardly at her lack of guile in not even selecting a more masculine shade.

'Well, well,' he only said. 'That doesn't matter now. We must get him to plead not guilty, and to contest the charge.'

'*"Doesn't matter"?*' cried Merry. 'But how can there _be_ a charge? You can see my brother meant to kill himself by my husband's hand.'

The moment that Merry met Sir Henry's gently admonishing gaze, she realised what he was thinking. She looked down at the shred of ridiculously coloured paper, and saw it as he must.

'But… but…' Merry realised to her chagrin that a woman, even a lady, carried little or no weight with the authorities, especially one fighting to save her husband.

'Yes, well, my dear Lady Rothsea. It was a very brave attempt but a little foolish you will admit?' he prompted, with an avuncular tone.

Merry leapt angrily to her feet.

'Oh, God save me from foolish men!' she cried. 'So now I must prove the origins of the paper? Very well! Where is this gambling den where the duel was instigated?' she demanded.

'Heavens, my lady! You cannot be thinking of going there?'

'Clearly I must, and drag the owner back here by his ear!'

'Forgive me, ma'am, but you will not do it. The rogue would be guilty of running an illegal gaming establishment,' said Sir Henry. 'And it would still not provide evidence that your brother wrote the note and not you yourself.'

Merry made a sound of complete exasperation, and then gasped with a sudden realisation.

'If I were able to produce an unimpeachable witness to the paper and to the writing of the note?'

'Well, if he or she might be produced before sentence is passed… and if his lordship might be persuaded to plead not guilty at the arraignment …'

'And when is that to be?'

Sir Henry rang a bell on his desk, and a clerk entered shadowed by Mr Worton, who stood goggling at the sight of the victim's sister dressed to the nines.

'Ah! Worton! That other matter is all cleared up.'

'The boy?' said Worton.

Merry and Sir Henry exchanged a look.

'Safe,' said Sir Henry, adding significantly: 'This is _Lady Rothsea_, who wishes to know when the arraignment will be so that she might speak to her husband beforehand.'

THE RELUCTANT LADY

Light had not entirely dawned for the Runner, but he had news.

'It's been and gone, your honour,' said Mr Worton. 'I just come from the court. Lord Rothsea pleaded guilty, as he said he would.'

'Oh!' gasped Merry, her heart plummeting as she saw Sir Henry blench.

'Begging your pardon, but Judge Bracton's in a pother about it and asked if you might wait on him at your earliest convenience,' said Worton.

Merry, who had earlier jumped up, had to sit rather quickly, as she felt a panicky sickness come over her for a moment. After a few steadying breaths, she stood again, straightening her back and lifting her chin.

'Sir Henry,' she said in a voice that sounded a lot calmer than she felt. 'If you could kindly keep Judge Bracton from killing my husband until I return, I should be very grateful. Now, I must do what others have failed to, and prove my husband innocent of any crime bar a lamentably volatile temper.'

As she stepped out of the room, where Brooke and Chantal awaited her, she kept her head high until they were outside by the carriage, then she clutched Brook's arm.

'He's already been arraigned and pleaded guilty,' she gasped, still feeling horribly light-headed, regretting that she had not eaten in the last four and twenty hours.

Brooke struck his forehead with his palm and swore, then begged her ladyship's pardon.

'Don't worry,' she said, wringing her hands. 'I thought precisely the same thing when I heard.'

'He could be sentenced as early as tomorrow,' said Brooke grimly. 'A guard at Newgate said they're rushing cases through for Mr Brunskill's last hanging before he hands over to the new executioner.'

'Oh God!' said Merry. 'And once he's sentenced, I've lost him Brooke,' she said, her voice breaking.

'We won't say that until we see him dance on air, not before, d'y hear?' Merry nodded, pulling herself together, despite the horrific picture that phrase painted in her mind.

'I've laid a little lard around the Newgate guards, and I think I can get in to see him, and maybe take a note and a little food.'

'Oh yes! Damn! I should have asked Sir Henry to vouchsafe me a visit.'

'He won't see you, my lady,' said Brooke. 'The fool lad's given orders, and paid handsome too, to prevent you or me going in. But I told them I'm his lordship's valet, just wanting to bring him a clean change of clothes and a few victuals so he doesn't disgrace us by fainting on the gallows.'

Merry bit her lip so hard to keep it from wobbling that she could taste the blood in her mouth. She tried to channel her emotion into anger.

'The wretched, wicked idiot! How dare he refuse to see me!'

'Aye, there's nothing like him for being a fool when he sets his mind to it,' said Brooke grimly. 'He thinks we'll do aught we can to save him, and he'd be right. Even if you hated him, you wouldn't let him hang, would you?'

Merry shook her head miserably.

'Aye, so he knows,' said Brooke. 'I expect he thinks he's being noble in sparing you from lying to his face.'

Merry had to bite her lip even harder.

'So, I'm to be smuggled in at midnight when the shift changes,' said Brooke. 'Is there anything we can do in the meantime?'

'Yes,' said Merry in a constricted voice. 'You said Harry's here in London?'

Brooke blinked but nodded.

'Then take me to him, now,' she said. 'I'm in the perfect mood to beg him for help on my knees, if necessary.'

As they were pulling up outside the elegant little house on Half Moon Street, Lord Ventnor, who had just descended the steps, on his way to his boot makers, spotted Brooke climbing down from the box.

'Brooke! Is that you?' declared Lord Ventnor. 'I hope you are well, my good fellow.'

'I've been better, my lord,' said Brooke.

'Ah, yes,' said his lordship. 'Nasty business …'

But here he was interrupted by the carriage door opening and a young lady jumping down, without the aid of steps or assistance.

'Come along, Brooke,' she said impatiently. 'You can catch up with your friend when we have Rafe safe.'

Brooke choked and tried to suppress a grin, as Lord Ventnor reached for his quizzing glass to survey the wand-slim virago before him - a piece of perfection, elegantly attired in a short grey, silk twill pelisse, trimmed with fine silver thread, over a trim lavender crepe walking dress and with a stylish matching hat - only to find as he began his inspection that she was staring quite openly back at him with her hands on her hips and a martial glint in her eye. He dropped his quizzing glass and blinked, nursing the distinct impression that she might have boxed his ears if he had continued. Then Rafe's words *"grey-eyed bantam"* came forcibly back to him, and he knew precisely who stood before him.

'Ah! Lady Rothsea, I believe,' he said. 'May I take the liberty of introducing myself? I am Lord Ventnor.'

'Oh, yes,' said Merry unencouragingly.

Charles looked down at his fob, choosing his words carefully.

'I was a friend of your husband's,' he said.

There was a momentary pause.

'Oh devil take it, man!' snapped Merry, looking at him in disgust. 'I forgave him. Can't you?'

In an instant, all Lord Ventnor's renowned self-possession and urbanity left him. His mouth fell open and he looked like he'd been slapped.

Then Merry turned from him, as if he were of no account whatsoever, and demanded of Brooke: 'Is this the house?'

'Yes, m'lady,' he replied, chewing his lip to keep from grinning at Lord Ventnor's stunned face.

His lordship swore under his breath and followed in her wake. She did not wait for Brooke to knock for her, but performed the office herself.

Noticing that the impudent fellow, who had just introduced himself, had followed her up the steps, Merry turned and looked at him warily.

'Are you following me?' she demanded.

'I live here,' said his lordship, resisting the strong urge to apologise for the fact.

'You do?' said Merry, staring at him, her eyes wide in confusion as the door opened behind her, and then she glanced for reassurance to Brooke, who nodded.

'Lives here with Lord Stowe, my lady,' confirmed Brooke.

'Oh, yes, I remember now. Harry told me,' said Lady Rothsea, turning away again, as Charles realised, with gleeful fascination, that he was, once again, dead to her.

Charles had to accept that it was a sad reflection on him as a gentleman that he did not immediately command her admittance, but he had to confess ... he would not miss this for the world.

The footman who had opened the door, and was waiting patiently for the young lady before him to announce her business, before he denied either of his masters, looked immediately across to one of these masters, who stood two steps behind her, smiling at him non-commitally.

'Please would you inform Lord Stowe that Merion Gri... er, no ... Lady Rothsea ... er ... his friend Merry would be grateful for a few words with him.'

The footman paused, expecting to be handed a card. When this did not come, and Lord Ventnor's eye sported a perplexing twinkle, Thomas the footman wavered and stepped back, allowing her ladyship to enter but felt obliged to whisper: 'Do you have a card, my lady?'

Merry looked swiftly at Brooke for guidance, but he shook his head.

'No,' confirmed Lady Rothsea, and Charles bit back a chuckle.

At this point, Mytchett the butler arrived, somehow expressing the severest disapproval, though his face bore no visible signs of life whatsoever.

The barest flicker of a glance at Lord Ventnor told him that his lordship was in one of his funning moods, but that the lady, who now stood impatiently looking about her in the hallway, was by no means an unwelcome guest, though not his lordship's own it seemed.

'This is Lady Rothsea for Lord Stowe,' intoned Thomas woodenly, knowing with a sense of doom that he would cop it when Mytchett caught up with him in the servants' hall later.

'If you would follow me to the morning room, my lady, I will ascertain if Lord Stowe is at home.'

THE RELUCTANT LADY

'Look here,' said Merry bluntly. 'You already know he's in or you would have said so … and he won't be pleased to see me, but I would rather introduce myself just the same. So why don't you just tell me where he is, because I haven't got all day? I'm in the most dreadful rush … and it's literally life or death.'

Not all Mytchett's forty years of training, man and boy, could freeze his features at this brutally forthright little speech. His brows lifted in surprise of their own accord, and he glanced, rather weakly, as he later confided to his particular friend Mr Price at the Wig and Brush, to Lord Ventnor, who, though laughing, managed to nod approval, thereby taking all the consequences upon himself.

'His lordship is in his book room,' said Mytchett a wavering hand indicating a short corridor to the right of the hallway.

Both Brooke and, to his shame, Lord Ventnor surged forward to follow her, as Merry headed off, but she suddenly turned sharply and held her little black-gloved hands out to forestall them.

'No, I have to do this alone,' she said, then turned, tugged her coat straight and hurried down the corridor.

At this, Lord Ventnor caught Brooke's arm and steered him into the morning room for interrogation, while Mytchett staggered off below stairs, a broken man.

Chapter Twenty-Three
Shadow of the Noose

Merry was nervous as she tapped softly at the door of the book room.

When she heard Harry's familiar voice shout: 'Come!', she felt a warm wave of nostalgia wash over her. Opening the door, she stood for a moment without speaking, watching her friend's head bowed over his correspondence. It made her ache a little to see him.

Harry looked up in enquiry, and then his expression transformed into one of stunned delight.

'Hallo Harry,' said Merry, still standing in the doorway, uncertain of her welcome.

'Merry!' cried Harry jumping up, and walking round the desk to greet her, his hands outstretched.

'Oh, Harry!' she said, ignoring his hands and putting her arms round him in an impulsive hug. 'I need your help … but I'm very sure you won't want to,' she said into his shoulder.

Harry returned her hug in blushing surprise. It was an unexpectedly feminine gesture from Merry, which was oddly disconcerting, as was the fact that holding Merry in his arms did not feel quite how he had once imagined.

After a moment, he held her away from him, looking anxiously at her face.

'You've left Rafe? Did the blackguard mistreat you? I'll kill him!'

'Wrong on all counts, old thing,' said Merry, reverting back to her boyish tone, which made Harry smile despite himself.

'He married you... immediately,' he asked hesitantly, with a slight blush, drawing her to the sofa, and sitting beside her, still holding her hand until she gently withdrew it.

'Yes, of course,' she answered, not pretending to misunderstand. 'In name only, at first, but I went to him willingly when I realised how much I loved him.'

'You do?'

Merry nodded, earnest confirmation in her candid grey eyes.

'But, you were engaged to me.'

'Yes, ...' she began.

'Damn him!'

'... But I should never have accepted your offer, Harry, and we would all have been unhappy in the end,' she finished. 'Eventually I would have realised that I loved him ... and then *our* marriage would have been a sham. Can you imagine how awful it would have been for you to be bound to me knowing all the time that I was wishing I were with him?' she reasoned. 'And I should have had to watch him go to the devil, for I know now he would have done so without me. He is doing it now, because he thinks he's lost me. But you haven't gone to pieces Harry...'

Harry coloured a little guiltily.

'Are you truly happy with him, Merry?'

'Yes, Harry,' she replied. 'Quite dreadfully.'

Harry sighed.

'I love you most dearly as a friend, Harry, but I know what true love is now,' said Merry. 'And it's not what either of us felt for each other.'

'Well, be that as it may, his actions were unforgiveable.'

'Do you think he is not deeply sorry for hurting you?'

'Oh, he's *always* sorry, but it does not stop him doing the damnedest things.'

'I know,' said Merry, quietly but meaningfully. Rafe's latest act was torturing them both most effectively. 'Ah, Harry... won't you forgive him?'

Harry put his head back and gave a couple of long sighs, and then finally spoke in a rather different voice, older somehow.

'I know how much it would have hurt him to hurt me. I was the nearest thing to family that he had.'

'When he forced me to marry him, he said it was because he feared he'd force a quarrel on you … and kill you,' said Merry remembering.

Harry thought about this, but shook his head.

'Oh, he would have wanted to, but he would not have,' said Harry. 'He'd have been more likely to put a bullet through himself. But I should have known that there was no way that he would have just stood nobly by and let us marry. Not when he had fallen so deeply in love with you and was certain that you loved him too.'

'No, we were both a little naïve about that,' said Merry. 'But I can't be sorry for what he did, Harry. I can only be sorry that I did not know my own heart sooner. I should have realised that I wanted to be your friend forever, not your wife.'

'And now he's been arrested, from what I read this morning in the Post,' said Harry wearily. 'And you want me to help him?'

'Yes, Harry,' said Merry, smiling ruefully at him.

'And why should I?'

'Because you're the truest friend two people could ever have,' said Merry, reaching out and gripping his shoulder.

'Oh God, very well,' said Harry, capitulating hopelessly. 'But I'm not taking part in a jailbreak, Merry, no matter what you say!'

Merry laughed and shook his shoulder, as a reluctant smile twisted his lips.

Merry then gave him so rapid and jumbled a summary of what had happened that Harry was obliged to keep stopping her to ask questions.

'Let me call Brooke…' said Merry.

'Brooke is here?' interrupted Harry. 'Oh, thank heaven! Yes, call the fellow in!'

'Yes,' said Merry, getting up and dashing for the door. 'He's been to Newgate and is to visit Rafe tonight in the condemned cells.'

'What!' cried Harry.

'Yes, didn't I say?' said Merry, as she left to call for Brooke. 'Rafe has pleaded guilty to murder.'

Merry returned a moment later with Brooke and, rather resentfully, with Lord Ventnor in tow.

THE RELUCTANT LADY

'So, Rafe's to be forgiven, is he?' asked Charles of Harry, a ghost of a smile in his eyes as he felt the scorch of the grey-eyed glare.

'It would seem so,' said Harry with a significant look for his friend, as he shook Brooke's hand in welcome. Brooke held a special role in all their lives, having helped each of the gentlemen out of predicaments at some point in the last twelve years.

'It was only a matter of time, dear boy,' said Charles, with a warm smile. 'You forgive us black sheep all our sins.'

'Look here,' interrupted Merry rudely. 'I don't know why you followed Brooke and me in here, but this is a private matter between us and Harry.'

'I thought I might lend my support, if needed,' said Charles, with a bow.

'Well, if you wish to stay,' snapped Merry, her temper flaring. 'You had better not say anything bad about my husband again, or I'll dashed well darken your lamps, and don't think I couldn't do it!'

But instead of seeing Lord Ventnor's face go rigid with shock, Merry watched in fascination as it lit with the most radiant and infectious grin, which caused Merry to abandon her ire and smile hesitantly back in surprise.

For his own part, 'Fatal' Ventnor now perfectly understood the fascination this young lady held for both his friends.

Merry was correct. Brooke managed to explain the entire situation in a handful of crisp sentences, but it still left the two gentlemen shaking their heads in concerned dismay. It said much for their knowledge of their friend that no one questioned his deathwish given the circumstances.

'Oh, God, Rafe!' cried Harry. 'Have you ever known *anyone* so bent on his own destruction? I'm sorry, Merry, but it seems like his stock in trade! He holds his life pretty cheap ... cheaper than your happiness, that's for certain. I suppose one must give him credit for that.'

'All or nothing,' confirmed Brooke. 'I've told him time out of mind.'

'We must employ a lawyer!' said Charles, with the first practical suggestion.

'A lawyer!' gasped Merry. 'Oh, why did I not think of that?'

'I'll send Fuller to engage one and bring him back here,' said Charles, excusing himself.

'Merry, you said you had a note of some sort from your brother?' said Harry. 'A confession, you said?'

'Yes, here it is! But Sir Henry thought it was my work, on my own paper, the pompous rogue! As if I would do such a thing, … or use such ghastly paper!'

'Wait a moment, I recognise that stuff!' declared Harry.

'Yes, I hoped if you might consider testifying that the paper came from the same gaming house … or even that you saw my brother writing something there,' suggested Merry. 'Not a lie, of course, but perhaps you *did* see him writing?'

'I might do better than that,' said Harry, striding to the door and shouting for the footman to fetch Clayton immediately.

'Your brother wrote me a note too, with his direction on it,' said Harry. 'On the same colour paper, I believe.'

Merry and Brooke exchanged hopeful glances.

Harry's manservant appeared in the doorway a few minutes later, standing aside for a moment to allow Lord Ventnor to rejoin the party.

Harry showed Clayton the piece of lilac paper.

'I had a piece just like it, Clayton,' said Harry. 'With a direction on it. Tell me you did not throw it away, there's a good fellow.'

'Certainly not, m'lord,' said Clayton, with a relieved smile. 'As it had a direction on it, and I could not be sure it was not a vowel, I placed it in your desk,' said the manservant, with a nod towards the desk in front of them.

Harry gave a whoop, and commanded Clayton to fish it out, while Merry gripped her hands together in fervent prayer.

Clayton, very conscious that his moment of glory was upon him, opened one of the drawers in his lordship's desk and presented, with the hint of a flourish, a piece of paper, identical to the one in Harry's hand.

All five of the people in the room, levelled by curiosity, gathered round the desk and stared as Harry placed the two torn edges of the paper together, and they matched precisely.

Merry put her head back, her hands still clasped together and gasped: 'Oh! Thank God!' putting both Harry and Charles in mind of Joan of Arc.

THE RELUCTANT LADY

'Aye, that tells the story, all right,' said Brooke, his relief palpable.

'This is proof, surely?' cried Merry, and then her face fell with sudden realisation. 'Oh, but Harry, it will implicate you, if you testify.'

'Much I care about that, Merry,' said Harry, with a slight frown that she could even think that he would cavil at it.

'Well, if you prove it was not murder, then there will be no charge to answer ... yes?' said Charles logically.

'Of course!' said Harry.

'But what about the witness ... the surgeon?' said Merry.

'Huh! He has a cool monkey lining his pockets,' said Harry. 'No doubt he will simply say he was mistaken because of the fog.'

Merry grinned thankfully at Harry.

'So, we must present this to Sir Henry together,' said Merry.

'Will that be enough?' asked Harry. 'The charge has already been made, and the imbecile has pleaded guilty.'

'He is *not* an imbecile,' growled Merry. 'He is trying to be noble ... the idiot!'

'Well, then, could we have the *'noble idiot'* declared insane?' suggested Charles.

All five, for Clayton remained an interested bystander, pondered this possibility, each with their own opinions of what constituted Rafe's 'right mind'. But, in the end, all were shaking their heads.

'No,' said Harry. 'He's acting like a lunatic, but no one will take him for one, more's the pity.'

'Then I suggest we await the lawyer, and put the matter to him,' said Charles. 'Has Harry here offered you refreshments, Lady Rothsea?'

'Merry! Where are my manners?' said Harry suddenly. 'I'll bet you haven't eaten a thing since it happened, have you?'

'Well, no, not much,' admitted Merry. 'Actually, I think I *could* eat something now, if you didn't mind?'

Harry grinned.

'Well, I don't think we have any sausages in the house,' he said with a twinkle. 'But I think cook can pull together a cold collation while we are waiting.'

'That would be marvellous,' she said, returning Harry's smile

Then Harry spotted Clayton still lurking interestedly beside Brooke.

'Hey! What are you still doing here?' said Harry with a vexed frown.

'You did not dismiss me, my lord,' said Clayton reasonably.

'Well, take yourself off and have cook lay out a nuncheon in the morning room as soon as can be.'

Then he turned back to Merry, with a faint enquiring smile.

'So you two have been introduced?' he said, indicating his friend Charles, who suddenly wore a comic expression.

Merry looked Lord Ventnor up and down for a moment, and then, with a slight hesitation, held out her hand.

'Well, I suppose you're all right,' she said, shaking his hand and then colouring faintly as she saw him grin and then remembered how rude she had been to him from the first. 'I'm sorry if I was a little uncivil.'

Harry, whose shoulders were shaking at hearing the famous 'Fatal Ventnor' damned by Merry's faint praise, couldn't speak for a moment.

Charles, who was used to lavish praise of his attributes - his looks, wit, charm and his physical prowess in a variety of activities - bowed meekly with only the ghost of a smile. It was odd, but somehow Lady Rothsea's 'all right', so grudgingly bestowed, felt like the highest praise he had had in some time.

'You may call me Merry, if you like?' volunteered Merry. 'Instead of all that Lady Rothsea stuff ... since you're Rafe's friend, after all.'

'I should be honoured... er... Merry,' said Charles, with that astonishing smile that Merry had glimpsed before. 'Pray call me Charles,' he said, according her the rarest of honours.

'Will do,' said Merry absently, in the process of turning away from him to Harry, her face reanimating as she steered him to the sofa and demanded to hear everything that had happened since they had parted.

Harry could not resist a slight grin of triumph over his friend. There was, at least, one lady in England who thought Harry Maitland more fascinating than Charles de Ferres.

From force of habit, Lord Ventnor's eyes narrowed for an instant in speculation, his hunting instinct aroused, until he caught

THE RELUCTANT LADY

one brief hard look from Harry, as uncompromising as the click of a cocking pistol. Charles blinked and coloured for a moment in surprise, and then smiled and shook his head reassuringly. But it was certainly interesting to glimpse steel in his affable friend's eye. Clearly, Harry would protect Merry from *all* harm, though she was another man's wife. Then looking down at the valiant little lady, so fearsomely loyal to Rafe that she had threatened to punch him in the eye if he denigrated her husband, Charles realised that she, quite unconsciously, commanded his loyalty, too.

Not for the first time that year, Charles began to warm to the notion of taking a wife himself.

Mr Cardross, the lawyer, arrived a little after three o'clock. A harassed-looking man of middle-age, who gave the appearance of having been dragged out of his chambers by the coat-tails, as he very nearly had.

He listened to the various strands of the story, delivered by the three and sometimes four voices, often overlapping. After some ten minutes, Mr Cardross raised his hand, arresting the conversation, and put his finger on the nub of the problem.

'His lordship has been arraigned and has pleaded guilty to the charge of murder?'

'Yes,' replied the chorus.

'Why did he do so?'

The voices erupted again, and were ceased once more by a lifting hand.

'Might he be induced to change his plea?'

This time, Mr Cardross waited in vain for an answer. His audience were looking at one another with doubt, anxiety and exasperation amongst their various expressions. It was Brooke who broke the silence.

'No, sir,' he said dourly. 'I think it unlikely.'

'Then there is little more to be said, I am afraid,' said Mr Cardross. 'Unless you can prevail upon the Prince Regent to issue a pardon.'

'But we have evidence!' cried Merry.

'Which could be presented at a trial, my lady,' explained Mr Cardross. 'But there will be no trial, only a sentencing … and no new evidence is presented at a sentencing.'

Merry felt her high hopes crashing around her.

'Moreover,' said Mr Cardross, warming to his subject. 'I'm sure you have been informed that there can be only one outcome from the sentencing as a result of his lordship's plea?'

'Damn it, man!' snapped Charles, a glance at Merry's horrified face sparking his rare temper. 'I'm not paying you to state the bloody obvious! Give us options, you fool!'

Mr Cardross choked and straightened his cravat nervously.

'Yes, my lord,' he muttered. 'Well, if you could only persuade Lord Rothsea to change his plea, I could offer you a dozen options. We could persuade the judge to reduce the charge to manslaughter or argue self-defence or even chance medley, though it has not been done for decades. The point is that no judge would convict Lord Rothsea of murder, given the evidence, and certainly not sentence him to hang. Indeed, he is far more likely to be acquitted of all but affray … but he *must be made to change his plea*!'

'And if he does not?' said Harry.

'Then, as I said, our dependence is on a royal pardon,' said Cardross. 'If you have any connections with his Highness or with the King's Cabinet, you may obtain a pardon, or perhaps a plea for mercy from his family? Lord Northover, his lordship's father, may have some influence there. Is he aware of the situation?'

Again, there was the strange exchange of glances.

'Well!' said Charles. 'I suppose I had better go and find out where Prinny is.' Then looking down as his seemingly immaculate outfit, he shook his head. 'I will have to change first. These rags will never do for Carlton House.'

He bowed to Merry, waved an airy hand towards Harry and Brooke, and departed briskly, calling for Fitch, his valet.

'Is there no way the charge could be changed or dropped altogether?' asked Merry. 'I mean, my brother initiated the crime, quite deliberately it seems.'

Mr Cardross frowned, trying to recall any precedents from his memory.

'Charges are more often amended or part-judged during the trial, not later.'

Then Brooke shared a notion.

'Well, it was the inquest that declared it murder, so perhaps if there was another inquest that ruled Mr Griffith's death a suicide?'

THE RELUCTANT LADY

There was a moment's silence and then both Harry and Merry looked at each other and cried.

'Sir Hector!'

'You know Sir Hector Parfitt?' asked Mr Cardross.

'Yes,' said Harry and Merry in unison.

'Well, Cardross? Could it work?' demanded Harry.

'Well, I know of no precedent, but if you can prevail upon him to reopen the inquest, consider the new evidence and change his ruling from unlawful killing to *felo de se*, then I cannot think that a man could be hanged for a murder when it is established that the premeditation was the victim's. Though Lord Rothsea performed the act, I believe we would have an exceptional case to persuade the issuing judge that he was offered no choice, and therefore to revise the charge. But I have to tell you, the sentencing session is set for eleven o'clock tomorrow morning, and Lord Bracton has demanded a formal identification of your husband to precede it at ten. I have heard he is in hopes of Lord Rothsea changing his plea. After sentencing, we have but two days, as you must be aware, and a great deal to do. Will Sir Hector reopen the inquest tomorrow?'

'He *must*!' said Merry, pale but determined.

Rafe sat on his hard bed, with his back against the wall, feeling the chill damp creeping through his clothes and pervading his body. He held the pillow to his chest, imagining it was Merry, though it felt more like a small sack of potatoes. He was remembering the time Merry had turned to him for comfort, had slid her slender arms around his neck and rested her chin on his shoulder. He recalled how it felt as her shuddering had slowly stilled as she had calmed but had not pulled away. She had remained in the reassuring circle of his arms, trusting him before she ever knew she loved him. Another memory so precious, so fine, that it could crush him to dust.

Yet, these were the images that kept the howling demons at bay; the demons that made him watch Merry sobbing on her chamber floor; then made her turn to look at him with freezing hate, as if he had never meant anything to her.

More often than not, the demons won, but now Rafe fought to conjure up the image of Merry wearing female attire for the first time and unconsciously looking up at him for approval. For the thousandth time, Rafe cursed himself for not bringing Merry's shirt with him, so that he might savour her sweet scent one more time before he left the world.

No matter. The suffering for both of them would soon be at an end.

Harry and Merry spent a futile two hours or more searching for Sir Hector, who, with no inquest to oversee that day, had led them a spirited chase from his tailor, to his snuff merchant, to Tattersall's, where he had stopped to look at a new carriage horse. Discovering that he would be dining at home that evening, Harry left his card and told the butler that he would do himself the honour of waiting on Sir Hector after dinner, as he had something of great importance to ask him.

Harry delivered Merry at Albemarle Street but would not come in, nor did he invite Merry to dine with him that evening. When Merry gave him a rather hurt look, he grinned and flicked her cheek.

'Have you forgotten everything I taught you in Quemerford, you little scamp?' he said. 'Your reputation will not benefit from entertaining a gentleman, even a friend, when your husband is from home,' he said. 'And still less, if you dine at Half Moon Street, the home of the notorious Lord Ventnor.'

'Why is he notorious?'

Harry grinned.

'Well, though *you* seem impervious, he is held to be fatally attractive by the ladies.'

'Really?' said Merry incredulously, and then she remembered that astonishing smile, and then conceded: 'Well, I suppose he is not so bad when he is not looking one over like cattle.'

She could still hear Harry laughing as his carriage pulled away.

Discovering that Brooke was in the kitchens preparing a small basket of food for his lordship, Merry hastened down to join him, taking over this duty, while Brooke went upstairs to gather some clothes.

Merry then braved Rafe's beautiful library and sat down to pen a long, heart-rending note, in the sad certainty that Rafe would not believe one word of it. After several attempts, which lay like confetti around her, Merry looked into her soul with sudden clarity and awful certainty. Then she picked up the quill once more

THE RELUCTANT LADY

and wrote four short lines, before folding and sealing the note. It would not do for Brooke to read it.

Then she only had time to bathe, change and eat a little dinner before Harry was knocking at the outer door, ready to convey her to Sir Hector's.

The interview with Sir Hector began rather delightfully, for Lydia was dining with her uncle once again. This had not been planned, but hearing from Sir Hector that Lord Stowe was expected had been a temptation too great to miss. When the visitors were shown into the drawing room, both Lydia and Sir Hector were waiting for them. Lydia's eyes had flown first to Harry, whom she clearly admired, and then, with a hint of dismay, to his rather stylish companion. Then she blinked as she saw the familiar grey eyes twinkling back at her, and then gasped.

'Merry?'

The stylish young lady nodded and grinned. At that, Lydia had run forward to give Merry her hands, but, after a moment's awkward hesitation, they laughed and embraced, Lydia finding herself squeezed in a fierce little bear hug, that crushed her best blue silk gown, but was no less welcome for that.

Sir Hector had looked a little bemused as he tried to place the young lady's rather familiar face.

Merry turned to Sir Hector and curtsied as Harry performed the introductions. Merry noted Lydia's relief as Harry introduced her as Lady Rothsea, but it seemed, regrettably, that Harry seemed not to return Lydia's obvious regard. He was his gentlemanly self, but he was not in love with Lydia.

'Er ... Lady Rothsea,' said Sir Hector, his brows reflecting his puzzlement. 'Is it possible that we have met before?'

Merry and Lydia shared a look and laughed, and then Merry explained everything, with Harry taking up the discussion to outline the purpose of their visit.

It took several minutes for Sir Hector to come to terms with the fact that the poor beaten boy he had met in Grafton House had been, in fact, this elegant young lady, who was now happily married to Lord Rothsea, the fellow who had shot her brother.

It took even longer to persuade him of the necessity of reopening the inquest. Like Mr Cardross before him, he could not fathom why Lord Rothsea could not simply plead not guilty. But, with Lydia as their ally, they finally managed to convince him that with the new evidence that had come to light, his own Coroner's verdict was now inaccurate and that this might precipitate a miscarriage of justice.

'Well, I shall send a note to Mr Kent in the morning. Then, let us see what can be done,' he said finally. 'But we will be cutting it very fine, for the Grand Jury will need to withdraw the charge, and if the accused has already pleaded guilty… well, you can see the difficulties, so I earnestly beg you not to get your hopes up, my lady,' he said shaking his head, anticipating disaster.

As they drove away, Merry declared her intention of attending Rafe's sentencing session the following day.

Harry begged her not to.

'He would not wish you to see him like that.'

'It may be the last time I see him at all, for I won't watch him hang, Harry!' she sobbed in a low, hoarse voice.' I won't!'

'Blasted idiot! I could strangle him myself for putting you through this hell.'

'But we both know he is putting himself through worse.'

Harry sighed and nodded.

'Very well, but let us see when the inquest is set for, as you must appear at that yourself, to provide the provenance of the suicide note, and to explain the circumstances that precipitated your brother's actions.'

Merry nodded grimly. She had not yet forgiven her brother.

As the din of the prison's daily routines had abated, Rafe's demons had crept ever closer with the night, when the sobs and wails of the unfortunates awaiting their various fates seemed amplified as the competing sounds diminished.

Rafe tried desperately to reanimate one of his happier memories, but now his self-loathing had returned to blight every image with the cruel taunt that all these happy moments had been shams. Now, he knew how Merry truly felt, even if, for one glorious week, she had forgotten in her first heady experience of love.

THE RELUCTANT LADY

But, came the insidious voice, *Merry was _made_ to be loved. How many men will now step forward to take your place?* Rafe writhed in torment at that thought. This was a new lash with fresh bite ... and his inner tormentor had no mercy.

'My lord,' came a familiar voice, as the door to his cell was unexpectedly opened and a lantern was lifted, blinding him for a few moments.

'Dear god!' the voice said.

It was Brooke, the rogue!

'Look at the state of you!' said Brooke, genuinely shocked.

'I thought I gave orders ...' began Rafe, in a ragged voice.

'Yes, well you can stuff your orders up y'r arse!' said Brooke, in a loud, angry whisper. 'I could kick you around this room for what you're doing to yourself and your lady, only in your present mood, you'd probably thank me for it.'

'Go away,' groaned Rafe, turning away from the light.

'No!' said Brooke. 'I paid a mort o' my own hard-earned blunt for these few minutes, and I damn well mean to use them.'

'Here,' he said, dragging Rafe upright. His palm itched to slap the boy, but as he looked into those harrowed blue eyes, he felt more like hugging him and weeping himself.

Brooke had seen all of Rafe's black moods, but this was undoubtedly the worst.

'You've broken her ladyship's heart, m'lord, I'm sure of it', said Brooke, trying to break through his master's despair.

'So am I, Brooke,' said Rafe darkly.

'But why, m'lord? I thought you loved her?'

'I do, with all my heart,' he responded brokenly.

'But she loves you too, lad. Loves you fit to bust!' said Brooke.

'She loves me? Really?' said Rafe, his eyes narrowing. 'Do you think I'm an imbecile, man?'

'Yes, sir, I do! We all do!' said Brooke. 'Her ladyship is frantic trying to get to see you herself, m'lord.'

'I'll bet she is, but you must prevent her!' he declared anxiously. 'Tell her that she need be patient a little longer. It is harder to hang than I thought.'

'She doesn't _want_ you to hang! She wants you back the way it was,' he said desperately, starting to strip his master of his grimy clothes. His money had only bought him ten minutes and a can of hot water.

'Pathetic,' said Rafe dismissively, as he submitted to Brooke's ministrations. 'Did you seriously think I would believe you?'

'No,' said Brooke, 'But I'm telling the truth, nonetheless.'

'I saw her! I heard her! Oh God!' Rafe's hands flew to his face, seriously impeding Brooke's attempt to remove his shirt.

Brooke jerked them away and roughly continued his task. Stripping off the shirt, before pushing Rafe to sit down as he yanked off the rest of his clothes.

'Well, you misunderstood, you dunderhead!' snapped Brooke. 'It wasn't you she was mad at. It was that brother of hers. She found his suicide note and was in a passion about that when you saw her. Here! Here's a letter from her ladyship explaining everything and begging you to come back to her!'

There was a moment's silence. Brooke nursed a hope.

'*She's* put you up to this, hasn't she?' said Rafe hoarsely. 'Sounds like one of her mad schemes. My sweet, noble girl …' his voice broke. 'Trying to save my worthless life, … but she doesn't know it won't be worth living without her.'

Brooke grated his teeth and shook Rafe hard by the shoulders.

'God, give me strength!' he growled. 'That's what I'm telling you! You won't be living without her! She loves you, you daft, iron-skulled bastard! Read the letter.'

Rafe only shook his head disbelievingly.

'Oh, sir! Even if you don't believe us, why can't you plead not guilty and self-exile?'

'Because I'd only come creeping back to trouble her again. How could I stay away while she is in the world? I'm not that strong. The only way I can free her and myself is by leaving it.'

Brooke sighed and shook his head. He knew it would be this way. *The wretched, self-hating fool was in one of his depressions.*

Brooke was right. Rafe was locked into a spiral of despondency. Reason couldn't touch him. A lifetime of rejection and loathing by those who should have loved him had taught him that forgiveness never came, ever. To live another day knowing that his beloved wife felt the same way about him as his father did was excruciating. He longed for the release that the noose would bring.

THE RELUCTANT LADY

Brooke had no doubt that the poor lady's letter would only further convince his lordship that this was a desperate attempt to keep him alive, only to take away his reason for living when he was safe.

Brooke took soap and a piece of flannel and scrubbed him down like a grubby child. If his master *was* going to get himself hanged, he would go to the gallows as a gentleman.

As Brooke shaved the coarse beard from his master's face, he heard him sigh, as that familiar process calmed him. He still clutched his wife's letter but had not opened it.

'She's here in London?'

'Yes, my lord,' said Brooke. 'Running round with Lord Stowe trying to save you from yourself.'

'H... Harry,' whispered Rafe, his eyes closing and his throat constricting. 'Of course.' The demon was grinning at him from the shadows, wielding the new lash.

Brooke frowned. This was not the reaction he had expected.

'He's forgiven you, sir.'

Rafe gave a harsh laugh.

'Yes, well, now I suppose he might.'

'And so has Lord Ventnor, thanks to her ladyship.'

'What?'

Brooke saw the sharp glint of jealousy in his master's eye, quite like his old self for a moment. With an inward hope, Brooke fanned the flames.

'Yes, they seem to have struck it off very quick. It's "Merry" and "Charles" between them already. Well, you know her ladyship's friendly way, and Lord Ventnor's taken a powerful shine to her, though I'm not sure Lord Stowe is so happy about that.'

Rafe caught Brooke's wrist in a bruising grip.

'You're to keep Ventnor away from her, do you hear!' he snarled.

Brooke looked innocent.

'Well, with you out of the picture, sir,' he said reasonably. 'There's not much I can do. Her ladyship will be an innocent abroad, as they say.'

Rafe gave him a sharp, suspicious look, and then, to Brooke's dismay, he relaxed.

'No,' he sighed. 'Harry will protect her. Charles is a hound, but he would not cross Harry, no matter how tempting his quarry.'

Brooke rubbed his face and grunted in frustration.

There was a warning scratch on the door.

Swiftly, Brooke got Rafe dressed in the fresh clothes he had brought and put the basket of food on the bed beside his lordship.

'Her ladyship prepared this with her own hands,' he said earnestly. 'She begged me to make sure you ate a little. The flask of brandy's from me. If we can't get you out of this, you drink that before they take you down. Might make your last walk a little more bearable.'

'You're a good fellow, John, and a good friend,' Rafe's voice broke.

'Oh, sir! Won't you change your plea?' said Brooke, his own voice breaking.

Rafe only shook his head miserably.

Brooke held his shoulders for a moment, and then hugged the young man hard and kissed his forehead.

'Oh, God bless you, son, you foolish lad!' he croaked, and then turned for the door, which had been opened to hasten his departure.

Then, recalling something, Brooke put his hands in his pockets and threw the contents around the floor.

''Ere! What's that?' whispered the guard anxiously.

'Lavender 'eads,' said Brooke hoarsely. 'His missus didn't want him sitting here in this stench.'

'Yeah, well, I'll be the one sweepin' 'em up,' complained the guard, closing the door. Brooke blinked and two tears slid down his face as he heard the sound of Rafe's hoarse sobs as they walked away.

When Merry heard all that had passed, she too broke down and wept, and Brooke was hard put not to join her as he patted her back.

Harry cursed.

At Merry's insistence, they had awaited Brooke in a closed carriage outside the prison. Merry had wanted to be as close to Rafe as she could, and both Harry and Brooke had known she would have come alone, if they had not relented.

'There, there,' croaked Brooke, as the poor girl wept against his shoulder. 'Lord Ventnor will get that pardon, never fear. Very thick with his Highness he is.'

Merry shook her head despairingly, a look of dread in her drowning eyes.

Brooke looked to Lord Stowe in alarm.

'The Prince is in Southampton inspecting the fleet. Charles left this evening in pursuit.'

'God help us!' whispered Brooke, the look of dread now in his own eyes.

Not even Mr Kent, with his habitual efficiency, could organise the re-opening of an inquest before noon, not least because his primary witness had already been hauled away from his breakfast by a constable to attend the identification of Lord Rothsea in Lord Bracton's chambers. Almost as soon as he stepped out of that difficult interview, the unfortunate surgeon, who was using his douceur from Lord Stowe's father to move his surgery out of easy reach of gaming houses, found himself collared again, by Lord Stowe himself.

Harry and Merry, working to hasten Mr Kent's tasks by gathering the original witnesses, nearly missed Rafe's sentencing, which followed hard on the heels of the identification.

Word had got about that a real member of the Quality was being sentenced to death, so the court was packed. Harry and Brooke had to fight to make a path for Merry into the gallery. She was still climbing the stairs as she heard the last fell words of the sentence being pronounced.

'… wherefore it is the sentence of this court that you shall be taken hence to the place from whence you came, and from thence to the place of execution, where you shall be hanged by the neck until dead, and thereafter your body buried within the precincts of the prison and may the Lord have mercy on your souls.'

Merry clawed her way wildly through the goggling, gasping onlookers to the front of the gallery and saw her beloved Rafe, pale and distant, at the centre of a line of eight poor wretches, in different states of distress.

At the sight of his gaunt beautiful face, the ripping, wrenching pain in her heart made her knees buckle, and she had to clasp the gallery rail to remain upright.

As the prisoners began to turn to be led away, she screamed: 'Rafe! I beg you! Don't do this!'

She saw him falter and look up wildly in the direction of that agonised voice, before his manacled hands came up to shield himself from the sight of her, as if he were under attack. Then, he and his fellows were bundled away by the guards.

Rafe's spirit was now utterly harrowed. Seeing Merry's beloved face, horrified and incandescently angry, had been torture, and then in the last instant he had glimpsed Harry's arms folding around her, drawing her away as the ushers closed in on her.

Merry was cursing herself as Harry helped her out of the courtroom in the wake of Brooke, who was barging a way through the crowd for them. When she had seen for herself the state that Rafe had driven himself into, seen him standing there calmly accepting a sentence of death, all through his blind belief in his own worthlessness, she had been as incensed as she had been upset.

This impossible man, who had fought so hard to bring them together, who had made her love him more than her immortal soul, was killing himself before her eyes … deaf to reason and as determined on his course to divide them forever as he had once been to unite them! If she'd had a pistol at that moment, she'd have damn well shot his other leg and wielded the brine herself!

But now she fretted that his last memory of her would be an expression of rage and not the aching love that underpinned it.

She was not entirely right.

Rafe had been returned to his cell. All eight of the condemned were to be hanged together at noon the day after next.

Well, there was some fellowship in that, he supposed.

As he sat, tormented by the fact that Merry had been allowed to witness that awful pronouncement, which would join the catalogue of unpleasant images in her young mind, Rafe remembered in startling clarity his wife's words and the look on her beautiful face. Merry had been furious, undoubtedly, but though his demons wanted him to believe that this illustrated her loathing of him, but Rafe had also seen her exasperation.

Her cry had been the last desperate ploy of her sweet scheme to save him. Merry despised suicide, for the cowardice and for the damnation she imagined that followed. Rafe knew this lay at the heart of her refusal to believe that her brother had taken his own life. She had not resorted to it herself, even when her plight had seemed unspeakably grim.

Though she might never forgive him for killing her brother, Merry would do anything to prevent her friend Rafe from damning his soul in the hereafter. Little did she realise that, stripped of the love they had found together, Rafe was already in hell.

As it turned out, Rafe was not entirely right either.

Early the following afternoon, Rafe sat with his head in his hands, embracing despair. Merry's distress, her agony beside her brother's jacket, was burned on his memory, casting all other images into shadow.

At first he had tried to cling to the happier memories, but as his depression had deepened, these had fallen away and he was now more often picturing her grim disdain when she would hear that he was dead.

His jacket lay on the bed beside him with the cravat he had removed as soon as he had returned from sentencing. Rafe had thought he could at least go to the gallows looking respectable. Merry might be there to watch – his heart twisted violently at the thought.

She would not be ashamed of her husband.

He did not look up when the key turned in the lock and the heavy cell door creaked open. It would be the man who changed the slops bucket or brought the bread and brackish water, the condemned man's fare in this godforsaken hole.

Merry stood in the doorway for a second taking in the scene. It wrenched her heart so badly to see him so desolate that she could scarcely breathe. At his feet lay the basket that she had put into Brooke's hands herself, with food, untouched, and a flask of brandy, empty. Merry could not see his dear face, and for a moment her resolve faltered, but she had determined on a course of action and her chin lifted as she called up the courage to see it through.

After a few minutes, the lack of expected movement from the doorway seemed to penetrate Rafe's consciousness, and he looked up with a puzzled frown. Merry felt her knees almost give way when she saw that dear face so ravaged by anguish.

It took only an instant for comprehension and fury to bring him to his feet.

'Merry! What the devil! Who the hell let you in here?' he cried, his voice raw and hoarse with emotion.

Merry said nothing, not trusting her voice for a moment, but threw aside her muff to reveal a small pistol. Then, her expression intent but unreadable, she pointed it at Rafe.

Rafe looked alarmed and bemused.

'Good God!' he gasped. 'Merry! What are you doing? There's no need for this! The hangman will do the job for you tomorrow. There's no need for you to swing, too. I couldn't bear it!'

Merry was very still, but emanating a suppressed energy. Then she spoke in a low tense voice.

'Did you read my letter?'

Unconsciously, Rafe's hand lifted to his heart, where Merry's letter still rested, unopened, in the breast pocket of his waistcoat. He shook his head, his eyes begging her not to make him do so.

'Open it,' she said, levelling her pistol at him.

'Merry,' he whispered, his voice a plea for mercy.

'Now!' she said, waving the pistol.

Rafe paused, and then reluctantly drew the small sealed note from his pocket. He glanced at her implacable expression, and broke the seal.

'Read it!' she commanded.

Taking a deep breath, Rafe unfolded the sheet and scanned the words, once, and then read again with dawning horror.

We are One. God and our Love made us so.
Understand, my dear Husband, that I Cannot and <u>I Shall Not</u> Live without you! If you choose to Die, so be it, but I will Follow you from this world within the Hour of your quitting it.
Your wife forever,
Merry Wolvenden

Rafe looked up aghast, to find the pistol was no longer pointed at him. The muzzle now rested against Merry's right temple.

'Merry! What does this mean?' he croaked.

'Why?' asked Merry. 'Is my letter unclear?'

'You can't mean to … to …' stammered Rafe horrified.

'Why not?' demanded Merry, her eyes holding Rafe's in a stern, intent glare. 'When my brother and my husband have set me such an excellent example?'

'Merry! I beg you …' gasped Rafe.

'No, Rafe!' she said, her voice shaking a little with passion now. 'You forfeited your right to beg anything of me when you decided to put me through the agony of watching you die. But, then I thought… why should I not accord you the same privilege? Why should I wait until they cut you down,' her voice broke a little, 'Before I follow you to hell?'

'Merry! Listen to me …'

'Why, when you would not listen to me?'

Merry saw he was moving a little towards her, rapidly assessing his chances of disarming her without injuring her. It would only be a moment before he pounced.

Merry cocked the pistol and heard the breath catch in his throat as his arms reached out helplessly towards her.

'How does it feel, Rafe, to see the one you love put a period to their existence before your eyes? Well?'

Rafe opened his mouth but could not speak. There were no words. He just looked at her in anguish, slowly shaking his head, his eyes pleading with her.

Merry's gaze held his, the stern mask falling away and her eyes gave him a glimpse of the torment she spoke of.

'I couldn't put it better myself,' said Merry, a tear slipping down her cheek, as she closed her eyes and poised to pull the trigger.

'<u>NO</u>!' cried Rafe, darting forward and grasping the muzzle of the pistol, jerking it away from her head so fiercely it almost wrenched her fingers off. Flinging the weapon aside, his hands wildly checked her for injury, before he crushed her to him in a bruising hug.

'Merry! Merry! My darling! My precious girl! You must never, *never* ...' he murmured brokenly.

Suddenly, Rafe felt her wriggle to be free, and swiftly held her off from him a little, unwilling to let her go. He looked anxiously at her face to find her beaming back at him with a wobbly tearful smile.

'Well, kiss me, you idiot!' she said.

Rafe stared at her in astonishment, unable to move or comprehend for a second. Then, his arms closed about her, almost lifting her off her feet, and pressed her hard to him again. His lips found hers in a desperate kiss, eloquent of relief, longing and the haunting fear that it would be his last before the hereafter.

Merry met his passion in full measure. As her arms twined around his neck and her fingers buried and tangled in his hair, Rafe groaned, his body shaking a little as passion rocked him. Their kiss grew hungrier and their bodies twisted as close as their clothes would allow. Rafe resisted the overwhelming urge to drag his wife to the bed and make love to her there and then for one last time. With a Herculean effort, he suppressed his more wanton desires and instead deepened the kiss, concentrating on making it a caress she would remember all her life. His lips now moved with a gentler rhythm, intimate, loving, as if each movement were cherished. He slowly caressed her back with one hand, while the other tossed her charming hat to the floor, so that he could cradle her head, revelling in the silky touch of her tawny curls.

Merry moaned softly, one hand breaking its grip on his neck to draw trembling fingers down his rough cheek. It paused a moment as she felt him sigh with pleasure and then continued, tracing an exploratory journey down his neck to his collarbone, then pushed aside his open shirt to slip inside and curve around his bare shoulder, ripping another loud groan from him.

Where this new surge of passion might have led them would never be known, because they were suddenly brought back to their senses by an embarrassed cough from the doorway. Rafe clutched Merry to him protectively and looked anxiously towards the door, fearing that the guards had come to arrest her. Then his arms dropped through sheer astonishment when he saw Harry standing there, his lips still pressed in a dry line at the sight of Merry locked in Rafe's arms, but a lurking wry humour at the back of his eyes.

THE RELUCTANT LADY

'Shall we go?' asked Harry, almost conversationally.

'Then, you *are* with Harry now?' said Rafe numbly, trying to mask the hurt as he looked for confirmation from Merry.

'I married an idiot, Harry,' said Merry, moving to the bed and reaching for Rafe's cravat and jacket.

'That's not news to me, Merry,' replied Harry, starting to enjoy himself, as he bent to pick up the pistol.

Rafe looked from one to the other in complete bafflement. Merry had reached up to wrap the cravat around his neck and was now starting to tie it when Rafe's hands closed about her wrists, stilling her effectively. His eyes searched hers for answers, unwilling to dare to believe what her glowing, laughing expression was telling him.

'Harry means shall we *all* go, my love,' she said softly.

'A jailbreak?' cried Rafe, causing the guard waiting outside the cell to peep in, before recollecting himself and disappearing again.

This was too much for Harry and Merry's sense of humour and they dissolved into laughter.

Rafe was perplexed and irritated, *but Merry was here, laughing, a heavenly sound, and she seemed to still love him, a miracle, and they were talking about his leaving with them!*

'Merry, for God's sake, what does all this mean?' he cried, shaking her wrists gently to break into their hilarity. But it was Harry who answered.

'Not that you don't deserve to hang, old fellow …'

'Harry!' gasped Merry, in sudden ire.

'But it seems,' continued Harry unabashed, '… that that happy event no longer features in your immediate future.'

'My sentence has been respited?' asked Rafe, stunned, thinking that somehow Harry had made an appeal to the Prince.

'There's no sentence, my love,' said Merry.

'No charge, in fact,' added Harry

'Wh…what?'

'Merry found the evidence to clear you …'

'We both did,' interrupted Merry irrepressibly, despite a quelling look from Harry.

Rafe's arm had slid unconsciously to circle his wife's waist. The horror that had locked him up for a week was ebbing. Rafe was returning to normal. Merry's heart had wings.

'Griffith left a suicide note and another with his address on matching scraps of paper. Sir Hector reopened the inquest and changed the verdict to suicide, then had the charges reduced to affray. Didn't Merry tell you?' asked Harry, knowing the answer.

Rafe's eyes raked round in incredulous outrage at Merry's face, now wearing a comic, mock-angelic look, which then transformed to one of unholy triumph, as she stepped quickly out of his reach and faced him.

'I told you, Rafe Wolvenden, that I would make you pay one day for your sins,' said Merry pointing a finger at him with baleful glee. 'That's for drugging poor Harry and me, and for putting all of us through the worst week of our lives, which, given some of _my_ previous worst weeks, took some doing!'

Importantly, Merry no longer numbered her brother's death amongst his sins, Rafe noted.

With a look that promised that she would be punished, quite deliciously, when he got her home, Rafe responded: 'It's only borrowed Merry, it's only borrowed,' his old manner now quite returned.

'Ah, by the way, Rafe,' said Harry affably. 'I have something for you.'

Rafe turned towards him with a look of enquiry, and so positioned his jaw perfectly for Harry's cracking right, which knocked him cleanly to the ground.

'Harry!' screamed Merry, rushing to the aid of her husband, who was slowly sitting up amongst the lavender heads, nursing his jaw. 'How could you!'

'Very easily,' responded Harry dryly, reaching down to help his friend up.

'Very neat right, you have there, Harry. I believe I've remarked upon it before. I suppose I deserved that.'

'You did,' confirmed Harry. 'It was that or call you out.'

'At least have the grace to admit that you caught me unawares,' said Rafe, 'as a salve to my wounded pride.'

Harry chuckled.

'Damned right, I did!' admitted Harry ruefully. 'Wouldn't have popped you such a flush hit, if you'd had your guard up.'

'Wouldn't have touched me at all, dear boy,' bantered Rafe.

THE RELUCTANT LADY

'Hah! We'll see that! Happy to meet you at Gentleman Jackson's at your next convenience.'

'You'll do nothing of the kind,' snapped Merry, turning her husband round to face her, as she resumed tying his cravat and making him presentable. Rafe looked down at her indulgently, a broad, tender grin on his face as he watched her expert hands go to work. No doubt he could do a better job, but it was too sweet a pleasure watching the dearest face in his world, the one which had haunted him for four long days and nights, now so close, absorbed in her task. Her eyes strayed once or twice to meet his rapt gaze, causing her to blush divinely and a smile to play about her lovely lips.

His hands had crept to her waist again, but then Harry broke into the moment once again, speaking as a man goaded to exasperation.

'Oh, don't start all that again! Here!' he added, holding up Rafe's jacket, obliging him to let go of Merry, who had now finished tying the cravat in a manner that better reflected her distraction than her skills, and thrust his arms into the sleeves.

'Well, I suppose you look as good as any prisoner leaving Newgate might, but I'd give a pony to see Lain's face if he saw you now,' said Harry critically. 'You've been nine kinds of a stubborn fool, Rafe, and you'll be hearing that from a number of quarters when you come back to town.'

'We won't be coming back to town for some time, Harry,' Rafe replied, his eyes holding Merry's and glowing with a promise.

'Italy,' murmured his delighted wife, her quick intelligence reading her husband's mind and seeing his ready confirmation in his glinting look of approval.

Harry groaned again, pushing them both out of the cell before he had to witness another kiss. It was the first time anyone could remember when the corridor of that grim establishment had rung with such happy laughter.

Rafe still had to endure a brief interview with Lord Bracton.

'You may still have to stand your trial for affray, Lord Rothsea. But the Coroner has ruled that you were provoked by one determined to die at your hand. You may do well to reflect in what light your character is perceived that poor souls in search of a quick despatch might choose to seek you out, and I hope you will mend your ways so that it does not happen again.'

Both Harry and Merry cast anxious glances towards Rafe, but it was significant to note that his recent experiences had substantially mellowed his temper. So instead of rounding on the pompous fellow and damning his impudence, he took his wife's hand and merely bowed towards Lord Bracton.

'When a man has something to live for himself,' he replied, 'he is less inclined to hazard his existence in a duel, nor put a period to another's.'

As they emerged from that dread place into the bright sunshine and bustle of Newgate Street, Rafe saw his coach waiting outside with Brooke sitting anxiously on the box. They exchanged a glance, and as Rafe smiled ruefully he noted his manservant's tense shoulders relax, as he sighed with relief. Rafe walked over, holding up a hand to shake Brooke's.

'You might have told me she still loved me,' remarked Rafe.

'I did, sir, many times,' replied Brooke matter-of-factly. 'But you took it into your head not to believe me … and we both know how difficult you can be when that happens.'

Rafe laughed. Such a welcome sound that it brought a smile to Brooke's face.

They were interrupted by Merry, who twinkled up at Brooke conspiratorially, before pulling her husband towards the door of the coach.

'Come on, Blackbeard,' she said, cupping his rough cheek with her hand. 'You're going to have a shave before I kiss you again,' she said, ruefully rubbing her face reddened by his stubble during their passionate embrace. 'And I very much want to kiss you again.'

Harry groaned.

'If you're going to coo like lovebirds, I'm taking a hackney!' he declared in a long-suffering tone. 'It was hard enough to see that Merry was so happy, when I was certain that she'd have shot you with your own pistol at her earliest opportunity.'

'She did,' Rafe reassured him, ushering his friend into the coach.

THE RELUCTANT LADY

Merry blushed crimson. She had not shared that story with Harry.

'What?' cried Harry, diverted and much heartened.

'We duelled ... and she shot me in the leg.'

'The leg! Merry! I thought you said you were a crack shot?'

'He was kissing me at the time,' said Merry apologetically, laughing as she saw Harry roll his eyes in disappointed disgust. 'The pistol went off and fired into his boot.'

This comic picture, together with Rafe's dry expression as he watched his friend's glee, caused Harry to burst into delighted laughter, which lasted all the way to Piccadilly.

'Priceless!' gasped Harry, when he could speak again. 'What a story! How I wish I could tell Charles. He'd appreciate that one.'

'Harry!' cried Merry.

'I know. I know,' he reassured her. 'I shan't tell a soul.'

'So, if you have both had quite enough pleasure at my expense,' said Rafe. 'Could one of you kindly explain precisely how my transformation from condemned man to free man came about?'

Merry and Harry explained in a jumble of anecdotes that took all Rafe's concentration to unpick. He winced when he heard of Merry's distress at finding him taken and his refusal to see her in prison.

'But I heard you cursing me in your room,' said Rafe, his brows locked together in hurt concern. 'You said you hated me and would never forgive me.'

'Not you, ... Bryn!' she explained. 'I had just found his suicide note.'

'So Brooke was telling the truth?' cried Rafe, his hand rubbing his eyes, as he groaned: 'I shall never hear the last of that.'

'Yes. You can understand why I was so upset. Bryn had taken all our money and squandered it, forcing a quarrel on you to secure his own escape from the consequences, but leaving me to face everything alone and penniless. I _still_ can't believe it! And I can't believe I almost lost _you_ to suicide, too!'

Rafe crushed her in a sudden hug.

'Some things can seem just too awful to live with,' said Rafe in a suffocated voice.

'Wrong! No matter what happens in the future, Rafe, you must promise me you will never, ever, do such a thing again!' cried Merry fiercely.

'I promise,' said Rafe solemnly, folding his wife against his chest as he remembered the terror of seeing Merry holding that pistol to her head.

Harry, feeling like a fifth wheel, looked longingly at a passing hackney.

'Harry was wonderful. He made everything happen once I asked for his help.'

Rafe met his friend's eyes in a long look that sought forgiveness, received it and conveyed his gratitude. They were brothers again. No need for words.

Then Merry and Harry finished their tale with the final scene, when Sir Hector had then secured the withdrawal of charge, and Judge Bracton had very willingly overturned his sentence and signed the release papers.

'That's when we discovered that you would never have hanged after all,' added Harry.

'What?' croaked Rafe.

'Bracton had sent a recommendation for full pardon to the King's Cabinet.'

'And poor Charles had already gone haring off to Southampton to seek one from the Prince Regent,' lamented Merry.

'Hey! Less of the "*Charles*", if you please, minx!' snapped Rafe, a jealous glint in his eye, as he heard Harry suppress a chuckle. 'You keep away from that fellow, Merry! Trust you to be on first name terms with the most shameless rake in England within five minutes of making his acquaintance!'

'I thought *you* were the most shameless rake in England,' said Merry naughtily, causing Harry to laugh out loud.

'Well, *I* have reformed, minx! *He* has not!' said Rafe, his eyes kindling. 'So you can damn well call him "Ventnor" like everyone else!'

'Actually, they call him "Fatal Ventnor",' said Merry confidentially. 'He has the most remarkable smile, hasn't he, Harry.'

'Oh, yes,' confirmed Harry, his eyes brimming. 'When he isn't looking one over like cattle,' he gasped, before bursting into laughter with Merry, while Rafe watched them, a lurking smile behind his martyred look of long-suffering.

'That's it,' said Rafe. 'Enjoy the roast! But I should like to see any man's face when his wife calls Ventnor by his given name like she's done it all her life!'

Merry merely shook her head at him, her eyes still alight with laughter.

'And when, pray, did you hatch the plot to put a pistol to your head and give me the worst scare of my life?'

'When I knew you were safe,' said Merry. 'Since you had given me the worst scare of *my* life, I thought I would punish you in kind.'

Rafe looked down at his wife, who was smiling unrepentantly, with that same kindling look that she had seen in his cell.

'I shall reserve my own revenge for that trick until we get home, minx!' he said in a silky voice.

But they had pulled up at Half Moon Street to drop Harry off at his house.

'Well, whatever you do, I'd recommend you have a bath first and burn those clothes. You smell like a stable,' said Harry affably, as he closed the door on them with a wave.

Only as he walked away, Harry remembered that he had not imparted to Rafe some extraordinary news about their friends. But watching the carriage disappear around the corner, he knew Rafe would have little time for others, wrapped up in this new private world he had found with Merry, from which all their friends would be excluded, at least for the time being. This recent glimpse into that world had persuaded Harry more than ever that it was time that he, too, found a bride

Rafe put his head back on the squabs, holding Merry against him.

'A bath, a good dinner and bed,' he sighed. 'Not necessarily in that order,' he added with a smile, winning a giggle from Merry, who nestled against him.

As they pulled up at the house in Albemarle Street, where their acquaintance had first begun, he and Merry exchanged a glowing smile of understanding, before he jumped down and, quite unnecessarily, lifted his wife down from the coach.

As Brooke took the carriage around to the mews, Rafe told the porter to have them put on hot water for his bath. He had no wish to delay that first essential activity on which his next would depend.

Then he and Merry scampered up the stairs to his rooms like excited children. When they entered the sitting room, he turned rather boyishly and said:

'This is where it all began.'

Merry nodded and smiled that sweet, provocative smile that made his heart and body leap.

'So you won't kiss me until I've shaved, hey?'

Merry shook her head slowly, teasingly, her eyes twinkling.

Rafe took a step closer, his arms snaking round her waist, and looking down at her with an achingly loving glow in his eyes.

'Are you sure?' he murmured.

Merry shook her head again with laughing uncertainty, then gasped with delight as she found herself once again locked in a thrilling kiss.

Brooke entered the room a little later, rolled his eyes, then retreated to set up the bath in the dressing room. No matter what ideas his lordship might have, her ladyship would thank him for getting his master clean first.

He had to ahem loudly several times to get the couple's attention, before announcing that his lordship's bath awaited him. Rafe followed him, dragging Merry with him by the hand.

'Thank you, Brooke, but we won't need you for a little while. My wife has kindly volunteered to assist me.'

'So you'll let her ladyship shave you, then?' said Brooke dryly.

'Er ...,' Rafe glanced doubtfully back at Merry. 'I'll shave myself.'

'Very well, m'lord. Good luck with that,' said Brooke, a wry glint in his eyes. 'Shall I ask the kitchens to prepare dinner ... in a hour or so ... on a tray?' he added meaningfully.

'You're the best of good fellows, Brooke,' said Rafe, with a nod of assent.

Merry had blushed several times during these exchanges, only saying with offended dignity.

THE RELUCTANT LADY

'You are a shameless rogue, ... and I am extremely adept with a razor.'

'I have no doubt that you are correct in both regards, my love,' he said, with husbandly complaisance, which was undermined entirely when he added. 'Now help me strip, there's a good girl!'

Merry only laughed and pushed him into a chair to help remove his boots and stockings. As she undid the buttons on the legs of his breeches, they exchanged a secret smile. Then Merry helped him shrug out of his jacket and Rafe made light work of the rest of his raiment, flinging them off in all directions, before easing himself, with a gusty sigh into the heavenly hot water. Merry rounded up the errant clothing and stuffed it through the door to the servants' stairs, so that Brooke could take them away for burning. She turned to see her husband beckoning her with a broad grin on his face. He held out a sponge to her and pointed to the bar of soap on the side table.

'Come, wife! Do as your lord and master commands,' he said, sitting back in the bath as though he were a pharaoh.

Merry took the sponge obediently from his hand, dipped it into the water and, as he closed his eyes in anticipation of the pleasure of being pampered by his beloved wife, slapped it into his face and rubbed it around as if he were a five-year-old with mud on his face. Rafe choked and joined in with Merry's laughter. But she would not surrender the sponge and they both relished every second of that bath. Merry washed his hair, massaging her fingers through the dark soapy curls as he murmured his pleasure at the discovery of how a commonplace activity could be rendered sensual in her hands. Brooke had discreetly placed two more cans of hot water outside the dressing room door, so Merry rinsed Rafe's hair and shoulders and saved the rest for his shave. This she achieved very respectably, despite Rafe's comic expression of mock-terror.

Finally, Rafe stood up. The sight of his muscular body sleek and wet made Merry's mouth go dry with desire.

'Here, hand me that towel,' he said, reaching towards her, smiling at the hungry, admiring expression on his wife's face.

Merry shook her head with that playful smile.

'For that,' he said, stepping out of the bath, dripping wet and achingly handsome. 'And for your little trick in Newgate, my dear wife, you are going to pay,' he added, closing on her with a broad smile.

'Rafe! You're soaking wet,' she shrieked laughingly.

'And whose fault is that?' he demanded, his arms closing round her and his mouth descending on hers, dragging a delighted moan from her. Merry, still holding the towel, tried to wrap it around his waist, but he whisked it away. Then, his muscular body still glistening and gloriously naked, Rafe swept Merry up in his arms and carried her through to the bedroom, kicked the door closed, set her on her feet and began unfastening the buttons on her gown.

'Rafe! It's the middle of the afternoon!'

'And you won't be leaving this room until breakfast,' he assured her.

'But Brooke will know what we've been doing!'

'My dear girl, he thinks we're doing it now.'

'Oh no!'

Rafe laughed as Merry covered her blushing face with her hands at that.

Then as her gown and stays dropped to the floor, he carried her to the bed, and effectively silenced any further complaint.

Only later that night, as Rafe awoke from a nightmare and drew his sleeping wife into his arms with relief, did he remember with a pang of shock that Merry's note had been given to him long before she could possibly know he would be saved.

It had not been part of her plot!

A shiver ran through him and he clasped her even more tightly. It was a long time before he went back to sleep.

Chapter Twenty-Four
New Life

The night that Merry gave birth was the worst and the best of Rafe's life.

When they had discovered that Merry was with child, during their early weeks in Paris, Rafe had wanted to turn back, but Merry would have none of it. Only when she threatened to continue on to Rome without him did Rafe capitulate. But as he now anxiously paced the floor of his own room, while Merry laboured in the next, he was grateful for those precious memories from their honeymoon.

The sky had been streaked with a blaze of pink and gold as Merry had stood in his arms on a balcony in Rome and watched her first sunset over the rosy rooftops and familiar landmarks that she had longed to see.

'Is it how you imagined it?' he had asked, after a long moment.

'Oh, so much more beautiful,' she had sighed, smiling at the warm touch of his lips on her cheek and hair.

The following evening, after a day of sightseeing, with Rafe indulgently being towed here and there in Merry's quest to see everything at once, he had taken her into a lovely chapel, decorated everywhere with white flowers. Then, to Merry's amazement, he had slowly sunk to one knee and, in an unsteady voice charged with emotion, had formally asked for her hand in marriage.

Rafe smiled as he remembered how she had looked down mistily at him and whispered: 'Yes, my love, with all my heart', her free hand softly cradling his cheek.

With Brooke and Chantal once more their witnesses, an English divine had married them again, there and then, remarking that he had never united two people so deeply in love.

They had remained in Italy for three glorious months, travelling upwards from Rome in easy stages, through Florence, Sienna, Pisa, Padua and finally to Venice, for the last month. Though rather less fragrant than she had expected, this magical city was everything Merry had dreamed of, and they had fallen out mightily when, when Rafe, panicking about his wife's enciente state, finally stated they were to return to England.

Merry had held out for a day, before padding across to him in her nightgown one morning, putting her arms round his stiffly disapproving body, as he tied his cravat in taut, frowning moves, and had said, meeting his eyes in the mirror: 'Very well, you impossible man, you win! Let us go back to the Fall, if you wish, but in heaven's name let's have an end to your infernal pouting. You didn't even kiss me when you got up this morning. Though I don't blame you if you have gone off me,' she had added, looking down at her swollen belly. 'I look pretty rum …'

'*I* didn't kiss *you*!' he had cried, turning round, his hands at her waist. 'You didn't kiss me, more like, you little minx! Gone off you! As if I ever could! You're more beautiful every day … and more maddening! And if you want kissing, I have kisses aplenty for you!' and he had proved his point immediately, taking her lips in a bruising embrace that slowly softened into a gentler, arousing caress.

'May I really take you home?' he had murmured into her hair, his breathing now heavy and erratic.

'Yes,' Merry had replied, her breathing no less unsteady. 'But if you cosset me just once, I shall leave you.'

'You wouldn't dare.'

Merry had wriggled free and skipped nimbly just out of his reach, a playful grin twisting her lips.

'Oh, would I not?' she had teased, a defiant glint in her eyes.

Then as Rafe had lunged to catch her, Merry had ducked out of his reach with a squeak of delight and dashed to the other side of the bed. After a few minutes of high-spirited chasing, he had caught his wife and tumbled onto the bed with her, a bundle of laughing, protesting loveliness. He had kissed Merry soundly for her waywardness, only breaking off to laugh as she tugged his shirt free of his breeches.

'So you would leave me, would you?' Rafe had demanded, stripping off the last of his clothes, eagerly assisted by Merry, who had already tossed her nightdress onto the floor.

'Absolutely!' she had gasped, as their bodies came together, warm and aroused, their lips meeting in a melting kiss.

'Hm ... I wonder what I can do to persuade you that that would be impossible,' Rafe had mused, before proving his point to Merry's complete satisfaction.

They had started for home the following day and Rafe had driven his independent wife to distraction by fussing over her like a mother hen for the next few months. But as her time had approached, Merry had submitted to his cosseting just to cherish the time with him in case it would be her last.

During the long hours of her labour, Merry had called upon all her experience of concealing pain to keep from crying out, but in the end even her astonishing stoicism broke. Rafe thought he'd never forget those last cries, when he feared he was losing her and broke into the room at the last minute to be met with the wonder of seeing his son come into the world. The even greater wonder was the expression on Merry's face as the child was held up for her to see. Having been put through such agony, there was a look of such stunning joy on her face that Rafe could barely speak. To have both his beloved wife and son survive this ordeal was the greatest blessing he could ask for.

Rafe stroked his wife's damp face, never more lovely to him than in this moment of shared joy, as the midwife quickly bathed and swaddled the child, who after a few hiccoughing squalls let out a bellowing cry that only his adoring parents could love. Merry and Rafe exchanged rueful smiles, lit from within by a glowing happiness.

This tender scene was cut short as the midwife stepped in briskly, placed the child into Rafe's arms and chivvied him through the connecting door, so that she and Chantal could help Merry bathe and prepare for bed, while a maid changed the sheets and cleaned up.

Rafe threw Merry a look of panic before the door snapped shut, leaving him alone with his son for the first time.

Terrified of dropping the tiny, wriggling bundle, Rafe sat in the nearest chair, and rested the child carefully on his lap, cradling its fragile head with his hands so that he could take a look at this precious life that had sprung from his own and Merry's. Reverently, Rafe touched his son's soft dark curls, his cheek, his nose, his mouth, awed by the miniature perfection of every feature.

As the babe wailed again, his tiny arms breaking free of his wrappings, Rafe said: 'Hey, hey, hey, little man! What's all this fuss, sir?'

The sound arrested the child's cries. He lay blinking his large cobalt eyes up at his father and at the bright, wide world around him, waywardly waving his strong little fists in the air, experimenting with their new freedom.

As father and child stared at each other, the timeless spell was cast. Somehow, Rafe's great love for Merry had expanded to embrace his son. A fierce, bone-deep, lion-love that would endure a lifetime; a duty of protection welcomed as a privilege.

'You know you caused your mother a great deal of pain, little man,' he said, to the child's apparent fascination, for the tiny face returned his gaze with an oddly serious expression. 'You must never do so again, or we shall assuredly fall out.' But Rafe's stern words were belied by a glowing look of pride and delight.

Then Rafe thought of his own birth.

Thank God Merry had not suffered his mother's fate! If she had ...

Rafe's expression suddenly froze as he looked at his son.

How would he feel if this babe had been cut from his mother's body in the same horrific way that he himself had been? How could he have looked at the child who had cost Merry her life and not have thought of what he had lost?

Rafe knew the answer. If he had lost Merry to gain a child - even this bright, beautiful boy - he would not have been a better father than his own.

And he had compounded the hurt by causing his younger brother's untimely end.

This had been at the dark heart of Rafe's self-contempt, but even this now fell away. It was time to forgive himself ... and his father.

THE RELUCTANT LADY

Slowly, a lifetime of resentment and self-blame began to crumble and blow away like dust.

Rafe had his own son to think of now. This helpless babe, who would look to him for example, and then one day surpass him, as nature demanded.

What a journey they would take together!
Yes, it was time to put aside the past and focus on his family's future.

Merry was sitting up against a bank of pillows when Rafe was allowed back into the room. She looked drained but beamed and eagerly held out her arms to receive her child. After a few moments of caressing his little face, she took him to her breast, and Rafe sat with his arm around them both, kissing Merry's bowed head as their son learned to suckle.

'Rafe,' murmured Merry, her tiredness telling in her hoarse voice. 'I should like to call him Kit, well, Christopher Bryn, if you have no objection?'

Rafe pressed his lips against the top of her head and stroked their baby's cheek.

So, it seemed all were to be forgiven today.

'A wonderful idea, my darling,' he said in a raw voice, forced with effort past the lump in his throat. 'I love you, Merry. You've made me doubly the happiest man on earth.'

When Kit had drunk his fill and begun to doze off, a nursemaid came forward to take the child, so that her ladyship could get some well-earned sleep. But Rafe waved her away and stood, reaching down to take his son into his proud, protective arms.

Merry felt such a surge of aching joy at the sight that tears pricked her eyes, then she smiled tremulously at Rafe's instant concern.

Quick understanding brought a tender, answering grin to his own lips.

'The doting father?' he guessed softly. 'Who would have thought one brave girl could have wrought such a transformation in the space of a twelvemonth?'

Rafe bent to kiss her lips in a long, gentle salute, eloquent of his love and gratitude, and then said: 'Sleep, my darling. We will both be waiting here when you awake.

The End